TRUE REPUBLIC

A NOVAK AND MITCHELL THRILLER

ANDREW RAYMOND

HUNTERHILL
BOOKS

ALSO BY ANDREW RAYMOND

Novak and Mitchell

1. Official Secrets

2. Capitol Spy

3. Traitor Games

4. True Republic

Duncan Grant

1. Kill Day

2. Dead Flags (pre-order now)

PROLOGUE

HATHAWAY PARKER HOUSE HEAD OFFICES, PIMLICO, LONDON - 8.05AM

Ian Ferguson was pale and sweaty as he rushed along Vauxhall Bridge Road on the west side of the River Thames. He was dishevelled. Unshaven. He had spent the night on a train travelling nearly the entire length of the UK. He hadn't slept, surviving the night on a large flask of black coffee, writing feverishly and combing through the information he'd found the previous night – still disbelieving.

The roads were rammed with rush-hour traffic, solid on both sides. Drivers looking disgruntled at yet another sequence of green lights and no movement ahead. A van driver leaned on his horn. Ian's insides jumped at the sudden blast. He wasn't sure if he'd shown any outward sign of reacting, but it felt like he'd jumped three feet in the air.

He did another shoulder check.

Still clear, for now.

Although the Underground stop at Pimlico was closer to his destination, he'd got off at Vauxhall, using the expansive sightlines from the bridge to ensure he hadn't been followed.

Still clear.

He'd feel better once he was somewhere safe. The head offices of his publisher, which, thanks to a recent merger, had become the biggest publisher in the world.

Hathaway Parker House.

The Pimlico office was the most traditional of HPH's three in the capital. Occupying an old red-brick office block and rising eight storeys high, it would have been pretty unremarkable apart from the iconic HPH logo on the outside. Although Hathaway had merged with Parker House, Hathaway retained its famous lighthouse logo that had adorned so many books since the company's founding in the forties. An almost instantly recognisable publishing icon.

Ian took a heavy, steadying breath as he entered the reception area. To his left was a wall covered with framed prints of Hathaway's most famous titles. Titles that had become part of everyday language, to the point that many people didn't even realise the phrases or sayings had come from book titles.

He felt like genuflecting in front of them. They represented his heroes. His idols. The reason he became a writer.

Several of his own titles had been framed among Hathaway's modern thriller line-up. Titles like *State of Truth*, *Cold Open*, and *Lies of Power* had become staples of the political thriller genre in which Ian wrote. He not only sold in huge numbers, he was also loved by the critics. As far as thriller writers went, he was a unicorn.

But all of that felt far away from his current crisis.

For now, he was just trying to figure out exactly how much trouble he had got himself into.

He was already rushing past reception when the young woman behind the desk called out in delight, 'Good morning, Mr Ferguson! Anne is expecting you.'

He pursed his lips and gave a worried nod, agitated at being recognised. Anonymity was the reason all of his meetings there took place outside of normal business hours. It had even been written into his contract. As a rule, thriller writers were rarely recognised in public. There were many million-selling authors that could comfortably walk around London all day without so much as being asked for a photo or autograph. One of whom was Ian.

He reached the editorial offices on the third floor, clutching a copy of *The Bookseller* magazine in his free hand, his worn leather messenger bag in the other, ready to begin the speech he'd been preparing on the Underground.

Before entering his editor's office, he removed his mobile from his pocket and left it on the floor by the glass door. The nameplate on the wall said, "*Anne Cochrane – CEO Hathaway Parker House UK.*"

He dropped his bag on the floor. While Anne was in the middle of saying good morning, Ian took her mobile off her desk, then placed it alongside his on the floor outside.

'Three months working with him and–'

Ian put up his hand abruptly. 'Don't use his name. Not in here.'

'You're as paranoid as a Cold War spy,' said Anne. 'The door's closed, our mobile phones are outside, there's all of three interns in the entire office, and all of them are too terrified to come within fifty feet of me.'

'If the receptionist downstairs knows that we're taking secret, unscheduled meetings in here, then it's no surprise *The Bookseller* is onto me.'

He dropped the magazine onto Anne's desk, already open at an article rounding up the week's acquisitions news. A small headline read, "*Ian Ferguson rumoured to be ghostwriting the autobiography of Griffin founder Hugo Byron.*" He took a seat opposite her, the chair a few inches too short to be optimal for the height of Anne's desk. It was no accident. She liked that it kept whoever ended up sitting there – interns, authors, junior editors – in a position of weakness relative to her. The moment anyone sat down in Anne Cochrane's office they were on the defensive.

Ian hammered a forefinger on the article accusingly. 'That's the biggest publishing-trade magazine in the country telling everyone that I'm working on a biography of a man that every intelligence agency in the world is trying to catch. It quotes an anonymous source from this office, leaking my involvement.'

Anne took it calmly in her stride. 'In my time I've been yelled at by far more powerful people than you, Ian. Prime Ministers. Royalty. The Archbishop of Canterbury gave me an earful once. You think an intern in my office leaked this? They know if they leaked anything I'd tell every publisher in this city – which is all of them – to blacklist them like they're communists in fifties Hollywood. These girls are coming in at half six every morning on the off-chance someone will notice them ploughing through manuscript slush piles before the overhead lights have come off night mode. They didn't leak this.'

'Then who did?' Ian asked.

'I did.'

Her candour left him dumbfounded. 'You?'

'Don't be so surprised,' she said. 'We have to start building hype on this thing. That's what I do, Ian. That's why I asked you to do this. That's also how I sell it in forty other territories and make you even more money than you've already got.' She squinted ironically. 'Or are you new to the publishing industry?'

'I'm rich enough.' He pulled back from the desk, reeling. 'If I'm working on a book about Hugo, that suggests I know where he is. Have you any idea the tonnage of shit this is going to cause me with the Security Service? They're probably bugging my place right now.'

Anne replied, 'You're the biggest thriller writer in the country, Ian. You ghosting a book for Hugo Byron is like Marco Pierre White cooking with foie gras. Georg Solti conducting the Vienna Philharmonic. Boswell writing about Samuel Johnson.'

'You wouldn't be so flippant if you knew what I found last night.'

Anne waited. She said nothing.

Ian reached into his bag, being careful not to disrupt the audio recorder he had secretly running, and produced several printouts. 'I know what's been going on,' he said. 'What's been going on this whole time.'

The sense of awe took a moment to appear on Anne's face as she realised what she was looking at. There was a long pause. Then, with a hint of fear, she asked, 'Who else knows you have this?'

'No one.'

'Apart from the source who gave it to you.'

'Naturally.'

'Who's the source?'

Ian shook his head. 'I can't tell you.'

Anne's gaze turned to steel. 'This isn't a newspaper, Ian. You don't get the luxury of anonymous sources on a project like this. We've got shareholders. Liability. Which means we have to fact check, because if this is real–'

'It's real.'

'–we'll need the entire legal department working on it.'

For the first time, Ian hesitated.

Anne said, 'You do realise you can't take this elsewhere. Or were you too hungover to read your non-disclosure agreement? Who's the source?'

He wouldn't renege on his promise, but he knew that Anne would need more than a tease to let him off. 'I can't tell you that.' he said.

'You don't get an anonymous source. Not on something this damaging to the royal family.'

'Damaging?' He laughed, gesticulating with the paper. 'Do you think I don't know what this is? This could take down the whole bloody lot of them! The end of the constitutional monarchy. I know the monarchy, the intelligence services, and Westminster inside out. I know what this is. I know what I've got and what it could do. In fact, I would say that the end of the British monarchy would be dramatically *under*playing what this could do.'

Anne swivelled in her chair to look out her window, lost in the implications. Each one worse than the last, accumulating like a gathering snowball racing down a hill. She turned back to face Ian. 'Lose it,' she said.

Ian nearly fell off his chair. 'You're kidding.' He stood up. 'Right? Tell me you're kidding.'

Anne held up a hand, demanding he hold his tongue for a moment. She marched to her door then yelled across the office, 'Gayle. I need coffee. You'll have to go out. The machine's broken.'

With a well-practised combination of keystrokes, the young intern hit COMMAND+TAB to come out of the Word document she'd been in – named 'ARHD Manuscript' – to toggle into her work email account. It happened so quickly that even someone standing over her shoulder would barely have noticed it happen. She did it whenever anyone walked near her desk, said her name, even when her phone rang, as it was always easy to get sucked into a conversation and absent-mindedly leave her manuscript up on the screen. Not a good look when you're one of twelve unpaid interns striving for only three full-time junior editing positions. On an average day, Gayle could toggle between the two tabs upwards of fifty times. She couldn't help it. She knew she should have been doing actual work for the company, slogging through slush-pile manuscripts, looking for that forgotten gem that had been overlooked by an overworked, overstressed editor several months earlier. It was straight economics. Interns were paid next to nothing – actually nothing, in Gayle's case – and just one successful manuscript could make Hathaway millions. Enough to write off all the hundred or so failures it published each year. Because that was just how it worked. It astonished Gayle once she got into the numbers. In no other business would a ninety-five per cent failure rate be accepted.

Except in publishing.

Because all it took was one *Fifty Shades of Grey* or *Da Vinci Code* for everyone to get rich.

But most of the manuscripts Gayle looked at in a typical day were so bad they could be discarded within a few lines. Basic grammar and spelling errors were rife. Showing not telling. It was Day One Writer Stuff, as Gayle saw it. All that haste left her plenty of time in the day to write her own masterpiece. A political thriller she'd been crafting for the past seven months called *A Right Honourable Death*. Writing from before dawn until late at night. Capturing the odd three hundred words while a chilli for dinner reduced on the hob, which was inevitably forgotten about five hundred words later, leaving the chilli stuck to the bottom of the pot. A price worth paying, as far as Gayle saw it. She even dictated chapter ideas on her wireless earbuds during her weekly food shopping. Slowly, painstakingly, over months it had come together.

With every word she typed, she could taste the pending literary success that would mean she would no longer have to eat cucumber sandwiches for lunch.

Every.

Single.

Day.

She was convinced that she had spotted that crucial gap in the market. And if she worked her backside off, she'd be done in time to leave a copy with Anne Cochrane before her internship was through.

The Anne Cochrane. Who had edited Prime Ministers' memoirs. Corrected the spelling of some of the world's greatest authors. And was now presiding over the most successful and profitable decade in Hathaway Parker House's history.

First of all, though, Gayle had to fetch her and Ian Ferguson coffee.

She'd noticed the broken machine earlier when she'd been the first one in the office. It had confused her. It wasn't so much that the machine wasn't working. After pulling out the machine, it looked more like the rear pipe had been intentionally damaged.

By the time she reached the lifts, the machine had already gone out of her mind. She was too busy focussing on Anne Cochrane's coffee order.

* * *

A small branch of an upmarket coffee chain was right across the road. The staff were used to dealing with stressed assistants and interns running out from the many nearby embassies. There were few coffee shops in the land where receipts were so often demanded by customers, all to be filed into various expense accounts.

Gayle was waiting patiently – though with one foot tapping anxiously on the ground – at the end of the counter for the two cups to be delivered. The shop was as busy as it got all day, the square footage of the branch insufficient for the number of people squashed inside. It was a hectic, stressful place just to walk into. Absolutely everyone was in a rush, and absolutely no one had time to waste.

Such was modern life, thought Gayle. Never before had there been a time when so many people fought so hard for their free time and did so little with it. She let her mind drift off to the chapter she'd been working on. That was the beauty of being a writer. While everyone else was having their time 'wasted', there was no such thing for a writer with a work-in-progress. She thought of an unexpected reversal of fortune to end the chapter. Teasing the next one that would rob a reader of another half hour of sleep, telling themselves 'just one more page...'

She didn't notice the barista dwelling slightly with the takeaway cups, pouring two drops of a clear liquid into each of them from a glass vial she'd hidden up her fleece sleeve.

Gayle's mobile was ringing as she reached for the two cups. One marked with the initials "AM", the other with "IF".

Any fear the barista may have had of Gayle noticing the surreptitious addition to the coffees vanished when Gayle rushed off with the cups, struggling to answer the phone at the same time.

The mere sight of Anne's caller ID sent Gayle into a tail-spin, exiting the shop straight into the path of a commuter on an electric scooter. The left side of the handlebar clipped Gayle, sending the cup for "IF" tumbling out of her hand.

She cried out in frustration and anger as the rider carried on, headphones on, carefree. Gayle looked forlornly at the cup on the ground, its contents spilled all over the concrete. Then she looked at the queue that was now out the door.

She couldn't go back up with only one coffee. But she also

couldn't rejoin the queue and take another ten minutes before she could explain.

In the time it took her to jog back to the office, wait five seconds for the lift that never came and opt for the stairs instead, Gayle rehearsed her apology. Better to hurry back and explain in person, she thought.

But she never got a chance. When she reached the third floor, Ian Ferguson was stomping towards the lifts.

Gayle tried to say something about how much his books meant to her, but he blazed past.

Then, after taking a few tentative steps into Anne's office, she was told in no uncertain terms by Anne that she and the coffee should both disappear.

Shaken by the frantic episode at the coffee shop, then being blanked by one of her literary heroes, and shouted at by her boss, it was with some relief that Gayle returned to her desk with the coffee.

With a black marker, she scored out the initials "AM" on the side, then did what she so badly needed to do.

Had a drink of hot, black coffee, then typed the triumphant last words of her manuscript: *THE END.*

* * *

At the coffee shop, the barista removed her latex gloves after carefully disposing of the glass vial she'd handled with such care all morning. She didn't bother making any excuses for disappearing from the counter to the back, towards the broom cupboard that made up the staff room. She collected her things and left out the back door. It was the last the rest of the staff would ever see of the young Russian woman who had only started that morning.

* * *

At first, Ian was too angry to think straight. For now, he just wanted to get as far away from Hathaway Parker House as he could, as quickly as possible, running for a bus that was bound for Charing Cross and idling at the stop. As he hurried towards it, a man and a woman in their forties were sauntering past in the other direction. They held hands, but neither smiled nor talked. They were a little overdressed for the benign late-autumn weather – both in woollen beanie hats – but London was always full of tourists from warmer climes braced for ten degrees celsius like it was deep winter.

Nothing about them raised any flags to Ian and his mind was elsewhere. So when the woman lost her balance and crashed into him, he paid it little mind. He didn't even notice that the hand she touched his with was in a clear surgical glove.

She apologised with a slight accent that Ian couldn't immediately place.

Once he was on the upper level of the bus, he took out the audio recorder from his bag and checked that his conversation with Anne had recorded correctly. It had. He attached the recorder to the USB socket on his laptop and uploaded the audio file to his cloud account with a password. When it was done, he took out his burner phone and entered a search into the Maps app.

"*Upper Brook Street Mayfair.*"

As the map spooled, he reconsidered and closed it down. Using his normal phone, he rapidly tapped out a message to his agent, Julian Darby.

"*We need to talk. Cochrane screwed me. I need you to get me out of this. I think I'm being followed. I'm scared.*"

A few seconds later, Darby replied: "*Come by the office, Ian.*"

The Darby Agency, one of the most powerful in London, was on Bedford Square in Bloomsbury. Still a little way to go on the bus.

It was fine, Ian told himself. Julian would tell him what to do.

By the time the bus reached the heart of Westminster, Ian's vision had gone foggy. He couldn't focus on anything outside the window. Everything a blur.

He told himself not to panic. That it couldn't possibly be what he thought it was.

But he kept replaying the scene with the woman bumping into him.

The touch on his hand.

Her accent.

Their unnecessary headwear.

A cough rose through his chest. He barely managed to cover his mouth in time. Now acutely aware of the other people on the bus with him, he grabbed at the support rails and bars, swinging wildly from side to side as he made his way down the stairs.

He looked down at the crook of his elbow where he'd shielded the cough. The elbow was covered in blood.

He kept on down the stairs, trying to warn the people near him to stay away. He looked like a drunk. At night, Londoners would smile along with a public drunk. But in the morning, there was no chance of receiving any sympathy.

'Get help,' Ian croaked, swatting at the air to keep people away from him. He didn't know how infectious he might be.

The doors opened out onto Trafalgar Square, but he only got a foot out in mid-air before he collapsed to the ground.

Foam bubbled out of his mouth. His eyes were open although he'd already passed out – they were almost totally white.

* * *

Outside Hathaway Parker House a full unit from the Metropolitan Police's Chemical, Biological, Radioactive, Nuclear, and Explosive Incidents team appeared amid blaring sirens and flashing blue lights – along with five BMWs of what appeared to be regular police, and three grey vans of the Counter Terrorism Command unit. A Mercedes Sprinter ambulance was also on the scene, "POLICE" written on the back and sides where it normally said "AMBULANCE". It had barely stopped when the rear doors flew open, and a team dressed in full HAZMAT suits jumped out carrying metal suit-cases of varying sizes.

A silver van with a trailer attached to the back was quickly unloaded, and a ten-foot steel barrier in a concertina design was unravelled and placed around the front entrance of the building. It was a solid fence with glass partitions designed specifically for response to chemical attacks – though it had only ever been seen on London's streets to, controversially, cordon off political protestors at a recent march around West-minster.

The police had already erected a similar wall around the Nelson's Column side of Trafalgar Square, bringing the entire area to a standstill. Which, in turn, had brought most of central London to a standstill.

Police officers in HAZMAT suits swarmed through the building, sealing off one floor at a time. On the third floor, Anne Cochrane watched in horror from her window as the police presence grew outside by the second.

She marched out to the office floor to assemble her employees, who were all standing around Gayle Ademi's desk.

Her eyes were entirely white, as if replaced by large marbles. She was foaming at the mouth.

Someone optimistically checked her pulse.

On Gayle's computer was the manuscript for *A Right Honourable Death*. If it were ever to be published, it would be posthumously.

A takeaway coffee cup sat on Gayle's desk. The colour of her lipstick around the edge. The initials "AM" scored out on the side, out of Anne's view.

As she reached for it a CBRNE officer in full HAZMAT suit shouted from a distance away, 'Don't touch that! Move back!'

Officers gave everyone respirator masks and led them away for examination while the floor was taped and sealed.

Anne couldn't get a straight answer from the police about what was going on. Her speech was muddy and indistinct behind the mask. 'Where are you taking us?'

'St Thomas's,' the officer replied. 'They have a secure wing where we can run some tests.'

'How bad is it?'

The officer tried to up Anne's pace. 'It's going to take some time to figure that out,' he explained.

'My daughter...'

'If she's in the building, I'm sure–'

'No, you don't understand,' said Anne. 'We haven't spoken in a while. And she's in New York. If I'm in trouble I want to call her.'

'We don't have time for that yet. We've got another dead body at Trafalgar Square with similar symptoms. We've got to get you out of here.'

1

THE REPUBLIC HEADQUARTERS, NEW YORK CITY - 5.15AM LOCAL TIME

ONE WEEK LATER

Stella Mitchell walked into the lobby of the ten-storey sandstone building in central Manhattan clutching a long black coffee in a travel mug. Her eyes might have been open, but she was in a place somewhere between asleep and awake. Between dreams and nightmares. She had her dream job: chief editor of *The Republic*, which had become one of the most prestigious news publications in the States and across Europe. Thanks to the conclusion of her and her partner Tom Novak's biggest story six months earlier, subscriptions were at record highs. Ad revenue was still through the roof and showing no signs of slowing down. All Stella had to do was set the course and steer the ship.

What no one saw was the endless work days required to make it all happen.

Stella had already been working hours more familiar to a trainee doctor than a news editor. She didn't understand how her predecessor, the irrepressible Diane Schlesinger, had managed it for so many years.

The night security guard had stopped commenting on Stella's early arrivals. He didn't even look up from whatever tattered paperback novel he was reading.

Stella felt empty as she made her way across the newsroom, her only company the vibrating phone in her pocket. In the background, the *Republic* logo was emblazoned on the wall in 3D letters:

THE TRUTH. FIRST.

It had been months since the cleaners had had to turn on the main lights on the *Republic* newsroom's fifth floor. Stella was always in ahead of them. Each morning they'd find her, in her glass-surround office, alone. Glasses on, hair tied back in a ponytail that would fray and disintegrate as the day went on in tandem with her energy levels, her increasingly gaunt face lit up by the harsh blue-light glow of a 4K computer monitor.

Since becoming chief editor, Stella had kept her normal dress code of trouser suits, and sensible shoes that allowed her to navigate the crowded Manhattan streets in a hurry. In the newsroom, she looked like any other reporter. She liked it that way. One of the board's older female members had recommended she "dress for power", the way Diane Schlesinger had, but Stella refused to. The way she saw it, there was no point in trying to be like Diane. Stella's authority came from her reputation. By how she carried herself. Her actions. There was already plenty for her to live up to. She didn't have time to worry about the cosmetic comparisons.

She checked her phone. Another text message. The same number again. But this one was different from the three previous days. Instead of the polite request to call back, this time they had written: "*We need to talk...*"

Stella stopped in her tracks when she read it. Tapping on the screen revealed the rest of the message. "*It's business, not personal.*"

She deleted the message, blocked the number, then did what had become routine. Lights on. Computer on. Coffee. Check the overnight wires left on her desk by a night-shift intern. Then her right desk drawer. Two of the pink pills. One of the yellow pills. She had stopped trying to remember their names. They would both have been worth a lot of points on a Scrabble board, with their abundance of Xs and Qs and Zs. All that mattered was that they were both by miles the most popular legal drugs on American college campuses in the run-up to term paper deadlines, and could keep Stella awake all day on three hours sleep without making her jittery or look wired – like too much coffee did. In short: they allowed her to think her to keep her eyes open when all her body wanted to do was shut the hell down.

Fifteen minutes later, when her coffee had kicked in and the pills had entered her bloodstream, Stella would ride a wave that would take her all the way through to the morning editorial meeting at ten a.m. It was as if she had just dropped her head for a moment when she looked up and saw the newsroom full. Bustling with activity. She'd been so fully in the zone that entire hours had flashed by and she felt like she'd done nothing.

The reality was quite the opposite. She had been working endlessly. Feverishly. She had completed line edits on three separate stories totalling twenty-five thousand in word count. She had had a Zoom call with her European correspondent in Berlin. She had answered several emails from the *Republic* legal team. Then the pills really kicked in when she was in the middle of another line edit. She suddenly stood up and decided to hold an impromptu motivational meeting on the newsroom floor. Everything in the office stopped in its tracks while Stella waffled in circles for eleven minutes about the importance of using the word "nonplussed" correctly, and another six on why use of the phrase "as to..." when a reporter means "on" or "about" or "for" made her want to drive her red pen through her eye socket. Much to everyone else's bafflement.

She then returned to her office so pumped about the meeting that she forgot to eat breakfast. Which meant that instead of being able to eat at her desk, she would lose at least ninety seconds – she'd timed it one day – to walk to the communal microwave and heat something up. And that was being conservative. The chances of a staffer not using the opportunity to pitch her a story was exactly zero. Because reporters are, above all, sales people. Selling themselves, their stories, or both. Which meant that Stella was looking at a loss of at least two minutes, maybe even three, just for breakfast. It was unacceptable. So she ploughed on. Hungry, but productive.

Until a knock on her door broke her spell. Part knuckle, part ring.

It was a young female reporter, standing hunched, too terrified to make eye contact through the glass.

Stella called her in whilst texting on her phone.

The reporter, Jennifer, had red around her eyes as if she'd been crying recently. Most of the morning, in fact, though she'd managed to get it together in the last twenty minutes. 'You wanted to see me?' Her voice was filled with doubt, as if hoping she'd been mistaken.

Stella was now typing an email, her movements frantic, chaotic. Stella hit the ENTER button on her keyboard then gave a delighted click of her mouse. Email sent. Just to continue keeping her hands busy, she pulled out her hairband

and scraped her hair back into a fresh ponytail. 'The clicks on your last three stories have been under average,' she said, as if it was information that Jennifer should already be aware of.

The strength and resolve that Jennifer had been building up in the ladies' staff toilet was ready to crumble. She was sure this was a preface to her being fired.

Finally Stella stopped, relaxed.

Jennifer could feel the beginning of tears. Then something unexpected happened.

Stella asked, 'Are you okay?' While Jennifer tried to readjust her thinking, Stella pulled out hard copies of Jennifer's recent articles. 'Your word choice lacks your usual colour. Your tone is timid. You're normally strong and declarative. I was thinking you might not be okay.'

Now that Jennifer had permission, she let all of her concerns flow. It was her personal life. A guy. Finances. And a million other things going on in the competitive environment of the office, where if you weren't working on your best-ever story you were dying a slow death. 'I don't think you realise how intimidating it is working in the same newsroom as you and Tom. I look at what you two have done here...' She shook her head, flashing her eyebrows up, overwhelmed at the mere thought. 'I can't be like either of you. I don't have it in me.'

Stella thought for a moment, trying to remember what it was like being in Jennifer's position. Young enough to be full of dreams, but not successful enough yet to feel close to attaining them. Stella said, 'I read this thing about Picasso once. It taught me a lot about how to get good at something. Near the end of his life, he would do these little drawings for people at art shows and exhibitions and charge huge amounts of money for them. Little more than a squiggle of lines in his typical style, but people were happy to pay it because, hey, it was Picasso. After handing one to a woman in the queue, she told him, "I'm not paying five hundred dollars for something that took you thirty seconds to do." Picasso replied, "No, madam. It took me all my life." It's amazing how it can look like some people aren't even trying. It takes most of a career to get there. You're young, Jennifer. You're standing at the bottom of this mountain, and all you can see is the summit. Because that's where you want to get to. Those stories that made Tom and I an overnight success? In reality, they took our entire careers to write.' Stella reached behind her to a long row of heavy volumes. The sort of books that people only keep in the house to weigh things down. She handed Jennifer a copy of *Garner's Modern English Usage*. 'Diane Schlesinger gave me that on my first day here. Read the section on active verbs. That's how you climb the mountain.'

Jennifer tried taking the book with one hand, then quickly realised she needed two. 'Stories like Goldcastle. Hilderberg. These are generational stories. I mean, thanks for this, but how are active verbs going to get me somewhere like Goldcastle?'

Stella replied, 'Let me pitch you a couple of ideas for novels, Jennifer. The first one is about a man who walks around a city all day thinking about his life. The second one is about a woman getting ready for a party. Which one should I write?'

'Neither,' Jennifer answered. 'They both sound... well, pretty crappy.'

'Congratulations. You just talked me out of writing both *Ulysses* and *Mrs Dalloway*. Your problem isn't that you can't find a big story. You're just not using the right words.' Stella smiled at her. 'That's it. It's harder to write when you're unhappy. But Jennifer, if you wait around until you feel ready, you'll get half the work done in this life that you should. This is a blood sport. If you want to make it, you have to suffer. Put in the time.' She pointed at the Garner book. 'Starting with active verbs. Now go and rewrite that Bitcoin piece.'

'Okay,' Jennifer said. 'Thank you.' She was grateful because Stella could have bulldozed her the way so many other editors might have in the same situation. Instead, she left with a smile on her face, ready to get back to work.

As soon as she was gone Stella dipped into her right drawer, extracting two pills, one pink, one yellow, then downed them with a sip of water.

Everyone was too busy with their work to notice – apart from Mark Chang. It was little more than a subtle upwards glance from his desk but it was enough. He'd also noticed the increasing regularity with which Stella had been knocking back water with something. And they'd been far too regular to be vitamins.

Chang was one of the last senior members of staff from Diane Schlesinger's heyday. He had only recently returned after an extended leave of absence to nurse his wife at home while she recovered from chemotherapy. Chang had seen it all through the years. Pill-popping behaviour was once an accepted norm for reporters under stress. He'd found that it stopped in one of two ways. Either the reporter realised they weren't writing any better than before and managed to stop. Or the pills stopped them before a choice could be made.

Chang tapped out a message on his phone. *"Her first top-up now. An hour earlier than last week. Time to intervene?"*

The recipient was Tom Novak.

Stella closed her desk drawer then shuffled some papers. 'What's next?' she wondered aloud.

After clicking into her computer's calendar – every hour until seven at night accounted for – she stared in incomprehension at the screen.

Ralph Ogden. Zoom call.

Stella called reception. 'Why am I talking to Ralph Ogden?'

All reception knew was that she had okayed it the previous evening.

Stella didn't remember. It wasn't as though her memory was hazy or patchy. It was like reception was simply inventing something. Then Stella remembered the extra pills she'd taken. And the used dinner plate she'd found in the kitchen that morning. A microwave meal she didn't remember eating.

Her stomach lurched at the thought of it.

Walking blackouts. A side effect she'd read about online in the case of abusing dosage recommendations.

In a panic, Stella said, 'Message him. Cancel it. Whatever it is.'

It wasn't just about the not remembering. Saying no to almost everything was a necessary part of being an editor. Stella was always being pitched. It could be directly, whilst waiting for something to cook in the staff room. Or indirectly, when staffers worked out logistical contortions to accidentally end up in the lift with her. Small talk would then lead to the inevitable, 'It's funny you mention that, Stella. I've actually been working on this piece...'

Stella tried not to be too hard on them. It hadn't been so long ago that she'd been in their shoes. Always hustling. Always trying to make yourself indispensable. But as editor, she had to be wary of anything that would be too costly, take too much time, wouldn't work, didn't fit with *Republic*'s tone or style, or as she and Novak had directly experienced, cause expensive legal troubles.

It was easier and faster to just say no. Very little can go wrong as an editor when you say no to things. "Yes" is generally the point at which trouble starts. It was a standard that Hollywood movie executives and book publishers had embraced for the best part of a century. Saying yes was committing to something, which meant money or resources. There was a chance that a project could be successful, but mostly there was a chance it wouldn't work, and the executive or publisher or editor would have to shoulder the blame.

Why? Because they'd said yes.

But sometimes saying no meant that you missed out on a hit. JK Rowling was rejected by twelve publishers. Even the one who said yes believed in it so little that Rowling was given an advance of just £1500. John le Carré's agent was once assured by a publisher that his author "hasn't got any future" in the spy genre. A publisher for Louisa May Alcott told her after reading the manuscript for *Little Women* that "You can't write. Stick to teaching."

Sometimes saying no could also have its costs.

As Ogden's profile picture appeared along with a green button to accept the call, Stella knew it would be the easiest thing in the world – the easiest option as far as her day was concerned – to hit reject and forget all about him.

But what if he really had something?

She couldn't help it. It was in her blood. She had to know.

The mouse wavering over the red "REJECT CALL" button, she opted instead for green.

2

'Good morning,' Ralph said. He was sitting at his kitchen table, holding a crying toddler – a little girl. The table was covered in the detritus of an attempted lunch, which had been abandoned with most of the puréed food he had prepared smeared across every available surface.

Stella winced at the shrill noise. 'Is this a good time, Ralph?'

He soothed the girl's cries, and got her back in her high-chair just out of shot. 'Sorry. It's fine. She was unwell through the night so I've kept her out of nursery today.'

Ralph's laptop camera was low resolution and dim. From the wide angle showing the kitchen, the house he was in looked cramped, with laundry in a pile on the floor, kids' toys everywhere, and dirty dishes from the previous night filling the sink. Stella's stress levels were going up just spectating the scene. Ralph, however, seemed impervious to it all.

He lived in a small semi-detached house in the working-class area of Romford, east London, having been pushed to the edge of the city by inflating house prices. He was in his early forties and looked like an accountant who had been job-swapped or had unexpectedly been given the day off halfway through dressing. He wore a white shirt from a cheap multi-pack with no tie. His hair was aggressively side-parted, overly long at the back and around the ears. Evidence of cutting his own hair at home with clippers and letting it grow out. His physique was slender but what flesh he had was soft, with barely an ounce of muscle – what modern parlance had christened as "skinny-fat" – from spending almost his entire day sitting down. His little girl was the heaviest thing he would lift in a day. Coding on a keyboard the most strenuous workout in a week.

He spoke softly. He did all of his talking on Twitter or on his website, Verax. He may have looked underwhelming – like middle management at a second-tier mortgage broker – but Ralph Ogden had been growing his one-man operation into a small, tightly knit collective of self-taught 'internet detectives' who used open-source online tools to investigate the same stories that major broadsheet newspapers and television media went after. War crimes. The seemingly accidental downing of commercial planes. Identifying Russian spy networks.

Verax was certainly a niche interest, but Ralph was convinced that he was about to break them into the mainstream.

All Stella could see was a man that was probably going to waste her time. 'Ralph, I'm very busy this morning, so I'm going to have to limit this to three minutes. Go.'

Ralph was undeterred. 'That's fine. I only need ten seconds.'

For Stella, this was confirmation of what she already suspected: it might only be ten seconds, but it was about to be ten wasted seconds.

Until she heard what he had to say. And saw what he had to show her.

With no further preamble, he showed a still CCTV image that had become familiar to anyone following the news in the past week. The shot looked down on a seemingly ordinary man and a woman walking hand in hand. Both were dressed for winter despite autumnal conditions, wearing jeans, boots, puffer jackets and beanie hats. But anyone familiar with the pictures knew them as the suspects in the poisoning of novelist Ian Ferguson.

Ralph said one thing. 'I know who they are.' He checked his watch then gave a confident, defiant nod. 'Five seconds to spare.'

Stella asked the only question she could in the circumstances. 'Who are they?'

Ralph replied, 'I could give you three guesses, but you'll only need one.'

'Russian.'

'Very.'

'That's not exactly news, Ralph. How sure are you?'

'I'm pretty sure.'

'Pretty? You don't come to someone like me with a story like this unless you need something. What is it?'

Ralph shifted in his seat. The confident part of his pitch was definitely over. Now the power dynamic between them had returned to normal: Stella with all the power, he with practically none. 'I need money,' he said, lifting his hands to demonstrate candour. 'I'm incredibly close to finding out who these people are – their names, real names – but I can't prove it without another source.'

Stella admired the fact that Ralph had a potentially huge story but wasn't going to rush out part-evidence, part-hope.

'Say I could help you,' she said. 'You get what you need, and you identify this man and woman. What then?'

As a one-man operation for the first nine months of Verax, Ralph had been a lot of things. Reporter. Editor. Graphic designer. Podcaster. Now it was time for him to be a salesman.

He said, 'I'm proposing a co-publication with *The Republic*, once we have confirmation on the suspects' identities. You get to catch up on a story you've been falling behind on because Tom Novak is away on a book tour.'

'And you get what?' asked Stella.

He gave a wry smile. 'We have two hundred thousand followers on Twitter. *Republic* has three million. Our last four big stories barely scratched the surface of the wider media. Sure, we're respected by people like you in the industry. Reporters cite us when asking question in press conferences, but this is a story that matters. This isn't just a hostile government taking out one of their own dissidents on foreign soil. This is the assassination of a British novelist on British soil. It's unprecedented, and the country needs to know who did it and why.' For want of a better phrase, he said, 'Brass tacks: we need your clout.'

Stella tilted her head slightly. 'That you're doing this call from your kitchen table tells me you don't need our clout. You need our legal department for libel protection in case the shit hits the fan. Libel tourism is a killer these days. If you were to get sued, you could lose everything in paying the damages. Your home. What will you do then?'

Ralph was only too aware of what was at stake for him. The fear that kept him up some nights. That had given him such pronounced bags under his eyes and prematurely aged him. Still, he replied, 'I just heard a lot of words and none of them were no.'

Stella smiled. She liked his resolve. Here was a guy with little more than a cheap laptop and a broadband connection going toe to toe with a journalistic behemoth. And now he wanted to take on the Russian state. 'If we do this – *if* – I'd want Novak on it with you. No one has more experience with what you could be running headlong into.' Stella looked up at the intern standing at her door holding a laptop. 'Ralph, I've got to go, but I'll call you later once I've talked to some people.' She hung up while Ralph was halfway through expressing his gratitude, then waved the intern in. 'How bad was it?'

The young woman hesitated. 'Pretty bad.'

'God help us,' Stella muttered, taking the laptop from her.

'I put timestamps on the parts you'll want to watch.' The intern beat a hasty retreat to the newsroom.

Stella hadn't had time to watch the livestream of Novak's book event. That was what the intern had been tasked with doing. Still, it gave her pause that while she had been stuck in the office since the crack of dawn, Novak was out publicising his new memoir.

She didn't have to dial in to the video feed on the New York Book Festival's website to see how big a draw the event was. He'd been on tour for over a month now.

She was happy for him, but there was also a part of her that felt lonely. Disconnected from him.

It reminded her of a magician from the 1920s she had once read about, who designed an intricate trick involving trapdoors and a lookalike. Every night the payoff to the trick was the magician disappearing behind a closed door, only to reappear almost instantaneously across the stage behind a different door. The crowd would be in raptures. And every night the magician would end the trick under the stage, having fallen through a trapdoor, leaving the lookalike to take the applause and adoration of the crowd. The magician would hear their faint roar and bow to no one, on his own. Eventually, he decided to swap the roles around, but then the magician missed drawing out the tension and suspense in the crowd in the run-up.

After trying both roles and failing to enjoy either, the magician retired the trick and his act died with it. Frustrated and his career in ruins, the magician took to opium, seeing out his premature last days in a poorhouse, lost in the brain-fog of addiction.

The story had stayed with Stella through the years, but it wasn't until recently that it started to play on her mind.

Was she okay with being the magician who orchestrated everything, having to satisfy herself with a bow under the stage, while the bright lights and cheers landed on Novak?

What was she willing to sacrifice to keep the Novak and Mitchell act going?

3

THE NEW YORK BOOK FESTIVAL, DAVID H. KOCH THEATER AT LINCOLN CENTER

There were many standouts in the line-up of the annual New York Book Festival. It seemed that almost every major Western author of the last twenty-five years had chosen the same year to publish new work and go out and talk about it. One of the biggest draws of the programme as far as non-fiction went was undoubtedly Tom Novak, who was there to discuss his latest book, *True Republic*.

Novak's slot had fallen victim to the abundance of talent at the festival, having been rescheduled twice in the last week, thanks to the prima donna antics of a well-known literary writer who demanded the prime-time evening slot. It had left Novak with one of the lesser morning slots, but that hadn't stopped his event selling out in record time.

Novak was no stranger to literary celebrity after the publication of his first book, *The Hidden State*. But the events surrounding the subject matter of *True Republic* – a memoir covering his time being indicted under the Espionage Act, then reporting with Stella on the Goldcastle, Angela Curtis and Hilderberg stories – had elevated Novak to a position he hadn't been prepared for. While Stella toiled behind the scenes at HQ, he was doing *The Tonight Show*, taking a seat alongside Hollywood actors promoting comic-book movie franchises and stand-up comedians with Netflix specials. He was photographed going out for coffee in Brooklyn on Saturday mornings, dressed down in jeans and white t-shirt, his short hair still bed-shaped. He had been romantically linked with several celebrities (only three of which had been accurate). His book had sold more copies than he thought there were readers in the country. It had been one of those perfect moments that publishers dream about, when subject matter, the fame and popularity of the writer, salaciousness, and newsworthiness all collide into a great big pile of cash.

Novak had been given an advance of $50,000 on his royalties. By week two of publication it had earned out. Since then, each day had brought a veritable ring of cash registers. To everyone but Novak.

Three months in, the excuses for lack of payment had become tiresome.

Six months in, it was looking damn near fraudulent.

Novak's patience had run out. He was about to get his answers. Just not the ones he was hoping for.

He stood backstage, peeking out from behind the curtain at the capacity crowd. The interviewer, Marty Remnick of *New York Times Magazine*, was already out there, giving the long rundown of Novak's plaudits. Novak was due out any minute, and he wasn't listening to a word of Remnick's. He was listening with increasing dread to Linda, his publisher's public relations and press officer – who surely had drawn the shortest straw in publishing that day.

On book tours, the major publishers always sent a representative to accompany the author. They weren't months-long odysseys like a band on tour promoting an album. They were rarely longer than a few weeks. The press officer was there to make sure the venue had promoted the talk or signing, and there were plenty of books for sale. Their job was simple: maximise book sales. If they happened to keep the author happy in the process, all the better.

It was often said that there were two myths in the publishing world: the overnight success, and the author who doesn't want to talk about their book. Most authors are more than happy to be out on tour. Judging by the evidence of the past week, Novak was proving to be an exception.

It had all started well. Venues were packed, the book was selling, and the critics were in increasing numbers declaring the book a masterpiece of reportage and memoir, capturing a bewildering moment in time when Tom Novak went from newsman to being The News, and placing his and Stella's reporting in the context of a post-privacy cultural moment like no other. Then, as he and Linda travelled from city to city, bookstore to bookstore, Novak started noticing something happening to his audience. A lot of them had some crazy ideas. About 9/11 being an inside job. About Roswell and UFOs. The leadership of the Democrats being involved in a satanic child-abuse sex ring. That there was a secret Nazi government that wanted to enslave the world. That the earth was flat. And about Tom Novak and Stella Mitchell's part in unmasking the Hilderberg conspiracy.

To them, Novak and Mitchell had managed to do what no one else had: expose the dark underbelly of corrupt politicians and big business, with evidence, indictments, and convictions in criminal courts in both the US and the UK.

They represented a victory and validation for all conspiracy theorists. If the Hilderberg conspiracy was true, then everything else they believed must also be true. In their eyes, these conspiracy theories weren't wrong. They just hadn't been proven yet, and the fact that they hadn't been proven was proof of how well they had been covered up.

Night after night at the Q&A, Novak braced himself for another barrage of their circular, faulty logic. And night after night he did his best to appease them without too obviously agreeing with their wacky theories.

He could see them out there in the crowd. In their red baseball caps. Their plaid shirts. Their t-shirts bearing the slogan of whatever batshit theory they'd found on Reddit that week. Some of them didn't even wait for Marty Remnick to get through his introduction before they started heckling with popular conspiracy theory mantras – 'We are Q!' '5G is a weapon!' – along with the ever-popular 'We love you, Tom!'

The New York Book Festival was meant to be Novak's victory lap. The biggest crowd of the tour. For writers, it didn't get bigger or better than the Koch Theater at Lincoln Center. It was the Madison Square Garden of the publishing world. A literary Wembley. Instead, he had found his platform sullied, the Q&A sessions often derailed by conspiracy theory talk.

To top it all off, the event was also turning into a wake for Novak's finances. It was a situation that had been brewing since Novak hit the *New York Times* bestseller list and his advance had earned out. The days of author earnings only being paid out quarterly had largely gone. The Big Five publishers pulled kicking and screaming into the PayPal age and monthly royalty statements.

Except, what Novak had been receiving wasn't tallying with what Hathaway Parker House was reporting and what their accounting division was sending to his bank account.

He had been stonewalled on the issue since the Midwest leg of the tour. Now that Novak was approaching ninety days of royalties, the grim reality of what had happened to his money could no longer be hidden. Forensic accountants had been called in. Investigations completed.

The findings weren't just bad. They were beyond Novak's worst-case scenario.

Linda had done her best to keep the information from Novak until the event was over, but Novak was refusing to go out on stage until he had some honesty.

Once Linda had given him some, it took him a good few minutes to come down off the ceiling. Struggling to lower his voice, he exclaimed, 'How can it all be gone? Where? The guy didn't spend, like, a million bucks in six months!'

Linda was shaken and felt out of her depth. She and the Hathaway Parker House executives had been crafting language for the last forty-eight hours, trying to figure out how best to tell Novak the devastating news that a fraudulent accountant had stolen the vast majority of his royalties. Just another hour and Linda could have hidden behind an email. That option had now been taken off the table. She tried to use calming gestures. 'Tom, why don't we wait until–'

'No,' he cut her off. 'Why don't we talk about the house I just bought. My overdue mortgage payments. Car payments. Let's talk about the money that Hathaway *owes* me. I don't give a shit what that guy stole. Because I'll tell you this, I will get *paid*.'

That was the part that Linda feared most. She gulped, noticing that Marty Remnick was close to wrapping up his introduction. 'The thing is, Tom... You're not the only author that this has happened to. The accountant has been funnelling cash out of the company for years.'

'How much?' asked Novak. 'From all authors?'

'It's hard to say for sure.'

Through gritted teeth, he said, 'Try.'

Linda paused. 'About ten million.'

Novak exploded, 'Ten *million*?'

A few people in the front row squinted in the direction of the muffled sound behind the curtain. Even Marty Remnick hesitated for a moment, wondering what was going on.

Novak closed his eyes and took a deliberately long breath.

Linda continued, 'HPH will of course cover all of your royalties, but it's going to take a little time to work out exactly what they are.'

'What are you talking about? How can you not know what they are?'

'The accountant has been altering sales data to cover his tracks.' She braced herself. 'We don't know what your real sales have been.'

Novak had already shifted to the anger phase about his loss. 'I've not left the bestseller lists for a month. Cut me a cheque so I can at least pay my mortgage this month.'

'We can't do that, Tom. We're a Fortune 500 company. We can't write cheques for random amounts without sales data to back it up. Do you know what an IRS investigation on a company our size would look like? It could shut us down for weeks.'

Novak knew he was getting nowhere. 'So basically I'm f–'

The crowd suddenly rushed to their feet with applause as Marty Remnick beckoned Novak to the stage with his arm outstretched. '...Tom Novak, everybody!'

As he stepped out, Novak was blinded by a spotlight tracking him across the stage, making his way towards two chairs at the front that looked tiny against the grand backdrop. The crowd were on their feet, applauding. Novak raised his hand in reluctant acknowledgement and sat down.

He managed to get through the first five minutes of softball questions on autopilot. They were the same ones almost every on-stage interview had started with.

Then he zoned out. The lights were so strong he could only make out faces in the first ten or so rows. He told himself not to, but he couldn't help it. His thoughts drifted to calculations of how much money he might have lost. What if the sales data couldn't be recovered? Like Linda said, Hathaway Parker House wasn't in the business of blindly cutting cheques.

Most of all, he felt like an idiot. For buying a house he couldn't really afford. For buying a car he didn't really need. All on the promise of money that would be coming to him later down the road.

Then he thought about having to tell Stella. He'd kept the exorbitant purchases secret from her, because he knew that she would tell him it was a bad idea spending so much on credit.

Now what was he going to do?

One word reverberated in his mind.

Bankruptcy.

4

'Tom?' Marty Remnick repeated.

Novak squinted, pretending to have been distracted by the bright lights. 'Sorry,' he said.

Remnick said, 'I was saying, more and more we're seeing changes in how the news is being reported: open-source journalism like Verax, using free tools on the internet to break stories that mainstream media outlets can't afford to spend time on. And then there's Griffin, of course.'

Novak pursed his lips. 'I was wondering how long it would be until we got to that.'

Naturally, he had followed the Griffin leaks closely in his role as national security correspondent at *The Republic*. Anyone who had paid the slightest attention to the news in the last three months had heard of Griffin, the non-profit website that published news leaks, where sources could upload sensitive or classified material with total anonymity. Even the coders and staff behind Griffin had no way of knowing who their sources were.

Novak thought the way that they had disclosed files

without any redaction was reckless in the extreme. But there was also something brilliantly cavalier about what they were doing and how they were doing it.

'I have to ask,' Remnick insisted. 'Your breakthrough NSA Papers story came from a classified intelligence leak. In the last six months Griffin has published a series of damaging and embarrassing intelligence leaks from anonymous whistleblowers. It seems that no one's safe from these disclosures. Politicians, celebrities, the military. My question is: do you worry about losing future stories to organisations like Griffin?'

Novak paused, trying to give a diplomatic answer. 'I really respect what they've done. Though as a competitive reporter I can't help agonising over the stories I've missed. Journalism is a zero-sum game. A source taking their information to Griffin is information *The Republic* doesn't get until Griffin publishes it. A story for Griffin is a story that I don't get. Mop-ups never have the same impact.' He explained to the crowd, 'That's basically reporting on someone else's story after the fact. Breaking the story has always been the thing for reporters. So far, their founder Hugo Byron has proven he's willing to get his hands dirty with governments and intelligence agencies around the world. The challenge for him in the future is going to be deciding what he thinks is newsworthy. Do they publish everything, or does he editorialise? They say they're apolitical.' He held a long shrug. 'How true is that? Only time will tell.'

'There's a lot of mystery about Hugo Byron. Almost nothing is known about his background, other than having been a pretty proficient hacker in his teens. He then dropped off the grid completely for nearly twelve years, before resurfacing as the founder of Griffin. What do you make of him?'

Novak said, 'I haven't seen any compelling evidence that Hugo Byron is even real.'

Some in the crowd laughed.

'I'm serious,' he clarified. 'No one from the organisation makes any appearances, in public or on video. The fact that Byron's name is out there at all took a hell of a lot of digging. And even that could just be a pseudonym for a collective behind Griffin. We all know that you can be almost anyone online now.'

Remnick grinned. 'Can I ask a question I think a lot of us would like to know the answer to?'

'Go on,' said Novak, intrigued.

'Are you Hugo Byron?'

Through some gentle laughs from the crowd, there was a genuine sense of suspense.

Novak drew out the moment for as long as he could, then shook his head. 'So far, Griffin has been responsible for leaks leading to the resignations of the US Attorney General. Fifteen members of Germany's *Bundestag* resigned in disgrace after an arms-for-cash scandal. The President of the Governorate of the Vatican left over continued child abuse allegations. And the Deputy Secretary-General of the United Nations was outed as embezzling foreign aid. If I *was* Hugo Byron, I'd damn well keep my mouth shut about it, because he's made some very powerful enemies.'

Remnick smiled along with the crowd's laughter. 'Griffin have been talking up how big their next drop is. What do you think it could be?'

Novak said, 'I don't know. There isn't much left! I do know that people in power have been waiting for Griffin to fall prey to hyperbole in their press releases, but they haven't failed yet in delivering. If they say they have something that trumps everything else so far? In that situation, I'm not a reporter. I'm like you guys. I'd like to see it. What matters is that Griffin has changed the way news is reported. They're influencing elections with their choice of what they leak and when. We've seen this in Presidential elections. One well-timed leak with damaging information can change the course of history. That's a dangerous game to play.'

'Speaking of dangerous games,' said Remnick, 'you and Stella Mitchell found a story with a cast of characters and a conspiracy that doesn't come along very often for reporters. Watergate. Iran-Contra. British newspaper phone-hacking all spring to mind. Goldcastle and Hilderberg comfortably sit alongside those...'

Before Remnick could get to his question, there was a heckle from deep in the crowd. 'Jozef von Hayek's still alive! Hilderberg is still alive! The Dems are Hilderberg!...'

Security smothered the rest of the man's desperate cries.

Novak shook his head and rolled his eyes. He was used to it at this point of the tour. 'Welcome to my life now,' he muttered.

Remnick said, 'As I was saying, you and Stella have had not one, but two, generational scoops. The pair of you risked your lives for this story, and nearly lost them on numerous occasions. You're a million-copy bestseller, you're on late-night talk shows, followed by the paparazzi. Where do you go from here?'

Novak was distracted, looking towards the table at the back of the auditorium where fans were already starting to queue for the book signing. 'I think the biggest mistake I could make as a reporter would be trying to find a story as big as the one Stella and I found with Angela Curtis. There are still indictments being handed down in Washington related to the case. Grand juries. Subpoenas issued to find out who knew what. A lot of people are already in jail or awaiting trial. I doubt I'll cover any of it. Stella wants newer reporters to cut their teeth on that.'

Remnick seemed surprised by this. 'Why?'

Novak thought for a moment. If he had been able to voice the thoughts flooding through his head in that moment, it would have taken an hour to get them all out. All the sacrifices made. All the lives lost along the way. The egotistical, narcissistic young man he was when he started the story, and the man he was now. He understood the reality of the modern world. The shameless self-regard and self-interest of politicians. The greed of their backers.

And above all, the terrible things people will do for money and power.

Novak said, 'You never really finish a story. You just choose to stop working on it. Or your editor tells you you're done and that they're publishing. For me, I know I *could* write about Angela Curtis and Hilderberg for another three years. I *could* write a sequel to *True Republic* – I'm sure my publisher would like me to. But you either move with the times or the times move you. I know that Stella and I have different feelings about that.'

Remnick's experienced ear told him that Novak had let something slip. 'I know that the Hilderberg story has increased *Republic*'s readership immensely in the last six months. But your partner on that story is now your editor. It must be hard if there's a conflict between the two of you in how you continue to cover the story...'

Novak inhaled sharply. He knew he'd messed up and now had to backtrack without making it look like a backtrack.

Remnick was too wily an operator to let it drop. 'Do you think it's a mistake for *The Republic* to keep giving such prominent coverage to what is essentially an old story?'

Novak didn't do a good job of hiding his irritation at Remnick trying to drive a wedge between him and Stella. 'I trust Stella to do the right thing for *Republic*. That's why Diane Schlesinger wanted her to take over.'

'But surely Diane couldn't have imagined Stella would be required to take over for at least another five or ten years. Probably longer. As it stands, at thirty-eight Stella is the youngest chief editor in *Republic*'s history. Given the tragic circumstances of Diane's death, there must have been a lot of pressure for Stella to accept the editor job. Now *The Republic* is at record high readership and subscriptions, it's making a lot of money. Yet she's an editor with very little actual experience. The weight of that must be huge.'

Novak answered definitively, 'There's nothing Stella can't handle.'

It was nearly time for Remnick to wrap up, as evidenced by larger sections of the audience heading towards the signing queue. Sensing one last opportunity to throw out a difficult question that might elicit a quote-worthy response from Novak, Remnick leaned in for the kill. 'As we've seen tonight, you've become synonymous with a very vocal part of the internet. The message boards and Facebook groups where a lot of conspiracy theories are discussed. How do you feel about being associated with that?'

Novak tried not to rise to the bait, falling back on the stock answer that Linda had suggested. 'That's really out of my control. All I do is report the news as it relates to national security.'

Remnick bowed his head, combing through his notes as if he were improvising even raising the topic. He peered over his glasses as he read. 'Holocaust denial. The murder of Princess Diana. The earth is flat. Mass shootings are false flag attacks. Top politicians are in a child-sex ring.' Remnick removed his glasses. 'These are just some of the topics that the Hilderberg conspiracy has become a part of. The narrative there is that in proving the organisation's existence and criminal conspiracy, you have somehow lifted the veil on all of these other conspiracy theories. There are now millions of people coming to them through the Hilderberg and Goldcastle stories, and possibly through this book–'

In the wings, Linda looked on, hopping from foot to foot in anger. She'd warned Hathaway that getting Remnick as interviewer would be a mistake. He'd seen his own publication's readership depleted thanks to *The Republic*. More eyes on *Republic* meant less ad spend for his magazine. And that meant job cuts. As Linda saw it, Remnick had nothing to lose. He wasn't there to help Novak and Hathaway sell more books.

Now Remnick went in for the killer blow. 'Do you think you bear some responsibility for bringing conspiracy theories into the mainstream? And what if those conspiracy theories end up having real-world consequences?'

Novak smiled as he looked out to the crowd. He said, 'In nineteen fifty-eight, there was a poll about professions that the public trusted the most. The only jobs above reporter were doctors, teachers, and members of the clergy. The same poll was taken a few weeks ago. Do you know the only professions now *lower* than reporter?' He counted them off on his fingers. 'Car salesmen. Stockbrokers. And members of Congress. That's how far we've fallen.' Novak stood up and turned to Remnick. 'You ask me about conspiracy theories? I've seen a lot in the last three years. We as a society are at a critical time now. Are we going to live in a world of lies and fairy tales, where hacks can peddle any kind of fantasy and sell it as fact for political or material gain? If you want to throw me under the bus for telling the truth, Marty, that seems to me a strange hill to want to die on. But if that's all that's on offer, I don't want any part of it. I can't control who reads my work, or shows up to my events.' He gestured at the crowd. 'Clearly. I'm done. With all of this shit.' He pointed to the back of the auditorium. 'If anyone wants their book signed, I'll be back there. Anyone wondering if I think we faked the moon landings can jump straight to the cab line outside.'

He left the stage to enthusiastic whoops from the crowd. Along with several boos.

As he passed Linda in the wings, she remarked, dripping with irony, 'That went well.'

* * *

The rain was pouring when Novak hurried out of the venue, past the fountain, towards Columbus Avenue. He draped his jacket over his head, focussed only on a waiting yellow taxi at the edge of the square. The only one in sight.

The desperate dash to the sidewalk was the culmination of an exhausting three years on a rollercoaster. All political conspiracies, all the time. Now he wanted off.

He was beat up. Exhausted. Now finally released from his publicity duties, it was time to stop and take stock.

He saw a young man upping his pace towards the cab.

No chance, Novak thought. He ran full tilt, beating him to the cab by a few steps.

'Son of a–' came the inevitable response as Novak quickly shut the door.

'Midtown,' Novak told the driver, wiping the rain from his face before sinking back into the seat in relief.

Seconds later, his phone rang. The number began with area code 212. A Manhattan landline.

'This is Tom Novak,' he answered.

'Tom.' The voice was pure Upper East Side, the wealthy Manhattan neighbourhood. 'It's Wendy Halbach.'

CEO of the American arm of Hathaway Parker House.

'Hi, Wendy,' said Novak, hoping his voice hadn't cracked too obviously with nerves.

What the hell? he thought. Had his performance gone down so poorly that word of it had reached Hathaway HQ already? Is this what she was calling about? Had Linda, now free of Novak's mood swings and ego, ratted him out to her boss?

Halbach said, 'I caught the online stream of the talk. Before you try to explain, let me tell you that I know what Remnick was trying to do. It was a mistake to get him to chair. I just wish you hadn't given him exactly what he wanted. You gave him a ninety-second video clip that his magazine is going to run all week.'

Novak tried to protest, 'Wendy, really...'

She spoke over him. 'I'm not calling about that. You can have that argument with Stella when you get back to the office. I wanted to reach out, personally, about this accounting disaster. I think you know when I tell you that every cent you're owed will be paid. Eventually.'

That simple word. *Eventually*. It sank Novak's spirit. He didn't need *eventually*. He needed *immediately*.

Halbach went on, 'I gather Linda explained our predicament regarding payments. I'm also aware of your frustration with your reporting duties. Excising yourself from the tinfoil hat brigade. So, I have a proposal.'

'What kind of proposal?' asked Novak.

'A book proposal, actually. A project.'

Assuming that she wanted a sequel to *True Republic*, Novak said, 'I don't know, Wendy. I've barely finished promoting this one. I think I should talk this through with my agent, because there's a bit of urgency on the financial front for me.'

'I suspected that,' she replied. 'It's not a sequel. It's a new project. Writing plot lines with your specialty knowledge for others to then write the full book.'

'A ghostwriter?'

'Kind of.'

'Who would I be writing for?'

'One of the biggest thriller writers in the world.'

Novak paused in confusion. 'They don't plot their own books?'

Halbach laughed. 'You really are cute sometimes, Tom. The job is in London. If you want it, I can set you up with my colleague in our office there.'

'Gee, Wendy, I don't know…'

Halbach then got to the kicker. 'There's cash in it for you.' The silence at the other end told her Novak was listening. 'As a new project, you would be entitled to an advance for any work you produce for us. My accountants and lawyers tell me that we could use this to funnel back some of the money that you're owed.'

'How much?' he asked. His phone pinged.

'I just emailed you the offer now.'

He opened the email and scrolled to the only section that mattered to him. "Remuneration". He was amazed by the amount. 'You must want one hell of a plot.'

'I want the biggest there is,' she replied. 'Hop on the red-eye and you can talk it over with the editor in charge. She'll give you the full pitch of what's required. If you like it, you keep the money and do the job. If you don't like it, you keep the advance and go home.'

Novak's mind was racing. About who he might be working with. And seeing his bank balance flush again. Creditors paid off. Payments made.

Then he remembered where he was heading. 'I need to talk to Stella about this first. Give me a few hours.'

'I can give you one. Then I call the next name on my list. And Tom, I should tell you. I had to fight to get your name ahead of them.'

'Why is that?' he asked.

'Because picking them doesn't involve cutting a cheque for three hundred thousand dollars.'

Novak could see his window of opportunity already closing. He said, 'Let me talk to Stella.'

He wanted to smile, but there was a part of him that wasn't sure. Why had Halbach been so soft on him about the interview? Not only did she gloss over Novak's part in a PR disaster at his biggest media event, but she took the blame for having hired Remnick in the first place.

Whatever Hathaway had going on across the Atlantic, they wanted Novak for the job. Badly.

5

THE REPUBLIC HEADQUARTERS, NEW YORK CITY

Novak felt a cloud hanging over him as he crossed the newsroom floor to his desk. He was asked several questions on the way there and answered none of them. He was dressed casually but expensively. His blue shirt looked at first glance like any other blue shirt that millions of men went to work in. But Novak's cost what a lot of people would spend on a dinner for four people. Normally it made him feel good. It wasn't about showing off how much money he had. It was for him. But walking through the newsroom in such expensive gear, with very little actual money to his name and not much coming anytime soon if he didn't take the job in London. He felt like a fraud. Like someone playing at being a big shot. Something he'd have to get used to if he didn't take Wendy Halbach's deal.

The divider around his desk was covered with various items printed from the internet in his research on Hugo Byron. Among them were pictures of Pyongyang in North Korea, the North Pole in a blizzard, and the moon. Above those, a note from Novak:

"*Possible Hugo Byron hiding locations?*"

Mark Chang stopped by. 'Hey, Tom. Making any progress with him?'

'Trail's cold,' said Novak.

'He's your Satoshi Nakamoto.' Chang nodded to himself in satisfaction.

'Who's that?'

'The inventor of Bitcoin. At least, the man rumoured to be. No one really knows for sure. Nakamoto was just a name attached to the first research paper on the technology. It could be a collective. An Aussie called Craig Wright claims to be Nakamoto. But he can't actually prove it.'

'Hugo Byron is just another message board invention. A name for Griffin to hide behind.'

'Could be.' Chang looked towards Stella's office and lowered his voice. 'You get my message earlier?'

Novak drew his eyes away, his expression changing to concern. 'I'm about to speak to her.'

As Chang moved on, Novak went quickly through the pile of notes left on his desk. All of them sounded semi-urgent, and all of them were put back on his desk without a further thought.

From behind him came a female voice. English. Stern. The kind of sternness that suggested a you-don't-know-what's-good-for-you vibe.

'I can't work out if you love trouble or if trouble loves you, Tom Novak,' said Stella.

He turned around slowly, sensing he had some of what he called the hairdryer treatment coming. Diane Schlesinger had often used it to get through to Novak when he'd *really* screwed up – it consisted of a tirade so loud that it was like having a hairdryer pointed at your face.

Stella went on, 'In forty minutes you managed to piss off

Marty Remnick, the entire staff of *New York Times Magazine*, conspiracy theorists, your own publisher, and most puzzlingly of all your own readers. It takes a special kind of talent to piss off all those people in one go.'

The rest of the staff made as if carrying on with their work, but they were all staying well and truly tuned in to what was going on. Technically, they were all colleagues. To the regular junior staff on twenty thousand a year starting salary, Tom and Stella were celebrities. They saw them on TV and on their phone screens more often than in the flesh.

Novak asked, 'How do you know all that?'

'The festival was showing it online.'

'You're sitting watching a livestream?'

'No, I had an intern do it. A legal necessity, I said.'

'We should be giving interns real jobs.'

'She took notes, Novak. Notes. Look at what she gave me.' Stella held up a wad of paper. 'One of these is headed "Potential controversies" Another, "Urgent controversies." Do you get the overall picture?'

Novak sensed an audience forming, and he knew that Stella was only getting warmed up. 'The intern's obviously a good listener. We should keep her,' he said, steering Stella back towards her office.

She wriggled out of his grip but kept walking. 'You announced on a stage to a live audience that you disagree with where I'm taking *Republic*. That isn't a joke, Novak.'

Every time they ended up in one of these confrontations, Stella was reminded how recently they'd been partners. Reining in his more harebrained ideas had been far easier when they were working side by side. She could keep him on an invisible leash. Now she had to make peace with the fact that he was out there on his own, day to day, answerable to no one.

Novak made sure to close the door behind them once they reached Stella's office. The walls may have been glass, but they were reliably soundproof.

Stella sat behind her desk, resuming her paperwork. She didn't need Novak's antics to drag her any further behind schedule than she already was. 'Go on then,' she said. 'Give me your side before I get the call from upstairs.'

Novak stood, hands on hips. 'I was asked to sign a Confederate flag.'

Stella stopped her work.

'No joke,' Novak continued, raising his hands in innocence. 'Is that who my audience is now? *Our* audience?'

Stella said, 'Don't be ridiculous.'

'Is it ridiculous, though, Stel? Have you seen my email inbox lately? My Facebook messages? They're nuts! One of them thinks that the moon is a hollowed-out alien space station, and that the British royal family are shape-shifting reptiles.'

'In fairness, I think the jury may still be out on the latter.'

'And the really crazy part–'

'This isn't already crazy?'

'The *crazy* part is that these look like pretty normal people. When it started, I thought their profile pictures would be them standing at the Lincoln Memorial wearing a tinfoil hat. But these are housewives writing me. People with respectable jobs. And some of them have started to turn on me.'

'Why?' asked Stella. 'I thought the crazies were your people.'

'That's the problem. I'm the wrong *kind* of crazy now. It turns out our Hilderberg-Angela Curtis story was an elaborate ploy. That secretly we're on Hilderberg's payroll, and our story is part of a deep state cover-up to hide the fact that Jozef von Hayek is now hiding on an island owned by Hilary Clinton and George Soros.' Novak pulled out the chair facing Stella's side of the desk and fell into it, exasperated. 'I'm done, Stella. Done with conspiracies. Being shouted at in the damn street.' He hesitated. Enough that he had to look away. 'Maybe with the newsroom too.'

Stella said, 'I see,' trying to comprehend what she'd just heard. Tom Novak not report the news?

He added, 'For a while, at least. I need a break.'

Stella looked to the ceiling in frustration.

'What is it?' he asked.

'I took a call from Ralph Ogden this morning,' she said.

'Why?'

When Stella had finished explaining, she concluded by telling him she wanted him to take the story on with Ogden.

Novak's body language had been growing increasingly strained throughout, rubbing his forehead intensely. 'I can't do it, Stel.'

'Why the hell not?'

'The thing is...' He suddenly became fascinated with his hands, the floor, the bustling newsroom beyond Stella. Anywhere but her eyes. 'There's something I have to tell you.'

He explained his money problems, the missing royalty payments. He felt shame radiating out of every pore. Then he explained about Wendy Halbach's offer.

Stella paused to absorb the news. She tried to ask in such a way that made the question appear inconsequential. Under the surface, she was doing calculations that Novak had no idea about. 'So if it's a writing job in London that would be with Hathaway, right?'

Of all the details to enquire about, Novak didn't understand why she was getting stuck on *that*. 'Yeah. And I need this money, Stel.'

'How much are you owed?'

'My agent thinks it's in the region of half a million.'

'How much do you owe?'

'Embarrassingly close to half a million. It doesn't matter. Without this book gig I can't even afford the interest payments. This time next week I'll be a Chapter Seven.'

'Bankrupt?'

He shrugged. 'I called Kevin Wellington from the cab for some legal advice. He was honest with me. It doesn't look good.'

Fearing the next thing from Novak might be a resignation letter, Stella put out a reassuring hand. 'You're upset, Novak. Let's wait and see what Kevin says about the money.'

'Geez, Stella, I'm not talking about the money! Or the massive house in Brooklyn, or the stupid car. I'm talking about what I *do*.'

'Exactly,' said Stella. 'You're a reporter. You're about finding the truth. Holding those in power accountable. Exposing secrets.'

Novak fired back, 'And look where it's got me! Handed Confederate flags by racists at book signings, and strangers shouting "mainstream media fake news!" at me in the street. I spent so long in this Hilderberg bubble, all I see are conspiracies everywhere. I don't even know what's *real* anymore.'

Stella said, already shaking her head, 'What about Diane?'

'Diane's dead, Stel, and it's time we started acting like it. We've kept this ship running way longer than anyone expected, but I look at what's happening to us and I don't like it.'

'Us?'

Novak paused. He knew that what he was about to say next could end with her storming out of the room, or possibly even the end of their working and personal relationship. For what was at stake, he thought it was a risk worth taking. He looked right into Stella's eyes when he said it. 'You're high right now, aren't you?'

She froze.

'Do you want me to open that drawer by your right leg?' he asked.

Her head dropped. Deep down, she had been hoping to be caught.

Novak clarified, 'When someone you care about is in trouble, all you want is for them to be well again.'

She said, 'You have no idea what I've been trying to handle all this time. Since Diane died.'

'I know I don't,' he replied.

'I'm the hammer *and* the nail around here, Novak. If I don't do it, it doesn't get done. In the time it takes me to clear ten emails another twenty have come in.' She gestured at the tall piles of paperwork skyscrapered across her desk like a mini-Manhattan. 'This is what it looks like on a good day. If it's a bad day, I can't tell the board I need a time out. I have to be *on it*. Every damn day. For you. For them–' she pointed to the newsroom '–for our competitors like Marty Remnick who would love nothing more than to see us crash and burn. And not least for Diane.'

Novak's head dropped. 'Stel. You were put in an impossible position because of circumstances that Diane could never have anticipated. She wouldn't want this. I've been here before. With pills. And Diane was the one who stopped me.'

'What happened?' Stella asked.

'I was twenty-two and thought I was hot shit. Indestructible. And I wasn't. I burned out and got into pills. Codeine. Anything to take the edge off that allowed me to still do my job. We've both worked with drunks.'

'Yeah, that never works. You can edit drunk, but only

Martin Fitzhenry is capable of writing good copy while drunk.'

'So I figured out that I could grind up co-codamol and filter it with water through coffee filters to extract the codeine without risking overdosing on the paracetamol they put in it. Three weeks in, what had taken me four pills now took me twelve. Then there was the fact that I'd watched my mother chew Prozac for years.'

Stella sat in silence. In their three years together, Novak had never talked about her.

He continued, 'I was seven years old when I found her hanging in our garage. I used a set of ladders to try and get her down, but my fingers weren't strong enough to unpick the knot in the noose she'd tied, or to take the weight of her in my arms. I finally called nine one one. The EMTs said she'd been dead a few hours. I was sleeping while my mum was killing herself. I'm not going to sleep through you, Stella. You're too important to me.' He reached his hand across the desk.

She took it in hers. 'I'm sorry, Novak. That must have been horrible. I didn't meant to bring it all...' Her eyes started to fill.

Novak glanced towards the newsroom, thinking about whether or not he should hug her. He decided to go with the hug.

'No,' she said, turning away so that no one could see her face. 'I don't want them thinking something is wrong. I swear we need to get rid of these bloody glass walls!' As she composed herself, she said, 'I was waiting for it to stop. You know?'

'It's never going to stop, Stel,' said Novak. 'This is what the job is. Diane missed both her boys' high school graduations because she was sitting behind that desk.'

'That's what we signed up for.'

'No, it's not,' replied Novak. 'And you know it's not.'

'I don't mind us missing a story. That happens. But Ralph Ogden's story on the Ian Ferguson poisoners is exactly what we should have. Right now we're being out-reported by a guy at his kitchen table.'

'I agree,' said Novak.

'It's not good enough.'

'Is this about Ian Ferguson or *True Republic*? Because I asked you to write it with me...'

Stella pushed her chair back from her desk. It smacked into the glass wall, which didn't go unnoticed in the newsroom. 'God, Novak,' she exclaimed, pacing to the other end of the office. 'It's everything! We're falling behind.'

He took a beat, trying to lower the temperature in the room. 'There are these lumberjacks working in the forest. Everyone's working really hard, chopping wood for the same length of time each day. Except for one guy who every day without fail disappears for an hour in the middle of the day. And every day he chops more wood than anyone else. It goes on for months like this. Eventually, someone says to him, I don't understand. Every day we start at the same time, every day we stop at the same time. And every day you chop more wood than us. How? What are you doing in that hour? The lumberjack says, that's simple. That's when I go home and sharpen my axe. Writing *True Republic* and doing promo, that was me sharpening my axe. And if I want to avoid swinging from a rope in a garage, or seeing the same happen to my best friend, then I need to understand when it's time to chop wood. That's something I don't think you understand.'

'What do you suggest?' she asked.

'Come with me to London. You take the Ferguson story with Ralph Ogden.'

'I can't do that.'

'Why not? You need to be a reporter again, Stella.'

Her full name. He really was being serious, she thought.

He continued, 'But if we do this thing, you have to be clean.'

Stella opened the drawer by her right leg and placed both bottles of pills on the table. 'What about the office?'

'Mark's here. The team love that he's back. They respect him and they'll work hard for him. He was by Diane's side for years. We didn't have him when she died, but we have him now.'

'You think he's up to it?' she asked.

'Well, he edited me for three years, so he knows how to deal with disruption. Remember his work on Goldcastle? It was Mark who made me call back Walter Sharp. Keeping our foot on the gas.'

Stella agreed. 'That's what every newsroom needs.'

'He was also the one who realised what you were doing with the pills. He sees more than you realise.'

Stella let out a heavy breath, thinking the worst of it was over. The plaster had been ripped off. Now all there was left was the healing part. 'I didn't think anyone would notice while you were away.'

Novak paused for a moment. 'After everything we've been through. Don't you know I could never let anything happen to you? Ever? I'm going to help you get through this thing. But I'm only going to London if you come with me.'

Deep down, she knew it was the right choice. The only choice, really.

She nodded. 'Okay. I'll come with you.'

Novak picked up the bottles. 'That's all of them?' he asked.

'Yeah.'

It came out so easily. She had expected some kind of

unconscious pushback from lying to Novak. Instead, it felt easier than the truth.

Novak pocketed the pills, not wanting anyone in the newsroom to see him holding them. 'You're going to feel pretty shitty for the next twenty-four hours.'

'Not as shitty as I feel right now.'

Once he was gone, Stella messaged Ralph Ogden: '*We're on. I'll be in London tomorrow. Further details to come.*' She then put her phone in her handbag, covering up two small bottles. One containing yellow pills. The other pink.

She got straight onto her computer and did an internet search for "*Hathaway Publisher London*".

The first result was a snippet from Wikipedia, detailing the company's rich history. The next three were from Hathaway's website, followed by links to their Facebook and Twitter profiles. Only a small fortune in search engine optimisation can bring such clean results on the first page of a search.

Stella clicked on to their official website. The homepage showed a carousel of autumn's biggest books. Autumn was all about literary fiction. When the potential award-winners were sent out into the world. But Stella wasn't interested in their books. She was interested in their personnel.

She clicked into the "About Us" section, and was presented with the full array of Hathaway's empire. All the other imprints they had gobbled up and bought over through the years. The non-fiction arm – Testimony – where all the big-hitting cookbooks, celebrity biographies, and lighter non-fiction went. Children's, audio, Hathaway Classics, and three other fiction imprints. The copywriter had tried to give them all different identities, but the truth was they were all much the same: previously the competition, packed to the gills with best-selling crime, thrillers, and fiction, then bullied into a buyout with an eye-watering valuation that made selling the only rational option for shareholders. What had once been the Big Six in the UK was now down to the Big Four. Of those four, the smart money was on Hathaway ending up as the Big One.

Stella clicked into the "Our People" section. The face she was looking for was at the top.

Anne Cochrane. CEO, Hathaway Parker House UK.

The short profile on the other side of the link had obviously been written by some committee to ensure all the necessary soundbites were ticked off. Lip service paid to all the PR talking points.

Books can change lives. Or even the world! Check.

I like taking risks... Check.

Embracing diverse voices... Check.

There was no mention of background or basic details like place of birth. And certainly no mention of Anne having formerly been married. Or being a mother.

In Stella's eyes, Anne Cochrane (formerly Mitchell) had stopped being that to her a long time ago.

6

THE MALL, LONDON

His name was George Asquith Villiers, but it was his title that had loomed largest in his life.

The 6th Earl of Carringdon.

There were nearly two hundred earls around the country, the third class of peerage in the UK below duke and marquess. The Queen had the final say on who was given a peerage, and having been the third generation of Private Secretary to various royals through the years, there was never any doubt that George Villiers would be given the title of earl at some point in his life.

Since he was a child, the weight of history in his family had followed him around, an oppressive and intimidating force for an only child. He had known only great men. Naval commanders. Politicians. Titans of finance. Women had featured little in his life, apart from a nanny who took over most mothering duties while Villiers' actual mother spent most of her time receiving guests in their twenty-room grand house, or attending the most lavish society events in London. After distinguishing himself in a brief navy career, it became clear that George Asquith Villiers was made for higher service. In many ways, the highest the country had to offer. Or as close as a civilian could get to it.

It had been made clear by George's dad – the 5th Earl of Carringdon – at an early age that being a Villiers marked young George out. It was nice of George to want to fraternise with the cleaners and gardeners and cooks, but it simply wasn't the done thing. There were lines drawn in society about the class of people you interacted with. There were people like the Villiers, and then there was the sort of people who travelled on buses and the Underground. Who wore trainers. Who didn't know the correct cutlery to use for different courses. Whose main source of entertainment was a television.

Such arcane rules were easy to drum into young George because he had no interaction with anyone outside of his economic sphere. He didn't live near them. He didn't go to school with them, or university. And when he entered the world of work he was coddled and protected thanks to his family connections. Over time, adult George tried to shrug off such appendages. He didn't think of himself as better than anyone. He had simply spent too long existing not in the real world, but in a world with a tiny population. Of obscene, almost grotesque wealth. Who had tried to keep alive a world that no longer existed. Something approximating the inter-war years. A kind of eternal *Brideshead Revisited*. Where all there was to do was go to white-tie dinner parties, play backgammon 'at the club', and race cars in the countryside with all those Helenas and Humphreys and Horatios. And every year that world became harder to keep alive.

Which was why Villiers enjoyed walking into work from his stately flat in central Mayfair so much. As he strode along the Mall, he knew that he looked like an anachronism. Almost a parody of an ageing English gentleman. White hair swept to one side underneath a navy trilby hat. A suit that looked dull and grey, but close up had been impeccably tailored. A tasteful thickness to the lapel. A tie dimple. A pair of perfectly polished antique rosewood shoes by Barker's – some would say the last great English traditional shoemaker. Villiers was fine with all of that. Because walking to work was his chance to be part of a world that had been denied to him. He enjoyed rubbing shoulders with what his father had called the 'common man'. Picking out ripe bananas in the busy metro supermarket. Saying good morning to strangers. Offering his umbrella during a rainstorm.

On the Mall, he carried himself like the gentleman he believed himself to be. By the paperwork tucked under his arm, he could have been a lawyer. Perhaps a fund manager. Maybe even a politician – you could throw a rock around those parts and come close to striking one. And many would have implored you to throw it hard.

This outwardly genteel appearance was offset by his determined walk. A man of purpose.

His back straightened slightly as he passed by a group of Italian tourists in their late teens, a few steps off the pavement onto the Mall's iconic – and recently repaired – red road to get a better angle as they excitedly took pictures on their phones of Buckingham Palace. Too excitedly to remember which direction traffic travelled in.

Villiers called to them in Italian, 'Get off the road!', just in time to prompt them out of the path of a taxi that had already taken evasive action into the centre of the road.

The tourists could have been French, German, or Spanish and Villiers would still have been able to communicate the danger. If they had been Swedish, he would have been able to shout a less specific warning, but it would have got the job done. Nothing sharpens the linguistics like having to liaise with foreign embassies before a royal visit.

The blast of the taxi's horn confirmed how close the Italians' trip had come to ending prematurely.

A few of them laughed out of fear. The others were too scared to do anything other than hold their chests in fright and give grateful thanks to the old Samaritan.

Villiers tipped his hat to them, then made a right halfway down the Mall towards the heavily guarded black gate on Stable Yard Row. Behind the gate, Clarence House. Royal residence, and home to a type of secretive gathering thought to have been ended over a decade ago.

The tourists thought that Villiers was just a nice old Englishman, carrying papers of no great import.

They couldn't have been more wrong.

Villiers' papers were of national importance. As all his papers were.

That was what came with being Private Secretary to Her Royal Highness Princess Rose – first in the line of succession to the British throne.

* * *

As the official royal residence of Princess Rose, Clarence House was the location for most of the meetings involving the principal secretaries of the various Royal Households. Apart from the Queen's, who always had sufficient business to take up entire days on their own, so their business was kept to Buckingham Palace. Not that the meeting Villiers was about to attend was in any way official.

The Board of Green Cloth had been named after the green baize tablecloth that covered the table where its members sat. Historically, its role was to audit the accounts of the Royal Households around the land, from the most well-known to the most minor royal that most people could pass in the street without batting an eye. The Board arranged all royal travel, both foreign and domestic, and analysed all the spending habits, bills – anything that was paid for using public money went through the Board. It had even run as a court to judge criminal offences committed on official palace grounds. As one by one the Board's powers were revoked or rehoused in obscure Whitehall accounting departments, the meeting and its Board were finally disbanded in 2004 as part of a drive for modern transparency, after accusations that the Board was there to cover up some of the more embarrassing and flagrant spending habits of the royal family.

Unofficially, the meetings had been kept going behind closed doors so that the most privileged information among the Private Secretaries could be shared and discussed. The politicians might have stolen some oversight of accounting, but the information behind it would always be kept within the bounds of what men like Villiers had always known as the Firm – the royal establishment within Buckingham Palace. Just as Westminster has its spin doctors and senior advisors who pulled the strings, so too did the royal family.

Whitehall may have taken over most of the number-crunching, but there were still many private royal matters that Her Majesty insisted only the Board would deal with. As it had been put to Villiers, "Discussions of a nature that allowed the secretaries to work with discretion." The translation couldn't have been clearer to Villiers: don't let anything embarrassing get out to the public.

In kinder language, the Board was a place where Private Secretaries could speak candidly about matters within the Royal Households, and there was a clear understanding that whatever was said at the Board of Green Cloth would be treated as totally confidential. Who was no longer sharing a bedroom with their wife or husband. Whose child was falling in with a bad crowd at school. In short, who was going to cause any negative press for Buckingham Palace. As the most senior and respected Private Secretary, it fell to Villiers to decide what action to take. Or, if it was serious enough, take matters directly to the Queen herself.

A non-royal hadn't been granted as much influence over royal affairs since Thomas Cromwell in the court of Henry VIII. A royal family member couldn't travel from their front door to the edge of the palace grounds without an invoice for petrol ending up in front of Villiers. He saw everything. He heard everything.

It was rare for anyone to be in a senior role such as Private Secretary for longer than ten years. Villiers was entering into his seventeenth. There was good reason for that: he had proven himself utterly indispensable. There had always been rumours among the Royal Households that Villiers knew where all the royals' bodies were buried, mostly because he had been the one that put them there. To Villiers, it was a laughable premise, but one that he had done nothing to disprove.

* * *

As secretary to the first in the line of succession, Villiers sat at the top of the table. The other secretaries then sat across from each other in descending order, depending on where their boss fell in the line of succession.

As usual, Villiers had been first to arrive. Diligently organising his papers in front of him so that he was ready when the ten others filed in.

It was a light day for order of business. The mood in the

room bordering on jovial. For Villiers, the only time and place for joviality was at a Gilbert and Sullivan opera. Outside of *The Pirates of Penzance*, he didn't really do light-hearted, as the others were about to be reminded.

Already chuckling at an earlier remark, the Secretary for the Earl of Wessex said, 'Have any of you seen that awful man from the BBC skulking around at your events? His Royal Highness called him "that ginger pillock" the other day at Ascot. Luckily the microphone wasn't hot or we might have ended up on the front pages.'

Fiona Bingham, sitting nearest Villiers at the top, piped up. 'Your man's tenth in line, Ed. The only way he's making the front pages is if he's talking about my guy.'

Her 'guy' was Prince James. The Duke of Salisbury. Who, for a man sixth in the line of succession, had been spending a lot of time on the front pages of the newspapers. None of it positive.

In the last month, the Palace had brought in Fiona Bingham, from a background in corporate public relations for global brands to firefight the prince's crumbling public image, which was starting to rub off on the rest of the family. When an oil company had a catastrophic spill, Bingham had been the person who crafted the press releases in response. Having grown tired of years of covering up shameless corruption, she had moved into more progressive areas of concern: the environment and social issues. Bingham found herself crafting campaigns to convince the public that a multinational company that made jeans really cared about trans rights. Or that a sports drink brand had an opinion on racial injustice. Or a major supermarket chain really did have a deep concern for the plight of refugees.

The concept of any of them should have been laughable, but a credulous public on social media was only too eager to share, retweet, and rebroadcast Bingham's campaigns. Reaching hundreds of thousands of people – for free.

Rehabilitating Prince James wouldn't be nearly as easy.

Villiers looked up slowly from a particular spreadsheet, and removed his glasses with disdain.

'Ms Bingham...' began Villiers.

'It's Miss, George,' she countered. 'As I've mentioned several times now.'

He gave a tiny bow, accepting the correction. 'Miss Bingham. We are representatives of the British royal family. This is not a competition.'

'Oh please,' she said. 'That's all we do here. Negotiating over who attends what charity dinner, in what order. Who briefs the press, who doesn't. It's not like there's no hierarchy in this room.' She gestured around the table. 'Everyone literally has a number. Or are you just sensitive about the fact that I've been brought in to fix what you couldn't?'

There was silence around the table.

Villiers looked down at the table and smiled. 'Everyone. I'd like the room with Miss Bingham. Consider today's meeting adjourned.'

The other secretaries shuffled out, disappointed at missing what was to come.

Once the door closed behind the last to leave, Villiers said, 'The concept of hierarchy might be frowned upon in whatever Palo Alto tech company board meetings you may be used to, Fiona. But in this room, hierarchy matters. I have dedicated most of my adult life in service to the royal family, and I think I have earned the right to some respect in front of my subordinates.'

It was only now that the room had cleared that Villiers was able to appreciate how well-dressed Bingham was. Private secretaries earned very comfortable salaries, but Bingham was dressed like the CEO of a major corporation. Effortlessly stylish in a subtle, tasteful Armani business suit. She had the look of a young woman at a point in her life where she no longer to be at her desk by seven a.m. Now was the time of drinking fruit juice at a relaxed pace after a morning gym session, before taking in the first editions. She was svelte. Her dark skin smooth and glowing from a supremely healthy diet that bordered on monastic. It worried Villiers, because it meant that she didn't really need to be there. She certainly didn't need the money. The question now playing on his mind was: what did she really want?

Villiers knew there was only one answer to that.

'Look, George,' Bingham began, as if what she had to say would be even more confrontational than it already had been. 'You might see your move to Clarence House and Princess Rose as a promotion. But I see it for what it is. Putting you out to pasture.'

Villiers retorted, 'I know I might look like I'm over the hill, but I can still recognise a power grab when I see one.'

'I don't know what you mean.'

'The Palace brought you in, Fiona, as a trial run before taking over with the princess. You don't have to school me in the art of coronations. At some point in the next ten years – God forbid it to be sooner – Princess Rose will be the next monarch of the United Kingdom. I'm just a steady pair of hands to iron out the rougher edges of her character. To refine her understanding of the ceremonial traditions and protocols. But you and I both know that come the time, the princess will have someone that looks like you standing next to her. Not an old white man like me.'

'I'm surprised to hear you say that,' Bingham said.

'Historically, yes, an older gentleman, experienced, the right background, etcetera, would be the obvious choice. But even I can see that times are changing. I must say it's rather high time that a young woman of colour such as yourself be brought into the fold in the Royal Households. I must also confess to a fear that you're too young and inexperienced for my job, which I have been given because the Palace understands the value and dependability that I bring. So if you think I'm going to gracefully step aside when I am *this* close to serving in the Palace, after all these years, you are sorely mistaken.'

Bingham was glad to see that she was at least dealing with a worthy adversary. Someone who saw the angles of power the way she did. 'You have no idea what I've had to do to get where I am. Forget money – I'm thirty-three and I've already made more money in the private sector than I can spend. I took this position because it's about power and influence. I've stepped over way too many bodies to be stopped by you. We also both know that the Palace giving you Princess Rose is a favour. A few last camera flashes for you before retirement.'

Villiers gave another smile. Briefer this time. He backed his chair away from the table and made his way to the window, looking out to Friary Court where the Queen's Guard were marching in formation, their red tunics bright against the dull autumnal light. 'During the summer, the prince was at the Tour de France as part of his trade delegation duties. Being a man of tradition myself, I was rather taken with something that happened during one stage. You see, whenever the Tour passes through the home town or village of a rider, all the others allow that rider to go ahead on his own. To lap up the applause as the local hero. I found this rather charming, but curious. So I asked one of the French delegates if the other riders felt it risky to let someone go up the road on their own. What if they took advantage of their good grace and tried to stay away to win the stage? The Frenchman laughed. Such a thing would be frowned upon, he told me. There are unspoken rules to this kind of thing. But the local rider could still get away with it? I asked. The Frenchman shrugged in agreement.' Villiers turned around to face Bingham. 'You see me as that local rider, waving to the crowd as I go past. At the head of the race only because you've allowed me to be there, knowing that eventually the pack will swallow me up again as they charge ahead. But what if I decide to ignore the unspoken rules? A private secretary in your position can't afford any scandal. And we both know that what the papers have printed about Prince James barely scratches the surface. One mistake and I'll be so far up the road you'll never reel me back in. Then all you'll be surrounded by is the echo of applause. For me.'

The threat had little impact on Bingham's demeanour. In the parlance of public relations, she had the eyes of a "killer": someone unshakable. 'George, I've got to tell you: that's the politest threat I've ever received in my career. There's a flip-side to that, though. Yes, if more scandal about Prince James comes out, then I go down. But one scandal involving Princess Rose and you're out for good. No free ride through your hometown. No applause. Just gone. Run over, most likely, by the cars behind.'

He rocked on his heels. 'Then we understand each other.'

* * *

When Bingham left, there was a timid knock on the open door as Villiers packed up his papers. The mere sight of the green cloth on the table was enough to trigger a wave of excitement in the junior secretary standing in the doorway. Whispers about the Board regularly made their way around Clarence

House and the Royal Households, but the young man knew better than to make any reference to it.

'Mr Villiers,' he said, 'I've been trying to reach you.'

Villiers squinted, then put his glasses on. 'It's Pembridge, isn't it?'

'Durbridge, sir,' he replied. His expression suggested he was pleased that Villiers had even got that close. 'I was asked to handle press requests on behalf of Ms Bingham while she–'

'Miss Bingham,' Villiers corrected him. 'She prefers to be called Miss.'

'Yes, sir. Miss Bingham. While she settled in with Prince James's media office. I received this last week, but I'm afraid it got somewhat lost in the shuffle.' Durbridge handed the message to Villiers. Then gulped. Hard.

It was an official request for an interview with Prince James. The name attached was Ian Ferguson.

Villiers froze after reading it. 'Who else has seen this?'

Durbridge looked terrified. 'No one, sir.'

'Keep it that way,' he replied quickly. He thumbed through a file underneath. 'Ferguson sent this with the request?'

'Yes, sir.'

'Go back to work,' said Villiers, then told him, 'And Durbridge? The men who rise in this place all have one thing in common: discretion.'

Durbridge nodded.

Villiers took the file back into the meeting room and locked the door. His heart started to race as the information in front of him took hold.

It was a copy of a bank statement from the Sovereign Grant, the public system of funding the British monarchy. But it wasn't the simplified, public version that was published on the royal family's official website. This was from the inner sanctum of Hunter & Company, the illustrious private bank that handled the monarchy's finances and investments.

One particular line on the statement was highlighted, showing missing funds. Ian Ferguson had added a question mark along with the annotation "unaccounted for".

The document showed a snippet from the travel records of Prince James's Foundation, records that weren't released to the public. In the middle of the page was a flight to Tel Aviv that had been marked as missing from the official Foundation records.

Villiers shook his head.

Prince James had taken a flight to Tel Aviv, then tried to cover it up. That alone wasn't news. It was what the missing flight coincided with that would be problematic: a payment by James into a series of shell companies in the Cayman Islands for the amount of £274,000. Paid as a 'donation' to Griffin.

Ferguson knew about it and had wanted to put on-the-record questions to Villiers and Clarence House. The question now was how many others had he told about it before he was killed? What the hell had James been up to in Tel Aviv, and why was he paying the most controversial website in the world £274,000?

Villiers rolled up the documents and hurried past the row of open office doors that made up the administration of Princess Rose's Royal Household. He explained to the staff in the bullpen area, 'I'm going out for an hour.'

There was a spring in his step along the Mall. A plan forming. Of how he was going to get rid of Fiona Bingham for good. Once more proving himself indispensable to the Palace.

7

BALMORAL CASTLE, SCOTLAND

Balmoral Castle had been one of the Queen's residences since the original building had been purchased by the royal family in 1852. Although it was still private property owned by the Queen, it was run by trustees and wasn't part of the Crown Estate – meaning that no revenue generated on the estate went back into the public purse or to Parliament. The financial separation tied in to a sense for the royal family that Balmoral brought a physical and psychological escape for them. The physical isolation was the cherry on top.

Situated west of the Cairngorm mountain range in the Highlands of Scotland, Balmoral estate sat near the River Dee, and stretched for fifty thousand acres into the surrounding land, from Braemar ten miles away, and as far as thirty miles south to Glen Cova. Although a private estate, when the Queen was in residence Scotland's right-to-roam laws still technically applied. For walkers keen to explore the rich, undulating landscape, it was a legal grey area. One day they could walk freely along the estate tracks on Deeside. On others, royal security guards – some in uniform, some not –

could demand they turn back. Generally, the advice was to avoid the area if any royals were on the property. As they currently were.

While the rest of the family posed for pictures with the official royal photographer on the front steps of the castle, Prince James roamed the hillside of the Coyles of Muick – pronounced "Mick" – with a Rigby Highland Stalker hunting rifle under his arm. His companion, Sir Christopher Benedict, motioned to James to get low to the ground.

Fast-moving clouds passed overhead. Single shafts of sunlight speared down then disappeared, like swords plunging into the landscape then retracting. The grass turned golden then black in an instant, then golden again as the sky cleared, illuminating a single red deer higher up the hillside.

James lay on his front in the heather next to Benedict. Both of them dressed in traditional hunting tweed.

'Your shot, James,' said Benedict.

The prince took aim at the fattest part of the deer's body, the iron sight set for the 250-yard shot. But before he could pull the trigger, the clouds shifted over the deer. The sudden darkness prompting it to run off into heavy ferns and purple heather.

'Shit,' cursed James.

Benedict shifted, as if about to get to his feet.

James said, 'Not yet.'

Thinking it odd, Benedict bowed to the prince's superior hunting experience. They had also been on the go since the early hours, climbing to the summit of the Coyles of Muick to scope out deer, so Benedict was only too happy to rest his legs a little longer. The hillside was exposed, the only shelter for miles around being "Coyle's Cottage", a tiny bothy made out of rocks. From the men's vantage point, they saw wave after wave of hilltops, and no one else in sight. Benedict wondered how much more remote and alone they would need to be before James raised whatever topic he had invited him out to discuss.

Benedict remarked, 'It must do something to you, owning all this land. The enormity.'

'It's not mine, though, is it?' replied James. 'It's her's. Mama's.' He emphasised the second syllable in a way only someone in the aristocracy or royalty could get away with.

Benedict found it faintly ridiculous to hear a grown man talking of his mother like he was a five-year-old. Even if she was the Queen.

James switched on the safety and laid the rifle on top of his canvas and leather gunslip. He surveyed the landscape with a pair of binoculars. 'So,' said James. 'Where are we?'

'Still operational,' replied Benedict. 'But we had to shut down for a while. Because of the investigation.'

'The investigation's been dropped. Fiona made sure of that.'

'No thanks to your man Villiers.'

An edge to his voice, James said, 'Ex-man. Leave Villiers out of this. I'll deal with him. You can handle Griffin at your end?'

'Of course. Hugo's eager to proceed. He wants what we want. Though for different reasons.'

'All that matters is Rose will be gone.'

'We're still up on her phone and her laptop. She's given us plenty already. More than enough.'

'Stay on it. I want it all.' James lowered the binoculars and looked at his companion. 'You realise what's at stake now, don't you?'

'Of course,' said Benedict, who looked troubled by something. 'Are you absolutely sure that you want to do this? Once it leaks, there's no getting the toothpaste back in the tube.'

James snorted with derision. 'They think they know me so well. My dear family. Everyone does. The public. The press. To them, my life is just a story. Disposable column inches to make them all feel better about themselves. As if they wouldn't have lost millions like I did in my position. Now I'm a persona non grata. Frozen out of the public eye. It's embarrassing to admit it, Chris, but I loved all of that shit. The fame, the cameras, the photographers calling, begging me to turn their way for just a moment. You can hear it in their voices, the desperation for you to look at them with the right expression for half a second so they'll have a photograph they can sell. Only you have the power to do that for them. Or when you walk the red carpet, how the public reaches out for you like you're a bucket of water to someone on fire. All that's been taken away. Now I'm some fugitive, hiding out, waiting for the storm to pass. Too embarrassing to the family to even be invited for some bullshit official photograph.' He turned to Benedict once more. 'She's going to pay. They're all going to pay.' His eyes lit up as Benedict reached down to the pocket of his wax jacket.

'This is early,' said Benedict, 'but if you're sure it's the right course of action, it might give a glimpse of how we could proceed.' He handed James a mobile phone, showing a series of text messages that Benedict's agents had extracted from Princess Rose's mobile phone. How this had been done, Benedict never specified and James didn't ask. He didn't care how Benedict did what he did. All James wanted was the information.

His eyes widened as he read. 'This is it,' James said. 'She'll never be Queen once this leaks.'

'If you use it,' he warned, 'there will be no going back.'

'There already is no going back.'

Benedict reached again for his pocket. This time he

showed James a picture of Ian Ferguson. 'This man could be a problem.'

'What are you talking about? He was killed last week.'

'He was in contact with the press office at Clarence House before he died. My people think he might have had some inside information.'

'About what?'

'About you.'

'What did he have?'

'I have people working on it. I'll know within twenty-four hours.' Benedict checked his watch. 'Shouldn't we think about moving on?'

James scoffed. 'People who are new to hunting, they always make the same mistake. You look in one place, and if there's nothing there you move on to somewhere else. Meanwhile, you're visible and making noise trying to find the deer's next grazing spot.' James reached for his rifle as he saw the same deer from before re-emerge from the heather higher up.

Benedict understood now. He whispered, 'You don't go to it.'

'You let it come to you.' James took aim, waiting for the breeze to die down. 'What Ian Ferguson found, it's only a matter of time before someone else finds it. We find them...' He fired, felling the magnificent animal. '...then we take them down.'

8

There is a good reason that most people flying from New York to London recommend leaving in the morning instead of getting the red-eye. Leaving New York at night, as Novak and Stella had, meant that they would be arriving at 6.30am, poorly rested, and facing the gruelling journey into London, fighting through morning commuters with rolling luggage – and there was nothing London commuters had less patience for than tourists with luggage.

Most passengers were trying to get at least a few hours of sleep in. Novak and Stella, however, knew that it was fruitless, and had already accepted their exhausting fate. With little else to do, Stella announced, 'I have a confession.'

Novak lowered the fat paperback novel he'd been reading. *Defence of the Realm* by Ian Ferguson. 'No good conversation ever started with that.'

'Not so much a confession as a warning,' said Stella. 'I think I know why you've been offered this job in London.'

Novak closed the book. 'Why?'

'The woman that you have a meeting with. Anne Cochrane. She's my mum.'

Stella had mentioned her mother to Novak in the past, though not by name. With Anne's frequent business with the New York arm of Hathaway, she could have made time to meet with her, and hadn't. She hadn't called when Stella and Novak broke the Simon Ali and Goldcastle story. Or after the Senator Adams Russian spying debacle. Not even after British Prime Minister Angela Curtis's demise when they were both in London again, however briefly, and she and Novak found themselves the most famous reporting duo on the planet. Anne had never really been there. Books had always been her real children. Her clients and novelists her real family. Why this had been the case had never been made clear to Stella, even as she pleaded with her dad to help her understand. But she never got anything out of him.

Novak said, 'You told me last year that you two rarely spoke. How long has it been? Really?'

'Since we last spoke... About a year. We get by fine with texts and emails.'

'When were you last in the same room together?'

Stella didn't have to think very hard to remember that one. 'Five years.' She thought better of mentioning the location. Room B of the Conville Crematorium, laying her father to rest after a brief battle with cirrhosis of the liver.

Novak asked, 'Why did you call this a warning just now?'

Stella replied, 'I think she's trying to get to me through you.' She looked down, as close to embarrassed as Novak had ever seen her. 'She's been trying to reach me. Since last week.'

'Why?'

'I don't know. I never got back to her.' Anticipating Novak's complaints, she said, 'I didn't have time. I've been completely buried this whole quarter.'

Quarter, thought Novak. She was already talking like a real editor. Reporters counted in stories. Editors counted in yearly quarters because that was how their ad buy and spend was calculated.

She said, 'I called it a warning because of this.' She took her phone out of the seat pocket in front of her, tapping to a news story she'd bookmarked five days ago from *The London Evening Standard*.

The picture heading the story showed police blocking access along Vauxhall Bridge Road to the offices of Hathaway Parker House. The headline: "*Police investigate second 'chemical contamination' site.*"

Stella said, 'The police confirmed that a Hathaway intern, Gayle Ademi, also died from the same poison that killed Ian Ferguson.'

Novak nodded along. 'He was in the building that morning. I thought the police said they aren't treating her death as suspicious.'

'They aren't. Because according to my source in the Home Office, that's what MI5 ordered them to do.'

'I don't understand.'

'If Ian Ferguson supposedly killed this poor woman because he was already contaminated with something so poisonous that it killed him less than an hour later, why was Gayle Ademi the only other person in that office who died?'

'And why would MI5 close down any investigation?' he added.

'That's why I'm warning you, Novak. There's something else going on here. And until we find out what it is, you have to promise me one thing.'

'What?'

'To not trust my mum,' Stella said.

'I already don't.'

Stella was surprised.

He explained, 'Since I was offered this job, I knew something wasn't right about it.' He did a quick shoulder-check and lowered his voice. 'Three hundred grand to write thriller plots? Sure, they want me to recoup the stolen royalties, but if this thriller writer is such a big deal, why does all of this feel so rushed? The news about the accounting broke at Hathaway forty-eight hours ago. Between then and yesterday afternoon they had a contract ready to go for me? I know book contracts and I've read mine, and that wasn't written in one business day. You're right, Stel. There's something else going on here.'

* * *

An hour later Novak had nodded off, his thumb still lodged in the paperback now resting on his thigh. Stella slid the book out of his hand, keeping his place before sliding his bookmark in.

She wasn't nearly as relaxed. All she could do was obsessively check how long it had been since her last pill. She had taken a yellow one in the taxi on the way to the airport. She would have taken another one at the airport if Novak had left her side for more than a minute. Passing through security and waiting at the gate, Stella could feel the drugs leaving her body. The more she thought about it, the more vividly she could visualise the effect on her brain. Shrinking. Shrivelling. Turning grey.

She had put up with it as long as she could. Now that Novak was asleep, she knew it could be her last chance before London, and that was still a good three hours away, plus however long before she could be on her own to take more pills.

She took her handbag and got out of her seat as gently

and quietly as she could. Once she was in the bathroom she was already well on her way to a high again. It was knowing that nothing now stood between her and the pills. She was going to feel it again any minute now. The awesome wave. That warm buzz in her stomach. For the typical pill-popper, the anticipation is half of the high.

Earlier that afternoon she'd dashed out of the office and bought ten different bottles of vitamins in a drug store. On the way home, her handbag sounded like she was carrying some sort of musical instrument. In the safety of her kitchen, she opened the bottles up one by one on her counter to compare the shape and size of the pills. It was hard to find both pink and yellow pills, but she managed to find a brand that was close.

There was a little voice in her head that told her what she was doing was risky, but ten minutes of research on a Reddit forum told her that American college kids were routinely flying across the country with uppers and downers hidden in vitamin bottles. And it was true. Homeland Security only cared about dealer-level quantities or explosive devices. It wasn't feasible to spend an hour searching and testing every suitcase with a bottle of pills in it. Half the country was medicated. Homeland Security knew it, and so did the vast number of pill-takers who flew in the States. Knowing that some recreational drug use would get through the airports was just the cost of business.

It was only as Stella glanced in the mirror that she confronted herself. The risk was low, but it wasn't zero. She closed her eyes and told herself, 'You haven't taken them yet. Put them away and stop this madness. If you stop now, that shows bravery and determination. What does it say about your control of this thing that you need to pop pills whilst flying over the Atlantic? You're going to close this bottle and put it back in your purse, then sit back down next to Novak and fall asleep. At least that way you'll be able to look him in the eye when he wakes up.'

It was a great little speech that she gave herself. One that she completely ignored.

She opened up the bottle and picked out the ever-so-slightly different shade of pill. After swallowing it dry, she thought for a moment. Then picked out another one. Because, after all, it would be longer than usual until she could take another. Once she had swallowed that one, she felt what almost every drug-taker feels after a dose. A mixture of elation and complete dissatisfaction. Of having failed to stop. Again.

When she returned to her seat, sliding back in as quietly as she'd got out, she didn't notice Novak opening his eyes a little. He asked if she was okay.

Whilst looking straight ahead, she said that she was.

9

Hathaway's secondary headquarters in London were in a new business development site on the south bank of the Thames, next to the US embassy building. Everywhere you looked was glass and steel, with pockets of urban greenery that only drew attention to how unnatural it was to have trees and grass and ponds in such a setting.

'Book sales must be decent,' remarked Novak, as they made their way into the expansive lobby.

The ceilings were fifty-foot high, tall enough to fit some more trees inside. It was a marvel of modern architecture, and the home of Hathaway UK's business side, while the creative and editorial work took place across the river. While that office remained closed until it could be made safe again, the staff from the Pimlico office had been temporarily rehoused on the fourth floor, along with Anne Cochrane. She rose quickly from her seat when she saw Novak and Stella approaching, being shown the way by an intern.

Anne was only halfway towards a smile for Stella. 'It's been too long,' she said. 'It's lovely to see you.'

Stella, not wanting to cause an atmosphere, leaned in for a cautious hug, keeping her body half in profile. 'You too,' she replied without any emotion.

Anne shook Novak's hand. 'Tom, so glad to get you here.' She beckoned them inside, then was sure to close the door all the way. 'I'm sorry everything's so sparse in here. They wouldn't let me take anything from my own office.'

All there was on the desk was a computer, a mobile phone, a leather notebook and a pen. The walls were all blank. There was a cable coming out of the wall for a landline phone connection, but there was no phone to attach it to.

Anne added as she sat down, 'Possible contamination, the police said. They might end up destroying everything. Thank god we mostly deal with digital manuscripts or our interns would have a lot of printing to do in the next few weeks.' She smiled at Novak but kept returning to Stella. 'You should have told me you were coming.'

Stella replied, 'This has coincided with some time off from the office, so Novak asked me to come along.'

Anne asked Novak, 'Do you call her Mitchell?'

He shrugged with a slight smile. 'I'm Novak. She's Stella. That's how it is.'

She asked Stella, 'Why the time off? Is anything the matter?'

Stella shifted in her seat. She didn't like Anne sitting there making out like she was a regular concerned mother. That Novak might mistake there being any closeness between them. 'This is about Novak,' she said. 'I don't want to distract the conversation.'

Anne nodded, then asked him, 'You received the contract okay?'

'The contract's fine,' he answered. 'What's a little less clear is what the actual job is.'

Anne reached for her phone and removed the battery.

'Do you do that for all your business discussions?' he asked.

'It was something that Ian insisted on,' she replied. 'Something I should probably have taken more seriously. So if you wouldn't mind...'

Stella and Novak each removed the battery from their phones, nullifying any chance that their conversation could be listened in to.

'I'm not coming up with plots for a thriller writer,' said Novak. 'Am I?'

'No,' replied Anne. 'You're not.'

Stella already knew that, and was glad to not have to be the one to say it. She wanted Novak to see for himself what she believed Anne Cochrane to really be: untrustworthy.

'It's a ghostwriting job,' Anne went on. 'And it needs to happen quickly.'

'For how long?' asked Novak.

'Two weeks. A month at most.'

He laughed. 'That's insane. You can't write a book in that length of time.'

'Your predecessor was already seventy thousand words in. I need you to bring out the colour. The political and technical side of things.'

'But that's still...' he tried to do the calculation. '...fifty thousand words? More?'

'You're a reporter, Tom. I'm sure you've had harder deadlines than this before. What's your concern?'

'I don't know... What about buying space in the bookshops?'

'We only buy space in supermarkets now. Buying space for books to be displayed certain places in bookshops stopped twenty years ago, even if we could afford it. There are too many other costs with publishing that are far more important. Editing alone is about one hundred hours of work. Then there's cover design and marketing. That's an endless back and forth. Then you have audiobook recording. Publicity. Serialised extracts. On this book, Hathaway is in for close to three million pounds. And that's before we've sold one copy.'

'I'm looking around this building, Anne, and it doesn't seem like Hathaway is short of cash. Where's it all coming from?'

'The five hits you have in a year pay for all the other failures. A book that lands, I mean, *really* lands, can bring in ten thousand dollars a day on Amazon. Half again from bricks and mortar stores. The book you'll be working on is going to be one of those hits. Trust me, I know from experience. If I want a deadline hit, I need a reporter. I have two young women from *The Guardian* working on something else for me right now. Not as hot as this, mind you.'

'Three million pounds,' Novak said to himself, puffing at the huge amount. 'Anne, who am I writing this book for?'

'A paranoid, egotistical narcissist. From what Stella tells me, the two of you should get on like a house on fire.'

'That was years ago,' Stella snapped, then repeated it to Novak. 'I said that before we got to know each other.' She said pointedly to Anne, 'Novak's different now.'

'Who is it?' asked Novak.

Anne replied, 'Hugo Byron.'

He laughed. It was the only natural reaction. 'Hugo *Byron*. *The* Hugo Byron.'

'Yep.'

'He's *here*? In this building?'

'We have him somewhere secure. Far away from here.' Anne checked the time on her computer monitor. 'So far, actually, if we want to get there before dark we have to leave soon.'

The extent of what he was being brought into then hit him. 'This is the job that got Ian Ferguson killed,' he said.

Anne paused, trying to choose her words carefully. One wrong move and she knew she could lose her ghostwriter before he'd even begun. 'I'm not going to lie, Tom. It seems unlikely that there's no connection between Ian's murder and this book. Which, to me, tells me that he was on to something important. Something someone thought it worth killing for. We've got to see this one through. We can't give in.'

Stella now understood. Since she'd found her mother's picture on the Hathaway website the previous day, she had been racking her brain to figure out why it had to be Novak. Now she knew. It wasn't that her mother wanted Stella back in London. It wasn't personal. Anne's text message to her had been honest. It *was* business.

She knew she shouldn't have been feeling anything after years of training herself not to care. But she had to admit to herself: she was disappointed.

Stella said, 'You don't want a ghostwriter. You want someone to investigate.'

'I want you to do both,' Anne replied. 'I think Hathaway's three hundred thousand dollars buys us that much. I believe in this book, Tom, and I believe that what Hugo Byron is doing at Griffin is important. If you don't want it–'

'I'm in,' Novak announced, then said, 'but Stella meets him too.'

Stella, who was clearly more reluctant, shifted in her seat. 'Novak, I'm not–'

'Just to help sound him out at the start.' He turned to Stella. 'It's Hugo Byron, Stel. I need your radar on this.'

Stella said, 'I have this meeting tomorrow, Novak. I really don't think it's a good idea–'

Anne cut in. 'She doesn't want to share a car back to London with me.'

'I'm sorry,' said Stella, addressing her. 'Am I not allowed to finish a sentence in this room?'

Anne gestured that the floor was Stella's.

'Fine,' Stella said. 'I'll do it. One night only.'

10

Anne had been evasive about where exactly Hathaway had hidden Byron away. All she would give them was that they would be heading north – very far north; about as far north as you could go on the mainland – along with assurances that there would be plenty of time for all their questions.

They took a British Airways flight from London City Airport at the docks of the Thames Barrier, only a few miles from Canary Wharf. From there, they were barely in the air an hour before wheels down in a dreich and grey Glasgow. But their journey was only just beginning.

Novak and Stella had so many questions, and none of them could safely be answered on the plane. If Anne and Ian Ferguson had been removing their phone batteries, then she wasn't about to get into any details within earshot of a dozen strangers.

A blacked-out Land Rover Defender was waiting for them at the airport, which Anne drove. She wanted as few people as possible getting between them and Byron's location.

'You'd better get comfortable,' she said, pulling out of the airport multi-storey. 'We've got six hours ahead of us.'

Novak and Stella exchanged a look with each other. Everyone had their location data switched off for security reasons, so they couldn't check any online maps. As it wouldn't make sense to be driving five hours south, the pair realised they were bound for the far north tip of Scotland.

Novak could only make it as far as Stirling – halfway up the country – before curiosity got the better of him. 'I'll bet that the Five Eyes have had people looking for Byron for the last six months. How did you find him?'

'I didn't,' said Anne. 'He came to us. Through an intermediary.'

'Who?'

'His literary agent. I haven't pressed the agent on the details, but at some point a representative from Griffin reached out through encrypted email and set up a meeting at the place we're going to.'

'Aren't you worried that whoever killed Ian Ferguson might target Byron next?'

'Of course I am. Every possible precaution has been taken. Hathaway is spending tens of thousands to keep him secure. The guards protecting the property don't even know who's inside. We pay for discretion. And we pay well.'

Novak said, 'If Byron's broken cover, he must have a good reason. Is it related to whatever Griffin's next big drop is going to be?'

'You'll have to ask him that.'

'Don't you know?'

'We signed him up for a ghostwritten autobiography. It's unfinished. I don't read unfinished work.'

Novak could have pressed on, and Stella certainly had to hold her tongue. The notion that Anne hadn't read a word of a manuscript that had most likely cost the life of one of the country's bestselling novelists didn't seem credible.

Novak said, 'I'm trying to get some idea of what the expectations are. Because if the first line of this book is supposed to be something like "It all started when my great-grandfather was born in eighteen whatever..." then I'm not your guy. I tried to read a biography on James Joyce that was like that. When I got to page seventy and realised Joyce's parents still hadn't been born, I gave up. Sent that book wind-milling across the room, and it was a big-ass book. To this day I think about the hours I saved myself abandoning that.'

Anne's eyes narrowed. 'It wasn't written by Richard Ellmann, was it?'

The pause that followed gave Novak away. 'Maybe.'

'That's regarded as one of the best biographies of all time.'

Novak looked out his window, unconcerned. 'I'd throw it again if I had the chance.'

In the passenger seat, Stella covered a stifled laugh with her hand.

* * *

They had been driving up the spine of Scotland for close to three hours when they reached Inverness and kept ploughing on north up the A9. When Novak and Stella asked for some indication of how much longer it was going to be, all Anne would give away was, 'A while yet.'

Fifty miles later and they were on a B road where it had been twenty minutes since they'd last passed another car, and longer still since they'd seen a house or cottage. The sun was setting behind the hills on the horizon.

Novak had nodded off in the back seat, leaving Anne and Stella partly on their own for the first time.

'Did you get my messages?' asked Anne.

'You know that I did,' Stella replied. 'You want me to explain why I didn't write back.'

'You must have heard there had been an incident at the office. You knew that I worked for Hathaway in London.'

'It's been a while, mum. I actually didn't know if you were still there or not.'

The word sounded strange, leaving her mouth. *Mum*. It required effort to say.

'It's nice to hear you call me that,' Anne said.

'Just out of habit,' replied Stella.

'It's not the same reading it in a text message or an email. Some day if you ever have children–'

She laughed in alarm. 'Please tell me you're not about to give me advice on how to handle children.'

Anne couldn't think of any reply that wouldn't anger Stella further.

It didn't matter. Stella had some things she'd felt like saying for the last hundred miles, stewing away, thickening. 'I was ten years old,' she said, then checked that Novak was still asleep. He was. 'You walked out. In the middle of the night. I went to bed with a mum, and woke up without one. Who does that?'

Anne could never have imagined when she was pregnant with Stella that one day the child inside her would come to detest her so much. 'I knew you wouldn't be able to understand back then,' Anne said, 'and I don't blame you for not understanding now.'

'You know that's what made him drink, right? It started when you left.'

'Someone who drinks their life away only has themselves to blame. I'm sorry, but that's the truth.'

'No, he drank because he blamed you and you weren't around to take it. So he turned it on himself.'

Anne wasn't for giving an inch. 'Your dad drank because that's what he was: a drinker. Like his dad was before him, and his dad before that.'

'What,' said Stella, 'like we're all destined to turn into our parents?'

'Most of us, yes.'

'Then I must be really screwed.' She flicked her head back again to check on Novak. Seeing him still out for the count, she took the opportunity to reach into her handbag for a pill.

'You should really take them with food,' said Anne. 'Your vitamins.' She dipped her head slightly, peering out from the upper half of her eyes. A knowing-mother expression.

'Don't worry about it,' Stella replied.

* * *

The darkness grew, and the road veered off onto a single track. Passing places dotted the sides of the road every hundred yards or so, some no more than half a car's width. The total lack of lighting and seemingly suicidal sheep running free across the road made for a tense final leg of their journey. It didn't help that the locals drove like maniacs, every bend and rise and fall deep in their muscle memory, only slowing down at the sight of oncoming headlights.

They were now deep into the Sutherland countryside, one of the biggest – and emptiest – counties in Scotland. Scattered clouds were flecked with the pink and purple dregs of sunset light, illuminating an utterly barren landscape of peat bogs as far as Stella could see. It had been half an hour since they'd last passed a house or cottage. The single-track road shared only with occasional stray sheep. Stella's only solace came from the sky that was already twinkling with stars: she could only imagine how lonely and frightening such a place would feel in a snowstorm.

'That's us,' Anne said, indicating to a faint light in the distance, several hundred yards off the road at the foot of a long glen. Then a large white house came into view, almost comically remote in its surroundings. Badanloch House.

A dirt track peeled away left towards the house. In the back, Novak stirred from the pitch and yaw of the Land Rover's progress along the track, the tyres hitting potholes and boulders, and puddles that had been there for weeks.

As they got closer, Stella noticed several figures in dark clothes patrolling a wide perimeter around the house. She peered through the darkness to see what they were holding. It was only when Anne pulled up outside the front door that she could make out what they were.

Submachine guns.

The men and women holding them weren't in uniforms of any kind, and Novak was trying to figure out if they were private security or not. Before he could ask Anne, she was already heading inside, receiving the warm welcome of the host.

Novak slowed Stella's progress to the front door. 'Is that who I think it is?' he asked.

'That explains a lot,' she replied.

Magnus Hofstadt was a Norwegian tech-entrepreneur who had made his fortune investing early in some of the world's most successful social media companies. He had stepped back from the business world in favour of spending his fortune on progressive social issues. His speech at the Davos Economic Forum urging the 1% of the world's richest to pay more tax had gone viral. But all he'd got was a ton of views on YouTube. The business community had ostracised him, and Hofstadt retreated to the remote wilderness of Sutherland, becoming an honorary Scot. And Hofstadt had gone all in on playing the part.

He was wearing a Harris Tweed three-piece suit and smoking a pipe. With his long blonde hair cascading down to his shoulders, he looked every bit the rugged Scandinavian. After kissing Anne on the cheek, he opened out his arms to Novak and Stella. 'Come in, my friends. The fire is on.'

As they stepped into the hall, their feet sinking into the plush tartan carpet, they savoured the warmth after the bitter cold outside. Novak's eyes were everywhere, looking for Hugo Byron.

'You must be hungry, yes?' said Magnus. 'We have made mince and potatoes.'

He led them towards voices in the kitchen, where a ten-place farmhouse table dominated the room.

Stella held back, allowing Novak to take the lead. This was his job, after all.

He seemed reluctant to follow Anne into the kitchen, where a man and a woman, both in their mid-twenties, were sitting at the table with their backs to the door.

Hugo and his female companion sounded like they were coming to the end of an argument between themselves. Before they realised company was approaching, Hugo raised his voice as he said, 'I don't want to *talk* about it, Sofia.'

Anne cleared her throat. 'Hugo. This is your new ghostwriter.'

Novak wasn't easily star-struck, but as one of the most mysterious men on the planet turned around, Novak felt a rush of adrenaline.

The couple were wearing knitted sweaters that were a size too big for them. Almost two sizes on her.

Stella wondered if they had been borrowed from Magnus.

Novak wondered what his voice would sound like. What would it give away about his background, where he was raised? What sort of person he was? He had so many questions, and hardly any of them were about to be answered.

Hugo got to his feet and, instead of shaking Novak's outstretched hand, threw down his napkin. 'I've lost my appetite,' he said, then stormed off up the stairs.

Magnus didn't even seem to have noticed anything untoward. He had been living with such behaviour for a while now.

Hugo's companion rose. 'I'm Sofia,' she said, shaking Novak then Stella's hands. 'I'm sorry about Hugo. He's been quite delicate since Ian...'

'They were getting quite close,' added Anne.

Novak said, 'I thought the point of ghosts was that you couldn't tell when they get close.'

'No,' said Sofia, heading towards the kitchen door, bound for the garden. 'When there's a ghost on your shoulder you can feel it alright.'

Novak moved, as if to follow her, when he felt Stella's hand stopping him.

'I'll go,' she said.

11

Stella had dressed for late autumn in London, which was far different to late autumn in Sutherland. The light breeze effortlessly pierced her trousers. Only her leather jacket offered any respite from the windchill and rapidly falling evening temperature. She hugged herself as she approached Sofia from behind, making sure to scuff her boots on the ground to let her know she was coming.

Stella knew that Novak was better off getting cosy with the most powerful person in the house, which at that point wasn't Hugo Byron. If Magnus Hofstadt was keeping Hugo at his house, he would be instrumental in keeping him onside. But the real information that mattered resided with a slender woman of twenty-four, with brown naturally curly hair, South American colouring, and an unmistakably Hispanic accent.

Sofia was already two drags in to a cigarette, staring out towards the silhouette of the hills in the distance. 'The stars here are so beautiful. They're one of the few things here that remind me of home.'

'Where is that?' asked Stella, joining her then refusing the offer of Sofia's cigarette packet.

'Colombia. A town called Miraflores. There's a river that runs through it, but it's nothing like the quiet and peace around here.' She stopped to exhale, impossible to tell where her cigarette smoke ended and her warm breath meeting the cold air began. 'Every day I wonder if this is really my life. How I made it so far from there to here.'

Stella asked, 'How long have you known Hugo?'

Sofia paused. 'Everything I tell you is off the record. You cannot print it anywhere. I know who you are.' She looked towards the kitchen where Novak was sitting at the table with Magnus and Anne. 'I know both of you. Who doesn't.'

'Of course. We're off the record. Always, until you say otherwise.'

'We met online about five years ago. I was living in Bogotá and starting to make my name on the hacking scene. We talked about everything. Life, movies, politics. I'd still be in Colombia if it wasn't for Hugo.'

Sofia didn't even notice Stella slipping into reporter mode.

'You do work for Griffin?' she asked.

'I code. Dear god, do I code. It takes thousands of lines to keep Griffin safe. We get about a hundred DDoS attacks a day. Most of it from foreign governments. Some of it from hackers trying to make a name for themselves. Hugo and I have big targets on us now.'

Distributed denial-of-service attacks were a way of taking a website offline by flooding it with requests. In hacking, if you couldn't infiltrate then you took down instead.

Sofia sucked hard on her cigarette. People like her were the reason so many people started smoking: she made it look cool. Sixties French Cinema cool. 'Look at them.' She gestured towards the group through the window. 'So comfortable. So protected. I never thought Griffin would end up like this.'

'In what way?' asked Stella.

'Magnus might have once been an idealist, but not anymore. Financially backing Griffin and protecting Hugo has become the new fad in London society circles. All these millionaires who want to kid themselves that they're changing the world. Magnus is just paying to stay in the game. They can't stand to be away from it. They want to be close to the throne. The crown. The seat of power. They love their money but they hate their money, if you know what I mean. Once they have it, they can't do a thing without it. They don't know how. Their entire adult lives, their solution has always been to pay more than the other guy. That's how they get what they want. Griffin isn't about that. It doesn't care about what you have or what you don't have. All that matters is that you want the world to know tomorrow what it didn't today. It doesn't require money to make a difference in this world. What it takes is the decision, to do whatever is necessary for change. Money, it gives people like Anne and Magnus the freedom they crave. They don't realise that it also puts them in a box. They see people like me and Hugo and they can't stand it. They want what we have.'

'And what is that?'

'The less we want what they have, the more power it gives us.'

'What about Hugo and this book?' asked Stella. 'Doesn't that cede some of that power back to the rich? Making Griffin reliant on people like Magnus?'

'Compromise is necessary in every walk of life.' Sofia stepped on what remained of her cigarette. 'Even the Taliban are willing to negotiate.'

As Sofia went back inside, Stella looked up at a flicker of

light between two curtains upstairs. It was Hugo. He had been watching them and wanted Stella to know it.

* * *

Stella followed Sofia inside, who walked straight through the kitchen and took up a place on the couch on her own. Stella sat at the long table beside Novak, trying to catch up on their conversation. Anne immediately spooned out some mince and potatoes onto a plate and handed it to Stella. She took it then mouthed thanks.

Magnus and Novak sat close to each other like long-lost friends, both of them eating.

'This is why I feel very protective towards Hugo, and everyone else with Griffin,' Magnus explained. 'Look at how broken the system is. People like me. You know how much tax I paid last year?' Before anyone could guess, he said, 'Seven million. You know how much I could have paid? Less than two. But I paid the seven. You know why? Because unless everyone buys in, everyone suffers. In the US, you can build a company to a value of a billion dollars like I did, and then borrow against that wealth for years. Until you actually sell any stock, you don't technically have an income. Between twenty fourteen and twenty eighteen, the top twenty-five earners in the US made over four hundred billion dollars. On that amount they paid thirteen billion in tax. Is anyone here only paying three per cent income tax? Is that fair? The only way to break up this corruption is for the people to know. Without Griffin, we wouldn't know these things.'

Stella said, 'You seem terribly determined to change a system that's allowed you to build a mansion and protect it with armed guards.'

Magnus lifted his hands, accepting the argument. 'True.'

At the sink washing pots, Anne stopped for a moment, then resumed, as if irked by something she'd heard.

Novak gave just a hint of a smirk at Stella. She'd effortlessly got Magnus to admit that the guards were his, rather than Hathaway's.

He went on, 'But I'm not the only one, huh. My friends in London, many of them have more money than I do and they feel this way too.'

Sofia caught Stella's attention, flashing her eyebrows up to say 'told you so'.

Magnus continued, 'In fact, to go on as we have without change is actually more dangerous for our wealth in the long run.'

A voice from the hallway announced, 'You lose your power over the people when you take away everything they have.' Hugo entered, holding a glass of whisky and his closed laptop, and sat next to Sofia to conclude the quote. 'When you rob a man of everything, you no longer have power over him. You have made him free.'

Novak was first to identify it. 'Aleksandr Solzhenitsyn.'

Hugo was impressed that Novak knew it, and raised his glass to him. Then he had a drink and opened the laptop.

'What are you doing?' asked Sofia.

'Syria,' replied Hugo. His tone and body language suggested that he had been gracious enough to come back down to be company, but that no one should expect him to pay the slightest bit of attention to them.

Magnus continued dominating the discussion, creating a division in the room with Hugo and Sofia on the couch, Anne, Magnus, Tom, and Stella at the table.

Once dinner had been eaten, Stella flashed a sharp look at Anne, then flicked her head towards the hallway. 'I should probably turn in. It's been a long day.'

Magnus got up as well. 'I'll show you where your rooms are.'

Reading the situation, Sofia got up as well. 'I'm going to bed. Will you be up soon?'

The question seemed to irritate Hugo. 'That depends,' he answered. 'Who needs me more? You or the Syrian uprising?'

Sofia left, looking hurt.

Novak had ended up a long way down the table. The only way he could have been farther away from Hugo was if he'd left the room. He moved down to the other end of the table.

There was silence for a full minute. Novak swore he wouldn't be the first to talk.

He wasn't.

'Why did you get this job?' Hugo asked.

With the anger gone from his voice, he was softly spoken. The accent was English. Possibly privately educated, but he was trying to hide working class roots.

Novak thought it best to start with honesty. 'I have no idea. I'm not really qualified. I've never ghostwritten a book for anyone before, and I don't really know what you want from this project.'

'I have no idea why you got this job either.' Hugo didn't lift his eyes from the laptop screen, typing with his left hand, drinking with his right. He wanted Novak to know that of the number of important things going on in the room, Novak was barely in the top five. 'As far as I can tell, your most important subject in the last six months has been you. Whoring your book around.'

'If you'd read it,' said Novak, 'you'd know that it's not so much about me as it is how Stella and I managed to expose a global conspiracy stretching back decades. A conspiracy to steal elections and get away with murder. Thankfully Griffin has been around to let the world know that the rich get away with not paying their fair share of tax. Who knew?'

Hugo looked up and smiled for the first time. He would have respected Novak even less if he hadn't defended himself. 'So you don't really respect what I do. What Griffin is about.'

'I respect what it could be,' he replied. 'Right now, your leaks are the equivalent of a temper tantrum. Running into a room, screaming as loudly as you can, then running back out again. Your idealism isn't the problem. The scandals you're exposing aren't the problem. You don't understand yet how to present them to the public. If you care about that, I might be able to help you. Your antagonism towards me... that's your loyalty to Ian talking. Loyalty's important to you. It must be. Without it, you would never have made it this far whilst keeping your identity a secret. But you should want my name attached to this book.'

'Why is that?' asked Hugo.

'Anne Cochrane thought that a celebrated novelist like Ian Ferguson would bring this project prestige. I can bring that. The only person more respected than I am in the field of politics and security is Stella Mitchell.'

'It's not your prestige that worries me. It's your integrity. You wrote that book to publicise yourself, not the issues.'

'Then why are you publishing a memoir?' asked Novak. 'You don't want to. Not really. But it's the only way to pay for all those hired goons outside carrying M16s. Do they think they're protecting Magnus?'

'All I know is that they don't know who I am. The US government is trying to switch off our online donations system. Without that, I can't keep Griffin running. Magnus gives us a place to stay, and I cover the security costs with the advance payment on the book. It's an investment in Griffin's work. I wrote the code for our website that completely blocks any evidence of who sent us material. Or where. Or when. If I die, Griffin dies. This started as a way to pay the bills. But it's bigger than that now. There are powerful forces at play here, Tom. Forces that you'll never understand. And this–' he motioned between the two of them '–isn't going to work. Tell Anne to find someone else.' He went back to typing.

But Novak wasn't done yet. 'You had someone else and now he's dead. I'm only here because Hathaway had leverage on me. The truth about who you are and where you are isn't going to stay secret forever, Hugo. And when it comes out, you won't get another writer coming within a hundred miles of this. Not someone of my calibre. You're like every other big-time hacker I've ever met: you want respect. To be admired. You want the world to know how brilliant you are. That's why you signed on to this book.'

'You think you have it all figured out, don't you,' said Hugo. 'Ian told me about someone interesting. He said that if anyone ever had to take over from him, he hoped that they would find inspiration in him.'

Novak edged forward, intrigued. 'Who?'

'He was a Roman statesman called Cincinnatus. Lucius Quinctius Cincinnatus. Ian called him one of the bravest men who's ever lived, and no one ever talks about him. In the early days of the Republic there was an invasion in his region and his fellow citizens asked for his help. He did more than that, though. He took over the entire state, wielding powers that would shame any dictator. Then he did a remarkable thing. When the war was won, he handed back all of his power and went back to being a farmer. This man could have been emperor. When Ian told me about Cincinnatus it reminded me why I'd signed on to this book. It's my way of handing back power to the people.'

Novak didn't entirely follow his meaning, but he didn't

have to. All he needed was for Hugo to agree to his final demand. His only deal-breaker. 'If you want to work with the best, then Stella and I are it.'

Hugo closed his laptop and put it aside. 'Stella?'

'We come as a pair,' said Novak. 'She won't be here all the time, but if this is going to work, I need her. Hathaway will never hire some ghostwriter whose last job was writing a memoir for some retired soccer player with a drinking problem. So if you want to stay here and keep the security you can't afford without this book deal, then I'm your only shot. You've pissed off plenty of people in the UK government. They won't protect you from the Americans, or whoever else will pay good money to see you in a hole in the ground.'

Hugo nodded for a moment, thinking through his options. He didn't have any. 'Ian didn't really know what he was getting into. You can't claim that same ignorance.'

'It's a chance I'm prepared to take.'

'You get your pay day, fine. That's not enough for you. What else?'

'I want to find out who killed Ian Ferguson.'

Hugo stood up, then extended his arm to Novak. His fingertips were callused from years of coding and typing on deep-travel mechanical keys. 'You should start with Ian's manuscript. It's in your room. We'll start in the morning.' As Hugo left with his laptop, he added, 'Welcome to Griffin.'

* * *

Anne was closing her door for the night when Novak walked past. She wished him a good night's sleep. Across the hall, Hugo and Sofia were picking up their argument from earlier.

Novak tapped on Stella's door.

She pulled him inside quickly. Her suitcase was open on the floor, not that she had any intention of getting unpacked.

After each brought the other up to speed about their conversations with Sofia and Hugo, Stella told Novak that she'd heard Sofia crying in her room.

'So they're, like, together?' wondered Novak aloud.

'I guess so,' said Stella.

Hands on hips, he asked, 'What do you think?'

'I think that this is what you wanted. But I'm not staying here. I'm going back to London tomorrow with Anne.' She hesitated. 'My mum. I've made arrangements to meet Ralph Ogden.' Stella looked towards her toilet bag, realising she'd left it open. Her "vitamins" bottle was in there. If Novak noticed, it would be lights out for her stash. She also knew that dashing across the room for a toilet bag that she didn't immediately need would send up a flare to him. She sat on the edge of the bed, trying to turn his attention away from the bag. 'Do you really think it's safe here?'

'Ian Ferguson wasn't killed here. He was killed in a place where armed guards might have saved his life.'

Stella lowered her voice to a whisper. 'I don't know what we've walked into here, but that is not grief written on Hugo and Sofia's faces. It's fear. They're hiding more than a few things. Hugo looks like he's ready to explode.'

Novak couldn't disagree.

Stella warned, 'You have to entertain the possibility that Ian was killed because of something he found out about Hugo Byron and Griffin.'

Misunderstanding her point, he said, 'Totally. I mean, Byron has made a lot of powerful enemies the last six months...'

'No,' she said. 'I mean something that Hugo didn't want Ian to find out. What if he had something incriminating about

Hugo? Ian wasn't even a reporter. Whatever he had, you'll find a way of getting it too. And what then, Novak?'

He didn't have an answer to that. And he didn't have time to contemplate it. Ian Ferguson's manuscript was waiting for him in his room.

12

Novak had never slept in a dead man's bed before. Having spent the night in Ian Ferguson's, Novak hadn't found much about it to recommend. Though the bedding had all been laundered, there was an intimacy about the room that he couldn't escape. As he went to the window to view the frost that had turned the landscape white overnight, his eye was drawn to a fingerprint on the glass near the opening handle. Novak found a tissue and wiped away the last trace of Ian Ferguson from the room.

The manuscript itself was on a memory stick which had been left on the mantlepiece of the old fireplace, like an urn of ashes. Anne had also printed a hard copy in advance, which now lay upside down on the bed, last page on top. Novak had finished reading it sometime around four. It didn't read like a biography written by a thriller writer. The language was flowery, and it was deathly dull. Novak couldn't believe that a writer like Ian had made a life like Hugo's appear to be so uneventful. From their brief conversation the night before, Novak could see that Hugo might have been rude. He might even have been arrogant, but it was hard to believe that he was also boring – the way that Ian Ferguson had written him, at least.

The opening line gave a taster of the dryness to come: "*It was the celebrated Roman author Pliny the Elder who wrote that griffins were said to lay eggs in burrows on the ground, and their nests contained gold nuggets. Now, in the digital age, Griffin the website – along with its enigmatic founder Hugo Byron – is also known for guarding treasures in the form of priceless secrets.*"

As far as narrative excitement went, it somehow managed to get worse from there. What followed was oddly plodding and tone-deaf. A gift to insomniacs, and the opposite of what an exhausted and jet-lagged Novak wanted to be reading through the night.

At the start of the driveway a quarter of a mile away, five armed guards piled out of a black van, and the ones on night watch piled in. Wherever they were staying, it had to be far away. Everything was far away from Badanloch House.

Novak heard footsteps crunching across the gravel, and went to the window in time to see Stella lift her suitcase into the back of the Land Rover before heading back inside.

When he joined the others in the kitchen, the only notable absence at the breakfast table was Hugo. Everyone set quietly to work at their coffee and toast and steaming bowls of porridge.

Magnus was dressed for hillwalking, preparing sandwiches for a trek towards Ben Klibreck, one of the most northerly of the Munros. 'What time are you leaving?' he asked.

'After this,' said Anne.

Stella added, 'I have a meeting I need to take.'

'Ralph Ogden?' enquired Novak.

Stella nodded, her mouth full of porridge.

'What are you meeting him for?' asked Anne.

'He thinks he has a lead on the people who poisoned Ian Ferguson.'

The clinking of cutlery, and mugs on saucers, stopped.

Sofia got out of her seat. 'I should tell Hugo.'

'No, wait,' said Stella. 'It might be nothing.'

'It's more than what the police are telling Anne. Hugo will want to talk to him.'

Anne raised an authoritative hand. 'No. Hugo needs to start work with Tom this morning. Speaking of which... How is the manuscript?'

Novak stayed standing at the coffee maker, holding a large mug filled with the blackest coffee he had seen for a while. He stalled for time by taking a sip. 'It's good,' he said with a hint of doubt. 'It could do with a bit more pace. And a bit more ideology. It can't just be about a life. It has to be about the purpose behind that life. And that purpose is Griffin.' He took another sip. 'I don't get a sense of that yet.'

Sofia didn't show it, but she was relieved to hear that Novak wanted to bring out more of the politics and idealism behind Griffin.

'That's why you're the right choice to finish the job,' said Anne.

'Ian never seemed to care much about what we do,' said Sofia. 'I think he took the job for money. Nothing else.'

Anne replied, 'I wouldn't judge him too harshly. You wouldn't believe how little seemingly successful authors make.' She checked her watch then told Stella, 'We should make a move if we want to catch this flight.'

'Where are you flying from?' asked Novak.

'Inverness.'

Magnus added, 'We're about an hour and a half, two hours from there. You should be fine.'

Novak drained his coffee. 'I'll see you out.'

* * *

At the car, Novak was under-dressed in a pair of light lounge pants and a t-shirt until he threw on the padded jacket that he had insisted to Stella he didn't need.

'Call me when you land?' asked Novak, zipping the jacket.

'There's no reception, remember,' Stella replied. 'I'll WhatsApp you. At least Magnus has got fibre broadband out here.'

Novak checked that Anne was in the car before asking quietly, 'How are you feeling?'

'I feel fine,' Stella said.

She didn't look it. She had barely touched her porridge and Novak had noticed a tremble in the hand she was holding her teacup with.

'Let me know what Ralph has to say.' Seeing her roll her eyes, he asked, 'What is it?'

She said, 'You're out here in the middle of nowhere to ghostwrite a book. You've been up all night reading a manuscript, trying to get up to speed. Trying to be a writer. And you can't help being who you really are: a reporter. You have to know, don't you?'

'What happened to Ian Ferguson is a part of this book now, Stel. Whether Hugo or Anne or anyone else wants it to be.'

When Stella saw that Anne had opened the window and was watching them in the side mirror, Stella turned away from the car, and turned Novak away too. 'And there really was nothing in Ian's manuscript?'

'Yeah, really. Nicely written, but not much pace. I'm not even sure that it's Ian's writing.' He paused. 'If it is Ian's, it's still weird, though. Like he's gone out of his way *not* to get into Hugo's background.'

'A deliberate omission?'

'More like sleight of hand. That manuscript isn't a clue. It's a distraction, from whatever it was Ian really found.'

* * *

After half an hour on the glistening-white roads and entering something approaching civilisation, Anne could no longer allow the *Today* programme on BBC Radio 4 to do all the talking.

'Tell me,' she began. 'Are you and Tom...'

Stella's face was a rictus of embarrassment, praying that Anne wouldn't attempt some euphemism to complete her sentence. 'God. No, we work together. That's all.'

'He's handsome.'

'Don't.'

'Well, he is! He's smart.'

'Not always.'

'He's funny.'

'Not nearly as much as he thinks he is.'

'He's got a great job.'

'What is this, nineteen fifty-one? I'm the chief editor of the bloody organisation, mum. *I've* got a great job.'

'I'm just saying... He's handsome.'

'Yes, you've said that already.' What irked Stella was that the more Anne tried to be a mother, the more it reminded Stella of how poorly she had done the job first time around.

Anne's attention was broken by a call coming through.

Stella felt at her pockets for her phone. 'Is that yours or mine?'

The dashboard screen switched from the radio ID to "*Murray Morton CALLING*".

Anne replied, 'It's mine. It's never good news when your

lawyer calls you at quarter past seven in the morning.' As soon as she answered, she said, 'Murray, you're on speaker in the car and I have company.'

'Can you take me off?' asked Murray. 'This might be a little delicate.'

Anne considered the situation. 'It's my daughter with me. You can speak freely.'

'I tried to reach you last night. The police would like you to come in today for a follow-up.'

'A follow-up? I've already given them a statement.'

Murray paused. 'They have some further questions.'

'What does that mean?'

'It's probably nothing, but I think you should go and you should take me with you.'

When Anne didn't respond, Stella whispered, 'Mum?'

Anne kept on staring, her gaze landing somewhere towards the front of the car.

Stella snapped, 'Mum!' The motion of her grabbing for the steering wheel, coupled with the blast of the horn from the oncoming logging truck, snapped Anne out of whatever had taken hold of her.

She pulled the steering wheel left just in time to swerve out of the path of the truck's front wing. The rear of the car corrected. Regaining control, Anne caught her breath.

'Are you okay?' asked Murray.

'I'll be there,' Anne said.

13

Magnus had got a fire going in the drawing room before taking off for his walk. The fire was badly needed. Two cups of steaming coffee had lifted Novak's energy levels, but had done little to heat him up. Luckily, Magnus had left out a pile of spare warm clothes for him: a warm knitted fisherman's sweater, and a pair of tweed trousers that required the tightest hole on the accompanying belt.

Novak sat on the leather couch with a laptop and notebook ready, waiting for Sofia and Hugo to finish up what they had promised would take fifteen minutes. An hour later, Novak found himself pacing around in front of the window, getting a jolt as a guard dressed in black and wearing a beanie hat walked past.

Hugo spoke over his shoulder. 'Close those curtains, would you?'

Sofia pointed out, 'It's not like anyone is going to recognise you.' Her attempt at leaning in to him was brushed off.

'Not now,' said Hugo. 'I'm trying to deal with China.'

Novak closed the curtains, leaving only a crack of sunlight

coming through. He turned on two lamps. It amused him how pompous Hugo sounded when he claimed to be working on an entire country. When Novak enquired to Sofia about what they were doing – he didn't want to disturb Hugo – she told him that a hacker in China had reached out for help to break through the Chinese government firewall. Hugo was sending him a script via a hacker message board on the dark web.

Novak's childlike amusement was evident. 'That guy in China has no idea who's helping him.'

Sofia was equally amused. 'Even if Hugo could prove it, they would never believe him.'

Novak remembered what Mark Chang had told him. 'He's Nakamoto,' he said to himself.

Hugo finally stopped typing. 'What did you say?'

'Sorry, I meant that it reminds me of Nakamoto. How no one can prove who he really is.'

'That's the first interesting thing you've said so far,' Hugo said, closing the laptop. 'We should get started,' he told Sofia, turning his face as she tried to kiss him.

Once they were alone, Hugo joined Novak on the couch.

'So, how do you want to do this?' Hugo asked.

'Well, I read Ian's manuscript last night.'

'What did you think?'

If Novak could be honest about it with anyone, it was Hugo. 'It doesn't read like Ian Ferguson. I mean, he tries to make people sitting at computers sound exciting, but let's face it, coding and hacking is like jazz: it's a lot more thrilling to the person playing the instrument. As far as the philosophy and politics behind what Griffin does, all I know from what he wrote is that you were a hacker who, as you saw more of your contemporaries being jailed, became increasingly political. So you created a place where people could safely expose the truth, and Griffin was born.'

'What's wrong with that?' asked Hugo.

'It entirely skips over what made you a hacker in the first place. Didn't Ian ask you about that?'

'He did. And I was evasive. As I always am about the past.'

'Okay, but you realise that you have to give me some details if the book is going to work. This is an autobiography, not a manifesto.'

'Maybe it should be.'

Novak paused, confused. 'But that's not the book that Hathaway has bought. That's what they're paying me to write for you.'

Hugo got to his feet and sauntered around. 'I can't stand that David Copperfield shit. I was born on... I was raised in... My parents were... It's all so dull. It's all there in Ian's draft.'

'Forgive me,' said Novak, 'but it's not.'

Hugo crouched down by the fire, giving it an unnecessary poke. 'Ian was like this. Difficult. Always pressing me about my background. Like I was hiding something.'

He might have sounded like a sullen teenager at times, but there were moments like the one Novak was witnessing, where the orange glow showed a vulnerability in Hugo's face that made him look advanced beyond his years. A young man carrying the weight of the world on his shoulders.

Hugo said, 'The simple step of a courageous individual is not to take part in the lie.'

Novak leaned forward on his knees. 'That's twice you've quoted Solzhenitsyn. You must have read him a lot.'

Hugo sat on the floor, facing the fire. 'He's someone I identify with.'

'Why is that?'

'He was arrested for writing things about Stalin in private letters. He was imprisoned, but he got out of the Gulag and he told the truth about what had been done to him. I found it inspiring, you know. For the first time, I saw what my life really was. I know that this is as good as it will get for me. My fate is already sealed. I've done well to keep my identity a secret this long, but it won't last. The Americans will get me eventually. Then I'll spend the rest of my life being toured around CIA black sites. Water-boarded. Starved. Tortured with sleep deprivation. Or maybe MI5 will just take me out to the hills one night and I'll never come back.' He asked Novak pointedly, 'Would you willingly put yourself in the firing line for that?'

Novak took a long breath. 'I was held in Russia for a spell. Lubyanka.'

It took a lot to do it, but Hugo was impressed. 'You were in Lubyanka? How bad was it?'

He shrugged. 'They didn't make it easy.' Keen to move on, he said, 'Hugo, how many people today would be able to quote Solzhenitsyn if he hadn't have written *The Gulag Archipelago*?'

'I'm all for ambition, Tom, but aiming for something like that is setting the bar a little high, don't you think? I read social media and the press. People already think I'm a pompous arsehole.'

'If one word of truth outweighs the world, then how many truths can we tell in a hundred thousand? That's the opportunity we have with this book. It can be whatever you want, but I can't do it without you. Or without really knowing you.'

While Hugo mulled it over, Novak glanced towards the drawing-room door, where a person's shadow moved, followed by footsteps up the stairs.

Novak asked, 'Why and when did you start Griffin?'

Hugo got to his feet, retreating to the desk where he and Sofia had been working. 'You said that you took this job because Hathaway has leverage on you. Why should I trust you?'

'Because I was locked up in Lubyanka and I know what you're afraid of. I know who you're fighting against, because they came after me and Stella, and I know what they're capable of. I think you liked Ian, but you didn't respect him. His only demons were in a bottle of whisky. The only enemies he encountered were in fiction. People like you and I, our enemies are much more tangible. So when you know that I'm willing to go to places like Lubyanka prison for a story, you know that you're telling your story to someone who will do everything they can to protect you.'

Hugo gave a gentle nod of admiration. 'You didn't even have to think about it.'

Novak showed him his voice recorder and placed it on the coffee table. The screen illuminated as it started recording. Then he waited.

Hugo considered it, and ran his hand through his hair, still getting used to how long it had grown. 'My parents were both in the military. We moved around a lot, as all military families do. They don't know anything about what I do. Who I really am.'

'The name Hugo Byron wouldn't mean anything to them?'

'No. It was a name that popped into my head when I first signed up to this hacker forum on the dark web when I was eighteen. I thought it made me sound mysterious. Now I'll be forever known as someone who isn't real.'

Novak asked, 'Does your family think you're missing? Will they be looking for you?'

'They think I'm backpacking around Asia. Every couple of weeks I send them an email with Photoshopped pictures of me in Thailand or wherever. I loop them through a VPN to make it seem like they've been sent from there. Not that they'd even know how to trace an IP address.'

'Do you miss them?'

For a moment, Hugo let himself appear vulnerable. 'Every day...' It seemed like he wanted to say more about them, but he shook his head. 'I started out like most lonely kids online. You get into coding because there's a logic to it that's absent from the real world. The more I learned, the more I pushed things. I was always pushing too far. It wasn't enough for me just to build a website. I wanted to break into someone else's. Then I found the dark web and I went down a rabbit hole I never got out of. Even now, I wish I could go back and experience that again. The shock. The absolute terror. That there's a world out there hidden away. Where almost unimaginable things are taking place. Where you can buy drugs and guns almost with impunity. Where child porn is as easy to find as searching for the nearest restaurant on Google.' He shook his head in wonder. 'Ninety-nine per cent of people's experience online is Facebook, Instagram and Google. In reality, those people are only seeing about one per cent of what's out there. When you're a lonely kid without direction, the dark web is this chance to live a different life. You can do anything, be anyone, go anywhere. With that freedom I chose to hack.'

'What kind of hacks?' asked Novak.

'It started small. I'd hack friends' email accounts just to see if I could. It's quite the eyeopener when you learn what people are willing to say about you behind your back. So I moved away from that to strangers. Then I figured out what the next logical step up from that was.'

'Which was?'

'Organisations. They're harder to access and their secrets are way more interesting. That was when Sofia found me on one of the hacking forums. The more we talked, the more we discovered we had in common. We were young. We wanted to change the world. And we knew that we didn't want to end up in jail like most of the other hackers we met online. We all wanted to change things. Fight back. It was around that time that I started reading Solzhenitsyn. What can I say... *Gulag Archipelago* changed my life. It consumed me. That was the reason I started coding what would become Griffin.'

Novak couldn't have written a more romantic explanation himself. A dissident Russian writer inspires the first generation born with the internet to fight back against the corrupt worlds of politics, finance, and the military. When he heard such statements, it was hard for Novak not to lose his critical faculties.

Still caught up in Hugo's romantic notions about the origins of Griffin, Novak steamrolled into the next question with little thought. 'You believe very passionately in this idea of there being no secrets. There's huge anticipation about what the next Griffin leak will be. Could you–'

Hugo's head dropped. 'Don't do that, man.'

'Do what?'

'The next drop is irrelevant. By the time this book comes out we'll have moved on.'

Novak persisted, 'Still, if it's the biggest thing so far, as you've said, then it merits at least a mention.'

'We never comment on our leaks. You know that. We don't editorialise. All we do is release the information.' He shot Novak a withering look. 'What's so funny?'

'You have to admit, there's a certain irony in someone who believes so passionately that there should be no secrets, yet refuses to divulge any of his own.'

'I'm not the one whose secrets should be on trial here,' Hugo fired back. 'Try asking these questions to the police, MI5 or MI6, or the NSA, or GCHQ and ask them what they have to say about invasion of privacy, rampant curtailing of free speech, harassment, the complete abandonment of *habeas corpus*. Ask them, Tom!'

'I don't need to ask them. The American government invoked the Espionage Act against me. You're not talking to the damn butler, Hugo. I've lived this too.'

'You have no idea what I've lived through. What I'm *living* through.'

With things as heated as they could get, Novak decided to go for the jugular before Hugo could storm out of the room.

'Did Ian Ferguson find out about Griffin's next leak? Is that why someone had him killed?'

Hugo paused, as if he was considering responding. Then he simply got up and left the room.

Novak picked up the audio recorder then said into the microphone, satisfied with Hugo's response, 'The subject has now left the room.'

14

CENTRAL LONDON

Fiona Bingham felt at home in the young woman's modern flat overlooking the Thames. It reminded her of the first place she had rented when she was nineteen years old and moving up in the corporate world. It had felt like a palace after her student digs. Just having her own living room and kitchen was a novelty in itself.

Having sized up the woman from the file that her team had put together, Fiona was confident that she understood the lay of the land.

The complainant, Bianca, was a dancer at one of Prince James's frequent haunts, The Circle nightclub. Taking home north of fifty thousand a year plus tips – as well as what she made from her online "interactive modelling" – seemed a fortune to a young woman like Bianca. Living in a block full of junior bankers and trainee lawyers, Bianca thought she'd hit the big time. Fiona saw through all that. How temporary it would all be. Bianca had another four years, tops, as a dancer until the owners brought in someone new. A fresh face. Younger. Then Bianca would be in her late twenties, no school qualifications, no meaningful work experience or transferable skills other than grit and determination, and a massive mortgage to pay.

Taking the payoff was her only option.

Bianca sat on the couch next to her lawyer, her eyes raw from crying most of the morning, wondering if she was doing the right thing.

Fiona handed over the non-disclosure agreement for the final review before signature.

The lawyer gave Bianca a pen, eager to conclude the deal. His client could, of course, have pressed charges against Prince James for the sexual battery and attempted rape that had taken place in the bedroom across the hall a month earlier. But that would involve taking on the Palace's lawyers and he knew he wasn't anywhere near their level. All he wanted was his twenty per cent cut of the settlement.

Bianca held the pen, trembling, unable to sign. 'You know what he did to me, right?' she said to Fiona.

She didn't reply.

Bianca didn't realise it, but her case wasn't special to Fiona. She had seen it all before. From CEOs and traders over the years. Since becoming the prince's Private Secretary, she had already handed out NDAs to other young women, exchanging payment for silence. Immune to concrete concepts like The Law. Once they were signed, James was legally in the clear. Whatever anyone had seen, they hadn't really seen. Whatever James had done to someone, hadn't really happened.

'If you want my advice,' said Fiona, her voice full of compassion. 'Take this money. Forget it ever happened. And move on. Believe me, you'll be *shocked* at what you can forget, Bianca.' She held Bianca's gaze with an intensity that suggested she knew exactly what she was going through.

Bianca took one last look at her lawyer, who nodded encouragement.

She signed, then slid the NDA away towards Fiona.

'The money will be in your account by the end of the day,' Fiona said.

Bianca fled to her room, hand at her mouth to keep from weeping.

The lawyer reached out to shake Fiona's hand. His upside secured, he flashed a wide smile.

Fiona looked at him with contempt. 'You should check on your client.'

Downstairs, Fiona texted the prince to tell him the deal was signed. Another crisis averted. Another scandal disappeared.

Then Villiers got out of his car, which he'd parked next to Fiona's. Both Mercedes.

'Ah, this brings me back,' said Villiers. 'The good old days of mopping up after His Royal Highness.'

She kept her distance. 'What do you want, George?'

'I've been doing some digging, Fiona. About a memo I wrote for MI5.'

'What memo?'

'Detailing concerns about the security on Princess Rose's personal laptop and mobile phone.'

She held her bag in front of her, an unconscious closing-off of her body language. 'What sort of concerns?'

'That someone had stolen documents from the princess. I had requested that MI5 reopen their investigation.'

'Did they?'

'No. They never received the memo.' He chuckled darkly. 'Which is the oddest thing, because all communications at Clarence House go through a central server, and only Private Secretaries have clearance to access those.'

'Is there an accusation coming?' Fiona asked.

Villiers moved closer, hushing his voice. 'I know you're working with James to bring down the princess.'

'Why would he want to bring down his own sister?'

'Oh, please,' Villiers scoffed. 'The entire family is full of snakes. Greek tragedy meets Shakespearian backstabbing and betrayal. We're only here to make sure they don't break rule number one: don't ever spill blood on the front pages of the newspapers.'

Fiona unlocked her car and got into the driver's side. 'It might be a little late for that, George.'

15

CHARING CROSS POLICE STATION

Thanks to the lack of available parking and the labyrinthine one-way streets around the Strand and Charing Cross, Anne and her lawyer, Murray Morton, had made their way to Charing Cross Police Station on foot. A suggestion by Murray that he was about to regret.

Anne had come straight from City of London airport, leaving Stella who was on her way to meet Ralph Ogden in the east end.

The moment Anne and Murray stepped off the Strand onto the pedestrian zone, the swarm of photographers around the entrance to the station was already in sight.

'For pity's *sake*,' Murray muttered.

Anne seethed. 'What the hell are they doing here?' For a moment, she nearly stopped walking, but Murray pulled her on.

'Alright,' he said, formulating strategy on the hoof. 'Stay next to me and don't say a bloody word. And whatever you do, don't try to hide your face. Your job is to not look guilty of anything.'

Whether Anne was guilty of something was entirely beside the point to Murray. All that mattered for the next thirty seconds was perception.

The station was on Agar Street, a tight, winding one-way street with parked cars on both sides reducing space on the road, and the pavement was barely wide enough for two abreast. The paparazzi spilled onto the road, their flashes going off constantly as Anne got closer to the station entrance.

She kept her head bowed as Murray announced, 'Ms Cochrane is here voluntarily to assist the police with their enquiries. There will be no further comment at this stage.' He then repeated it verbatim. It was a form response he'd given to the press dozens of times before.

Anne bowed her head ever lower as the press swarmed around her – it was instinctual, and the only reasonable response to the paparazzi's clamouring.

The noise stopped once they got through the main entrance portico, surely the grandest entrance to a police station in the country. It was the jewel in the modern Met's crown, after a £35 million refurbishment had transformed it from a Victorian-era hospital into a gleaming cream three-storey station.

Anne and Murray were greeted in the lobby by what looked like a senior officer, who knew from the commotion outside and the look on Murray's face that all was not well with their invited guests.

Murray unbuttoned his jacket and took a quick glance at the officer's epaulettes – a bath star under a crown. 'I don't know what kind of show you're running here, Chief Superintendent, but in my book that kind of ambush is worth a quick heads up.'

She put out her hand. 'Chief Superintendent Lancaster. I

apologise. But I can assure you I know as little about that scrum outside as you do.'

'Yes, of course,' said Murray, unimpressed. 'Nice to see the Met still knows how to pick up a phone to the press for fifty quid a go.' He draped his jacket over his arm, then took up a defensive stance. 'I want a statement. From you. On those steps out there, making it clear to the press that my client is neither under caution nor suspicion...'

Lancaster put out her arm towards an interview room she had prepared. 'Why don't we all just take a breath and have a sit down. No one's under caution. I acknowledge that you're here voluntarily.'

If that was supposed to mollify Anne Cochrane it would be short-lived. There was already a male detective inspector sitting in the interview room, and an iPad had been set up on the table where a woman in a white coat was already streaming live.

Lancaster sat down next to the DI, while Anne and Murray sat opposite. Anne waited for a second to see if the DI would rise or acknowledge her presence in any way at all. He didn't.

The DI was combing through his notes and was still doing so when they introduced themselves. 'I'm Detective Inspector Scahill.'

Murray placed an audio recorder on the table and switched it to record. 'Could you spell that for me, please?' he asked.

Scahill waited, wondering if Murray was joking.

'For my tape,' Murray elaborated.

Scahill knew fine well the calibre of lawyer he was sitting across from. 'Mr Morton, this is all off the record. It's my and the chief superintendent's intention to keep this as informal as possible.'

Murray's eyes were piercing. 'Humour me.'

Scahill reluctantly spelled his name.

'And when were you going to tell my client that you're with Counter Terrorism Command and not regular Met?' Murray raised a bushy eyebrow as if to say you're not talking to an amateur. 'The red band on your epaulette.'

Scahill decided to turn his attention to Anne. 'I *am* with Counter Terrorism Command, Ms Cochrane. We are a Specialist Operations branch within the Metropolitan Police–'

Anne snapped, 'Let me guess. In charge of investigating terrorism? Can we move this along, please?'

Scahill went on, 'I am leading the investigation into the deaths of Ian Ferguson and Hathaway Parker House employee Gayle Ademi. I can tell you that both of these incidents are being treated as connected and terror-related.' He then gestured to the doctor on the iPad. 'This is Doctor Jenny Arishiro from the Defence Science and Technology Laboratory. They're a Ministry of Defence agency based at Porton Down. They have been leading the testing to establish exactly what caused the deaths of Mr Ferguson and Miss Ademi.'

'I'm sorry,' said Murray, his head wavering laterally from impatience. 'This sounds a lot like the sort of briefing that can happen over the phone.'

Anne put her hand in front of Murray to stop him. 'Murray, it's fine. Carry on, detective inspector.'

Scahill thumbed through his notes. He wanted to get every detail exactly right. 'Ms Cochrane, you sent Miss Ademi–'

'It's very polite of you, Scahill,' said Anne, 'but can we not play the surname game. We'll be here all bloody day.'

'You sent Gayle out for coffee on the morning of her death.'

'Correct.'

'When she returned from the coffee shop, neither you nor Ian received their coffees. What happened?'

Anne looked at Murray. 'This is all in my statement. Why am I being dragged back in front of the press for *this* a week later?'

Scahill said, 'Certain information has come to light that appears to contradict your statement.'

Murray whispered to Anne, 'You don't have to answer that.'

She answered anyway. 'It's my understanding that Gayle dropped the coffee intended for Ian, and I didn't end up taking mine.'

'You asked for it,' said Scahill.

'I did.'

'Why didn't you take the coffee?'

Murray had heard enough. Having failed to get through to Scahill, he now appealed to Chief Superintendent Lancaster. 'There's a shift in tone with that question to the adversarial, and I'm not happy about it. Are you suggesting my client is under suspicion in some way here?'

Anne spoke before Scahill could. 'I don't understand what the coffee has to do with this. Gayle died because she came into contact with Ian, surely? That was the impression the police gave me at the hospital when I was having about a litre of blood taken for testing.'

Lancaster said, joining her hands. 'And we now have the results of those tests, Ms Cochrane. Doctor?'

Doctor Arishiro spoke dispassionately, clearly. In her line of work there had to be no room for doubt. It was about data, not emotions or appeals for understanding. 'The tests have concluded that the poison used on both of the deceased is an organophosphate nerve agent A-234.'

Murray said, 'And for those of us who haven't gone to

medical school?'

Relenting to use the less specific term, she said, 'It is an agent more commonly referred to as Novichok. Both Gayle Ademi and Ian Ferguson's results show similar levels of the agent, leading us to conclude that Ms Ademi could not have been poisoned through secondary contact with Mr Ferguson. Or we would have seen similar results in other Hathaway Parker House staff, as well as significantly more casualties.'

'It was the coffee,' explained Scahill. 'She drank your coffee. Your initials were scored out on the cup.'

Anne was stunned. 'The poison was meant for me.'

'Thank god you refused it,' said Murray, then quickly corrected himself. 'I mean, I am, of course, heartbroken for the family of Gayle Ademi. As my client is.'

Scahill scowled. 'Sure. It was certainly lucky. Or maybe you knew something Ian Ferguson didn't.'

Murray appealed to Lancaster, 'Is this meant to be the civil part of this conversation?' He told Anne, loudly, 'Ignore that impertinent remark.'

Scahill ploughed on. 'Can you think of any reason why someone might want to kill you, Ms Cochrane?'

'Of course not,' she answered.

'Can you think of any reason why someone might want to kill Ian?'

'No.'

Scahill couldn't help but note the extra second it took Anne to answer.

'You were having a meeting with Ian,' said Scahill. 'Could you describe the nature of that meeting?'

'Business,' she replied.

'I'm thinking about the tone of the discussion. Argumentative?'

'It was fine. Spirited. With literature, it's common to have disagreements with authors, and they with you.'

Scahill reviewed his notes once more. 'Witnesses have described that before you two started this spirited disagreement, both you and Ian left your phones outside the office. Can you explain why you did that?'

Anne glanced at Murray who gave her the all-clear. 'Ian was quite particular about privacy.'

'Privacy or secrecy?'

Anne smiled. 'You'd make a good editor, detective inspector.'

'Are authors really that paranoid? What were you discussing that merited such paranoia?' Before Anne could answer, Scahill rephrased, 'Let me put it another way: what was Ian Ferguson working on?'

Anne glanced again at Murray. This time he shook his head.

'My client isn't prepared to answer that,' Murray said.

'This is a murder investigation as part of a wider terrorism incident,' said Scahill. 'If Ian was killed because of something relating to his work, then that's something we need to know about.'

'It's proprietary and irrelevant.'

'Your client doesn't know that.' Scahill then said to Anne, 'Or perhaps you do but aren't willing to say. Why would that be?'

'Move on,' said Murray.

'Are you in the habit of removing your phone from any office you speak in, Ms Cochrane?'

'It was Ian's request,' she said. 'He was a highly valued author to Hathaway. I might be CEO, but in our relationship I was the employee, not Ian. It's simple power dynamics. If Chief Superintendent Lancaster pointed out that your tie wasn't straight, would you not straighten it?'

Scahill looked down, and became aware that his tie was indeed not straight, but didn't want to draw further attention to it by adjusting it. 'On Ian's phone paranoia: you never answered. It wasn't privacy. It was secrecy. A precaution against agencies with the power to listen in on mobile phones being able to do so. Why did he think an intelligence agency might be listening in to his conversations?'

'No idea,' said Anne.

'Did he appear scared?'

'Not really.'

'Because some of the people in the office that morning said that your meeting was a good deal stronger than spirited. In fact, referring to it merely as an argument appears to downplay what one witness described as–' he checked his notes – '"vicious" and "a sustained attack on Mr Ferguson."'

Murray collected his notes and recorder, switching it off. He told Anne, 'We're done here.' He got to his feet and encouraged Anne to do the same.

She remained in her chair to speak to Doctor Arishiro, 'I'm still waiting for the results of my blood work.'

This took the doctor by surprise. 'Those should be with your GP already, Ms Cochrane. We confirmed results yesterday.'

Murray told her, 'Maybe they couldn't get through. You said there was no signal–'

Anne was a little too eager to cut him off. 'Yes, yes.' She said to Arishiro, 'Can't you tell me while I'm here?'

Arishiro said, 'You should talk to your GP, Ms Cochrane.'

'Because I was close to Gayle in the office after she had... And I don't know how airborne...' She broke off.

Arishiro repeated, 'You should talk to your GP, Ms Cochrane.'

Anne stood up. She asked Scahill, 'Why would someone try to kill me?'

'I'm going to find out,' he replied. 'In the meantime, I'd like to assign you a constable...'

'No. It's quite out of the question with my work.'

'For your own protection. At least outside your house at night.'

Murray tilted his head. 'You should take it. Whoever's behind this isn't screwing around, Anne.'

'No. I won't have it. If someone's going to get to me, a constable isn't going to stop them. All I'd be doing is putting someone in harm's way.'

Murray asked, 'Would you be so kind as to show us a back way out of here?'

Chief Superintendent Lancaster showed them the way. When she returned, Scahill was still standing in the same place. The iPad switched off.

'What do you think?' Lancaster asked.

Scahill said, 'Why was she so keen to downplay the argument? And so evasive about what Ferguson was working on?'

'You couldn't have pushed any harder. Not without a caution.'

'Did you hear what Morton said? About her not having a phone signal. He must have been trying to reach her yesterday, too. When was the last time you couldn't get a phone signal in this city?'

'Underground?' Lancaster offered.

'I think she went somewhere. I called five times for her yesterday. I was told she was out of the office. She must have been somewhere remote.'

'Find out where she went,' said Lancaster. 'With Murray Morton in her corner, you better have it nailed on.'

'Oh, I'll nail it on, ma'am. Watch me.'

16

ROMFORD, LONDON

Sitting on the far eastern edge of Greater London, Romford, in the borough of Havering, was one of the cheapest places to live in the capital. The sole reason that Ralph Ogden and his wife had decided to live there.

When Stella reached his street, she found traditional East End terraced houses, their continuity broken up by railway bridges. It was the sort of setting for the opening credits of a British soap opera. The hum and activity of London could be heard, but seemed somehow far away. A reflection of how many more green spaces there were in Havering. The population much less dense than the rest of the city.

Stella counted three separate St George's flags hanging from windows on Ralph's street. A reminder that this wasn't the London of the liberal media set. For London, Romford was as real and traditional as the city got. It amused Stella that one of the most progressive and technologically advanced media organisations in the world was based in such a place.

She had been feeling a vague anxiety in the taxi on the way over, prompting her to fire down a further two pink and yellow pills – on top of the pills she had taken at the first possible moment away from her mother's company. She knew what she was doing wasn't healthy, but it was the only thing she could think of to stem the quivering in her nerves. It was always there, like someone repeatedly tapping your shoulder for your attention. What concerned her was that she no longer had the excuse of being in the office. It was no longer about the practical benefits of the pills. She just needed – wanted – the buzz of them coming on. To reset the balance in her head. Stella was smart and knew the truth. She had also read the scientific literature that clearly showed that statistically it was far easier for low-IQ individuals to kick an addiction than for those with high-IQs. However she wanted to talk around her habit, what was undeniable was that it was growing, and as her dependency grew, the less difference the drugs made to her.

She knew she was both addicted and in trouble.

When she knocked on Ralph's front door, she could already sense the stress on the other side. Through the frosted glass, it was obvious that there was a mess all over the floor, given away by the haphazard mix of colours and shapes.

Ralph's outline came jogging down the hall. He couldn't say hello audibly as he had his phone clamped between his shoulder and ear, with various cuddly toys and soiled children's clothes gathered in both hands. He was explaining to the nursery at the other end, '...no, it should be in the yellow bag... Yes, the one with the zebras on it.' He closed the door behind Stella and gave an ironic eye roll of "*who says being a parent isn't full-time work?*"

Stella was surrounded by chaos in the cramped hallway. There were piles of laundry littered across the bottom stairs. Toys that erupted with obnoxious noises at the slightest hint of contact were scattered around like the pending evidence of numerous home-injury claims. The carpet was badly in need of hoovering, flecked with sock fluff and the random detritus of the everyday: but there was always too much mess on the carpet to make it worthwhile getting a hoover to it.

Once Ralph had confirmed the location of his toddler's favourite toy giraffe, he hung up the phone with the sort of joy normally reserved for receiving a large tax rebate or being cleared of liability in a car crash.

'Sorry, Stella,' Ralph said. 'You'd think this place would get easier when I'm the only one in the house. But it's the only time I can actually get anything done. When the house is full, everything else has to wait.' He threw up an arm in Stella's direction. 'Have you got any kids of your own?' As soon as he said it, a look of horror crossed his face. 'I'm sorry. What an impertinent thing to ask a stranger. I don't know why I said that. I think it's working in the house alone. The toddler doesn't say much, and the baby can't talk yet, so it kind of leaves me to yap away to myself. You know how they say you should try to explain the world to your children, rather than just plonking them in a chair in front of the TV.' He twirled his hand up around his head. 'It keeps them ticking over. Engagement. Anyway, I was apologising. Yeah, working from home… it breeds this false sense of familiarity. Whenever the phone goes, I forget I'm talking to a stranger. Because I'm just always in the house. Do you know what I mean?'

Stella had been trying to keep up with his mile a minute pace.

In his effort to prepare himself for the meeting, Ralph had taken on a few too many strong coffees.

'It's fine, Ralph,' Stella said. 'Don't worry. And I don't have any children, but I do sympathise. You must have a lot on your plate.'

He showed her into the kitchen, chuckling nervously.

'Come in to the office.' The kitchen was under marginally more control than the hall. There were clear boundaries about the utility of a kitchen. Anything that wasn't dirty washing, dishes, or food scraps, plainly didn't belong there and stood out. In the hall, it was anarchy. Anything went, because a hallway wasn't really *for* anything. It was just somewhere everyone passed through to get somewhere else in the house.

Stella spotted a well-worn copy of *True Republic* on the sideboard, full of multicoloured sticky notes. Ralph hurriedly put it away in a cupboard.

A small round table was in the centre of the room, most of it taken up by copious amounts of paper, printouts from the internet, and handwritten notes on A4 foolscap that were almost illegible to Stella.

Ralph clocked her noticing. 'I read about this rapper, Jay-Z, when he was growing up, he was so paranoid about someone stealing his rhymes he wrote in this tiny, almost microscopic script so that he was the only one who could understand what the words were. It kind of stuck with me.'

The thought of a middle-aged man wearing a packet white shirt, black trousers and slippers being in any way familiar with Jay-Z amused Stella no end.

Their small talk didn't last long, both keen to press on. Ralph because he had to pick his two children up before his wife finished her shift at the local Tesco superstore, and Stella because she didn't want to land squarely in rush-hour traffic going back to her mother's house. If Ralph was going to prove a waste of her time, she wanted to find out sooner rather than later.

She wouldn't be disappointed.

'Okay, then,' she said. 'What do you have?' She was pleased to see that Ralph wasn't about to hold back any details from her. He knew that this would be the only shot he had at collaborating with someone of Stella's prestige.

First of all, he brought forward the picture of the suspects. A man and a woman, both roughly in their forties. Ralph said, 'The Met released this CCTV photo a few days ago. Now, passport data is easy to come by for GCHQ and MI5. They'll have pictures of these two at Heathrow Airport, which–'

'How do you know they came in to Heathrow? I've not seen that reported anywhere.' As soon as it came out, Stella knew it was the pills. She could feel them kicking in. The adrenaline. Brain synapses firing like Hogmanay fireworks.

Ralph gestured, softly, for patience. 'I'll get to that... If the British authorities have them at the airport, that means they'll have their passports. If they haven't released the suspects' names, that means the passports are obviously fake. Otherwise, why appeal to the public for information? They *need* their real names.'

'Okay,' said Stella, not completely accepting the premise yet. 'What if MI5 or whoever just want the Russians to know they know?'

'I don't think that's the case, and again, I'll get to that. So...' Ralph reached for a cup of coffee that had long since gone cold. 'Can I get you coffee? Tea?'

Stella declined. Her heart was racing enough already. *Have I taken too many?* she thought. She tried to get control of her heart rate.

Ralph recoiled from the cold coffee's taste. 'The police rather helpfully released the dates when the suspects arrived in the UK and when they left. I've got some open sources that provide access to the passenger manifests...' He found the printout and showed it to Stella.

'How did you get this?'

'It was a Russian flight.' He paused as if it were obvious.

'In Russia, pretty much any data you want is for sale. In the open-source world, for publicly available data in America and Britain, they make you jump through all sorts of hoops, levy huge charges to access it. It can also take months to get even the simplest data points confirmed. Russia is like Disney World, by comparison. If you've paid your money, you're in and you can go on whatever ride you like as many times as you like. In terms of data transparency, Russia is light years ahead of the West. Very technologically advanced data systems for citizens to manage their lives online, particularly when it comes to dealing with official government data, like paying taxes, registering to vote and the like. What comes with such huge databases is an equally huge market in the trading and selling of data. Since I started Verax, I've been gradually acquiring a lot of these traded databases on the dark web and through torrent-file sharing. Then there's the email providers. Well... let's just say the Russian email providers don't take data security as seriously as Gmail and Hotmail. They're always being hacked or suffering data leaks. The black market in this stuff is enormous. Residential databases, travel, car registration, property buying and rental...' He lifted up a big pile of paperwork. 'I now have a considerable amount.'

Stella pulled it over, awestruck at the extent of it. 'Is this all searchable?'

'Oh yeah,' he said. 'I've made a master copy that I can filter by name, age, date of birth, passport number. You name it. There's plenty available for free. You can even go online and find out who has had a traffic violation in Russia. It's incredibly transparent. Then there are these...' He reached for a much smaller pile. 'This stuff has to come from inside the government departments. A lot of it has been leaked over the years to Russian newspapers like *Novaya Gazeta* who, in their opposition to the President and the government, have broken a lot of scandals with this data. A lot of it is sold. That's how I have the passenger manifests. We know from what the Met stated that the suspects arrived in London the morning of the attack and left for Moscow twenty hours later.' He passed Stella the passenger list that proved his next point. 'Only nine male-and-female couples in their forties travelled to both of those airports on those dates and at those times. After checking their passport photographs, I found our suspects: Alexander Gorkov and Ludmilla Nikolevka. Cover names, of course, but you can see that they match the suspects shown in the CCTV.'

'You have their passport data?' asked Stella.

'Oh yes,' he replied cheerily. 'When you know where to look and who to ask it's very easy to come by. A reporter with BBC's Russian Service bought his own passport file for two thousand rubles.'

'Two thousand?' said Stella, working it out. 'That's barely twenty pounds.'

'*And* I found a data broker who was charging one hundred euros to purchase phone records for any Russian individual, as well as precise location data going back a year. It's the wild west out there.' He pointed to a string of numbers listed beside each passenger on the manifests. 'These passport numbers are interesting. See how our two suspects are only five digits apart. You can see by all the other families here that no one else is even close in number to each other. Not friends, relatives. Yet these two come within five digits?'

Stella could see he was right. Everyone else's passports were number soup in comparison. 'What does it mean?' she asked.

'It means someone sat down and processed these passports manually. As part of a batch for cover identities.'

'For who?'

'The GRU.'

Russian spies operating on foreign soil. A very deadly version of MI6.

Ralph went on, 'The manifest shows when the suspects' flights were booked, when they checked in, etcetera. They booked their flights to London and checked in the night before their journey.'

'Devil's advocate, Ralph,' said Stella, 'that's what last-minute means. Thousands of tourists do it every year.'

'True,' he accepted. 'Except that the male's is not a typical passport. Russian passport files list a full history of addresses associated with that person, and all previous ID documents they have held. Expired or otherwise. It gives an entire catalogue of who a person is. This male's catalogue is empty. It's like he only started to exist a few years ago. It's impossible.'

Stella took a closer look at the copied image of the passport file. 'What is this stamp here? It's Cyrillic.'

Ralph grinned. 'I was hoping you would notice that. It means "Do not provide information." My sources in the Russian police...'

Stella loved that he had such a thing.

'...say that they have never seen this stamp before. As far as they're aware it doesn't exist. You can see the handwritten note under the stamp to explain it.'

Stella read it, 'SS.'

'It means "*sovershenno sekretno*". Russian for "top secret". Now we have proof that these are not civilian passports. It's a cover identity.'

Stella nodded, following his line of thought. 'Because the female's passport is so close to his...'

'We know they're working together. Which isn't really news, though. It's nice to have the proof, but we need to know who these two *really* are. Then we can say definitively either way.'

'Definitively what?' asked Stella.

'That the Russian government sent two assassins to kill a novelist in London. That's the story *everyone* wants, right?'

'Of course.'

Ralph pursed his lips, savouring the moment of revelation. 'Except, the Russians aren't behind this.'

17

Stella could see how passionate Ralph was about uncovering the truth. The only other person she'd ever seen with that expression – or anything close to it – was Novak. Ralph really was one of them. But as much as Stella was prepared to accept that Ralph knew far more about Russia than she did, the notion that the Russians weren't behind the murder of Ian Ferguson seemed ludicrous.

'That makes no sense, Ralph,' she said. 'These are two verified GRU officers operating under cover names.'

He corrected himself, 'Forgive me. The suspects are definitely Russian, but the Russian *government*, the *state* and the GRU aren't the ones behind this.'

Stella felt herself channelling Diane Schlesinger's spirit, with her constant invoking of a particular phrase, and Stella was ready to fire the same phrase at Ralph. 'How do you know that?'

He explained, 'The Kremlin has got wise to all of this data-selling. They had to make their agents' cover identities look real. Now the bigger risk is some reporter from *Novaya*

Gazeta or *Republic* or some berk in his kitchen in Romford being able to track down their GRU agents. So they started excising the data from cover identities from phone records, residential records, etcetera. This was idiotic on a few fronts, but principally it meant that anyone like me who already had a master copy of those databases could now simply compare the old versions with the new ones. All you have to do is look at which ones have been altered or removed.'

'That must have taken forever,' Stella pointed out.

Ralph shrugged. 'A couple of weeks with a very long spreadsheet. As I suspected, the Gorkov and Nikolevka names had been removed from most of the databases we have acquired. So we know that those are GRU identities.' Anticipating her next question, Ralph said, 'Why, then, do I say they're not working with the GRU? There's something not right about their passports.' He turned his laptop around to a tab he had prepared earlier. It showed a map of Europe with various plane flights tagged with dates. 'From the random Kremlin-approved cover identities I checked against the passport data I have, it appears that they all pretty much stopped functioning around the time that the databases were tidied up. Yet Gorkov and Nikolevka keep travelling across western Europe under these same identities like nothing has changed. Why?'

Stella said, 'Tell me I sat through all of this to hear a theory.'

'I think they've moved to the private sector, and they've continued using cover identities that were working for them. Until the Ian Ferguson hit.'

'But you can't prove that.'

'Not yet. I will.'

It was the answer Stella wanted to hear. She said, 'You're

not the only reporter with access to this sort of data, Ralph. If you wait, you run the risk of losing the story.'

Ralph then gave the answer that had become all too rare in the journalism field in recent years. 'I'd rather run the full story – the full truth – than just be first.'

'What do you need from me to make it happen?'

He leaned back in his chair and took what was supposed to be a celebratory sip of coffee from the cup of glory. Instead, he spat it back into the cup when he remembered it had gone stone cold a while ago. 'Excuse me... Like I said. Russia is very much in the data market. There's a lot of money to be made. In Russia, that means one thing.'

Stella sighed in disappointment. 'The Russian mafia.'

'If I was in organised crime, I'd get into data.'

She laughed.

'Seriously,' he said. 'The lower-tier guys? The guys on the street? This is what they're turning to now. Guns and drugs draw too much heat and the heaviest sentences. Data is going to be the twenty-first century's heroin. The new narcotic. The best thing is, there's always going to be plenty to go around. Every day we pump over a trillion megabytes into the world. There's no crop shortage because of civil war. No Taliban jacking up the price of poppies. No cartels gouging the price of cocaine. With the right data in a few key areas, I can close this story. I have a Russian contact in London who's connected to the people we need. All I have to do is set up the meeting and I can close this story.' He then said pointedly, '*We* can close it.'

Stella needed to check he was serious. 'You want to cut a deal with the Russian mafia?'

He didn't hesitate. 'That's right.'

'You've got a young family, Ralph. Ian Ferguson and

Gayle Ademi are dead. Is this really worth risking your family? For a news story?'

He stabbed at the table with his forefinger to press home each of his points. 'Every time Russians are caught in something like this, all we see is that one crime. What about all the other times they got away with it? How many other Ian Fergusons and Gayle Ademis are out there? How many murders that were never even treated as murders? The only thing that gave this away as murder was the dosage being so high. Whoever wanted Ferguson dead didn't want to take any chance of him surviving. I'll bet my life that the assassins would have known it was too much poison. That it would give them away. That means exposure. Which also means the person who ordered the hit must have significant funds at their disposal. We have to find out who these people are.' He pointed to the photos of the suspects. 'If we can trace where they've been, we can expose every job they've ever done, every hit, and with the right phone records we'll have their employers. People like Gorkov and Nikolevka are employed because they're trusted. Because they've done it before. With their prep time on the passports, I'd be staggered if this was their first job for this employer. They had them ready on standby, and when someone made the call they didn't flinch.'

'How much?' asked Stella. 'To find out who they are?'

'Ten thousand. Maybe fifteen.'

She puffed. 'I need to make some phone calls. I might be chief editor, but my petty cash allowance doesn't go quite that high. How much time do you have before you collect your kids?'

Ralph checked his watch. 'I've got half an hour.'

Stella had already decided. Ralph was in. He had won her over. She couldn't have been more convinced that he was very close to breaking a major story, and she wanted to be a part of it. The trade-off in bringing him in meant that she couldn't expect total transparency from him while he got nothing in return. If he was going to be up to his neck in data, then there was no telling what subtle name or date or number could be the key to unlocking the crime. She didn't have a choice.

'Ralph,' she started, clearing her throat. 'I have to tell you about something Novak came over here to do. Someone that he's working with. Someone who had a close working relationship with Ian Ferguson in recent months. You're probably not going to believe me, but I need your utmost confidentiality. It's not hyperbole to say that Tom Novak's life might depend on it.'

18

BADANLOCH HOUSE, SCOTLAND

Novak was on the phone to Stella, standing at his bedroom window – what he was still struggling to think of as anything other than Ian Ferguson's room – catching up on her meeting with Ralph Ogden and trying to decompress from his own earlier meltdown with Hugo. They'd had to do an online voice call, using Badanloch's wi-fi while the regular mobile phone signal flashed in and out of use.

Novak was excited to learn of Ralph's progress, but it was impossible to feel connected to whatever he and Stella had going on in London. He was simply too far away, and he was distracted by the ongoing argument he was witnessing between Hugo and Sofia outside.

It was loud enough for Stella to notice once Novak cracked his window open.

'What's going on there?' she asked.

He replied, 'It's hard to tell. Sofia keeps breaking into Spanish when she's really mad.'

'What's your strategy for handling Hugo?'

'I think I'm best leaving him alone for a bit. He was already sore from our argument.'

'You'll probably be the last person he'll want to see after Sofia. Which means you should be the first person that she sees when it's over.'

Novak wasn't so sure.

'She's got no one else to talk to,' Stella assured him. 'She might want to open up about things. Their relationship. You should be ready to find her when the argument's over.'

'Yeah, you're right,' he said. 'How are you feeling?'

'I'm fine,' she lied. She hadn't taken any more pills since her heart had felt like it was beating out of her chest earlier at Ralph's. The tremble of anxiety had stormed back with a vengeance since. 'A strange thing happened in the car on the way back. My mum's lawyer called, saying the police wanted to talk to her again.'

'What about?'

'Nothing specific.'

'I'm sure it's nothing.'

'If it was nothing then why does she need her lawyer? I don't know. I'll let you go. Call me later.'

Novak thought Sofia was wrapping things up, so he grabbed a jacket from the bed. Then, on his way to the hall, he realised that Hugo's bedroom door had been left open. Not only that, but his laptop was sitting on the bed, the lid only half-closed, the screen still glowing.

Novak looked left then right. Outside, Hugo and Sofia were still going at it. He knew that it could be his only chance. It was the first time Hugo had been anywhere without the laptop since Novak had got there. The screen could have gone to sleep at any second.

He hurried into the bedroom, stepping over the piles of laundry on the floor. He crouched down to see the laptop screen, which was filled with code. He gently opened the screen for a better look – being careful not to leave any fingerprints on the glass – but the code was more advanced than anything he'd ever seen.

'Where the hell is Rebecca Fox when I need her?' he said to himself.

He took out his phone. Scrolling around or moving to a different page on the laptop was too risky. If Hugo was running a key-logger, then he could see anywhere and everywhere Novak went, like leaving footprints from a dead body to your front door.

Novak opened the camera function on his phone and took a picture of the code before he was discovered. Once the phone made a satisfying shutter-lens sound, Novak froze, listening.

It had gone quiet outside. The argument was over. And if there was anything predictable about Hugo's mood swings, it was that he always retreated to his room.

Novak pocketed his phone and returned the laptop screen to its previous angle, ready to flee. When he turned around, he found Magnus stopping mid-stride in the hallway.

Novak gulped. How long had Magnus been there? How much had he seen?

'Finding everything you need?' Magnus asked.

Novak managed to channel the old adage that if you can fake sincerity, you've got it made. His insides may have been churning, but on the outside he was innocence personified. 'No,' he said, before adding coolly, 'Hugo. Have you seen him?'

'Last I heard he was outside.'

Novak patted him on the arm on the way past. It was like patting the trunk of a Redwood tree.

Magnus stayed rooted to the spot, his eyes fixed on Hugo's

laptop, then firing back to Novak, who was only too happy to get down the staircase and to the kitchen.

Hugo stormed past, muttering about having no space, directing it caustically in Novak's direction.

Through the kitchen window, Novak could see Sofia setting off through the garden towards the angriest rain cloud he had ever seen.

* * *

He managed to catch up with her in a few minutes. Before he could get alongside her, she called back, 'What do you want, Tom?'

He held his arms out for balance as he navigated the uneven surface of the frozen bog, in boots borrowed from Magnus that were two sizes too big. 'It's not exactly easy to sneak up on someone out here,' he said.

'I don't understand how it's so impossible to be left alone in a place this empty.' She motioned around the Badanloch grounds. 'The guards. Magnus. Anne. Ian And now you.'

'I'm not on the clock, Sofia. There's a time to be a ghost-writer, but I can also be a human being.'

'That's debatable: you're a reporter. Mainstream media.' Her brain was still in defensive mode following her fight with Hugo. She was magnanimous enough to realise it. 'I didn't mean that.'

Novak could see her slowly dropping her guard. 'Are you okay?'

She seemed embarrassed that he'd overheard their argument. 'It's work. Hugo wants to do something bigger with the next leak.'

'The big one?'

'Bigger than anything else we've ever had. It's funny. No one has any idea what's coming. It's going be huge.'

'But you have a difference of opinion on strategy.'

'Something like that. He's got it into his head that we should editorialise more. Edit the leak down and add some of our own commentary.'

Novak tried not to show how pleased he was that Hugo was taking his suggestion. 'You disagree?'

She flashed him a withering look. 'It's not what we do at Griffin. The point is that we're not biased like...' She broke off. There was no other way of saying it.

Novak said it for her. 'Mainstream media types like me?'

'*The Republic* are the good guys. I know that. We're in different disciplines, though. We don't taint the facts with opinions or points of view.'

Novak was struggling to keep up with her, not used to the terrain. 'How can you walk across this stuff so fast?'

She glanced down at his feet with a smirk. 'It helps to have boots that fit. Also, a lot of arguments with Hugo means plenty of practice out here.'

'Something like an occupational hazard?'

'Mood swings and anger are the price you pay for genius.'

'Or just being a son of a bitch,' he suggested.

Sofia wanted to laugh, but restrained herself. 'I'm sorry if I've been hard on you. I'm just very protective of Hugo. He's been so cut up since everything with Ian. He's the kind of guy who can't explain what's wrong with him. He lashes out in other ways. He's never known how to control his emotions.'

'Like anger?'

'Or guilt.'

'Why guilt?'

She recoiled, like she'd said too much. 'The last time he and Ian spoke was an argument.'

'What did they argue about?'

'I don't know. But Hugo was still angry about it the next morning. I've never seen him like that, actually. He was...' Searching for the right word, she slid her hand in front of her face like a mask falling. '...black with rage. When he found out about Ian, well... You can imagine how he felt.' She stopped walking, observing the black cloud tumbling over the peak of the nearest hill. She stamped a little on the ground. 'The rain will break up this frost in no time. This isn't the place to be in a rainstorm. We should go back.'

The walk back was more relaxed than the way out, sharing stories about their childhoods, and how strange it was for either of them to have ended up in such a place, doing such things with their lives. The two exchanging playful pushes. Trying to be a gentleman, Novak didn't push too hard, then Sofia gave a full-on shove that put him on his back. While Sofia wheeled away with laughter, he scrambled to his feet and set off after her as the rain started. It lashed down, soaking them through by the time they reached the house, where it quickly became clear that all hell had broken loose.

They kicked their wet boots off at the back kitchen door, rushing to find out what had happened.

Magnus had a phone to his ear and was listening intently to the person at the other end, while Hugo had on wireless earbuds and was engaged in frantic conversation via video call on his laptop. 'They can't get away with that!' he yelled. After being asked a follow-up question, he fired back, 'Trust me, I just know.'

The television was on, and it seemed like every screen in the house had been moved into the kitchen, for what had turned into a kind of crisis centre.

Novak managed to stop Magnus – also on the phone – to ask him what was going on.

Magnus covered the mouthpiece, still listening to the voice at the other end. 'The police have arrested three different sources for leaking documents to Griffin. Two in Washington, D.C., another in New York, and one in Manchester. A fourth has just been found dead in Berlin. I think this place is going to be next.'

19

The news was across all the major news channels. Online was on fire with intrigue, gossip, and conspiracy. Novak couldn't help wondering what the conspiracy theorists would make of his involvement with Hugo – if only they'd known.

There was little information coming out other than what Magnus had told Novak.

Hugo was nearly an hour deep into a video call with a lawyer that Anne had put him in contact with. A specialist in human rights law, Nadia Al-Aziz. As a favour to Anne, she was willing to waive her extortionate hourly rate.

Hugo stood over the laptop on the kitchen table where Magnus, Sofia, and Novak could all see, but so far Hugo and Nadia were the only ones doing any talking. Anne was also on video call, but seemed oddly subdued given the situation. Novak could see that it wasn't fear. Her mind was elsewhere.

'Legally,' Nadia explained, 'you're in a bit of a grey area.'

'You're not explaining why that is,' complained Hugo. 'I haven't committed any crime by running Griffin.'

'Technically, and to the letter of anti-terror legislation, there *is* an argument, Hugo, along the lines of knowingly distributing classified material of a harmful nature, and with the express intent of causing damage to national security. There's also a pretty compelling incitement argument to be made.'

'We haven't commented publicly on any of these leaks.'

'But you have published documents from people who have encouraged others to commit violence against politicians. And the tide of the courts is only going one way on that kind of thing, Hugo.'

Sofia was the calmest one in the room. 'They'll have to find us first,' she said, legs swinging as she perched at the end of the table.

Hugo said, 'This isn't about what we've done. It's about what we're going to do. Who knows who the hell these people are that they've arrested.'

'It's a fair point,' said Novak. 'There's no function within the website for Hugo or Sofia to identify the senders of classified material. How could he be accused of sheltering?'

'That remains to be proven,' said Nadia. 'All I'm telling you is that from a legal standpoint, you're not on concrete ground.'

Once the call had finished, Novak remarked to Anne, 'Well, that was a waste of time. Thank god we didn't have to pay for it.'

Anne replied, 'We need to have a frank discussion about where this leaves the book, Hugo.'

'Sod the book,' he snarled. 'There are lives at stake here.'

'Yes,' said Sofia. 'Ours.'

Anne didn't seem impressed. 'Hugo, the best thing you can do, that anyone there can do is stay put. There's no reason to believe that anyone knows where you are, or that you're in any immediate risk there.'

He retorted, 'Is that your advice to protect us, or protect Hathaway's investment? I mean, forget jail. Forget assassination. I'm just a commodity to you! You know what Ian said about you?'

Anne gave no indication that she wanted to hear it, but knew Hugo was going to tell her anyway.

'He said that it didn't matter to you whether you were selling books or tins of beans. It was all just units to you. Money spent versus money earned.' Hugo brandished a finger at the laptop screen. 'Oh yeah, I know all about what Ian thought of you.'

Anne shifted in her seat a little, looking beyond Hugo towards Novak. 'Tom, I hope you got some good material today. Keep me posted on your progress.'

Once Anne had gone, Novak tried to steer the conversation back to what Hugo cared about most: the arrests. Trying to let his experience guide Hugo's reaction, Novak rationalised, 'It's always hard for leakers to stay free. That's the harsh reality. Anyone who leaks information worthy of Griffin ends up drawing attention to themselves.'

Sofia agreed. 'They share information that only so many people can know... it's just a matter of time before the net closes in on them.'

'I'm sure that brings them a lot of solace right now, sitting in jail.' He gesticulated at the television. 'That poor woman in Berlin has been shot.'

Magnus added, 'They say she was armed and threatening to shoot.'

Hugo looked at him with disgust. 'Of course they're saying that. It's borderline assassination, is what it is.'

Novak was bewildered, and disappointed, that Hugo would jump so quickly to a position that all the facts contradicted. 'It was a member of the public who tweeted that she was armed, Hugo. Not the police.'

'Whose side are you on, anyway?' he shouted. 'It's a tweet. That person could be anyone. Of all people, you should know that.'

'It can't be a coincidence that they've all been taken in at the same time,' said Magnus. 'I know the plan was to release the next leaks tomorrow, but I really think we should consider getting out of here. All of us.'

Hugo replied instantly, 'I'm not going anywhere just to make your life easier, Magnus. They're going to have to take me out of here in a body bag. Those leaks are coming out tomorrow.'

Magnus had to restrain himself.

Novak was shocked at Hugo's ingratitude, and how quickly he was willing to turn on a supposed ally.

Sofia suggested, 'What about a non-extradition treaty country? We could claim political asylum.'

'It worked for Edward Snowden,' said Novak.

Hugo wouldn't hear of it. Which didn't come as a total surprise to Novak. Hugo didn't want to run off to Russia, where he would end up somewhere far less salubrious than his current surroundings, bailed out and housed by a tech millionaire. In Russia Hugo would become a plaything for the Kremlin. Going there would also undermine his credibility. It could even end with him being pressured into releasing anti-Western leaks. Hugo didn't want to hide away where the public would eventually forget about him. He craved the notoriety that would come from being arrested, followed by the inevitable trial, which any decent lawyer would be able to drag out to a series of pre-trial reviews and counter-proceedings, all of which would be covered by the media.

Sofia pleaded with Hugo to at least consider their options.

'You're going to get us all killed,' she exclaimed, then ran out the room.

For once, Magnus had to play the paternal figure rather than the intoxicated sugar daddy. He was so in thrall to Hugo, it wasn't a role that came naturally to him. He was keen to keep Hugo onside, regardless of his snarling attitude. 'Why don't I make a few calls...'

Hugo declared, 'I'm not running away.' He stormed out of the room, taking his laptop with him, muttering under his breath.

'Hugo,' Magnus called after him, feebly.

Novak found it strange to see such a powerful-looking man so emasculated by a thin, pale computer hacker. 'Should I go after him?' he asked.

'Leave him,' snapped Magnus. 'The selfish bastard has had enough attention. Do yourself a favour, Tom. Don't stick your neck out for that young man. Not like I have.' He left for the sanctuary of the drawing room, leaving Novak on his own.

Just then, a message came through to Novak's phone. It was from Anne Cochrane:

"*Keep it to yourself but I'm worried Hugo will be next. Need to press him more tomorrow. Running out of time.*"

Novak pocketed his phone and sighed. 'Yeah. I definitely didn't need that.'

He was surrounded by the shrill combination of voices from the news channels, coming at him from every angle.

After muting them all, he found the picture he'd taken of Hugo's laptop screen. He was fairly literate when it came to coding, but he couldn't fathom what he was looking at.

He attached the picture, then tapped out a message and sent it to one of the few people he knew who might understand it.

"*Kurt, do you know what this code means? Need answer asap.*"

20

BLOOMSBURY, LONDON

The Darby Agency was located on Bedford Square in Bloomsbury, in a black Georgian terraced house. While most of the other big literary agencies in London had moved to bigger, modern premises within glass-fronted buildings, Darby had remained stubbornly traditional. Only a small gold nameplate beside the door gave any indication as to who worked there.

Stella had called ahead of time, having to namedrop quite a few editors she and Ian's agent, Julian 'The Wolf' Darby, both knew before he would concede to a brief conversation. Even getting past the front door proved troublesome. After pressing the buzzer outside and explaining who she was, Stella received the receptionist's rote response that they didn't accept unsolicited visits. Two further buzzes from Stella and an intervention from Darby himself managed to get her in.

The receptionist looked sheepish as Stella entered.

'Sorry about that,' Darby said, standing at his open office door off reception. 'Don't blame Camilla. We get all sorts showing up here through the day. Mostly eager young men with manuscripts wrapped up in brown parcel paper like it's still the seventies.' He beckoned her inside his office. 'Do come in.'

He was wearing a black suit and black tie. Not to mourn Ian's passing. It was Darby's signature look. He was balding, with the thinnest collection of strands pushed backwards, but he had a youthful nature and glowing skin, making it easy to picture him as a young man, rather than a sixty-year-old.

She knew of him by reputation. It had become common for political journalists to have thrillers published, taking the extended Parliamentary break over summer as a chance to finally get some fiction down – although some would have said that they were already specialists in that category. Those who had approached the Darby Agency talked of him in hushed tones as a 'star-maker' but also volatile and extremely hostile if caught on the wrong day. The sort of agent who could secure mouth-watering advances for his clients. The problem was getting him to read the manuscripts in the first place, as he was famously reluctant to take on new clients.

His office was spotlessly clean, the antithesis of the image of a Bloomsbury literary agent Stella had expected: loose manuscript pages piled high on desks, a general sense of organised chaos, lovable looseness. Instead, Darby's office was all business: flanked on both sides by white bookcases. Clean, modern design, with thin bezels not for aesthetic purposes, but simply because it allowed him to fit more books in.

The day's broadsheet newspapers were fanned out carefully on a table in front of a long blue couch, each edition the same width apart so that the name of each paper was visible at a glance.

Stella took a seat on the couch as Darby had directed. He sat opposite in a sleek leather chair of minimalist design.

'I'm sorry about Ian,' she said. Her knees complained as

she sank into the couch. She had been doing far too much sitting down in the last twenty-four hours.

'Yes,' said Darby in a thick Anglo-American drawl. 'Dreadful business. He also left his business affairs in a total goddamn mess. Now I've got to tidy it all up. It was stipulated in his will.'

Stella titled her head in confusion. 'Isn't that your area of expertise?'

'An author has a lot of moving parts behind the scenes these days, Ms Mitchell. There are online sales dashboards, advertising reports for Facebook and Amazon, official email address, website... Ian was good with tech and liked being hands on with his book promotions, so he stayed in charge of such things. All he asked of me was to be me: namely, land him the biggest publishing contracts in the land.' He flashed a sharp smile. 'Which I always did.'

He had been born in the States, but had lived in England from seven years old, going through the boarding school system before returning to the States to attend Harvard.

Stella couldn't figure out exactly why, but he had an aura about him. It was more than his reputation preceding him. It was his small, narrow eyes, giving the impression that he wasn't watching you. He was spying, assessing. His voice was thick and heavy, commanding without requiring volume. Like a hi-fi where the bass had been turned up too loud on the equaliser.

'I'm afraid I don't have a lot of time to give you, Ms Mitchell,' Darby explained. 'But I know you're close friends with Martin Fitzhenry and as one of my clients he would want me to take this meeting.'

'I'm doing some background on behalf of my partner, Tom Novak.'

Darby tutted ruefully. 'How I would have liked my cut of a

book like *True Republic*. It's a shame he and Ian never met. They would have got on well. I know Ian was a thriller writer, but his fans always said how much they valued the effort he put into research. In the end, it could have been what put him in his grave.'

'What do you think got him into trouble?' asked Stella.

'Let's just say Napoleon did fine until he started crossing borders. Let's be honest here,' he gestured at the posters for million-selling thrillers framed on the wall behind Stella, 'I only represent big fish. Although ninety per cent of what literary agencies receive in submissions is unpublishable drivel, they still rely on the process to find books that go on to sell. It's a necessary evil, and requires dozens of interns – or "editorial assistants" – to read through endless piles of submissions.'

Stella said, 'Most agency websites I've looked on have long sections detailing their submission process. Your website simply states "We do not accept unsolicited manuscripts." Is that where your reputation comes from?'

Darby grinned. 'Whatever do you mean?'

'You have a reputation for stealing other agencies' authors.'

'And I get them bigger advances than they've ever seen. Better to be a wolf, Ms Mitchell, than a sheep. That's why Ian hired me.'

'It's my understanding that Ian attempted contact with you the morning he died.'

'Yes. He was barely ten minutes away. I can hardly stand to think about it. If only I hadn't brought him into the fold on this bloody book.'

'Why did you?' asked Stella.

Darby replied, 'Anne Cochrane hired him to bring credibility to a book project that Hathaway were worried would be derided in reviews as vanity on Hugo's part. It needed Ian's reputation for pace, commerciality, and research. If you brought in some reporter from *The Guardian* it would get swallowed up in arguments about political bias. With Ian, Hathaway knew they were getting someone impartial, and that would be important when it came time to promote the book.'

Stella asked, 'But ghostwriters are not generally acknowledged when a book is published, am I right?'

'Normally, yes. Hathaway's problem was that they needed to tie Hugo Byron to someone respectable, but it would have more weight if it was seen as Hugo's autobiography.'

Stella looked down at her hands, realising she'd been picking at the skin around her cuticles. She hadn't been aware of it until then, but she was wired, if not obviously from the outside. Inside, she was churning like she'd had ten coffees in quick succession. 'I saw Ian's books in the *Sunday Times* bestsellers all the time. I'm curious as to why he took the job in the first place.'

'Today, the number one book in this country will sell about four thousand copies through all retailers, including online. Do you know how many people today will watch the tenth-most-popular TV show on Netflix?'

Stella was stumped.

Darby said, 'Close to seventy-five thousand. Publishing is a boutique industry, Ms Mitchell, no matter how glamorous we try to make it. It's not only about my bottom-line, though I always encourage my writers to follow the money. The Hugo Byron book was about prestige. Ian wanted to go behind the scenes where the NSA, MI5, and Mossad would kill to get even a glimpse of. It was good business to stay in-house with Hathaway too if they were publishing the Byron memoir. Ian had a new contract coming up in two books' time, and I thought it would help if he had done Anne Cochrane a favour. That would have been moot, as it turns out.'

Stella had a way of pouncing on doubt the way that sharks smell blood in the water. 'Why is that?'

'After Ian had signed the contract for the Byron book, he came up with this crazy idea that he was going to self-publish his next book. Go straight to Amazon himself. To make matters worse, he was going to publish under a different name.' Darby reached back to his desk for a small cup of tea he had forgotten about.

Stella took his lack of offering her one to mean that he really didn't want her staying much longer.

He sipped his tea thoughtfully. 'Gary Shepherd, I think was the name. Why, I have no idea. I thought it all pretty fanciful and even took it to Anne, using it as a negotiation strategy for when the next contract came up. I could drive his price up.' He shook his head and gave a snort. 'It's fair to say she was not entirely amused. She accused Ian of using Hathaway's clout, and now that his reputation had been made, he was going to cut everyone out. Me. Hathaway. Everyone. Me? I didn't care what Ian chose to do with his next book. I make enough money. Not enough to make my family proud of what I do. Only a handful in this business make any, what they would call, *real* money.'

Stella suspected that coming from a family as illustrious as the banking Darbys, Julian Darby's barometer of "real money" was somewhat skewed.

He continued, 'Anne screamed bloody murder. So to speak... She said that self-publishing was like telling everyone who sang in the shower that they belonged in La Scala, duetting with Corelli or Callas. But that was nothing in comparison to when I told Ian about it. I'd never seen him run so hot. How could I do this, he screamed. I'd endangered everything, etcetera. I never figured out what it was all about. I was just relieved to hear that he had finished the book ahead of schedule. Believe me, in this industry that is a rare beast.'

Stella inched forward in her seat. 'Ian finished the book?'

'So he said, though he never got the chance to send it to me. As power of attorney over his business affairs, I have access to all his dashboards and passwords and email, and there was nothing with any attached files. No manuscripts.'

'Could he have used any kind of cloud software? A drop box?'

'Ian stopped using them. Said he didn't trust that they were safe from GCHQ and the like. We have the venerable pairing of Stella Mitchell and Tom Novak to thank for that one. No, he told me that the book was finished and ready to publish, but that Hathaway wouldn't be pleased.'

'His exact words?' Stella checked.

Darby took out his phone and scrolled to the email. He showed it to Stella. Date and time, and all.

'The night before he died,' said Stella. 'He never told you why Hathaway wouldn't like it?'

He put his phone away. 'I asked, but he refused to go into details over the phone. I can only assume that's what he and Anne Cochrane quarrelled about at their last meeting.'

'How do you know that?' asked Stella.

'According to the police. They asked me if I knew of any reason why Ian and Anne would have argued.' For the first time, Darby looked cagey. 'Ms Mitchell, my client and close friend was poisoned because of something relating to this Hugo Byron book. Of that, I'm in no doubt. If Ian finished the manuscript, frankly, that's information I'd rather keep to myself until the facts become a little clearer.'

'You don't trust Hathaway or Anne Cochrane?

'About a completed manuscript? Not as far as I could throw them.

'Mr Darby, do you suspect someone at Hathaway of being involved in Ian's murder?'

He paused, considering his words. 'Let me put it this way... The last contract I negotiated for Ian Ferguson was a ten-book deal worth seventy million pounds. His value is nearly double that now. That's the difference between Hathaway shareholders' value being up on the year, or down. I'll let you draw your own conclusions from that.' His body language said he wanted to wrap things up.

Stella interjected before he got any further. 'One more thing I was wondering... You said that it was good business to stay in-house with Hathaway...'

Darby gave a faint smile, enjoying the fact that Stella had quoted him verbatim. He loved precision.

She went on, 'I don't understand. You had already been approached by Hugo Byron and then sold the book to Hathaway?'

Darby pushed out his lips, confused. 'Anne Cochrane brought Hugo Byron to *me*. The book was pitched to Ian as a Hathaway book already.'

Stella felt the wind being knocked out of her.

He elaborated, 'Hathaway was onboard with Hugo Byron before either Ian or I were ever involved. I've already been through this with the police. Frankly, I no longer want any connection between myself and Byron. I have no wish to have to check my food at every restaurant I eat in for the remainder of my days.' He stood up, buttoning his suit jacket on the way. 'Find Ian's killer, Ms Mitchell. There will be a handsome reward in it for you.'

Stella shook his hand. 'Thank you, Mr Darby.'

'And Ms Mitchell,' he added. 'The next book that Tom Novak wants to write. Tell him to give me a call first. That agent of his? Total sheep.'

'And you're a wolf, Mr Darby,' Stella said.

'That's right.'

She got as far as Shaftesbury Avenue with only one thing on her mind: why had her mother lied about how she was introduced to Hugo Byron? And if it hadn't been Julian Darby who brought Hugo to her, how had she found one of the most sought-after people on the planet?

After trying and failing to reach Novak by phone, she wrote out a message to him:

"We need to talk."

21

When Novak got to his room, he stood in the doorway taking in the scene. Something wasn't right. The bedding was slightly rumpled, having been left tidy, and his laptop was now on top of his notebook on the desk, rather than the other way around.

They left in a hurry, he thought.

He moved towards the window, assessing the view. Anyone in the room would have seen him and Sofia returning from their walk.

Having already written up his notes on his discussion with Hugo, Novak turned instead to Ian's manuscript. He turned to the section about Hugo's background, which had been started but not finished. Ian had inserted a place-holding text: "FILL IN FROM RESEARCH NOTES".

When Novak had read the manuscript during his first night at Badanloch, he had assumed that Ian hadn't got around to bringing it up with Hugo. Then he remembered the transcript of his own conversation with Hugo, which he'd typed up to take his mind off how poorly it had ended.

He turned on his laptop, only to find the document had been deleted. Whoever had done it hadn't covered their tracks well. It took Novak a minute to dig into the hard drive logs and find evidence that the document had been deleted. The time showed that it had happened while he and Sofia were outside.

He patted down his pockets, relieved to find his audio recorder still on him. He scrolled through the conversation until he found the right spot.

Hugo: "*Ian was like this. Difficult. Always pressing me about my background. Like I was hiding something.*"

Novak checked the manuscript again.

FILL IN FROM RESEARCH NOTES.

If Ian had found out something about Hugo's background, he wouldn't have left his notes somewhere obvious. And he didn't know he wasn't going to return from London. His notes had to still be there.

Novak rushed through every drawer in the room. Checking for loose floorboards, pulling furniture out from against the wall. Nothing.

Ian's clothes and personal items had all been removed and sent down to his family in London, so the cupboards were bare, as Novak hadn't bothered to unpack yet. There was always the possibility, however unlikely, that Ian's notes had been found but were packed up with his clothes. What was most likely was that someone had found Ian's notes and made sure they were destroyed. Their secrets gone forever.

That was when Novak's eyes fell on it. One of the few things still in its proper place in the room: a short bookcase next to the writing desk. Novak closed the desk drawers, then kneeled down for a closer look at the books. He scanned across them, looking for something that stood out in any way.

He was almost at the end when he spotted a copy of *Natural History: A Selection* by Pliny the Elder.

When Novak opened the book, he found it hollowed out, with a memory stick and a mobile phone sitting inside. Having mentally derided the Pliny reference at the start of Ian's manuscript, he felt the strange sensation of having Ian help him.

He closed his door completely, then switched on the phone. There were no contacts saved, no messages and no call log. The classic signs of a burner.

Novak put it in his pocket and slid the memory stick into his laptop, taking it to the desk. 'That makes a welcome change,' he remarked. No passwords or encryption.

As he scrolled through the reams of documents that Ian had saved, Novak felt terrible for thinking that Ian had done such a crummy job with the book. He had been truly busy. He'd gone to town on Hugo Byron, gathering more information than anyone ever had on him.

The first that Novak clicked into showed old message board logs from Hugo's hacking days. The logs had preserved pages of conversations back and forth between Hugo and his hacking associates, and they weren't kind to Hugo. In the face of accusations of being apolitical in response to several close hacker friends from the board being arrested, Hugo showed total apathy. When someone tried quoting Solzhenitsyn to him, Hugo replied:

"*No idea who that is.*"

Novak stared at it for a moment. At first, it was sheer surprise. It was a far cry from the Solzhenitsyn devotee Novak thought he'd been talking to. He thought about what Hugo had said about wanting 'to fight back'. The message board posts didn't show him wanting much of any kind of fight.

Then Novak looked at the date of the post. Hugo was only

two months away from buying the domain name for the Griffin website. It didn't make sense that in that short space of time Hugo had somehow become radicalised, read the complete works of Solzhenitsyn, and then set up Griffin.

Novak's concentration was broken by footsteps running down the hallway, followed by a muffled warning from Sofia to the others downstairs.

'Someone's coming...'

Novak sprang to his feet to see out the window. There was occasional traffic on the single-track road, mostly birdwatchers heading for the RSPB watchtower five miles away. But the white van that Sofia had spotted was turning off the road, and onto the Badanloch House driveway.

Magnus, Hugo, and Sofia met in the main hallway.

'Are you expecting anyone?' asked Hugo, wondering if he was experiencing his last moments of freedom.

'No one,' Magnus replied, taking up a radio to talk to the guards outside. 'Back off until we know what this is.' The guards hid their guns under their long coats. The last thing anyone needed was someone getting shot.

Novak took up a crouched position under the drawing-room window, watching the van trundle nearer the house. The driver no doubt apprehensive about the strange figures in dark clothing patrolling the grounds.

'He's pulling up,' Novak said.

Across the hallway, Sofia and Hugo watched from the lounge.

Magnus covered the front door, telling Hugo, 'You should go. You might not get another chance.'

'I'm not running,' Hugo replied, his eyes wide with worry and panic.

He might have talked the good game of a brave political

dissident, but when the law came bearing down on him, he was scared like anyone else would be.

The driver got out, dressed in a typical delivery uniform. Cargo trousers, boots, a company fleece in a garish purple. Not knowing whether to go to the door or not, the driver called out, 'Tom Novak?'

Novak got a jolt of fear, like someone had attached jump leads to his heart.

The guards said nothing. Then one eventually pointed to the front door.

The driver took a brown padded envelope from the front seat and took it to the door, knocking cagily.

Magnus answered, opening the door as little as possible.

'Tom Novak?' the driver asked hopefully. 'I have a special delivery.'

Novak got to his feet, walking cautiously to the hall.

Magnus handed him the parcel and was about to close the door.

The driver leaned in a little, holding out a handheld device and a plastic dummy pen. 'I need a signature.' He glanced over his shoulder, checking out the guards' formation. They might have slid their weapons inside their jackets, but the driver knew that something strange was going on at Badanloch House.

Novak stepped into the light of the doorway and signed.

The driver said thanks with relief. He left twice as fast as he'd come in, giving no thought to the van's suspension in the driveway potholes.

In the lounge, Hugo slouched, sliding down the wall onto his backside. Sofia sighed.

Magnus wasn't nearly as happy. 'Who knows you're here, Tom?'

'No one,' he replied, then took the envelope upstairs.

His answer satisfied no one, and left the others tense and distrustful.

Novak shut the bedroom door behind him and placed the envelope on the desk – wondering what he was going to find inside.

He almost jumped out of his skin when the envelope started to vibrate. It quivered on the spot. Novak ripped the envelope open and took out the phone that was inside. The screen lit up and the ringer had been switched off. The call was coming through an online messaging app. The ID said "UNKNOWN NUMBER".

Novak answered but said nothing, playing it safe.

After a long pause, a genteel, male English voice asked, 'Tom Novak?'

There was no point in prolonging the non-committal strategy. Whoever had arranged the delivery clearly knew he was there.

'Yeah. That's me,' Novak said.

'You don't know me, but your life is in danger.'

'What makes you say that?'

'Because I tried to give Ian Ferguson the same warning. Unfortunately, Ian wasn't as careful as he should have been. I'm hoping your amateur tradecraft will be a little more robust than his.'

Novak took the phone away from his face for a moment to check something. 'How is this phone already connected to the wi-fi here?'

'It remembers the network because it's the same phone Ian used to talk to me on. He left instructions with his agent for it to be sent back to me. Should anything ever happen to him.'

'Who are you?' Novak asked.

'A man who has dedicated his life to something important. Now I'm a man with nothing to lose.'

'What is this all about?'

'You have no idea who you're dealing with, do you? He'll do anything to get what he wants.'

Novak's body was rigid. 'Who?'

'It will all come out tomorrow.'

'What's going to come out tomorrow?'

'When we meet.'

Novak looked hopelessly out the window. He might as well have been on Neptune. 'That's not possible.'

'I'll come to you.'

Assuming that the caller didn't know about the armed guards, Novak warned, 'That's not a good idea.'

'Because of the guards?' he said. 'Don't worry about them. I'll meet you at Forsinard Flows. You can walk there. There's a train station. Meet me there at six fifteen. And Tom,' he added, 'keep an eye out for delays. It's not the sort of place you want to be left alone for an hour. Not in your situation.'

Before Novak could respond, the caller hung up.

He scribbled down the meeting time and place in his notebook, then tore the page out and put it in his pocket. If someone was rifling through his things, he wasn't about to give up a crucial piece of logistics. The house may have been surrounded by armed guards, but Novak wasn't feeling safe.

22

Stella had put off her return to Anne's house in Primrose Hill for as long as she could. The thought of being in close quarters with her almost-estranged mother, trying to hide a pill habit, wasn't exactly attractive to her. But she couldn't get answers to her questions from a hotel room.

Anne's house was on a gently curving street of pastel-coloured Georgian terraced houses, each a different colour. Anne's was mint green, with pink and yellow on either side. Stella allowed herself a sardonic laugh at how similar the colours were to the pills in her handbag.

Once the epicentre of Britpop in the nineties, home to raucous parties hosted by artists with work in the Tate Modern and musicians at the top of the charts, Primrose Hill had become the place to be for those in the fashionable media set, from digital influencers on Instagram, to those like Anne in publishing. She liked the vibrancy and village-green charm that came with the surroundings, the tree-lined avenues, and the park that provided stunning panoramic views across London.

Stella slid the spare key into the door and found the house mostly in darkness. It took her a few steps inside to tell that Anne was even home. The music and dim lamp in the living room giving her away.

Pink Floyd's album *The Final Cut* was playing on vinyl from a ludicrously expensive turntable and hi-fi set. Anne was wrapped in a blanket with her feet up on the couch, drinking methodically from a glass of red wine. Stella noticed that the bottle on the table in front of her was already half-empty.

'Long day?' asked Stella, trying to be polite.

Anne replied, 'You could say that.'

'How did it go with the police?'

Instead of answering, Anne put her feet down, reaching for the remote to turn up the volume on the hi-fi. 'I always loved this song,' she said.

Anne had struggled sufficiently over her Ss for Stella to know that she was definitely tipsy, and coming up fast on drunk.

Stella picked up the vinyl gatefold. 'I thought this was supposed to be one of their crap albums.'

'It's basically a Roger Waters solo album,' said Anne. 'Left-overs from *The Wall* sessions, but it's had a bit of a critical reassessment recently.'

Stella sat on the armrest of the armchair opposite. As close as she was willing to get. 'What happened at the police station?'

When Anne reached for her glass again, Stella took it out of her hand and put it on the mantlepiece. Anne wasn't prepared to go that far for another drink. She was as drunk as she needed to be to get the words out.

'What happened?' asked Stella.

As one of David Gilmour's finest, haunting guitar solos started on the album's title track, Anne bowed her head. 'The police knew that Ian was poisoned after he and I had our meeting. I had sent Gayle out for coffee for us. She dropped Ian's and returned with mine. But I didn't take it.'

Stella squinted, wondering where it was all going.

Anne looked up at Stella, her eyes filled with tears. 'That was what killed her, Stella. The coffee that was meant for me.'

Stella rushed to sit down next to Anne, putting a hand on her shoulder. 'Why would someone try to kill you?'

'I don't know.' She paused. 'Turns out they did better than anyone thought.'

'What does that mean?'

'I spoke to my doctor today. They took blood work from me when they first took me to the hospital.' She turned to meet Stella's eyes. 'There must have been a lot of poison in the cup. I was at Gayle's desk. Only for a moment. They think that's when it happened.'

'When what happened?'

'When I was poisoned.'

The wine. The music. The tears. Stella knew it was all leading to something. But she needed to hear her mother say it out loud before she could believe it.

Anne said, 'The doctor says I've got six months, Stella.'

23

Novak returned downstairs to find the atmosphere strained. It only took ten seconds in everyone's company in the kitchen to figure out that he was the reason.

Magnus was trying to make tea, but couldn't because of the mess. Every mug in the house had been used and left scattered in every room. He couldn't even get into the sink to wash one because it was full of fetid water, where dirty pots and pans had been steeping for over twenty-four hours.

At first he tried to make his point with a combination of heavy sighs and clattering things around, followed by mumbled swearing in his native Norwegian. Finally, he directed his anger at Hugo. 'Would it hurt you to wash up every now and then? You are living here rent-free with armed security.'

Hugo was what he liked to call "wired in". Meaning that he was either answering emails sent to the Griffin website, or obsessively checking his Google Alerts: he'd set them up so that every mention of his name prompted a notification. At least that was consistent with his no-secrets ethos, thought Novak.

Hugo swiped his headphones off. 'Magnus, I'm trying to deal with Egypt here. Do you really think that washing dishes is a valuable use of my time?'

'Yes,' Magnus replied. 'It is. It's part of being a normal human being.'

'Normal is a revolting word to me,' Hugo scoffed.

Sofia sat in the corner on her own, knees pulled up to her chest, staring into space as she smoked a cigarette.

Giving up on the prospect of tea, Magnus dropped a pot back into the sink which caused a meteor-like splash, leaving the sink area far worse than it was before, then dried his hands on a dirty tea towel. Turning his ire towards Novak, Magnus brandished the tea towel at him. 'I'm not happy with you, either. Having parcels sent here. Are you crazy?'

Novak stood his ground, folding his arms to demonstrate how comfortable he was in such a hostile environment. 'I didn't get it sent here.'

'That's even worse. Someone else knows you're here.'

'Stella knows he's here,' Sofia offered.

'That's the problem,' said Magnus. 'Stella Mitchell knows. Anne Cochrane. What about these guards outside? We've got them holed up in a hotel in Lairg. Do you think that isn't raising eyebrows? People around here talk, Hugo.'

He pushed his laptop away. 'Clearly you're not interested in letting me work. So what do you want, Magnus?'

'This place isn't safe for you anymore.'

'Are you asking me to leave? Telling me?'

'No.' Magnus paused. 'I'm telling you that maybe it's time you moved on.'

Hugo spluttered a laugh. 'You bloody clown. Anne told you, didn't she? That I wouldn't write a foreword for your stupid book.' Hugo felt it necessary to explain to Novak, 'He's been touting a book to Hathaway. That's why he's been putting us up here. Buying influence by keeping me close. It's all part of his champagne socialist image.' Without a break in his speech, he opened a bottle of whisky on the sideboard and poured it sloppily into a glass that had dried remnants of the same whisky from the day before. 'The thing is, Magnus. I know the truth about you. Magnus Hofstadt and his many millions.' He swigged from the glass and told Novak, 'It wasn't even him that invested in all those start-ups. All those billion-dollar valuations they had in the early two-thousands. It was his fund manager that put his money there.'

Magnus leaned against the worktop, silent.

Hugo went on, this time to Magnus, 'Mate, everyone knows you didn't have the stomach for it. You're the luckiest guy in Silicon Valley history. And now you want to ride on *my* coattails? Dream on.'

'Guys...' Novak said, trying to step between them.

Magnus easily brushed him aside. He said to Hugo, 'Do you know how much money I've spent protecting you? Drinking my whisky. Eating my food. And this is how you repay me?' He marched off upstairs.

Fearing that their meal ticket was expiring, Sofia set off after him, telling Hugo on the way, 'You are such an asshole.' She called after Magnus, but he didn't stop until he reached his room and slammed the door shut.

Novak let the dust settle a moment then raised his arms. 'Who's next, Hugo? Me? You've gone through everyone else today.'

Hugo poured himself another whisky, then collapsed into the banquette against the wall. 'Don't be such a drama queen. They'll be fine tomorrow.'

'No they won't, Hugo. What if Magnus throws you out? What then?'

He shrugged. 'I'll go public. Screw it.' Hugo hadn't been much of a drinker until he came to Badanloch House. Alcohol affected the dexterity of the fingers and motor functions required for ten-hour coding runs. It was clear after two hastily downed glasses that Hugo had little tolerance for it.

Novak slid his audio recorder out onto the table in such a way that Hugo didn't even notice it happening. When he did spot it, he didn't protest.

The smoke from Sofia's cigarettes still hung in the air across the table, late-afternoon sunset light catching it through the kitchen window. Hugo wanted to keep throwing back drinks. There was a magical quality to being drunk at such a time. Alcoholics have understood this for decades, almost centuries. The unspoken agreement with yourself that you have checked out of the day. That it's a total wash, and it won't come back.

Novak sat across from Hugo. 'I've been reading old posts from hacking forums,' he said. He took out his phone to quote from some of the choicer selections.

The words flooded back to Hugo like rereading an old diary. 'Where did you get those?'

'Ian found them,' said Novak. 'It seems I underestimated his abilities. I think you did too.'

'He never gave you permission to read those.'

'I'm ghostwriting your autobiography! What did you think I was going to do with his research?'

'I always knew he was up to something. Like everyone else. Using me. Preparing to stab me in the back.'

Novak wasn't going to get pulled into the mud on that. He leaned forward. 'You told me yesterday that you started

Griffin after reading Solzhenitsyn. But it's clear from reading these posts that you'd never even heard of him back then.'

Hugo's eyes were pure evasion. 'What are you talking about? Of course I did. That's what I told Ian. That's what I told you.'

'Except it's not true, Hugo!' Novak showed him a screenshot. 'You wrote it right there.'

Hugo reached for the whisky bottle, but Novak pulled it away. 'This is bullshit,' Hugo said, escaping the banquette to take a beer from the fridge. He opened the bottle and let the lid fall to the floor. 'Ian's doctored those. He's trying to slander me.'

'Yes, Hugo. Everyone wants to destroy you. Ian did. So does Magnus. Anne. Even the police.'

Hugo's eyes went wide. 'They're trying to frighten off others from coming forward. Can't you see that?'

'Why are you so sure that those people who were arrested aren't your sources?'

Hugo leaned across the table and switched off the recorder. 'We're done.'

24

BALMORAL CASTLE, SCOTLAND

Prince James had four lines of high-grade Colombian cocaine chopped out on a mirror when he heard a knock on his bedroom door. He hoovered up two of the lines before shouting, 'Unless you've got another gram for me, piss off.'

Rose opened the door anyway.

James made no attempt to conceal the cocaine-smeared mirror, or to switch off the TV that had graphic pornography playing on it. The Balmoral staff had seen him in far worse conditions over the years.

'Bloody hell,' Rose said in disgust, averting her eyes.

James sneered, 'What? The drugs or the porn?'

'I have to pick?'

'You always were a prude.' He leaned over his desk and snorted the two remaining lines.

Still looking away, but unable to block off her ears to the ridiculous moaning and groaning from the TV, she asked, 'Can we talk? Without the two women being... whatever's being done to them. I'm going back to Clarence House tomorrow.'

Amused at her discomfort, he switched off the TV with the remote, then cleaned up the remaining powder on the mirror with his finger, rubbing it into his gums. 'Okay,' he said. 'Let's talk.' He poured her a glass of wine.

Surprised at the gesture, she said, 'Thank you.'

He was wearing a dress shirt and no trousers. On his lower half, only baggy boxers and socks that were pulled up high past his ankles.

'Can you at least put on some trousers?' she asked.

He sat on the end of his unmade bed. 'What do you want?'

'I want to know if we can get past this? Us.' She motioned back and forth between them.

'Why should I do that?'

'Because it's bad for business, James.'

He swigged straight from the wine bottle. 'It's not bad for *my* business. My business is already in the toilet thanks to you and the rest of the family.'

She took a sip. 'This is nice wine.'

'No, it's not. You're mistaken. It's the piss that we give the guests. The wine that civilians buy in supermarkets and think it's posh because it costs more than twenty quid.'

'You're drunk.'

'No, I'm being real,' he retorted.

'There is no *real*, James. Not in this family. It's just this. People pretending to be people. We're just statues. Ornaments that are taken from place to place to open things. To attend things. You couldn't even do that right. You had to have George Villiers mopping up whatever semi-illegal trail of destruction you left in your wake, handing out non-disclosure agreements like fliers at one of those depraved nightclubs you go to.'

'You know why I love being a royal? Because I can do

whatever I want,' he pointed the wine bottle at Rose, 'and I always get away with it. Everyone wants to be like us. Rich. Untouchable.'

'The world is just a big playground to you, isn't it?'

'Literally everyone wants what we have, Rose.'

'No, they don't.'

'Bullshit. Look at the list: everyone that's rich bloody loves it. Then there's everyone that's not, the poor, everyone else in the middle. Even the rich ones who make out that being rich is a burden on their mental health. They only say that because deep down they know that they will always be rich. I, for example, deserve it. Not everyone does. Look at footballers, for god's sake, with their Gucci bloody umbrellas and those stupid big white trainers. They don't know what the hell they're doing. And why?' He pointed again with the bottle. 'Good blood. Breeding. It can't be taught.'

Rose countered, 'You're confusing having purchasing power with good taste.'

'Honestly, I don't know why they go on living. These bloody people with their little grocery bags, their online betting, and Netflix subscriptions. Bloody insects, the lot of them. The other day, I got into the front seat of my car, just to see what it was like. I don't know how people do it. Carrying house keys and wallets? It's barbaric.' Finally registering her appalled expression, James protested, 'That's real.'

Rose had heard enough. 'You want to be real? Let's be real. I know that someone hacked my phone. That photos and messages were stolen. And I think you're behind it.'

'Thinking don't make it so, sis.'

She put her glass down as hard as she could without smashing it on the antique console table. 'What did I ever do to you to make you hate me so much?'

'Hate? I don't hate you, Rose. You're just in my way.' She

was about to leave, when James added, 'And you should have been more careful.'

She asked, 'What is that supposed to mean?'

He tutted. 'Rosey, Rosey... You of all people, especially having a black Private Secretary, must know that that's the one word you can never be caught saying. I mean, it's so bad, people don't even say it anymore. It's just a letter. The N word.'

The blood drained from her face. 'I don't know what you mean.'

He shook his head. 'You should. You said it a number of times in that voicemail about the footman.'

'That was to Uncle George.'

'Yeah. But you never know who's listening in these days, Rose.'

'You're already out. This will damage you as much as it does me.'

'Oh, I find that very hard to believe. And that is just a snippet of what I've got.'

'You mean you have...'

'Oh, yes. I've got it all, Rose. Soon, the British public – the whole world – will have it, too.'

'You wouldn't dare.'

'Really?' he asked.

'Why? Why would you do this?'

'Because I can. Because you and the rest of the family should have respected me more. Now you're all going to find out what it means to be on the outside. For the rest of your lives.'

'You don't want to go to war with me,' Rose warned him.

'I already have,' he replied.

25

BADANLOCH HOUSE, SCOTLAND

An hour later and the house had turned silent. Hugo was passed out on the living room couch. He'd drunk too much too quickly and was comfortably out for the count. Novak knew this because he bumped loudly into a chair across the room and Hugo didn't even stir, his mouth hanging open.

Novak went upstairs to check on Sofia, who was sitting on top of the freshly made bed that Stella had slept in the first night.

'I'm going out for some air,' he said, shuffling into one of Magnus's top-of-the-range Arc'teryx hiking jackets.

She leaned over to see out the window. 'It looks cold out there. Are you going far?'

'No, not far.'

She held his gaze, waiting for him to be more specific.

Novak broke the awkward silence. 'Hugo's asleep downstairs. Do you know where Magnus is?'

'I heard him go out about half an hour ago.'

'On foot?'

'No. The old Land Rover. Not that I blame him. It's not exactly a happy house right now.'

Novak turned to leave, but changed his mind. 'Sofia... how well do you know Hugo? I mean, *really* know him?'

'How much does anyone really know anyone?'

'You two met online, right?'

'Yeah.'

'And was he always quite political?'

'Of course.' She shuffled across the bed towards him, then kept going all the way to the door. She then closed it, blocking Novak's way out. She spoke softly. 'What's this all about?'

'You don't... I don't know how else to say it.'

Before he could, Sofia said it for him. 'You're worried that Hugo might be involved in Ian's death.'

He was relieved that she was the one to say it. 'Ian found some things online that suggest that the Hugo you know might be quite different from the real one.'

'I don't know what to think anymore.' She rushed into him, knocking him back half a step. When she held him, she clung to his back.

Novak had felt that kind of grip before. The grip that says 'don't leave me. Not right now.' What came after an embrace like that was often messy. He pulled back just as he sensed her lifting his chin, her lips about to seek out his. He said, 'I really should get some air.'

She exhaled as she retreated to the bed. 'I'm sorry,' she said, pointing to her head. 'I'm not thinking straight.'

The path to the door now clear, Novak opened it.

She started to say, 'Tom...'

'I'll be careful,' he replied.

It was hard to leave Badanloch House unnoticed. The grounds were flat for a mile all around, making any solitary figure stand out against the landscape. Novak even more so in Magnus's red jacket. It was supremely light, yet waterproof and windproof. The only problem being that it was sized for someone six foot five and two hundred and twenty pounds.

The guard nearest the driveway entrance got on his radio, watching Novak walking along the single-track road. 'The American has gone out on foot.'

'What direction?' came the reply.

After a handful of farms there was only one place in Novak's direction.

The guard said, 'Towards Forsinard.'

* * *

The online map Novak consulted before leaving told him that the train station was a twenty-five-minute walk away. But after checking his watch – showing he was twenty-three minutes in – all he could see ahead of him was the road stretching out as far as the eye could see, and no station in sight. It was a tundra-like expanse on either side, broken up by the occasional loch. Novak couldn't work out if the isolation was beautiful or terrifying.

He stopped walking, figuring that something was off in his calculations.

With all internet signals lost, he couldn't see his live position on the map. What he could see, though, was that he had only paid attention to the projected length of time for the walk rather than the distance. The total route was just shy of five miles. If he was able to complete that in twenty-five minutes then he should have been preparing for the next Olympics rather than ghostwriting a book. That's when he realised that he had selected 'Cycle' as the mode of travel rather than 'Walk'. With the data for both still saved on the page, Novak was able to toggle between them. When he selected 'Walk', the time range shifted from twenty-five minutes to an hour and twenty minutes. Factoring in how far he'd already walked, there was still a long way to go. And time was running out.

The source had pointed out that it wasn't the sort of place to hang around on your own. If Novak didn't make it in time, he could lose them for good.

He broke into a jog, but his energy levels already felt sapped at the thought of the gruelling task ahead. Book tours like the one he had just completed were not known for bringing about awesome levels of cardiovascular and athletic conditioning. They generally involved a lot of sitting around and eating biscuits. Still, he pressed on, determined not to miss out on his opportunity. He knew he was going to be late. That was a given now. What spurred Novak to up his pace was the timetable that he'd read. There weren't a lot of trains going through a wilderness like Forsinard, especially later in the day. As long as he could get there before the next train departed, he might still stand a chance of catching his source.

In a field to Novak's right, there was a herd of nearly fifty red deer. They all stood still. Heads slowly panning with Novak's progress.

He gave them a low-key wave. 'How you doing,' he wheezed on the way past.

One stag looked back in the direction of Badanloch, hearing the low-end rumble of a Mercedes Benz G-Class SUV. Formerly known as the G-Wagen, it was an off-roading icon, though less immediately familiar than a British stalwart like a Land Rover. It hurtled through the gloom, its classic silhouette of the spare wheel on the back broken up by rather eerie headlamps: each a thin ring of LEDs rather than a solid cylinder of light.

Before it got any closer, the stag bolted, prompting the entire herd to take off.

Novak dashed into a passing place so that he didn't get knocked down. When he took off running again, he hoped they weren't bound for Forsinard Flows. The last thing he and the source needed was company.

In the car on the way to Badanloch the road had felt quite flat, if tight and often winding. Now that Novak's feet were hitting the tarmac, he was finding out that even a tiny gradient rise of two per cent could feel like climbing the north face of the Eiger.

His legs ached. His chest burned. Then at the crest of a hill he finally saw a building. Down a short descent, in the middle of a massive bog was a cylindrical watchtower in a pale Scandinavian-style ash. The sun had set behind the hills to the west, where fog was rolling in like dry ice.

Further along the road was a copse of trees obscuring the train station behind it. Novak only realised it was there when the level-crossing lights started flashing and the barrier lowered with an alarm that pierced the evening air.

'No,' he cried out. It would have been the train after the one his source arrived on. If he wasn't still there, then it meant Novak had missed him by mere minutes.

He slowed his pace. There was no longer any point in fighting. The train wasn't going to stop for him. All he could do now was hope.

He gasped for breath as he stalked towards the level crossing, the barrier now lifting, the alarm relenting.

The train station itself was the original building, little more than an extended cottage, but with the modern signage of Scotrail everywhere.

The platform was empty.

Novak leaned on his knees. 'Damn it!'

The train was still in sight, setting off towards Inverness, achingly close. A few hundred yards away or in London. It didn't matter. Novak was sure that the source was gone.

Then a door at the station building opened behind him.

'You're lucky I'm a man of faith,' he said. It was the voice from the phone.

Novak turned around, struggling to explain while he still caught his breath.

'My train was delayed due to a landslide outside Thurso.' The source patted Novak on the arm. 'Let's hope that it isn't a metaphor for what awaits us both.'

Novak swallowed hard, setting off after the source who was walking towards the level crossing, carefully avoiding the security cameras' line of sight.

* * *

Across the road on the way to Forsinard Flows watchtower was an abandoned hotel. The Forsinard Hotel. Which a sign declared as "Mainland Britain's most remote hotel." Until the train station had been built, that had been true. White paint had peeled and flaked from the facade, and the garden was overgrown to a degree that suggested the hotel had been out of commission for at least a decade.

It was out of season, so there was no else around. There was an RSPB visitor centre on the other side of the train station, but they had closed for the day.

Forsinard Flows – or 'Flow Country' as the locals knew it – was a vast peatland, dotted with deep bog pools, where the RSPB had erected a watchtower for viewing ospreys and other rare birdlife.

The watchtower itself was easily accessed from the main

road, no fee required. Just a long, twisting boardwalk through a huge peat bog, leading to the tower.

The source said, 'The name's Dunhill.'

'Is that first or last?' asked Novak.

'Sebastian Dunhill,' he replied. 'I'm Vice President of Corporate Finance at Hunter & Company.'

Unfamiliar with the bank, Novak joked, 'That sounds great.'

'I'm not surprised you haven't heard of us. Even most Brits don't know we exist, despite the fact we turned over seven hundred million last year. We were founded in sixteen seventy-two, the tenth oldest bank in the world.'

'Sorry, I appear to have arranged a meeting with a Wikipedia article. Are we here to discuss Ian Ferguson or not?'

'Very well,' said Dunhill.

It was hard for Novak to get a handle on Dunhill's background. He was in his late fifties, well-spoken, and had made an attempt at dressing down for the countryside, which involved being dressed head to toe in Barbour outdoor clothing: a dark wax jacket, wine-coloured cords, and a cream Tattersall shirt that he would have preferred to wear with a tie. He looked like someone's idea of country dressing for a person who didn't get out of London very much.

Dunhill pointed towards the tower. 'I suggested the flows because you can see someone coming from miles away. What we have to talk about, I don't want to be looking over my shoulder or worrying about sharpshooters.'

'Sharpshooters? What is this, *Zulu*? You're talking about marksmen. Assassins? Out here?'

'As I said on the phone, Mr Novak. You have no idea who you're dealing with. You see people who look just like hillwalkers on the train. But you never know. These people are trained to blend in.'

Novak understood the theory behind going to the tower, but as far as tradecraft went it was a horrible approach. One that Walter Sharp wouldn't have entertained. If anyone ambushed them at the tower, there was nowhere to run. But now that they were out there in the middle of nowhere, there wasn't anywhere else to go.

Every fifty feet there were small signs stuck into the peat warning of the dangers of falling in. With the heavy rainfall earlier that day, the bog had been well topped up. They were dangerous places even in broad daylight, and the sun had well and truly set.

The tower was open all the time as there was no door or entrance. People often came to the flows to stargaze or take night photographs of the stars, which were abundant there. But not that overcast, foggy evening.

'You can record this if you like,' said Dunhill. 'It doesn't matter. For your own safety, however, I'd advise against it. Ian thought someone was going through his things at Badanloch House.'

'I know the feeling,' said Novak.

'I'm proud of my company's traditions, Mr Novak. Hunter & Company was tied closely with British royalty and the aristocracy going back centuries. We were used mostly as a clearing bank to the nobility and landed gentry.'

'What about now?'

'Our reputation stems mostly from our most notable client: the British royal family.'

'You're their banker?'

'Someone's got to do it, Mr Novak. Tell me. Have you ever pulled a muscle that you were never really aware of before?'

Novak was thinking of several in his legs currently. 'Sure.'

'Hunter is a muscle of this nation. No one knows much

about us, but were we to disappear, there would be a pain there for the country.'

They were at the foot of the tower now. Novak held his arm out, letting Dunhill go first.

'What sort of pain?' Novak asked.

Dunhill climbed ahead, checking that the upper level of the tower was empty. 'My position at Hunter gives me certain privileged access to documents concerning the royal family's affairs. Broad business interests. Investments. Their income would be quite static without our intervention, so we invest for them. As a prudent analyst, I was the one who first noticed that something was going terribly wrong with Prince James's finances earlier this year.'

'I read about them,' said Novak.

'Not about these, you didn't. Money was coming in from the sale of various properties in the prince's portfolio, all vastly over the asking price and paid via offshore companies.'

Novak was familiar with the set-up. 'A pay-off for something?'

'Unquestionably. These were companies I could connect – about ten rungs up the ladder – to Kazakh oligarchs. One of whom was the nephew of the Kazakh president.'

'What did you do?' asked Novak.

'I took it to my chairman, telling him I was concerned that we were effectively rinsing laundered money. Some of it came out in the papers, but vastly diluted.' Dunhill paused, leaning over the balcony on the watchtower. 'I was worried about the bank's reputation. Clarence House wouldn't entertain my concerns, and neither would my chairman. I couldn't trust going to the papers. The editors had all been kept on a tight leash. They had what I had, and still they wouldn't go to print. There was nowhere else to go.' He let Novak fill in the blank.

After a few moments, he got there. 'You leaked it to Griffin,' he said.

'I did.'

'This is the next big leak?'

'Gosh, no. As frightful as this is, what they have is far worse. That's what Ian Ferguson found out. It's what he was killed for.'

26

'Wait,' said Novak. 'If what you leaked to Griffin isn't what they're releasing next, what happened to it?'

'They never published,' Dunhill said.

'Why wouldn't they publish something like that? And why aren't you in handcuffs right now?'

'Excuse me?'

Novak remembered Dunhill would have been travelling through the afternoon, most of it with no internet connection. 'There were several arrests today. All people suspected of leaking classified information to Griffin.'

The blood drained from Dunhill's face. 'Then I could be next.'

'I don't know,' said Novak. 'I watched Hugo's reaction. I don't know what it was, but it seemed like he knew that they were innocent. He was convinced that British intelligence are trying to scare off anyone else going to Griffin.'

Dunhill seemed shaky for the first time. 'Well... regardless, I think the decision not to publish what I leaked is related to this.' He reached into his jacket pocket and passed Novak a series of itemised reports on Prince James's travel stamped "CONFIDENTIAL". 'As a trustee of the Prince James Foundation, I have access to travel records that the Palace don't release to the public. All they publish is what royal went where, and how much it cost.' Dunhill pointed to a flight documented in the middle of the page. 'The flight mentioned there is missing from the official records. It's been deleted.'

Novak read the listing. 'Ben Gurion Airport? That's Tel Aviv.'

'Right,' said Dunhill. 'The question then is, why would someone be so eager to cover up that Prince James went there?'

'Why did he?'

'The official reason is listed as an FCO visit – the Foreign and Commonwealth Office. Which is common. A royal in Prince James's position will often act as an unofficial trade envoy, wining and dining Foreign Ministers and ambassadors. Currying favour...' He broke off, unable to continue the euphemism.

'Paying bribes,' offered Novak.

'Essentially. This has always been the way. The problem with the date of this visit is that the Israeli ambassador, the Interior Minister, *and* the Foreign Minister were all in Katowice, Poland.' Dunhill showed a press photo of Princess Rose standing alongside them all, dressed in black, holding candles and laying down flowers. 'The Israelis were there with Princess Rose for the International Holocaust Memorial Day service. Prince James would never have gone to Israel for an FCO visit because there was no one of any standing there to receive him.'

'So why was he in Israel?' asked Novak, thinking aloud. 'There's the Tel Aviv stock exchange...'

Dunhill said, 'If anything, I think it's got to be tech-related. They call Tel Aviv "Silicon Wadi". All the tech companies that matter are based there. Especially computer security.' He revealed a page from the bank statement of the Sovereign Grant. 'These are official records of money paid by Prince James into a series of shell companies registered in the Cayman Islands and the British Virgin Islands. The amount of two hundred and seventy-four thousand pounds.'

'Who was the recipient?' asked Novak.

'That's where Ian Ferguson came in. As part of his research on Griffin, he'd been digging into their donation structure because it's no secret that the United States government is angling to cut them off by axing their ability to process credit-card and PayPal payments. He then reached out to me when he found a payment in Griffin's donations that stood out.' Dunhill showed him the printout.

Novak stared at the number in incomprehension. 'Two hundred and seventy-four thousand pounds.'

When their eyes met, Dunhill's widened, nodding assuredly that what Novak was looking at was very real.

Novak said, 'This is a direct financial link between Prince James and Griffin. Why on earth would he be funding them?'

'That's what Ian couldn't figure out on his own,' said Dunhill. 'Until I could link the payment to James's visit to Tel Aviv: the same day the payment was processed.'

Novak was shuffling the jigsaw pieces on the table, but he still couldn't quite make them fit. 'Griffin... Tel Aviv... It has to be related to computer tech or security, right?'

Dunhill's expression turned grave, and he looked out across the flows. 'I'm afraid that's where it starts to get very, very ugly.' He wouldn't even look at Novak when he said it. 'There are two memos underneath the bank statement you're holding. If they knew I was showing it to you...'

Novak skimmed the memos.

Dunhill explained, 'The first details concerns from GCHQ that Princess Rose's personal laptop and phone may have been contaminated with spyware of unknown origin. As with all threats against the government or monarchy, it was handed over to MI5, who investigated and concluded that there was no threat. No spyware was found on either the laptop or the phone. That should have been the end of it. But that's where the second memo comes in.'

Novak brought it to the top, shaking his head as he read it quickly to himself. 'George Villiers, Private Secretary to Princess Rose.'

While Novak read, Dunhill explained, 'Mr Villiers is one of the longest-serving Private Secretaries in the Royal Households. A stalwart. One of the old school.'

'It says here that he believes files have been taken from Princess Rose's laptop and phone. He asks for MI5 to reopen their investigation.'

'But they never did,' said Dunhill. 'They never received Villiers' memo.'

'Why not?'

'Because it was deleted from the Clarence House server before it could be sent to MI5. All communications at Clarence House are routed through a central server. A bit like airport security, so everything coming in or out can be scanned and checked. But Villiers' memo never made it through. I don't know how, but Ian found out who deleted it.'

'Who was it?' asked Novak.

'The Private Secretary to Prince James. Fiona Bingham.'

Novak stepped away from the balcony, the jigsaw pieces now forming a picture. 'She was covering for her boss...'

Dunhill nodded. 'As all ambitious people do.'

'The payment to Griffin,' Novak went on. 'It's the same playbook that the prince used in receiving bribes from foreign investors. You pay for something that looks legitimate to pay for the cost of something illegal. I buy your house for more than it's worth, you then secure me the contract I want.'

Dunhill kept nodding.

'James paid someone to get that spyware onto Princess Rose's laptop. Hugo has some connection to a company in Tel Aviv?'

Dunhill said, 'Ian had a theory. That Griffin's next leak is going to be something hacked from Princess Rose's laptop or phone. Something so damaging that it could stop her ascending to the throne.'

Novak tried to get there, but he couldn't see it. 'But Prince James is where in the line of succession?'

'Sixth.'

'After Rose's children, and they have children. Finding some kind of scandal on Rose doesn't hand the crown to James.'

'A position that Ian completely agreed with.'

Novak said, 'I've found evidence that Hugo Byron was not always the political firebrand he claims to be when he started Griffin. But what he is now isn't fake. Something radicalised him. If he's working with Prince James, it's not to clear a path for him towards the throne.'

'Again,' said Dunhill, 'Ian concurred. Keep going.'

'James is damaged goods already. He knows he can't come back from the scandals surrounding him. There's only one thing left for him. Revenge. And if he found something big enough, scandalous enough...' Novak couldn't finish his sentence. He could see the full picture now. All the jigsaw pieces forming the picture that Ian Ferguson had made.

Dunhill concluded, 'It could bring down the royal family altogether.'

'That's what got Ian killed.' Novak's mind raced with

suspects. Exposing the plot would destroy Prince James, but it would also destroy Griffin and Hugo. Novak asked, 'Is it even possible? To bring down the monarchy?'

Dunhill said, 'It's commonly accepted that there are four ways the British monarchy could end. First, parliamentary legislation to abolish it – that's not going to happen. The second would be execution – and not even an army could manage that. There would always be someone in the line of succession. The corollary to that is that they all rescind their positions – again, that will never happen. The fourth is a referendum pushed through by overwhelming political pressure. The kind that could only come about from a scandal so huge that there was no escaping it. Something that enveloped not only Princess Rose, but infected the entire monarchy itself.'

Novak needed a moment. It was over one hundred miles to the nearest city. He was surrounded by peatland bog and darkness. Even in such a desolate place, conspiracy and all the other remnants of his reporting gig that he'd tried so hard to escape had still managed to find him. 'You know, in Washington on Inauguration Day, the President is taken away for a security briefing where he gets his instructions on the nuclear football and where he gets taken in the event of an attack. In the White House Briefing Room, the older guys used to joke about how that's also the time the President gets taken into some smoky room in the basement. A table with a dozen guys sitting around it. No one speaks. There's just a projector running an old sixteen-millimetre film on the wall. It's the JFK assassination, but from an angle you've never seen before that shows who really killed him that day. The film stops, the lights come up, then someone asks the President, "Any questions?" It's bullshit, of course, but I've always felt like underneath it all there's a real truth in it. That the real power isn't at the top. It's at the margins. In the shadows. When you go there like Ian did, it gets dangerous. Trust me, I know. And it seems you know it too.' Novak gestured at their surroundings. 'Look where we're standing. Why are you doing all this?'

Dunhill pulled his collar up against the cold, as the fog thickened across the flows. 'Mr Novak, Hunter & Company has lived through the French Revolution, the reign of Catherine the Great, and saw George Washington as American President. What Prince James has done is risk my bank's reputation, its very survival, by playing with the monarchical constitution of this country. He thinks because he has money and power he can do whatever he wants. At some point, someone has to say enough. You *will* be held to account for your actions. No matter what your place in society may be.'

'Only if it can be proven,' Novak warned. 'I need to prove who owns those shell companies that paid Griffin. The FBI trailed Capone for years. In the end, it was paperwork that did him in. If Ian was killed, then he must have had a paper trail that connects Prince James to Hugo Byron and the Princess Rose hack. The answer has to be on Hugo's laptop. It's what he protects more than anything...' Novak's mind drifted to something that had struck him at the time, then promptly forgot because of what had followed.

Dunhill asked, 'More than what?'

'Earlier today, Hugo was outside, arguing with his assistant. He left his laptop in his room and I managed to get a picture of the code on the screen.'

'That was lucky.'

'Yeah. Too lucky. I glossed over it at the time because it felt like a big break. Like the file deleted from my laptop. He wanted me to know he'd been in there. But why would he want me to find something incriminating on him?'

Dunhill said, 'All I know is that Ian didn't trust anyone at Badanloch House, and neither should you.'

'I don't,' asked Novak. 'Someone has already gone through my things. And Ian hid his research in his room. Something as big as this, he would have taken it away from Badanloch.' Thinking out loud, he suggested, 'Anne Cochrane?'

'Or his agent. The police report said that was the last person he tried to contact.' As he checked his watch, Dunhill hunched his shoulders – he had underestimated the cold there. 'The last train will be coming in soon. You shouldn't be here when it comes.'

Before he left, Novak called after him, 'What about you? What will you do?'

Dunhill had a far-away look in his eye, seeing the distant lights of an approaching train snaking across the countryside. 'What I've done my whole life,' he replied. 'Protect Hunter & Company. By any means necessary.'

27

PRIMROSE HILL, LONDON

Stella was in the kitchen on her own, standing with a cup of tea. Drinks were always the first port of call when bad news was announced. Water. Tea. Whisky. Stella could see through her own facade in making the tea she no longer felt like drinking. In the wake of her mother's prognosis, Stella had felt compelled to do something, anything. Putting on the kettle had been the second thing she did. First, was getting to the bathroom for some more pills to take the edge off. They didn't even scratch the surface of what Stella was feeling inside.

The outlook wasn't great for Anne. The doctors reckoned they could squeeze an extra three months of life from her failing body, but it would require constant medical care. If she carried on without medical care, her body would eventually shut down over a shorter and less predictable time frame. But it would give her a few more months of activity in which she could get her affairs in order. She didn't want to spend her last days in a hospital bed, puking from medication side effects.

Stella poured the tea into the sink, then filled a tumbler with cold water and brought it to the living room.

Anne woke up with a start, having fallen into a wine-fuelled sleep when a nightmare made her shoot her leg out. She came to, her eyelids reluctant to let in any light from the lamps that were still on. 'Sorry,' she said, pushing off the blanket that Stella had left on her. Her whole body felt clammy from unnecessary insulation.

For Stella, putting the blanket on was easier than having to sit there and hold her herself. She put the mug down on the table. 'You should have some of that or your head will be pounding tomorrow.'

Anne struggled to sit up. 'Is that one of your hangover strategies when you're out living the New York high life?'

'No,' said Stella. 'I used to force dad to do it. When he'd had five or six too many.'

Anne knew what was coming next. As long as Stella was staying in London there was no avoiding it.

'Why did you leave, mum?' asked Stella.

Anne gulped down half the glass in one go, steaming the inside with her breath. 'It was complicated, Stel.'

'I don't like being called that.'

'Tom calls you it.'

'Tom and I are close.'

Anne had thought a terminal diagnosis would have bought her a little more charity from Stella, but apparently not. 'For what it's worth now, I *am* sorry that I left.'

'I believe you, but you don't understand how much easier it is to say sorry than to live through what I had to growing up. The man you married is not the man that I was left with. When you left us, he went to pieces. He used to be such a proud man. Who took pride in his clothes and how he presented himself. When you left, he stopped all that. Slowly, all these things that used to be unthinkable became common-place. He swore more often. He watched dumb movies. It made me so sad because it was so obvious that he didn't even want to think. All he cared about was getting home from work so that he could have a drink. I don't give a damn what the doctor said about cirrhosis of the liver. It was suicide. Just by other means. Because he was too scared to do it himself.'

'I'm sorry. I had no idea,' said Anne.

'I know you didn't. Because you never called. Like when Tom and I broke all those stories. All those times you were in New York and never looked me up.' Stella could feel tears forming and she hated it. She didn't want Anne to see her like that. Needing her. Wanting her. Which only made her tears heavier. 'That question, why did you leave... I thought it stopped mattering to me a long time ago. Like wondering why no one ever says goodbye at the end of phone calls in movies. It's one of those things that you just accept after seeing it a few hundred times. And I doubt there's any answer that you could give me.'

'There's not,' said Anne. 'And I doubt the truth will bring any comfort to you. It was as boring as me leaving your dad for another man. It was an affair that had been going on for about a year beforehand. Then, finally, one night, the strain between your dad and I got too much. And I left.'

'But without even saying goodbye, or explaining? Why wouldn't dad explain it either?'

'As you said. Your dad was a proud man. For a long time. Maybe I took away that part of him when I left. I don't know. All I can do now is try to make it up to you. With the time I have left.'

Stella wiped her eyes. 'I've been worrying lately... that I might be turning into him. Dad.'

Anne reached out to her, stroking her cheek. 'Oh Stella, what makes you say that?'

Stella tried not to jolt away too awkwardly, to show that

she was obviously uncomfortable with the contact. 'It's like... you see what's happening. What you're doing to yourself and you still can't stop it.' All of a sudden she felt much younger than she was, and she didn't like it. 'I have to go to the bathroom,' she said, getting up slowly in case the pill bottle in her pocket rattled.

The light in the bathroom was harsh. Much too harsh for the moment, filling the room with stark white. There was nowhere to hide in such light. She turned on the cold-water tap, running it hard, and took out her pill bottle – which was the extent of everything she'd smuggled into the UK.

The way Stella saw it, life was about choices. The fact was, the pills weren't making her feel any better. She could at least see that. What she had needed was the ritual: if she kept taking the pills, then they must have been doing something. But she was taking more than ever. She wasn't getting any more work done than before. She felt on edge all the time. And, if anything, it was getting worse the more she took.

Standing in that bathroom, the choice was clear: continue and get worse, becoming more like her dad by the day. Or stop and get better.

It wasn't easy, but it *was* clear.

She opened the pill bottle, not caring about picking out the bad pills from the vitamins. She just turned the bottle upside down over the sink and let the water sweep all the pills down the drain.

When they were gone, only then could Stella look at herself in the mirror. 'It's time to get up off the mat, Stel.'

She passed Anne in the hall, making her way to bed.

'I finished the water,' Anne said. 'Thank you.'

'Mum,' Stella said, stopping her. 'I'm sorry. About what's happened. What's happening.'

Anne pursed her lips in acknowledgement. She knew how

hard it must have been to say such words, because she knew how little she deserved them.

Hearing it brought little respite when she crawled into bed, still half-drunk. Her body and her brain weren't done with the nightmare from earlier. As she dosed back into sleep, the nightmare began its reprise: of what had really happened that fateful night so many years ago.

28

LUDLOW, SHROPSHIRE

TWENTY-SEVEN YEARS AGO

It was one of those crisp winter nights when the only place you wanted to be was indoors, under a duvet, or in front of a fire. Outside, everything twinkled and glistened in the moonlight. The outline of Ludlow against the sky on such a night was almost perfectly English: the church spire proudly above everything else; the Tudor-style half-timbered houses; the numerous quaint bridges crossing the River Teme, its surface mirror-like.

Yet Anne Cochrane was throwing the contents of her life into a suitcase.

Her husband, John, had been chasing her around the bedroom for the last half hour, trying to make some sense of what she was telling him. That, somehow, their marriage was over.

So far, they had managed to keep their voices down out of fear of waking Stella two doors down. Fortunately for them, she was ten years old, and still capable of the kind of deep sleep they couldn't even fathom at their stage in life.

'It's him, isn't it,' John said. It wasn't really a question.

Anne could hardly focus through her vale of tears. She was barely cognisant at all of what she was packing. It didn't matter in a practical sense. Where she was going would be the start of a whole new life anyway.

In desperation, John raised his voice. 'Answer me!'

Anne picked the suitcase up off the bed and swung it down. There was nothing she could say that would either make sense, or make any of it alright. The truth was rarely that easy.

She made as if to open Stella's door when John stepped in front of her.

'No,' he whispered. 'You don't get that luxury. I'll tell her. In the morning. This will only confuse her.'

'I really think–'

'You gave up your right to think anything about what goes on in this house when you started packing that case.' He gestured dismissively towards the stairs. 'Go on, then. Get out.'

She didn't protest. What she was doing was indefensible. Not being able to kiss Stella goodbye was the least that she deserved – she knew that.

When the front door closed behind her, it sent a shock of cold air up the stairs, which rushed past John and met Stella's face as she opened her bedroom door, bleary-eyed.

'What's going on?' she asked.

John crouched down and hurried her back to bed. Even at ten, he was amazed at how light she was. It reminded him how delicate children are. Those seismic events that adults are left to deal with – what they do to children, and how it changes them. He had no idea how he was going to get Stella through what was to come. What he wanted was another seven or so hours of peace, and then the war could begin.

He told Stella, 'It's fine, darling. We can talk about it in the morning.'

* * *

After walking to the centre of town carrying her suitcase, a car pulled up alongside Anne. She put the suitcase down, giving her another hand free with which to wipe away her tears.

The man inside got out. He was underdressed for the cold, having had the heating in the car turned up full. He didn't say anything until Anne's suitcase was in the boot and they were both in the car.

'I know this is painful,' he explained to her, 'but it's what we signed up for. Because what we do is bigger and more important than our own lives.'

Anne replied, 'It's the closest people to us that are punished, though.'

The man paused. 'You know you can't contact them.'

'I know,' she said, looking away.

'Ever,' he added.

'Just drive.'

He did. He drove them deep into the night, across the country.

He was prematurely balding, with bulbous searching eyes. The kind that could see through to the realities of a situation, or a person, with a short look. It was what had made him such a successful spy, climbing the ranks of MI5. Eventually landing a knighthood to become Sir Christopher Benedict.

29

BADANLOCH HOUSE, SCOTLAND

Novak was no longer exhausted as he marched back to Badanloch by torchlight. Unseasonably heavy snow was beginning to fall, breaking through the torchlight in a hypnotic manner.

At the forefront of Novak's mind was the donation from Prince James to Griffin, which was only the start of an avalanche of other implications related to Hugo and the real inner workings of Griffin.

Novak heard a distant car somewhere behind him, but the fog was so thick he couldn't yet see any headlights. For safety, he stepped off the road onto the grass verge which was covered in sheep droppings.

Novak kept doing shoulder checks until the headlights appeared faintly. He did a double-take, thinking there was something strange about them. They were the same as the car that had passed him earlier – that had frightened the deer away.

His skin broke out in a chill, thinking through the reasons why someone would be doubling back on such a road within a relatively short timeframe. There was nothing but empty road beyond Forsinard.

It wasn't the first time he'd been hunted. Experience and instinct told Novak to get further off the road, for his own safety.

That was when he saw the headlights breaking through his legs, casting his long shadow in front of him. Then the engine revved, unmistakably, at the sight of him.

He broke away from the road into the bog to his right. His first stride broke straight through the earth, all the way up to the knee. It was pure boggy stodge. He put out his hands, pushing on the mounds of snow-dusted heather on either side, and pulled his leg as hard as he could. But the vacuum was too strong. He was stuck.

The car pulled up where Novak had broken away. It was a powerful off-roader, but nothing could drive through such terrain.

One man got out of the front passenger side, while the driver turned the car so that the headlights pointed towards Novak. His face lit up, his struggle and predicament evident.

Novak's eyes widened further when he saw that the man was holding a handgun, and he was stalking towards him for a closer shot.

Instead of trying to release himself in one go, Novak twisted his foot from side to side, trying to create a break in the vacuum. It was working. Slowly. Possibly too slowly, as the man took aim at him from fifty yards away.

He fired just as Novak hauled himself out to one side – the bullet sinking into the peat where his torso had been fractions of a second earlier.

Novak was now in a bind. Without his torch, he couldn't see where he was going, but with his torch on, the shooter would be able to see him.

The man looked lithe. Powerfully built and quick. He was wearing dark outdoor clothing, walking trousers and fell-running shoes. Clearly prepared for a foot chase.

Novak wasn't going to give him any extra help. He tossed the torch aside, then bolted at ninety degrees. As long as they had the car, travelling in a straight line back to Badanloch was pointless. He was never going to outpace them over multiple miles. He just had to get as far away as possible.

The shooter had a torch of his own. A good one. The light illuminating the falling snow. The only thing in Novak's favour was the fog. He had managed to get far enough into the bog that the car's headlights now made no difference. If the headlights could barely pierce it, the shooter's torch stood no chance.

Running in the darkness and fog over such uneven ground was a lottery. Novak already knew the potential consequences of falling into the wet stuff. If anything, the warning signs back at the watchtower boardwalk had undersold the danger. If he went to ground again, it would be lights out for good.

He was encouraged by a sudden groan behind him. The shooter had come undone trying to catch up too quickly. Now Novak had the chance to make up some ground. He told himself to slow down. A fast stride that didn't end with him stuck in the bog would be ten times faster than a sprint that did.

He couldn't help wondering how many dead bodies were out there. How many problems had been covered up. Like the Las Vegas desert.

It had been nearly ten minutes and the shooter had apparently made no progress. Not that Novak could tell. The fog was getting heavier. His internal compass spinning uncontrollably.

He didn't know that the shooter had given up and returned to the car.

Novak stopped, hearing the engine gunning, accelerating away. Now that he felt the first wave of reassurance rush through his body, he held his hands up to his face. They were raw with cold. The temperature was only a touch above freezing, and the snow was getting heavier with each passing minute. Without a phone signal or a torch, he was now truly in dire straits. Making deathly slow progress when he needed to be getting out of there. Fast.

He tried to course-correct, but there was no way of knowing whether he was on the way back towards the road or not. He walked a good fifteen minutes, certain that he was going the right way. Then the terrain started drying out, the snow building underfoot. And the ground started to incline.

He let out a desperate groan as he realised he had been going completely the wrong way, towards the hills.

The only positive was that he now knew he just had to backtrack in a straight line away from the hills and he'd eventually find the road again. The problem was how long it might take to get there. And in the flows, sidestepping small ponds, it was easy to stray off-course. Out there, in that kind of weather, that would mean death.

There was also the risk that the Mercedes SUV could still be prowling up and down the road with its lights off hoping to catch him, but it was a risk he had to take.

His right leg that had been in the bog was tingling, his boot still filled with water which squelched like a sponge with every step. If he didn't get out of his soaking clothes he would have a one-way ticket to hypothermia. It was getting harder and harder to lift his leg, the cold draining his central nervous system, slowing his progress even further.

Magnus's jacket no longer felt very warm. What had

earlier been like walking in a warm blanket now felt like a thin paper bag. The cold had got deep into his bones, and no further layers of insulation on the outside of his body could do anything about that. He needed to get indoors.

The fog and snow grew heavier, disorientating him. Novak's progress stalled. He told himself that if he could just reach the road, then maybe he'd stand a chance. Then the headlights returned. This time, he didn't have the energy to run. It had been nearly two hours in the wilderness. It might have seemed paradoxical to become dehydrated in cold conditions, but he was. His body having to churn through energy and fluids to keep everything functioning. Not helped by the damage done to his leg, and the internal resources it had required.

Novak sank to his knees as the headlights stopped. As if the persons in the car knew exactly where he was.

There were four torches this time, their beams criss-crossing across the bog. This time, faint cries came with them. Indistinct at first. Then Novak made it out. It was his name being called.

It was Magnus. Accompanied by guards from Badanloch House.

Of course, Novak thought, his logic turning manic. Magnus, who had caught him in Hugo's room. Novak had wondered how much he had seen, and now he knew: everything. Magnus must have seen him taking the photo of the laptop screen and told Hugo and everything would have spiralled from there. Now he was coming after Novak with the guards he'd hired to finish him off. A multi-millionaire like Magnus could afford to pay for anything. Even body disposal.

Novak's chaotic thoughts kept running on, replaying all those moments with Magnus that now made so much more sense. But Novak couldn't run. His eyes were closing. He fought it as hard as he could, keeping them open until the moment Magnus leaned over him, flanked by two of the guards, then picked Novak up like he barely weighed one hundred pounds. He pulled Novak's arm up and over his shoulder, and dipped his head under his arm, carrying him safely to the Land Rover which was parked in a passing place.

He laid Novak across the back seats, slapping his cheek to bring him around.

Novak stirred, still covered in snow and lost in the head-fog of delusion that Magnus was there to kill him. Then he saw him tilt a bottle of water towards his lips. Some of it spilled down his chin, but some of it made it into his mouth. Hydration. It wasn't quite as extreme as being reborn, though not far off.

'They tried to kill me,' Novak groaned. 'There was a shooter. Mercedes... SUV... Bright silver...'

'It's okay, Tom,' Magnus said. 'They're gone.' He pulled him upright in the seat. 'Come on. We have to get back.' He emphasised to the guards, 'Quickly.'

Magnus sat next to Novak for the journey home, which seemed unnecessarily fast and rough. Novak had silver foil wrapped around him and had been given a flask of hot tea.

He swallowed it and groaned with comfort as the warm liquid worked its way down through his body, lighting up his nerve endings again. He closed his eyes. 'How did you find me?'

Considering the situation, Magnus's tone was severe and short. 'Recco reflector.' He reached under Novak's hood, pulling on a small red band. 'It makes you searchable to rescuers. I have them on all my jackets. When you didn't come back, Sofia insisted we go out for you.'

It was a passive transponder that didn't require batteries or activation. It was always on, always transmitting. The guards had handheld Recco detectors that echoed a signal from the jacket back to them, which gave a location within eighty metres. It had saved dozens of lives in the Alps. And had just saved another in northern Scotland.

'What were you doing all the way out there?' asked Magnus.

'I was walking,' Novak said, shuddering and shivering. 'I got lost.' Struggling to keep from spilling his tea, he asked, 'Do we really need to be going this fast?'

Magnus had more pressing issues on his mind. 'There's a problem at the house,' he said. 'Hugo has disappeared.'

30

When the Land Rover got back, Badanloch House was in a vastly different mode than the one it had been in when Novak had left. From beyond the driveway, he could see the security lights around the house's midriff, all angled outwards, all of them on. Lights that Novak hadn't even noticed before. Every available guard had been called in to cover the area, everyone shouting for Hugo. All Magnus had told them was that one of his party had gone missing, possibly involuntarily. It never occurred to any of the guards that the Hugo they were looking for could be Hugo Byron. There was no reason to make such a leap.

Novak staggered out of the back seat of the car, still shivering. There were blinding lights everywhere, Hugo's name echoing out into the night. Badanloch House was no longer a covert operation.

Sofia emerged from the hallway in tears, hugging herself as she tried to get on a pair of rubber boots. Magnus had to restrain her, telling her it was too dangerous to go out. That they had plenty of good bodies searching everywhere they could. And not to worry. That Hugo would show up.

'But the snow,' she cried. 'It's covering any footprints he might have left.'

'Exactly,' said Magnus. 'We're already doing everything we can.'

Novak was in desperate need to get out of his soaking wet clothes, but first he stopped in the hallway to ask Sofia what happened.

She was struggling to speak through her tears. 'I was in the kitchen washing the dishes, and I shouted for Hugo to come and help. He didn't answer. When I finished the dishes, I went to his room and he wasn't there. In three months, he hasn't once gone out after dark.' She turned mournfully towards the coat stand by the door. 'His jacket is still there. Why would he have gone out without a jacket? The only thing that's missing from his room is his laptop...' She snarled at two passing guards, 'and these creeps did something to him! I *know* it!'

Worried that Sofia might be next if she kept making a scene, Novak told the guards, 'She's just upset...' He asked Magnus, 'What are you going to tell the police about these armed guards?'

'The police?' said Magnus. 'Nobody has called them.'

Novak, who had started up the stairs, stopped. 'What are you talking about? The police can get mountain rescue out here. You need a helicopter to cover this terrain.'

'We can't call the police, Tom,' Sofia conceded.

'You actually support this?'

She and Magnus had already talked the issue out. 'We can't risk exposing Hugo's identity.'

'His identity isn't worth protecting if he's already dead.'

'If the police find out he's been staying here, we'll have MI5 crawling all over the place. We can't have that. It would mean computers impounded. Months of work compromised. Hugo wouldn't want that.'

'He'd be willing to die for it?' asked Novak.

Sofia was steadfast. 'If necessary.'

Seeing Novak's chattering jaw, Magnus told Sofia, 'He needs to get into some dry clothes. I need to get back out with the search team.'

'So do I,' she fired back.

'He's got damn near hypothermia. We're lucky to have him in one piece as it is...'

'Really, I'm alright,' said Novak, sounding anything but.

Magnus said with emphasis to Sofia, 'Someone needs to stay with him.'

The message now seemed to get through to her. As it did to Novak, even in his chaotic state of mind. It wasn't so much like they were worried about leaving him alone. It was as if they didn't want him to be free to snoop about the place unobserved.

'Come on,' Sofia said, helping him up the stairs to his room.

Each adjustment of a limb to wrestle out of his clothes was a struggle. He was so desperate to get out of them and into something warm and dry, the ten seconds of being undressed felt like being a newborn.

Sofia turned her back until he was decent again.

Once he had on dry warm trousers from the radiator and a thermal polo neck, Sofia pulled back his bedspread. 'You should rest,' she said.

Novak wasn't interested in sleep. He checked his phone to catch up on his messages. Nothing came through, but there was an unread message from Stella from two hours ago.

"*We need to talk.*"

He tapped a reply, telling her he would call soon, then pocketed his phone.

'Hugo's only been gone a short while,' he told Sofia. 'The next few hours could be critical. What shape is his room in?'

Sofia gestured towards it. 'I checked to see if he had left a note, that's all. There's nothing. His laptop is gone, though.'

With the blood beginning to flow through his legs properly again, Novak hobbled towards Hugo's room.

Sofia said, 'Tom, I really think you should rest. You need a hot bath.'

'I'm fine,' he said.

The room was a typical mess, with a notable space on the bed where his laptop would often be put down.

Novak closed the door. He spoke quietly. 'Did you hear any strange noises? Anything strange at all?'

'No, nothing. I had the water running in the kitchen. Why?'

'He didn't go out the back because you were standing right in front of the kitchen window. And if he left at the front, then why didn't any of the guards see him?'

In the panic of the moment, she hadn't yet thought it all through. 'He wouldn't hurt himself. That's not him. He hasn't run off, Tom. I know it.'

Novak was at least calmed by the knowledge that it couldn't have been Sofia. She was too small, too slender to carry Hugo – even if he had been incapacitated.

'Surely, then, that means Magnus and the guards are involved,' said Novak, watching him leaving the property in his Land Rover, accompanied by two guards. 'Except Magnus just saved my life tonight when he could have easily ended it.'

'Tom,' she said, almost scared to ask. 'Where were you tonight? You didn't go for a walk so far away in the dark. You barely made it back to the garden in daylight with me.'

Novak turned away from the window. 'I was meeting a source. A source that Ian Ferguson had been speaking to.'

'What source?'

'A man with powerful connections. He has access to documents that show a payment from the Sovereign Grant to a shell company.'

'What's the Sovereign Grant?'

'The royal family, Sofia. The British royal family. In this case, Prince James. He paid the shell company to hide the payment. A payment that ended up in Griffin's donations fund.'

'A donation to us. From Prince James?'

'More than a quarter of a million pounds,' he said.

Her face cracked, then she let out a burst of laughter. 'That's ridiculous.'

'I've seen the proof, Sofia. Ian found it. It's real.'

She backed away, trying to make sense of what she was hearing.

Novak knew that if she was protecting someone she would crack soon. 'Someone was spying on Princess Rose. They hacked her laptop and her phone, and MI5 has covered it up, along with Prince James's Private Secretary.' He could see she was getting lost in her own thoughts and theories, so he stepped towards her, trying to block her pacing back and forth. 'Sofia, listen to me: that was no donation. That was a payment through an intermediary for a hack. And I think Hugo did it.'

She pulled away from him.

Novak didn't let up. 'Did you know about the payment, Sofia?'

She broke free and sat on the end of the bed, her back to Novak.

'Was Hugo paid to hack her?' he asked, ramping up both

volume and intensity. 'I know that whatever was found is going to be the next Griffin leak. That was Ian's theory, wasn't it? That's what got him killed. He found out about it. Something so damaging it could tear the royal family apart. And if he exposed that, he also exposed Hugo. I think Ian found out that Hugo wasn't always as political as he makes himself out to be. Something radicalised him into what he is now. Sofia, look at me. Tell me the truth...'

When she turned around again, tears had filled her eyes.

Novak asked, 'Is Hugo working with Prince James to try and destroy the monarchy?'

The question hung in the air for a moment. Then as it fell to the ground under its own weight, something within Sofia wilted. 'I couldn't get him to tell me,' she finally admitted. 'That was what we were arguing about before.'

Novak crouched down to reach her eyeline. 'I know what these people are capable of. Believe me. There are people in MI5 and close to the royal family who would have wanted Ian dead. Likely the same people that targeted me tonight. I got lucky. Ian and Hugo haven't been so lucky.'

Sofia was still in denial mode. 'It's only been a few hours, Tom. You're talking like–'

There was no time to tread lightly around the reality. 'Sofia, Hugo's probably dead. I'm sorry. But we both know it. Two men chased me in a car earlier. One of them tried to shoot me because I know only part of what Ian knew. Now, you can take your chances with them or the police, or you can talk to me. But you have to tell me *everything* you know about the leaks. Because right now I would say I'm the only friend you've got in this house.'

She dug the heels of her palms into her eyes. When she released them, her vision went black, then slowly cleared. With Hugo gone, she was in bad need of an ally. 'Hugo told me that he had documents that would be the biggest thing Griffin had published. Something about the royal family. I mean, not just allegations, or a compromising, embarrassing picture. It was something that would end them for good. We knew how big it would be, so we didn't let anyone else near it. None of our other satellite coders or remote assistants across Europe. Just us. Then one night, Hugo caught Ian going through his laptop. He went crazy, accusing Ian of spying for Anne Cochrane. It was a huge fight. Ian left for London that night, and he didn't come back.'

'Did Hugo ever raise suspicions about anyone?' he asked.

'He never trusted anyone,' she replied. 'But answer me this: who was the one person here who thought that the leaks shouldn't go out tomorrow for some reason?'

Novak answered, 'Magnus.'

'Who had the time and resources to get rid of Hugo tonight?'

'Magnus. But why would he do that?'

'He only put us up here because Hugo was his ticket back to the limelight. The way for Magnus to relaunch himself. He lives out here acting like he wants to be far away, but he remembers, Tom. He remembers what it meant to matter. To not be invisible like he is now. And without Hugo's help, Magnus would remain invisible.'

Novak countered, 'I don't buy it. Magnus could have easily killed me tonight.' He stood up, trying to figure out how to lay the groundwork for his next assertion. It would be risky, and if it backfired could turn Sofia against him for good. 'There is another side of this that we can't ignore because Hugo has gone missing tonight.'

'Like what?'

'He doesn't have a jacket and he can only travel on foot.' Novak raised his arms as if to punctuate the question. 'There's a small army out there trying to find him: where is he? Why can no one find him? Even if he ran straight into the hills, why would he?'

'What are you saying?' asked Sofia.

'I'm saying there are two ways Hugo left his property: with the assistance of Magnus and the guards, and this whole search is an elaborate ploy to make sure no one finds him.'

'Or?'

'Or Hugo was in that car when it was chasing me.'

Sofia was adamant. 'Hugo would never leave me. He wouldn't just take off. Someone took him.'

'What happens to the leaks now that Hugo's laptop has been taken?'

'Nothing. They sit on the hard drive until Hugo uploads them to the server. Without his laptop, the leaks go nowhere. He must have been taken to stop us publishing.'

Novak shook his head at the lack of options available to them. 'They came for Ian, then they came for me and Hugo. Staying here is suicide. There's no choice: I'm leaving here tomorrow for the first train away from here.' He opened the door. 'I've seen how this story ends for other people, Sofia. If you want to stay alive, I would strongly urge you to come with me.'

31

When Novak reached his room, he found a handwritten note on his pillow. It looked like it had been written in a hurry, the paper torn off the page of a book. There was still a sliver of the title from the uppermost part of the page:

"*ELAGO*"

The only thing Novak could think of was *The Gulag Archipelago*. Solzhenitsyn again.

The note said: "*Tom, the only sentence from Ian's manuscript worth keeping is the first. The only thing left to do now is hand back all the power to the people.*"

It had to have been from Hugo. The handwriting was little more than scratches, indicative of someone more used to typing than writing with a pen.

Novak stood in the centre of the room, thinking back to Ian's manuscript. 'The first sentence...' he said to himself. He grabbed his copy of the manuscript.

"*It was the celebrated Roman author Pliny the Elder who wrote that griffins were said to lay eggs in burrows on the ground...*"

'Tell me you have, Hugo. Tell me you have...' Novak

lunged for the bookcase, removing the hollowed-out copy of Pliny the Elder where Ian had hidden his memory stick. Novak was in such a flap that the book fell out of his hands, spilling Ian's memory stick onto the floor.

He grabbed his laptop and inserted the stick, feeling all the momentum with him now.

Then the folder opened up as before, but this time with a password window.

'Damn it,' he said to himself. 'It was too much to ask to get through this thing without a damn password hunt?' He shut his eyes to reset. Whatever Hugo had put on the stick he wanted protected, but he also needed Novak to be able to work out the password. It had to have been something they had discussed.

'Power to the people...' he said, rooting out his audio recorder, scanning through his conversations with Hugo until he found the spot he needed. Where Hugo talked about the Roman statesman Cincinnatus. 'He gave back all of his power...' Novak started typing the name "*Cincinnatus*" into the password window. '...when he could have continued as a tyrant.'

When the password was accepted, Novak made a jubilant 'come on' gesture as the file opened, revealing something not in Ian's original research.

It was a cached webpage of a regional-news website from two months after the hacker message board logs were dated. It reported on a hacker whose identity hadn't been released and had been charged with hacking into over fifty NSA computers and stealing passwords and other sensitive data. There were also attempted hacks of GCHQ, major defence contractors in the UK and US, and the Ministry of Defence. It was unclear how successful the hacks had been, or what, if any, compromising material had been taken.

Novak went back to the Cincinnatus folder, where there was one other document. A scanned copy of what should have been a sealed Crown Prosecution Services file on the hacking case. If Stella had been there with him, she would have emphasised how hard it is to obtain a sealed CPS file – it had either been stolen from the CPS server itself, which was protected as heavily as any GCHQ database, or a judge had somehow been compromised. It had been the latter, a favour that had been outstanding for over ten years for Ian's literary agent, Julian Darby. The file had been provided on the explicit promise that Darby never contacted the judge again, even though they were both members of the exclusive and very private Portmyron Club – hangout spot to the retired men who once ran the country in various capacities. If Darby and the judge ended up standing next to each other at the bar, they weren't so much as to exchange a glance or a nod.

But Novak didn't know anything of the struggles to find the document. All he knew was that he was now looking at an arrest record from six years ago for a nineteen-year-old named "Gary Shepherd", and the photo attached was a mugshot of the man Novak knew only as Hugo Byron.

The file contained a statement from the lawyer representing him, explaining that the nineteen-year-old's parents had died when Gary was an infant. The mother in childbirth, the father a few months later by suicide. Gary had spent his childhood in a mix of care homes and with various foster parents.

'What happened to you, Hugo?' Novak wondered, his brain still hardwired to Gary Shepherd's pseudonym.

The appearance of the documents on the memory stick at least explained why someone had been rummaging through his things, and Hugo's reluctance to go into any details about his background. Giving Novak the files was Hugo's last act of cooperation before disappearing. Either by his own hand, or someone else's.

* * *

The futile search for Hugo continued into the small hours of the morning. Novak was lying awake, staring at the ceiling, a thousand thoughts rushing through his head. Sleep was never going to happen. There was also a part of him that was a little afraid to go to sleep. But then, if Magnus or the guards or anyone else wanted to to kill him, whether he was asleep or not would be irrelevant. From Badanloch House, screams wouldn't travel very far.

The lights outside finally went off. The sound of guards' footsteps on the gravel tapering away. They were calling it off for the night.

They had spread out in every direction, walking as far as they could, covering as much ground as possible in the snow that was now inches deep. Still no Hugo.

Novak wrapped the duvet a little tighter around himself, thinking about how cold he had been hours ago. It still hadn't fully left his bones. Calling off the search for the night was as good as calling it off for good. By morning, it would no longer be a search operation. It would be about recovering a body.

Giving up on sleep, Novak sent a message to Stella:

"Are you awake?"

A reply came through within a few seconds.

"Yeah. Call on Darkroom?"

Since the NSA and GCHQ's capability to intercept text and email metadata had become common knowledge among reporters, Novak and Stella had favoured apps with end-to-end encryption. Darkroom was an app that was a product of the age, offering encryption for instant messages, and video and audio calls.

Novak kept the volume down until it was at its lowest when Stella's call came through with a shrill ringing tone.

'I've been trying to reach you,' Stella said.

'I know, I'm sorry,' he replied. 'Are you okay?'

'I've been better.'

'Where are you? You're talking really quietly.'

'I'm sitting in Anne's kitchen drinking tea. I closed the door over, but you know how conversation carries so much more in a house in the middle of the night. Why are you still up?'

'Hugo disappeared tonight. No one can find him.'

Clinging to optimism, Stella offered, 'Could he have run off? There are all those guards there. How could someone have taken him?'

He clasped the bridge of his nose, feeling a headache coming on. 'I feel like I've not been seeing the full picture of what's been going on here at Badanloch. I don't trust anyone.'

'You sound scared, Novak. What else has happened?'

He loved how she just knew. Even though he'd been trying to sound okay. 'I met a source tonight, Stel. It's changed everything up here.'

He went through it all. Yet another chase and brush with death. The Dunhill meeting and everything that came out. Ian's research, the CPS file, Hugo's real name. The disparity about how Griffin started, and Hugo's accelerated radicalisation from hacker to political idealist on the cusp of decimating the British royal family.

Stella asked, 'You're the one who's been with Hugo. What do you make of him?'

'It doesn't add up. He was evasive, dismissive. Next minute he's leaving evidence about who he really is. But as long as he's gone there's nothing left for me up here. I'm coming to London tomorrow, Stel.'

'Good.'

'I actually need Ralph to do something for me,' he said, opening up his laptop. The white and blue light of the screen burned his retinas in the darkness of the room. 'I'm sending you Hugo's CPS file on IronCloud. I need Ralph to see what he can find on the real Hugo based on what's in there. I don't have access to the sort of databases and open sources he knows for the UK. Hugo hasn't given us much to go on, and Ian can't give us anything more. No one could find Hugo Byron because they didn't have a real name or a picture. Now we have both. We fill in the life of the real Hugo Byron, Gary Shepherd, then we find out the truth of what's going on here.'

Stella flicked through the notes that she'd jotted down sitting on the kerb outside Julian Darby's office. 'That's what I wanted to talk to you about, Novak. I've found out some things of my own about Hugo. I spoke to Ian's agent, and according to him–' her voice lowered further – 'he didn't bring Hugo to Hathaway. It was my mum.'

'How could she have known Hugo then? No one did.'

'I have no idea. That's not all. When we were on our way to Inverness this morning, she got a call from her lawyer to say that the police wanted to speak to her. She says it was nothing, but on the phone Murray insisted that–'

Novak interrupted, 'Stel, Stel... Murray *Morton*?'

'Yeah.'

He clicked into the Cincinnatus folder again. 'I've read that name before,' he said. 'In the CPS file I sent you. Do you have it?'

Stella opened up her IronCloud app and opened the file.

'Murray Morton was Gary Shepherd's lawyer in the hacking case.'

'How did a nineteen-year-old hacker get a lawyer like Murray Morton?'

'This all ties in. The disparity about how Griffin was started, and the fact that Anne was the one who brought Hugo to Julian Darby. I'm afraid to say it, Stel, but your mother is up to her neck in this.'

There was a tremor in her sigh that followed. Anxiety. Fear.

'Can you talk to her in the morning?'

'It's not that easy,' she said. 'She's sick. Because of the poison at her office. She got too close to whatever killed Gayle Ademi.'

'Too close? What are we talking here? Is it treatable?'

'She's got six months. At best.'

'I'm sorry, Stel. I really... I don't know what to say.'

Eager to move on, Stella added, 'She was a target as well, Novak. She was supposed to be killed like Ian was. It was total luck that she escaped.'

He wanted to be a friend, but the only way he really knew how to do that was to also be a journalist. 'You're going to have to confront her, Stel. If this was anyone else...'

'I don't know if I can. What if you talked to her?'

'Me?'

'If you're coming down here anyway, I really think you should talk to Julian Darby. I think he'd like a look at the completed manuscript.'

Novak paused. 'Stel, there isn't a completed manuscript.'

'Darby said that Ian told him the book was finished.'

'If it's finished then it's not here. The one Ian left is full of blank paragraphs and placeholder text.'

'That settles that,' said Stella. 'I'll see if I can set up another meeting with him.'

'What are you doing tomorrow?'

'Ralph and I are meeting one of his contacts about buying a database that's linked to the GRU.'

'And who's the contact?'

'Novak, I'm a big girl, you know.'

'I know, but it sounds like Ralph is being a bit cavalier here.'

'I'll be fine. We're meeting at Leicester Square.' Stella thought better of telling him the contact was mid-level in the Russian mafia and the database was costing *The Republic* £20,000.

32

Novak awoke to the sound of Sofia running along the hall with rapid footsteps. His eyes stung around the lids from lack of sleep. He'd nodded off around three, having tried and failed to get any results based on Hugo's CPS file.

The bedroom seemed much brighter, not only because Novak had fallen asleep without closing the curtains. The sun wasn't yet visible in the dawn sky, but its light was reflecting off a glacial white landscape – the snow still falling. Within the house were muffled, half-heard noises from the kitchen or some far-off bathroom. But Novak could also hear something outside. Coming from the road. The white noise of tyres on-snow-on-tarmac, multiple cars making slow progress along the driveway, in high gear to keep the revs low. Locals who knew how to drive in snow.

Novak threw off the covers to go to the window, throwing on a jumper and trousers as quickly as possible.

A BMW 4x4 in police livery and a navy estate car with 'dead' plates – not registered on any publicly available database; the letters and numbers in a non-traditional construction

– edged their way along the driveway towards the house. The guards were gone. As was any sense that the Hugo situation could still be contained.

Novak made it to the hall in time for the police pulling up outside: two constables from the 4x4, and three plain-clothes from the touring car – a not inconsiderable amount of resources in a place like Sutherland. Magnus and Sofia didn't blink, but Novak thought it strange that three detectives had shown up for a person who had been missing barely twelve hours.

Sofia stormed from room to room, demanding answers and receiving none. 'Who called the police?'

'Don't look at me,' said Novak. 'I can't even get a signal, and I wouldn't have woken the whole house to use the landline. It was probably a guard, worried about dying out there in the search party.'

A voice from the kitchen resonated through the hall. 'It was me,' said Magnus, throwing a wet dish towel over his shoulder.

'Are you out of your mind?' exclaimed Sofia.

'Hugo's either dead or he's not coming back,' Magnus replied. 'Either way, this has to end.'

For Novak, it was a perfect summation.

The constables appeared hesitant to approach the open front door, knocking pointlessly on the frame while eyeing Magnus, Sofia, and Novak in turn. 'Good morning,' one of them said. 'I understand we have a missing person.'

A missing person, thought Novak, was the very least of what was going on.

The constables deferred to the three in plain clothes following swiftly from behind. Two males, one female. The female was in charge, directing the men to search upstairs and down-. She was also the first to produce her ID. A Security Service card.

She spoke only to Sofia and Novak. She was English, London by the sounds of it, and had brought that typical officious metropolitan attitude with her of behaving like she was still in a major capital city: the fact that they were all in one of the most remote parts of Britain was irrelevant to her. There was protocol to follow. Laws to lay down.

She said, 'My name's Duffy. I'm with MI5,' she motioned to her two colleagues, 'as are these two men. The two constables with me are here to ensure that my warrant for a search of this property is carried out without interference, and the questions that I have to ask are answered. Magnus,' she said in a softer tone of familiarity, turning to him, 'can you get the kettle on? It's bloody Baltic out there.'

Sofia's mouth slowly opened as it dawned on her. 'You're with them?'

For the first time in a while, Magnus had regained his status. Back in charge of the house, he brushed past Sofia and Novak without a word.

33

PRIMROSE HILL, LONDON

Stella was surprised to find Anne already up in the kitchen by half past five, fully dressed, and zipping back and forth from coffee cup to toaster to sink as if she was about to leave.

'You're up early,' Stella said, feeling underdressed in her pyjamas.

Anne hurried over to give her a kiss on the cheek. The action took Stella by such surprise that it was over before she realised what was happening.

Anne sounded harassed. 'Has Tom told you yet?'

Stella turned away to hide a grimace of pain at the migraine that was setting up camp in her head. 'About Hugo? Yeah, we spoke last night.'

'I need to chair a crisis meeting at work. MI5 just showed up along with the police, so I wouldn't expect any communication from Tom for a while.'

'They can't keep him there indefinitely. On what grounds are they there?'

Anne smothered butter on her toast like a plasterer taking out frustration on a trowel against a wall. 'All they have to do these days is yell national security and they can do whatever they damn well please.'

Stella took out her phone and scrolled urgently through her contacts. 'I'll need to get a lawyer on this.'

'Do you really think that's a good idea?' Anne might have gone AWOL as a mother, but she could still do a good impression of one.

'Novak's your employee right now.'

'He's got nothing to worry about. All MI5 will want is to find Hugo.'

'Can't you send Murray Morton?' She watched Anne carefully, registering every micro-gesture in her body language.

Anne bided for time by taking a long final sip of her coffee. 'Murray works for Hathaway. Tom's freelance.'

'Hugo wasn't a Hathaway employee when Murray represented him in a hacking case six years ago.'

'What are you talking about?'

'I've seen the CPS file. Hugo was arrested on hacking charges and Murray defended him. Hugo was nineteen. How did he end up with someone like Murray on the case?'

Anne took out her tension on the toast she was buttering. 'You'd have to ask him that.'

'Hugo is not who he says he is, mum. Do you even know whose memoir you've bought? It's a hacker named Gary Shepherd. But I think you know that already.'

Anne dropped the butter knife with impatience. 'I'm paying Tom to find this stuff out for me. For the book. Whatever or whoever Hugo was, is a mystery to me.'

'Julian Darby told me that you were the one that brought Hugo to him. Not the other way around.'

'What?'

'How did you find Hugo if it wasn't Darby who proposed the book?'

Anne's defences steeled. Her back straightened. 'What you don't know about Julian Darby could barely be contained by the Thames Barrier. Just because you brandish a red pen in Manhattan doesn't mean you have the first clue about my world, Stella. Why would Julian Darby lie? I haven't a clue.' She brushed past Stella, collecting her house keys from a porcelain bowl, and headed for the front door. 'I'll be in meetings most of today. Do you have your spare key?'

Stella would have preferred if she had just stormed out. Stopping to ask a question that demanded a response seemed somehow unfair. 'In my bag.'

Anne stopped at the opened front door to fire her last salvo. 'I feel fine, by the way. Thank you for asking.' The slam of the door provided the missing exclamation mark.

* * *

Ralph had set the meeting via a series of encrypted online messages. Stella didn't like having little control of the situation. She was at the mercy of Ralph's trust in his contact, and little more than hope that they weren't about to be robbed blind by the Russian mafia. Stella made sure to look up at the cameras at King's Cross train station, in case the police had to put together her final movements in the next few days.

'Are you okay?' she asked Ralph, meeting him off the train. 'You look tired.'

'Matilda, our youngest, didn't sleep well,' he said, sipping on a large black takeaway coffee.

'On a scale of one to ten, how safe is this?'

Unfazed, Ralph replied, 'A seven.' He then added, 'You mean one being the safest, right?'

She blinked heavily in dismay. 'No, Ralph.'

'You were just hoping to be reassured?'

'Yeah.'

He sipped on his coffee again. 'Sorry about that.'

Stella couldn't tell if he was brazenly courageous, or dangerously naive about what they were walking into.

They found the bus stop they had been directed to, seeing a woman wearing a grey bobbled hat, standing back from the waiting commuters at the bus shelter with a copy of the previous day's *Evening Standard* under her arm.

'What am I supposed to do?' asked Stella as they closed in.

The woman joined the passengers massing at the kerbside as a bus pulled in.

Ralph replied, 'Stay with me.' Shifting his weight from foot to foot, he joined the queue behind the woman and asked about the crossword as instructed.

The woman turned Ralph away. 'Change of plan,' she said in a Russian accent. She quickly rounded the queue and left the bus shelter. A midrange people carrier cut in front of the bus, and one of its rear doors opened sharply. The back windows were tinted.

The woman got in the back and held the door open for Stella and Ralph.

'It'll be fine,' he said, sliding off his backpack.

'Are you telling me that, or yourself?' asked Stella.

The car took off the moment she closed the door.

The woman took off her hat, letting a long stream of blonde hair tumble down. She held out what looked like a wireless card reader. The screen showed the amount of £20,000 exactly. 'Enter the account number,' the woman said.

Ralph said with concern, 'That's not what we agreed.'

The woman said something in Russian to the driver, who brought the car to a standstill in the middle of Euston Road.

The taxi behind, seeing the road clear ahead, wasn't shy in letting him know what he thought of the move as he angrily overtook.

Ralph said, 'If you're pinning your hopes on my discomfort over holding up traffic, then you're sorely mistaken. The database, then the money. As agreed.'

Stella's whole upper body was rigid with tension, watching the driver for some indication of what was going to happen next.

The driver told the woman something, his body language indicating that stopping where they were wasn't the best option for not drawing attention to themselves.

Yielding to his pressure, she gave a dismissive wave of her hand and they set off again. To where, Ralph had no idea. They were already off script.

'You can call me Zara,' she told them. There was nothing about her that would have given anyone pause should they pass her on the street. Accent aside, she could have been any anonymous London commuter. No ostentatious jewellery or designer clothes. It wasn't just tradecraft, however. In the Russian mafia world, she and the driver were the equivalent of minimum wage.

Ralph took a quick look out the back window.

'Where are you taking us?' asked Stella.

'Nowhere. We keep moving,' Zara replied.

'I want to see the database.'

'Want?' She pouted. 'We all *want* something, Stella Mitchell.'

Stella didn't know how to respond. Ralph looked equally helpless.

'Relax,' Zara cooed. 'I recognised you from across the street. I'd rather be sitting here with two known journalists than two strangers I have to work out whether they're MI5.'

She reached down to a leather satchel, taking out a laptop that was already running. 'For your inspection.'

Ralph took it from her. 'It's recent? Like you said?'

'See for yourself.'

Stella leaned over slightly to see the screen, but all the writing was in Russian Cyrillic. 'Can you read that?' she whispered to Ralph.

'Enough to know it's real,' he answered. 'Phone records linked to every Alexander Gorkov and Ludmilla Nikolevka in Russia in the last ten years.' He asked Zara, 'Where did it come from?'

'What do you care?'

'Because every GRU agent in the country is going to be trying to keep this information secret. If this was ripped off from one of their databases, I want to know who will be looking for it.'

'Trust me, where this came from, I'll be first in line for trouble ahead of either of you. All you need to know is that it's what you want for the price you asked.'

Ralph ran some checks on the database to verify it was genuine, while the driver took them in and out of the surrounding side streets. When he was satisfied, he removed the memory stick and handed back the laptop.

Eager to be anywhere but in the rather cheap and dirty interior of the car, Stella asked, 'Are we happy?'

Ralph said, 'This will give us everyone they talked to, and everywhere they went. We're happy.'

Zara produced the card reader once more. 'Enter the account number.'

Stella followed the instructions on screen, thinking about what she would tell the board if Ralph's contacts were screwing them. They weren't exactly going to get a receipt for the information they were buying. All Stella had to go on was her trust in Ralph – and his trust in some Russian mafia gangsters he found on the dark web.

Stella pressed the green enter button at the end, and *The Republic*'s operating budget was drained of £20,000.

Zara was distracted by Ralph looking out the back window again. She promptly followed suit. 'You've done that twice now,' she said. 'Are you expecting someone?'

He took out his own laptop from his backpack and opened an app. 'No. Are you?'

Zara conferred with the driver, who signalled being oblivious.

'You've got a tail,' said Ralph.

Stella caught a peek at his laptop screen but wasn't sure what she was looking at. Worried that he was going off the reservation, she asked, 'What are you doing, Ralph?'

He spoke with good cheer as he typed. 'Everyone on the dark web wants credit card details, email addresses, passwords. But in your line of work, Zara, the most valuable resource is one that tells you who owns the vehicle that's been following you for the last five minutes, even though you've been essentially driving in a circle.' When Zara tried to see what Ralph was typing, he quickly angled the screen down. 'The inner sanctum of the DVLA. A record of every vehicle in the country. Including those registered to the Metropolitan police's Covert Policing unit, as well as MI5. Wouldn't that be information worth having?'

Stella waited with bated breath to see how the Russians would react.

'What do you want?' Zara asked.

Ralph answered, 'I want the online yearbook of the Suvorov military school–'

Zara was already laughing; the driver smiling, almost impressed.

'–and you're going to get it because taxis like the one behind us don't drive in circles with no passengers. One of Verax's researchers is a London cabbie. He tells me all sorts of things. If I were you, I'd want to know if that taxi is MI5 or not. Before you drive off to your next deal.' As if to push things further, Ralph added, 'Could be your last.'

'Maybe this will be *your* last,' Zara replied.

The driver veered off Euston Road again to a side street, keeping a close eye on the rear-view mirror.

Stella was halfway around to looking out the back window when Ralph stopped her. All eyes landed on the driver's tense expression via the rear-view mirror.

When the black taxi followed, it prompted a vicious back-and-forth between Zara and the driver. His conclusion caused her to curse in her native tongue.

'You were right,' she told Ralph. 'We have a tail.'

'Then we have a deal,' he said.

'What do you think I am? Some military general? I cannot get this for you.'

'The sort of person who can find the phone records of two former GRU officers can surely find some simple year-book pictures.'

'Do you think my head zips up the back, Ralph? I know what two people you're trying to find. Countrymen. Fugitives.'

Stella had no idea what Ralph was asking for or why, but she trusted that if he was asking for it, it must be worth it. 'Come on, Zara,' she told her. 'You're not some McMafia gangster tearing around London in a souped-up Range Rover with a bunch of goons in black leather jackets. You're just trying to earn a living. Not exactly an honest one, but then who am I to judge in a transaction like this. The moment you make a move that the Kremlin doesn't like, those two agents could just as easily be dropping Novichok onto the door handles of this car. Where will the Kremlin be when MI5 pulls you in over some minor infraction?'

The term "minor" was certainly a stretch in the context of Zara's business practices.

The driver suddenly spoke up in English. 'You give us the name of owner of taxi, we send you military school yearbook in IronCloud account.'

'And give away our only bargaining chip?' asked Ralph.

'That taxi isn't the only car I want to know about. When we give you yearbook, you send me full database of DVLA.'

Ralph checked with Stella who nodded in agreement.

'Done,' he said.

'So who is it?' barked Zara. 'Who's the tail?'

'It's owned by a Nikolai Chayevski. I assume he's the competition.'

The driver and Zara both swore in Russian.

'In our world he is a hyena,' said Zara. 'There's nothing he won't eat as long as it's free. He's low-ranking for sure, but not to be ignored.'

'We'll lose him before next meeting,' said the driver, pulling over. He turned around, looking Ralph up and down. 'You've got balls.'

As he shifted left to exit the car, the driver said one more thing.

'Screw us on the database, Ralph, it won't just be yearbook you miss out on. Molly is five next year, no?'

The mere mention of a name that Ralph said about one hundred times a day – a name that when said out loud provoked the most intense feeling of protectiveness – and said by someone as intimidating and unknowable as the Russian, sent a shiver up Ralph's back.

The driver continued, 'A big year. Starting school.'

Ralph gulped hard. He needed two attempts to say, 'You'll get the database. I promise.'

The driver didn't need to check if Ralph really meant it.

When they reached the sanctuary of the busy pavement, Stella wiped away the relief from her face. Ralph looked like he was recovering from a blow to the head.

The Russians' car dived in front of oncoming traffic to escape down a narrow lane. The taxi tried to follow but was blocked off.

Ralph and Stella hurried away as a series of blasted horns pierced the air, the taxi driver yelling at the car blocking his path with a heavy Russian accent.

34

HATHAWAY PARKER HOUSE HQ, LONDON

As CEO of Hathaway Parker House in the UK, Anne Cochrane had only one superior in the company: Wendy Halbach, CEO of the American, and parental, side. Anne always carried herself as if she was an equal of Wendy's, but the power dynamic was written into the DNA of Hathaway's structure. So when Wendy called a crisis meeting and the only others in attendance were from the legal department, Anne knew that it was serious.

The lawyers spent most of the video call scribbling down notes, leaving the talking to Murray Morton who was only a few miles away from Anne across the capital.

'What exactly is our liability here?' asked Wendy.

Murray rocked gently in his leather ergonomic chair. 'From a legal standpoint, I think we're solid. Anne has been cooperating fully with the police, and has gone far beyond her legal requirements.'

'I don't want to get a call from Anne telling me we're in trouble for sheltering a potential criminal.'

'The whistleblowers who actually leaked documents to Griffin are the ones in dire straits.'

Wendy retorted, 'That was before MI5 uncovered evidence of criminal conspiracy between Hugo Byron and a member of the British royal family.'

A pause. Murray said, 'Which was done completely outside of the knowledge of anyone at Hathaway Parker House.'

Anne looked to be zoning out, her eyeline somewhere to the side of her camera lens.

'Anne?' said Wendy.

She jerked her head, coming back to attention.

'You've been running a tight ship over there. You didn't have any idea that Hugo was up to all of this, did you?'

'Of course not,' Anne replied.

Murray bristled at the leading question she'd been given. But he wasn't there to find out the truth about what Hugo had been hacking from a royal family member, or his possible involvement in the murder of Ian Ferguson, and attempted murder of Anne Cochrane. His job was simply to protect his client: Hathaway Parker House. And so far, the company was in the clear.

Once the legal team and Murray Morton signed off, Wendy and Anne were left on their own.

'Between you and me, Anne,' said Wendy. 'I hate to say it, but there is upside if he turns up dead.'

'True,' she admitted.

Wendy added hastily, 'Of course no one wants that. Our first priority is Hugo's safety, regardless of what he's been up to.'

'Of course.'

The tick-box exercise of false concern dispensed with, the

two women could now console each other with the financial upside. Which was substantial.

Wendy said, 'We could be looking at the next true-crime phenomenon. I mean, Hugo Byron and Griffin, it was always going to be a hit for politicos and liberals. But this... it takes the book into a whole new territory.' She then uttered the words that make editors salivate. 'It could truly be mass market.'

'Netflix would option,' said Anne.

'For sure. This has got ten episodes written all over it.'

Anne threw out a hand as if the thought had only just occurred to her. 'We could go public at Frankfurt.'

Frankfurt Book Fair was the biggest publishing trade fair in the world, where millions were spent on upcoming projects, distribution deals cut, rights assigned, TV and film deals made, and every book that would matter in the next year was front and centre.

'That's tomorrow night,' said Wendy. 'You really think you could turn it around that quickly?'

'We always buy up the opening-night slot, right?'

'Sure. We bought that months ago.'

'I've had marketing working on the release since dawn. They'll be ready. All Novak has to do is get on stage and do what he's told.'

'He doesn't exactly have a great track record when it comes to that.'

'This is different. He needs the money now or he'll be wiped out.'

'I don't know,' said Wendy. 'What if they find a body in the search for Hugo?'

It was designed to sound like concern, but Wendy and Anne had been in the game too long not to understand her true meaning: if Hugo showed up dead, they'd sell book rights in fifty territories within hours of a Frankfurt Book Fair announcement.

There were a lot of industries like oil and gas and big pharma that took almost constant flak for putting profits over humanity, but Anne knew that when it came to sensitivity, book publishing wasn't too far behind. The moment a body hit the floor, some editor somewhere was thinking about how to spin a book out on it. What was inescapable was the reality that from a financial perspective, the best thing that could happen to Hathaway Parker House would be Hugo Byron's dead body being found somewhere out in the flows once the snow thawed.

Anne said, 'I'm sure we'll weather that storm. Hugo would want us to announce.'

Mulling it over, Wendy said, 'Make it happen.'

Anne excused herself when she saw her phone illuminate with an incoming call. 'That's Tom,' she said.

'Take it,' Wendy told her. 'And Anne. I want you to know how much I admire the way you're taking your news. I'm going to make sure Hathaway gets you the best care we can get.'

On the surface, Anne appreciated the gesture and the words. But she knew that all Wendy truly cared about was to stick the landing of the Hugo book at Frankfurt Book Fair.

'Tom?' Anne answered. 'Where are you?'

'I'm at Inverness Airport, about to get a flight down south.'

He was outside, having to raise his voice over the sound of taxis and minibuses slushing through the snow outside the small terminal building. The only things not covered in snow were the runway and the Moray Firth that the airport overlooked, the inlet that led out to the North Sea.

'Hugo's still missing,' he explained. 'And Sofia's been taken into custody.'

'What? By who? On what grounds?'

'MI5 had the local police do it. They're saying it's investigating Hugo's disappearance. They've taken hard drives, laptops, everything.'

'At least you got out of there–'

'Are you hearing me, Anne?' Novak wanted to stop his brisk pace so he could devote his full energy to channelling his anger and frustration, but he was running late for getting to his gate. 'Magnus has been working with MI5 all along. Did you know about this?'

'Of course not,' Anne replied distantly.

'But if Magnus has been working with MI5, why hadn't they moved in to take Hugo away before?' He had a million theories he wanted to air, but Anne wasn't interested in hearing them.

She had to cut in. 'Tom, I know that this is a lot to deal with, but I need you to focus on the book and what you worked on with Hugo.'

'Anne, we had two days together...' As a test, Novak decided to throw something else out. '...and all I've got to work with is two thirds of a manuscript from Ian.' He paused. 'Is that definitely all the material Ian left behind?' he asked.

'What makes you think there's anything else?'

'Because Ian told Julian Darby that he had completed the manuscript. But Darby never received it and I certainly don't have it.'

'Could it have been hidden somewhere in Badanloch?'

'I tore that bedroom apart. It's not there. Ian must have taken it to London the morning he died.'

'Tom, writers lie to their agents all the time about completing work.'

'I can't finish this book with a question mark still hanging over who killed Ian, Anne. Ian and Hugo are intertwined now.'

'That may be, but it's not the book that Hathaway paid Hugo for, and it's not the book I hired you to write. You've got thirty-six hours to turn this project around, Tom, before I start having conversations with Murray Morton and our legal department about breach of contract. And you know what that means.'

It meant no more advance money, which in turn would mean bankruptcy.

Novak slowed to a stop. 'Why thirty-six hours?'

Anne said, 'That's when we formally announce the book and your participation at the Frankfurt Book Fair.'

'You said Frankfurt would be too early. Out of respect for Ian. That we should wait for London Book Fair in the spring.'

'Things have changed.'

'I see that.'

'Tom, Ian's dead and Hugo's gone. I think we both know he's not coming back. Like it or not, you're the face of this book now. And Hathaway has a lot of money riding on its success.'

'That's why you wanted me,' he said, the reality hitting home now the threat had been made. 'You wanted someone who couldn't say no. Anyone else could walk away from a contract like this, but not me.'

Anne sighed. 'Tom, I think you need to get some rest. You've been spending too much time at Badanloch. That place is unhealthy.'

Novak eyed his gate a short distance away, passengers already filing in to the boarding bridge. There was still time to broach the subject. 'I don't know how you'll feel about this, but Stella told me. About your illness, Anne. I'm sorry.'

'Compared to Ian, Hugo, and Gayle, I appear to be getting off somewhat lightly. But I appreciate the sentiment.'

'I know this must be hard for you, but we need to sit down properly and go over some things.'

'Like what?'

What Novak had in mind was how Anne first came into contact with Hugo. Why did she lie about Julian Darby bringing him to her? And how did Murray Morton come to defend Hugo years earlier in his hacking case? But those were nothing compared to the truly big guns: were you involved in Ian's murder or Hugo's disappearance?

Then he thought about his contract. The legal consequences. And how easily he could end up under a medical tent like Ian Ferguson in the next thirty-six hours if he didn't play ball.

Novak said, 'Like what you want me to say at the book fair tomorrow night.'

* * *

When the call to Novak was over, Anne muttered to herself, 'Shit shit shit...'

She paced her office, running her hands through her hair. Having the blinds to her office closed for the earlier video call had ended up a saving grace. She didn't want her staff seeing her this agitated.

She unlocked a drawer in her desk and took out an old-style Nokia phone. It had no internet connection capability and held no contacts on the phone itself or the SIM. There was no need. It was only ever used to dial one number. A number she had long since committed to memory.

After dialling, the number rang and rang. She was about to hang up when, finally, a male voice answered.

Anne said, 'There's a manuscript out there.'

'You said we had that already.'

'No, a completed one. Ian told Julian Darby he completed a manuscript.'

'Then where is it?'

'I don't *know*,' she snapped, losing her composure.

A long pause. 'Calm down, Anne. We'll find it.'

'Bastard,' she mumbled.

'Excuse me?' His anger was evident.

So was Anne's. 'I said bastard! I *know*, Chris.'

'What do you know?'

'I know you tried to take me out, too. It was the coffee cup intended for me that killed Gayle Ademi. After everything we've been through together. After all these years. This is what you do to me.'

'It was a mistake, but it had nothing to do with me. I would never... We shouldn't talk about this over the phone. For god's sake, find that bloody manuscript or we're all going to jail.'

He hung up.

Anne held the phone above her head, desperate to smash it on the ground. Somehow she restrained herself. She knew she couldn't do it. The phone was the only thing that connected her real life with her secret life. And she wasn't ready to lose either of them. Not yet.

35

LONDON

When Novak landed at London City airport, he felt sick in his stomach. At first, he thought it was something he'd eaten. He sat in the back of a taxi bound for Hathaway's headquarters in central London, the architecture, the noise, the traffic, all coming back to him.

He was at the centre of the biggest story in the UK, a story that no one really knew about yet, and he was seriously considering not pursuing it. To protect himself. Being back in London brought it all back to him about how far he had come since his first story with Stella. After everything they'd gone through, he couldn't just walk away. Not now.

Passing Trafalgar Square, there was still a white tent erected where Ian Ferguson last fell. Tests were being run on the surrounding area to check that it was safe. Novak thought about how scared Ian would have been in that moment. The poison would have come on fast, but he would have known what was coming. People in car accidents have milliseconds to watch their life flash before them. Ian Ferguson had upwards of fifteen minutes. Which is a long time to stare death directly in the eye.

Novak couldn't abandon him. What Ian had fought for, to try to expose. He might have been a novelist, but everything he'd found in Ian's research told him that Ian was one of them. Like he and Stella: truth tellers.

'What am I doing?' he asked himself.

He said it loudly enough to get the driver's attention. 'What's that?' he asked.

'Sorry,' said Novak, taking out his card to pay the fare. 'I'm going to get out here.'

He took out his phone to check the name of Ian Ferguson's literary agent that Stella had spoken to, but when he turned on the signal for internet, the battery died.

He looked around in vain for somewhere he could get online information, but internet cafes in central London had gone the way of telephone boxes. Then he remembered that he had Ian Ferguson's old phone. The burner hidden in the bookcase.

Once he got it up and running, he opened the Maps function and was about to type in "literary agent", and hope he recognised the name. Before he could do that, a new map automatically scrolled instead.

'The route is being calculated...' said a robotic voice.

Novak grumbled at the delay, then realised the map was showing a route that Ian Ferguson had input the last time he was in London, but never completed.

He couldn't yet see the destination, but the screen told him he was thirty-one minutes, one point five miles away. After popping in his wireless earbuds to follow directions more discreetly, he scrolled across the map with sweeps of his finger to see where Ian had been planning on going.

The red pin marking the destination was stuck on Upper Brook Street, Mayfair.

While the audio directions continued in his earbuds, each turn of a corner, each new direction and yardage brought further anticipation and excitement. Marred only by the thought that he was walking the route of a dead man.

36

Ralph and Stella marched along Euston Road, back towards King's Cross station. But they weren't getting on a train. They didn't want to waste any time in examining the phone records that had cost roughly the same as what Ralph earned from Verax in a year.

'Have you ever been here before?' he asked. He was struggling to keep up. Any faster and they would certainly have been moving at what Ralph could refer to as a light jog.

Stella was embarrassed to admit that in all her years as a reporter she had never stepped inside the British Library at St Pancras.

Ralph said, 'It looks like a regional leisure centre on the outside, but it's nicer inside.'

Stella thought that the long red-brick building looked more like a modern young offenders' institution. Then they entered an expansive courtyard of large red squares and the entire complex opened out to a series of interconnected buildings with an almost oriental feel about the layered roofing and terracotta colouring.

When the library split from the British Museum in Bloomsbury, London lost its last great reading room: the circular room with its domed ceiling and illustrious patrons had marked it out as one of the city's most beautiful. Marx and Oscar Wilde had written there. With the reading room now banished as a mere exhibition space at the British museum, sold off to corporate sponsors, the British Library had been rehoused next to St Pancras and King's Cross stations in 1998.

Inside, light flooded through the building from the many skylights which made up for the distinct lack of windows.

Ralph knew exactly where he was headed: the Humanities reading room, for which he had a membership card.

Stella peeked past him to get a glimpse of the reading room. 'Is this really the best place to work?' she asked.

'It's okay,' he said. 'You're allowed to talk. And I know a corner where we'll be left in peace.'

The white ceilings and walls reflected the late-morning sunlight that poured in, filling the room with gold and yellow. There was a full spectrum of life around the desks: students young and old, retirees, amateur sleuths, crossword enthusiasts, as well as good old-fashioned book lovers who wanted to read in pleasant surroundings. Unfortunately, the room had neither the smell nor atmosphere of the old reading room, replaced instead with the hum of a hundred laptops and charging phones. In the old Bloomsbury room, books had dominated the setting. In the St Pancras reading room, their thousands of books had been banished to the edges like an afterthought. The majestic sweep and sense of history of Bloomsbury replaced by cleanliness and a priority on USB sockets.

Ralph led the way to a quiet corner near some engineering textbooks, which typically attracted little traffic. Stella slid off her jacket and threw it over the back of her chair, ready to get to work. Much like Ralph, she lived for the information. Finding that gem hidden in the dirt that unlocks the bigger mystery. That was where their passion for journalism came from. Not cloak-and-dagger rendezvous and dead drops. Discovery was the thing.

Ralph whizzed around the database, selecting a filter to show the English-alphabet version. He made a ta-da motion with his hands. 'The phone records for every Alexander Gorkov and Ludmilla Nikolevka in Russia in the last ten years.'

Stella said, 'So, first we have to figure out which ones are our guys. Any Gorkovs and Nikolevkas that have called each other.'

'That should be a healthy start,' said Ralph, filtering the data with a long spreadsheet equation. 'The chances of any Alexander Gorkovs also knowing a Ludmilla Nikolevka are pretty slim.' He was right. Once he hit the enter button, the total results were slashed down from tens of thousands to a few hundred.

'Okay,' said Stella, assessing their next move. She took out a notebook, flicking to a page filled with various times, dates, and locations. 'How about filtering to any of them who made calls in London between these dates in a twenty-four-hour window, when we know our Russians were here.'

The results cut again. This time to just one Alexander Gorkov, and one Ludmilla Nikolevka.

'That's them,' said Ralph.

'What else can you filter to?'

Typing as he went, he said, 'I can find phone numbers they both have in common.'

Twenty-one results.

'It's too high, still.' He filtered the results to the most

commonly used phone number by both Gorkov and Nikolevka.

Stella leaned in to the screen in anticipation, the number at the top of the list almost throbbing at them. 'Who are you?' she asked.

'That's a London number,' said Ralph, recognising the area code. 'Mayfair.'

'It's not one of your dark web Russians, is it?'

'I doubt it. Only the top ten per cent live in the really affluent areas, and most of the Russian oligarchs will be abroad at this time of year. Three quarters of foreign-owned property's lying empty in London, anyway. The guys we met today are just foot soldiers. They've got as much chance of living in Mayfair as we do.' Remembering the illustrious company he had beside him, he corrected himself, 'Well, I'll speak for myself on that.'

He pulled up a result on an online map. A red pin sitting on Upper Brook Street in Mayfair. 'We can't get an exact address on that, but the mobile phone tower that pinged the location is accurate to about twenty metres.'

Stella leaned across to take control of the map. 'May I?'

Ralph happily ceded the laptop to her.

Switching to street view, all it was showing was a narrow street with typically Mayfairian townhouses and terraced houses. 'They look like businesses, but it could be any of about half a dozen there.' She held a shrug. 'Only one way to find out, I suppose,' she said, then typed in "1 Upper Brook Street, Mayfair".

37

Novak followed the phone-map instructions, pacing towards the destination with intensity.

"You have now reached your destination," the phone informed him.

Novak looked from side to side but was none the wiser about what the destination was. The directions had stopped directly between two addresses on Upper Brook Street. Both looked like upmarket offices of some kind. One was an architect. The other had a gold plate outside its main door. It said "POLONIUS" in an elegant serif font. In a smaller font underneath, "Management consulting".

The main door was black. The windows shuttered, but clearly lit behind.

Novak searched Ian's phone for any internet searches, starting to type P-O-L...

The suggested search automatically filled out with what Ian had once typed in:

"*Polonius London Sir Christopher Benedict*"

The first result led to a spartan website for Polonius. The

site gave nothing away about what they actually did. Even calling it a website was a stretch. It was a single page that stated the company name and a list of three main offices.

London.

New York.

Then the one that confirmed to Novak that he was on the right track.

Tel Aviv.

Destination of Prince James's mysterious missing plane flight.

The rest of the website had no phone numbers. No addresses. No outbound links. No contact details of any kind. Not even a generic email address to send queries to.

If Novak hadn't been standing outside their London offices, he would have assumed the company was a fake.

He wandered away from the main door to avoid drawing attention. It was a street for professionals in suits. As an unshaven American in crumpled outdoor wear with a suitcase and backpack, staring helplessly at a phone, he looked lost.

He tried an internet search for Sir Christopher Benedict but could find precious little. He then added Hugo Byron to the search.

Again. No results.

Then he added Gary Shepherd.

Still no results. Not even accidental ones.

He needed help. Which, as it so often did, meant a call to Stella.

Not recognising the number, Stella answered with a quizzical, 'Hello?'

'Stel, it's me,' he said. 'I'm standing in Mayfair and I need to find out if a name means something to you.'

'You're in London?'

'Yeah, and I'm trying to find out about a link between Ian Ferguson and Sir Christopher Benedict. He searched for Benedict's name against the office I'm standing outside of. Polonius. Some kind of management consultancy or something.'

Stella relayed the information to Ralph, but he'd never heard of Benedict or Polonius. 'Sorry, Novak,' she said. 'We're at the British Library with Ralph's laptop. If you give us a few minutes I might be able to get something.'

He didn't want to wait that long. 'Something made Ian come here. The map on his phone automatically kicked in when I got into central London.'

In the background, Ralph was asking for the phone number for the office.

Novak scoured the building for any sign. 'There's nothing. And I've already looked online.'

'Hang on,' said Stella, passing the phone to Ralph.

'Tom. Ralph here. What street are you on?'

'Upper Brook Street.' Novak pressed the phone harder against his ear, hearing rapid typing at their end. 'What's going on?'

'Two seconds,' said Ralph, like he was finishing the final strokes of a watercolour painting. When he finished typing, he didn't say anything.

Novak could hear Stella, though.

Faintly, she said, 'Oh my god...'

Novak urged them, 'What have you got?'

'Tom,' said Ralph. 'We're looking at phone records for Alexander Gorkov and Ludmilla Nikolevka. I've checked the location data on the phones they used. The first place they went after arriving in London was Upper Brook Street. Polonius's offices.'

Novak turned around to face the building. 'Shit.'

'Yeah. Pretty much. I really think you should get out of there. Were you followed?'

Novak looked to either end of the street. 'I don't think so.'

'You weren't checking?'

'I had other things on my mind, Ralph,' he snapped. 'And I'm not going anywhere. Whoever's in there almost certainly had a hand in Ian Ferguson's murder. I've got to get in there.'

'I don't think that's a good idea, Tom...'

Stella took the phone from Ralph. 'Novak, you have no idea who's in there.'

'Yeah, but I have a funny feeling they're going to want to talk to me rather than the police.' He hung up.

Back in the library, Stella tried to curse under her breath but it came out far louder than she would have liked, prompting several dirty looks in her direction.

Ralph said, 'We better find out everything we can on this Benedict guy.'

As Stella set to work on Google, LexisNexis, and every other news source she had available to her online, Ralph asked, 'Does Novak do that a lot?'

'What?'

'Insane stuff.'

'Yeah. Mostly. What are you smiling about?'

Ralph was a little overwhelmed. 'So this is what it feels like?'

'When?'

'When you get a massive break in a massive story?'

'Yeah, this is it, Ralph. And no, it never gets old. Come on,' she said, shifting tone. 'Let's get to work. Novak needs us.'

* * *

Novak pressed the buzzer on the wall. It made no sound, and

he didn't know if it had actually done anything. After a full ten seconds, someone responded.

'Do you have an appointment?' She sounded in her sixties. Well-spoken. Matronly.

'I'm here to speak to Sir Christopher,' said Novak.

'We're appointment only,' came the reply, as if it was the end of the matter.

'Could you give him a message?'

'A brief one.'

'Tell him Ian Ferguson finally found him.'

There was a pause at the other end that was so long Novak wondered if he'd been hung up on. Then an older, male voice broke in.

'This is Christopher Benedict,' he said, sounding harassed. 'What's all this?'

'I'm writing a book about Hugo Byron,' said Novak.

'I don't know who that is.'

Although possible, it seemed an unrealistic claim that Benedict hadn't heard of someone who had been in and out of the news for the last three months.

'What about Alexander Gorkov and Ludmilla Nikolevka? You should know them. They were standing out here a few days ago.'

Novak could hear the woman arguing faintly with Benedict before he returned with a more welcoming tone.

'Why don't you come inside.'

38

After carefully closing his office door, Benedict met Novak in the tiled hallway. The white walls had framed abstract paintings along them, leading to two closed doors on either side of the stairs. There was no reception desk or place for a secretary. In fact, there was no obvious evidence of the address being a business at all.

The woman who Novak assumed he had spoken to on the intercom appeared in the doorway opposite Benedict's, only opening her door halfway to get a look at their unscheduled visitor.

Benedict wondered aloud, 'Mr?'

'Novak. Tom Novak.' He waited for Benedict to extend a hand that didn't come.

'We run by appointment only,' he said, forcing a smile.

Novak glanced towards the woman. When their eyes met she closed her door abruptly, and Novak heard the unmistakable click of a lock turning.

'I tried to find a phone number on your website, but there wasn't one listed,' said Novak.

'That's not an accident.'

'You don't want publicity.'

'In our line of work we have no need of it, Mr Novak.'

'Management consulting.'

Benedict gave his best poker face. 'What we do at Polonius is very simple: we gather information and intelligence that would be profitable for our clients.'

Novak had encountered plenty of operations like Polonius in the States, where private spy companies had become a multi-billion-dollar industry. Most of the American ones were a sort of retirement home for ex-CIA officers, the same way that ex-cops gravitated towards private detective agencies in their twilight years. Novak figured Benedict as ex-MI5 or -MI6. But he knew Benedict wasn't going to reveal such information.

Novak said, 'You don't want your time wasted by people who can't pay what I can only assume are huge fees. If people don't know what you do, then they shouldn't be contacting you.'

Benedict might have been trying to give the impression of showing patience and innocent intrigue, but he couldn't manage the same in his tone. 'What's this all about, Mr Novak?' he asked, leading him to his office.

'I'm writing a book about Hugo Byron.'

Benedict didn't flicker.

'A job I inherited from Ian Ferguson.'

His office was plush yet spartan. A glass desk with minimalist black leather executive chair. The ornaments on display were mere abstract shapes, knots of iron, and there were no photographs on Benedict's desk. Just a premium slimline computer set-up. If Polonius did keep any hard copy files anywhere, they weren't in Benedict's office.

'Ah, yes. Ian Ferguson. I heard about him.' Benedict

nodded like a muse as he took a seat on one of a matching pair of leather Barcelona chairs, somewhere between a two-seater couch and an armchair with no armrests. 'The other two names you mentioned...'

Novak could see him feigning forgetfulness. 'Gorkov and Nikolevka.'

'Right... These two names I don't know.'

'I got the impression that those were the names that got me in here.'

'I admit that I bowed to curiosity, Mr Novak. I don't quite understand what brought you here.'

'I was wondering what business Ian Ferguson had here.'

'I would rather think the only person who could answer that is no longer in a position to do so. I certainly have no clue.' Benedict tented his fingers. 'A horrible way to go. Poisoning. I expect the worst part is knowing that it's coming. Then once you realise, it's already too late. You're powerless to stop it. The truly scary thing is that it can happen at any time. You never know how. Did I touch something? Did someone touch me? Something I ate, something I drank?'

Novak gave no indication of being intimidated. 'It wasn't uncertainty that killed Ian Ferguson. It was Alexander Gorkov and Ludmilla Nikolevka. I've come into information that says they visited here.'

'That I definitely don't understand. When are they supposed to have visited?'

'The morning that Ian was killed. They must have come straight from the airport.'

Benedict nodded slowly.

'That doesn't frighten you?' asked Novak.

'Should it?'

'Two Russian assassins who are wanted for Ian's murder were here.'

'In this building?' Calling his bluff, Benedict said, 'I'd love to see your evidence of that.'

'You don't even seem surprised that it could be the case.'

'If they were here, I assure you I was not.' He dropped his hands on his thighs as a precursor to standing. 'I wish I could help you, Mr Novak. But I think you should recheck your information. Reckless claims can be very damaging. Very damaging indeed. I don't need to tell you that. You're the man walking in a dead man's shoes. As it were.'

Novak paused briefly in the hallway as Benedict showed him out. 'Polonius,' he said, considering it. 'In *Hamlet* he was a spy.'

Benedict's attempts at good cheer had long since faded. Stony-faced, he replied, 'Don't read too much into a name, Mr Novak.'

As if he'd just remembered, Novak said, 'Then Polonius tries something too clever for his own good, and ends up dead.'

Once Benedict had shut the door on Novak, the woman opened her office door again.

Benedict told her, 'Call it in. It's worse than we thought.'

* * *

Contrary to his expectations, Novak actually felt less safe once he was outside. It wasn't just the methodology of Ian's murder that created fear. It was that in the modern age, anyone could be hit by anybody, anywhere, at any time. Public spaces brought only the illusion of safety. So when a white van rounded the corner onto Upper Brook Street ahead, Novak swiftly turned the other way towards Park Lane. With his wheeled suitcase and backpack, he could only go so fast. First a light jog, then a trot, then a canter. The traffic on Park Lane seemed like Novak's only hope. If something were to happen to him – if the side door of the fast-approaching van were to open up and he was bundled inside by masked men – then at least there was a chance of someone seeing it, or a security camera catching a registration plate of the getaway vehicle.

Novak tried to move faster, but Park Lane remained tantalisingly distant. He grimaced as the white van revved behind him. He didn't dare look over his shoulder. Ignorance was now his only comfort.

As the van picked up speed beside him, the revs died as the driver approached the junction for Park Lane, then sped off towards Marble Arch.

Novak stopped running, his chest heaving inordinately at how far he'd had to travel. It had nothing to do with fitness. It was about anticipated fear. He heaved for breath.

The van had just been taking a shortcut.

Still catching his breath, his phone rang. Rather, Ian Ferguson's phone rang.

Novak recognised the number. 'Kurt?'

'Tom, I've been trying to reach you. Is your phone off?'

'Yeah. How did you get this number?'

'Stella gave it to me. It's about that coding you sent me.'

Novak had forgotten all about it. 'That feels like weeks ago.'

'It feels like weeks I've been working on it. I've seen a lot of messed up shit in my time with you, but this code is off the hook.'

'Is that a technical term?' asked Novak.

'I've never seen anything like it.' His voice turned hushed, as if covering the mouthpiece. Then there was the sound of a door closing to his tiny office that was littered with spare computer parts. 'This is Griffin, isn't it? This is code for a leaks program. Real advanced stuff. It has to be.'

After everything they had been through in the still-recent past, Kurt was one of the few people Novak would trust with the information. 'Yeah, it's Griffin. Hugo Byron's code. What have you found?'

'It's the weirdest thing. There's a massive vulnerability built in.'

'Built in?'

'Yeah, by design. It's a backdoor that allows someone to see the IP address of anyone who uploads material to Griffin.'

'Are you saying that someone at Griffin's end could identify leakers?'

'With an IP address? Match it up with whatever documents they were uploading? Yeah, it would be pretty easy to work it out. You're lucky you managed to see that bit of code.'

Luck again. He didn't trust it. Never did, and never would. 'Unless Hugo wanted me to find it,' said Novak. 'He was outside at the time I took the photo. Arguing. He knew I would know he was outside. He took his laptop everywhere with him. He was trying to leave it for me to find without making it seem obvious to anyone else watching.'

Kurt asked, 'Why would he want you to know that there's a backdoor in Griffin's system?'

'Cincinnatus,' Novak said cryptically. Lost in thought, he lowered the phone while Kurt impotently asked what that meant. Novak's thoughts turned to the meeting with Dunhill. Specifically, to Dunhill's reaction to Hugo potentially knowing who had leaked documents to Griffin. 'The password Hugo left. Cincinnatus. It was about handing back power to the people.'

'I don't understand, Tom.'

He told Kurt quickly, 'I've got to go.'

He tapped out an internet search:

"*Hunter Company London.*"

There wasn't time to search around for anything other than a main switchboard number. Novak hit call then ran for Park Lane, where he prayed there would be a taxi available.

On the move, Novak said frantically, 'I need you to connect me to Sebastian Dunhill.'

'Can I ask what it's regarding?'

'It's urgent!' He flagged down a taxi on the other side of Park Lane. The taxi pulled over, but instead of waiting for it to turn, Novak ran out into the road, barely pulling his suitcase clear of a car that had to brake heavily. So heavily and unexpectedly that the driver didn't even have time to blast his horn.

After an almost silent series of holding blips, the receptionist came back on the line. 'I'm sorry, Mr Dunhill isn't available presently.'

Novak yelled in distress, 'But is he in his office?'

A painful pause followed.

'I don't currently have that information, sir.'

The taxi driver looked at Novak like he'd lost his mind.

Novak piled into the back seat, his luggage in a tangled heap around his feet. He told the driver, 'Hunter and Company, Blue Nile Street in the City.' He then told the receptionist, 'Can you tell him to call me back on this number. Do you have it on your screen?'

'Yes, I do,' she said hesitantly, hearing the commotion and Novak's heaving breath in the background. 'Whose name should I give?'

He wasn't sure if it was safe or not to give his real name. 'Can you send someone to his office in case he's there–'

'Sir, I need a name before I can relay any–'

'Listen to me! His life is in danger.'

39

The headquarters of Hunter & Company were marked by a huge glass frontage that dominated the financial district of Blue Nile Street. Yet, to most people, Hunter was not a household name in the way that many other financial institutions were, giving a mystique as to what actually went on in the building. Secrets known only to men like Sebastian Dunhill, who had given their lives to the bank.

As Dunhill trudged inside, hours late for the start of a normal business day, he took his time going through reception, thinking about the illustrious figures that had built Hunter. In its early days, no one could have believed what it would become. Now it was all so perilously close to collapse and Dunhill was the only one who knew.

He had been on high alert since his meeting with Novak. The journey home had been made even more arduous by the unexpectedly heavy snowfall outside of Inverness that left them idling on the track. Dunhill had passed the time by assessing the relative danger of each passenger in his carriage.

In his stressed and exhausted mind, even the most benign-looking hiker with an overfull rucksack seemed to be a possible assassin or tail. Dunhill knew how these people operated. Their attention to detail allowed them to adopt any persona, any identity to obscure their real purpose: to do you harm.

Inside headquarters, Dunhill didn't assume he was safe. Even the very security team employed to keep danger at bay couldn't be trusted.

Waiting for his suitcase to be scanned, he felt the eyes of those behind burning into his back. Like they all knew his secret: that he had leaked sensitive documents to Griffin. That he was going to be found out. That he was the reason it was all going to fall apart. There were no limits to what they might do to him in retaliation.

A security guard at the scanner gate eyeballed Dunhill, wondering why he was sweating when it was so cold outside.

Dunhill quickly looked away.

The guard was new. Too new? Dunhill started to question who did the vetting of the guards. Was it outsourced? How much could anyone really know about someone hired for private security? Why was the guard looking at him like that?

Dunhill retrieved his suitcase once it had passed through the X-ray machine, then hurried towards the bank of lifts past reception. The guard kept a close watch, then set off after him. Slowly. Drawing zero attention.

It didn't go unnoticed by Dunhill, who pressed the button with increasing panic. He knew it wouldn't get the lift down to him any quicker – he could see it still descending – but his brain wouldn't allow him to just stand there and accept his fate. He wasn't going to let them take him down.

Then the lift two doors along suddenly opened.

Dunhill pushed past the small group exiting, doing a

shoulder check in the process to see where the guard was – pace quickening, but not fast enough. Dunhill battered the number six on the wall, along with the "close doors" button.

Once the guard saw that Dunhill was definitely going to escape, he returned to the X-ray machine, which he scrolled back to see what Dunhill had been carrying in his case.

No, he thought, trying to make out what he was looking at. That couldn't possibly... But it couldn't have been anything else.

The guard told his colleague, 'I'll be back in a minute,' then he ran towards the lifts, making no secret of his urgency now. He reached them as two lifts disappeared upwards, and the other two were on their way down. He swore under his breath, then made instead for the stairs.

When he reached Dunhill's floor, he slowed his pace. It was a trading floor, where confidential information was being spoken about over the phone, and was openly displayed on computer screens. The two reasons guards weren't allowed to be there during trading hours.

The guard stalked around the offices that lined the perimeter of the trading floor. Offices for the higher-ups. The people whose names were on their doors rather than worn on shirt badges. People who took lunch when they felt like it. Who had drivers. Who were almost blind to the presence of men in uniforms like him, who disappeared into the background, as relevant to the top brass as the artwork on the walls.

Ruling out each office in turn, there was only one left. A corner office. Blinds shut. Door closed.

The guard stalked towards it then knocked. 'Mr Dunhill,' he said gently. He looked around to check if anyone was watching. They weren't. 'Mr Dunhill,' he said, softer still. He looked around again, then tried the door handle. It was locked. 'Excuse me,' he asked the nearest trader, idling at his desk. 'Did you see Mr Dunhill go in?'

The trader wore an expression of *Who the hell are you and why are you even asking me a question?* 'Dunno,' he said after a cursory glance at the office.

'Do you have a key?' the guard asked.

'A key? It's Mr Dunhill's office, of course I don't have a bloody key.' The trader frowned. 'What are you doing here, anyway?'

The guard shook his head in frustration, marching towards the locked door. A few feet back from it, he extended his foot out and drove it hard into the door near the handle.

Everyone nearby flinched, rising from their seats. With no clue as to what was happening, only two traders approached, and they were tentative.

The guard was strong, but not as strong as the reinforced door frame. It didn't deter the guard, who shunted the back-chatting trader out of his chair, a £1000 Herman Miller Aeron with an aluminium base. The trader was upturned onto the floor. He hurled insults at the guard, yelling at his colleagues to call someone.

Without missing a beat, the guard pitched the chair straight through Dunhill's window then ducked under the shards of glass and dangling broken blinds to get inside.

Dunhill was swinging from a noose hung around the beam above a removed ceiling tile. The guard rushed to take his weight from the legs, pushing Dunhill up while he clambered up the overturned chair on the floor. With one hand free he managed to unhook the noose from the beam. The sudden full weight of Dunhill sent them both crashing to the ground.

As the traders edged around the shattered window, the

guard shouted to them, 'Call an ambulance!' He gave Dunhill CPR, blowing air into him, which brought him back on the third attempt.

Dunhill rolled to one side, coughing and spluttering. There was too much adrenaline coursing through his body to feel any pain yet. That was still to come.

A trader who was on the phone with emergency services described the scene to them.

The guard explained that Dunhill was alright, but he would still need medical attention. He lay on his back, thinking about the awful consequences if he hadn't reacted to the strange sight of a length of thick rope with a noose knot in Dunhill's case downstairs. He rolled over, gently slapping Dunhill's cheek to check he was staying conscious. 'It's okay,' he told him. 'You're still here, mate.'

Dunhill wasn't sure how he felt about that yet. The only consolation that had come from his decision to commit suicide was that there was no one in his life that his death would devastate. Both his parents were gone. He had no wife or children. No real friends. He understood that death was the only way to make it all stop. To protect Hunter & Company. It was about honour. Because no one did the honourable thing anymore. Unlike the Japanese ritual of Hari-kari, where cutting open one's own stomach was preferable to surrender, Dunhill's act was about something bigger than himself. It was almost impossible to get fired as a politician in the modern age. Now, the apparently 'honourable' and 'decent' thing to do was to cling on to your job and try to put right what you had messed up. That made no sense to Dunhill.

The guard tried to help him to his knees at least, to get more air into his lungs. But it was a struggle. 'It's okay,' the guard said, allowing himself to relax a little. The feeling didn't last long, when he leaned down and saw the foam bubbling from Dunhill's mouth. 'Hey, hey,' he said, trying to get Dunhill upright.

He flopped to the floor again, the foam building by the second as if it were being pumped from inside him. Distraught at the thought of losing him again, the guard yelled once more for the ambulance.

A trader suggested it must have been caused by the asphyxiation.

The guard said, 'That wouldn't do this.' As an ex-hospital porter, he knew it was no ordinary reaction. He cradled Dunhill, trying to get him to cough it out, then he was frozen by a terrifying sight.

Dunhill's tongue was bubbling. Like fatty meat left under a grill.

'Oh Jesus...' The guard backed away, looking at his hands in terror.

A trader reached for Dunhill but the guard waved her back.

'No, don't touch him, and don't touch me,' he warned. 'I think he's been poisoned.'

Dunhill slumped forward, his forehead planted on the ground. Then, like a falling building, he lurched to one side.

The guard stood up again, seeing a note on Dunhill's desk which contained a single line:

"*In defence of the realm.*"

* * *

Hundreds of miles away, the hiker that had shared Dunhill's train carriage the night before was crossing the pedestrian lane of the Forth Road Bridge at South Queensferry, Scotland.

The wind was howling, rain cutting in horizontally from the east. He slid his overfull rucksack off, being sure to slide on latex gloves before disposing of the glass vial over the side of the bridge into the churning waters of the Firth of Forth below.

40

Novak was sitting on the kerb of the pavement with his luggage, watching the police gradually get to grips with the crime scene. The evacuation of Hunter & Company's headquarters had already begun by the time he got there. Now the building was being sealed off by the Metropolitan Police's specialist chemical response team, who immediately doubled the depth of the perimeter from the main entrance to the pavement. Police officers in HAZMAT suits rushed inside, erecting their purpose-built steel barriers across reception, where access in and out of the building would be tightly controlled.

Novak managed to get his phone going after finding his mobile phone charger pack, getting enough juice into the zeroed battery to receive all the missed messages and voicemails from Kurt. As well as a message from Sebastian Dunhill:

"*In defence of the realm.*"

It wasn't the way he'd tried to go out, but Dunhill had got his wish to die.

Stella and Ralph arrived soon after in a taxi. She handed a twenty to Ralph for the fare, then hurried out to Novak.

'Are you alright?' she asked.

'I'm fine,' he replied. 'Sebastian Dunhill not so much.'

'What happened?'

'I talked to one of the traders. They said Dunhill tried to hang himself.'

Ralph pocketed the taxi receipt, taking in the disastrous scene. He spotted the vehicle that looked like an ambulance but with police livery. 'I'm no expert, but that doesn't seem the typical response to a suicide. I saw pictures of that police unit at Trafalgar Square.'

'They got to him too,' said Novak.

'Why the suicide attempt?' asked Stella.

'He knew what Kurt told me a short while ago. There's a backdoor in Griffin's system that lets them see the IP address of anyone who leaked documents to them.'

'Why would they do that?'

'I don't know. But Dunhill must have suspected it.' He shook his head disconsolately. 'I should never have told him how Hugo reacted to the Griffin arrests.'

'It's not your fault, Tom,' said Ralph. 'You couldn't have known.'

'He thought he was going to be exposed. He was trying to protect the bank.'

Stella asked, 'Why kill him, though?'

'Maybe he wasn't careful in coming to see me. I think the company that Prince James paid to get the spyware onto Princess Rose's tech is a subsidiary of Polonius. A shell company linked to Sir Christopher Benedict. Dunhill had the paper trail. Just as Ian Ferguson did.'

'As we now have,' Stella pointed out. 'Thanks to Dunhill.'

Novak took it in his stride. 'What if Hugo was blackmailing Prince James because he found out that he was behind the Princess Rose leaks?'

'Extortion?'

'According to Sofia, it was worth covering up. We need to find out who those Russians really are, and who hired them, before they get to us next. Because as long as we have that information, we *will* be next.'

Ralph and Stella shared a look, wondering who would tell him.

'We might have something on that, Tom,' said Ralph. He ushered them away from the fray as journalists and TV-news crews arrived. 'Come on. We need to get somewhere less visible.'

41

It was late afternoon by the time they reached Romford in the east end of the city. Small children were skipping and running home, some with parents, some without. Stella and Novak's experience of being followed by intelligence officials had given Ralph some comfort on the train there. He had thought it best to take a taxi before Novak pointed out that if they had a tail, that would mean you had dragged them right to your front door. Having the tail in itself wasn't the problem. Making sure you lost them before your destination was what mattered, and Stella and Novak were satisfied that they were in the clear.

Ralph's wife Christine was in the kitchen, preparing dinner for Molly (four years old), and Matilda (two). Having been in the house already, Stella was more relaxed in the surroundings than Novak, who held back right up against the inside of the front door.

He gestured to his luggage. 'I feel like we're asking permission to move in.'

After a brief explanation from Ralph, Christine called through. 'Tom! Stella! Come in. I've got a brew on.'

It was music to Stella's ears. Novak, on the other hand, didn't know quite what he was being offered.

'Tea,' Stella whispered to him. 'Just say yes.'

Molly was waving her toy giraffe excitedly in the air at the sight of Ralph, who quickly got in some kisses on the tops of the girls' heads before embracing his wife. He held on for a little longer than usual. 'I missed you,' he told her.

Wondering what had provoked the irregular intimacy, she pointed to the two spare wooden chairs around the table for Novak and Stella. 'Make yourselves at home. It's chicken and veg stew tonight,' she explained, pulling out a huge stock pot.

Novak was about to protest about imposing, but Stella overruled him. The two children being present kept shop-talk to a minimum, something that Novak, Stella, and Ralph were glad of. Molly in particular made it almost impossible to keep conversation flowing, breaking it up with abrupt non sequiturs about her giraffe, and Matilda blowing raspberries which was providing her endless delight.

Ralph mopped up Matilda's droolly mess with her bib. 'Hard to believe that they could ever turn into scientists or teachers or lawyers or just socially acceptable adults, but somehow they'll get there.'

When it came to dinner – served at least two hours earlier than any dinner Stella and Novak had eaten for years – Stella found something moving about the cosy domestic scene. The way Ralph and Christine weren't afraid their children might break at the slightest contact. Their loving fastidiousness in wiping up mess and delivering aeroplanes of food into their mouths.

Novak, deep in conversation with Christine about the current state of her football team, West Ham United, looked up from a hearty mouthful of stew, catching the warmth in Stella's eyes as she played with Molly.

After dinner, Christine took the children upstairs while the others remained in the kitchen. There were dishes to be done. Ralph washed. Novak dried. Stella was at the table with her laptop.

'We found out some things about Polonius while you were with Benedict,' Stella said. 'Not much. Enough to paint a picture. Ralph, what was that Greenpeace thing you found?'

He chuckled at the memory of it. 'There was this exposé by a Dutch newspaper. The CEO of an oil company asked Benedict if Polonius could get a man inside Greenpeace to help foil a campaign against their drilling in Nigeria. Benedict was using ex-spies. Infiltrating and disrupting a pro-environment campaign was easy money for field-hardened operatives. It was pro versus amateur. It wasn't just a different league, it wasn't even the same sport.'

'Benedict has a background in intelligence?' asked Novak.

'It appears so,' Ralph replied. 'That makes drumming up business a little easier. His liaisons from his MI5 days mean that his name and number are in the little black book of every major British business and institution with overseas interests. It's bolstered by the revolving door of politics and the private sector: when the politicians retire, they take all of their contacts and unreturned favours with them. Then they join firms like Polonius – and the twenty other similar firms like them – using their close relationships with the politicians they had mentored, or had got them cushy Whitehall positions. Everyone gets rich, and everyone gets what they want. It's a perfect system, and it's impossible to stop, no matter which party wins a General Election. They're all up to their knees in dirty money and reciprocal favours.' Fearing that this was all old news to someone like Novak, he added, 'I expect Washington, D.C. is much the same.'

'Sure. It's a universal system.' After drying a potato masher, Novak held it out as a way of asking where it went.

Ralph leaned down to a cupboard by Novak's legs. 'Just down here... So yeah, recruitment comes via referral only, no doubt passed through conversations in the private members' clubs where all the old spies spend their time, lobbying for easy paydays to top up their pensions. These guys don't care. Their loyalty disappeared long ago. When you look at the risks involved in the spy game post nine eleven, with such crap pay, I can't say I blame them.'

'Hasn't anyone ever raised a question in Parliament about these guys?' asked Stella.

Ralph replied, 'A few old lefties had nosed around about Polonius's close ties to the Foreign Office and Cabinet ministers, but it never came to anything. Too expensive.'

'Too expensive?' asked Novak.

Stella told him, 'Asking questions in Parliament isn't free. The politician asking the question doesn't personally pay for it, but it comes out of Parliament's operating budget. Due to the time required to research answers to tabled questions – like 'Is the government's relationship with Polonius, the private spy company, corrupt and illegal?' – a minister could claim that it would cost more than the stipulated limit of seven hundred and fifty pounds to answer the question.'

'So the Minister could just decline to answer?'

Stella scoffed at Novak's innocence to the so-called honourable British system. 'Just because we conduct our politics in ancient buildings doesn't guarantee decency, Novak. It's in the ministers' interests to shut down such questions. Companies like Polonius are feeding them tens of thousands in donations each year.'

Ralph pointed out, 'Confidence in a corrupt political system is a likely reason Prince James felt safe in taking his business to Sir Christopher Benedict and Polonius. He's protected. And no one wants to ask questions that could cause trouble for Benedict.'

A loud ping came through on the laptop.

Stella said, 'I think that's it.'

Ralph hurriedly dried his hands and took up a spot over Stella's shoulder. 'Gotcha.'

'What is it?' asked Novak.

'Ralph negotiated some extra source material for us.'

'What kind of material?'

Ralph was too involved with unzipping the encrypted file, leaving the explanations to Stella, despite the fact that he could have been crowing for extra credit from his new colleagues.

Stella said, 'The yearbook of the Suvorov military school.'

Mystified, he motioned a circle in the air. 'Okay, walk me through it.'

She let Ralph take over while he opened the documents.

He said, 'We know from the passport data on Gorkov and Nikolevka that we're dealing with agents with a focus on western European operations. They rarely travel east of Moscow. Okay, so we know their approximate ages from their photographs, and the ages they claim to be on their cover passports. We assume a plus or minus of two years on those, because with a cover identity there's no reason to lie any more elaborately than that about the age. All you do is draw unwanted attention. Next: where would operatives like them have been trained? I have a contact in Russia, retired military, who told me that we should be looking for military schools who specialise in foreign-language training, and overseas clandestine operations. That would be the Far Eastern Military Command Academy.'

Novak had to interrupt at this point. 'You're not telling me the Russian mafia are giving you the yearbook for that? It would give you the real name and faces of most of the GRU's active agents.'

'Of course,' said Ralph. 'That's why I never asked for it. I asked for the Suvorov military school. The main feeder for graduates of the Far Eastern. These people end up as general infantry soldiers, desk duty, civil servants, and, yes, the occasional spy. We have their rough graduation years,' he gave a semi-theatrical flourish of the hand at the laptop screen as the database opened, 'and now we have the faces.' He kept stills of Gorkov and Nikolevka's passport pictures in the upper corner of the screen for comparison.

Stella asked, 'Speaking of pictures, Ralph. Did you ever find anything on the Hugo picture from the CPS file? Or should I say, Gary Shepherd.'

Ralph paused for a moment, thinking. 'That's another thing. I couldn't find anything on a Gary Shepherd that matches the details on that CPS file. And trust me, I have a lot of databases I've acquired now.'

Novak asked, 'Is that strange to come up with nothing on a hacker like him?'

'You bet,' he said. 'It's day-one stuff that's missing. I'm talking birth certificate. Electoral roll. Debt. Credit files. You name it.'

Stella said, 'You know open-source data better than us, Ralph. Have you ever encountered anything like that before?'

'A few times.'

'What for?'

He pursed his lips. 'They were in witness protection programmes.'

That put a chill across the table.

Ralph continued, 'It takes big resources, and even bigger access to get something like this to work.'

'Could it be Polonius that wiped everything?' Novak wondered.

'But to wipe everything like that?' said Stella. 'You need access to state records.'

'We're talking about a plot to bring down the monarchy, Stella. Whatever Gary Shepherd was doing, he's clearly got some game.'

'Oh shit,' said Ralph, reacting to a breaking news notification on the laptop.

He clicked through to the full headline on the BBC News website.

"*BODY FOUND IN SEARCH FOR HUGO BYRON*."

42

Stella returned from the back garden after making some phone calls with Novak.

'Is he okay?' Ralph asked.

'Yeah,' said Stella. 'It wasn't a shock, at least. You?'

'Putting the finishing touches to the DVLA database I promised our Russian friends.'

Stella shook her head in wonder.

'What?' he asked.

'How do you do this?' She held out her arms, cradling the room. 'Nothing seems to faze you. Raise two small kids. Run the most dynamic news agency in the country, maybe the world. Cut deals with the Russian mafia. And I never see it affect you. You just keep smiling that smile like it's all going to work out.'

'You don't think it's all going to work out?'

'I don't know, Ralph. I'm looking at the world these days and I don't know. The people in this story are only making it worse. There's always been a gap between the wealthiest one per cent and the other ninety-nine per cent. That's everyone from you and I and the Prime Minister, to homeless people camped out at Tower Bridge. The growth of Western economies has all flowed to the upper end. We talk about Russia as if it's this crass plutocracy where five hundred people own ninety per cent of the wealth. But America and Britain aren't far behind. In America, four hundred people have as much money as the lower one hundred and fifty *million*.'

Playing devil's advocate, Ralph said, 'I mean, that's crazy. But what do you want rich people to do? Just give away all their money until there's no social inequality? Because Russia tried that already and it ended up with one hundred million people dead.'

'It's not that they won't share the money, Ralph, it's what they're doing with it to rig the system. I'm not talking about someone who turned their family business into a seven-figure turnover, or made smart investments with family inheritance. I'm talking about the one per cent of the one per cent. They're buying elections. Politicians. They invest in advocacy groups who agree with their conservative cultural outlook. Think tanks that decide whether we go to war or not. They're funding universities and filling them with lecturers who promote free-market economics and deregulation. All to ensure one thing: that these people do not pay tax. Ever. Prince James is buying people like Christopher Benedict to do their bidding, and every year they get a little more powerful and a lot richer. Then you throw in spying on journalists, legislating against publication of state secrets that have nothing to do with national security and everything to do with covering up illegality. You're talking about a tiny elite who have unlimited power and endless money, to do whatever they want, whenever they want. They've broken it all, Ralph, and it's not coming back. Yet here you are. In the middle of it all, and you're still fighting and you still have a smile on your face. How?'

Ralph blushed a little at the compliment. 'It's like my mum used to say. "Always tell the truth, Ralph. It's the easiest thing to remember."' He shrugged. 'That's what I do.'

A message came through on the laptop, unseen by Stella on her side of the kitchen.

"*You did well, Ralph. The database works. You have nothing to fear.*"

It was the reassurance he needed, to finally, truly feel safe for the first time since the Russian driver had made his threat against Ralph's children.

He excused himself to check on the girls. When he rose from the kitchen table, he automatically picked up two dirty tea cups to take to the sink on the way – the ingrained and necessary efficiency of a parent.

He had already tucked Molly and Matilda into bed, but something about the last few minutes compelled him to pop his head into their shared room. Through the crack of light coming in behind him, he could make out their peaceful faces. Mouths hanging open, lost in dreams. It still staggered him how much peace it brought seeing his girls sleeping. Safely.

Christine called for him quietly, asking when he would be coming to bed. Correcting his original answer of 'soon', he told her ten minutes. When she asked if he was okay, he told her that he was. He then excused himself and went to the bathroom.

He closed the door and ran the tap, even though he didn't need it. The door was thin and the hallway to his and Christine's bedroom was short. At night especially, the sound travelled easily. The water running was to cover up the sound of his sobbing into his hands, which were covering his face. It had been his job to hide his fear from his wife. The way he saw it, that was the problem now. Everyone wants the whole world to know how much pain they're in. Sometimes it's *good* to hide it. Not to suffer in silence, but to try to be strong. Whatever happened to resilience? he thought. It wasn't a fashionable word anymore. Ralph's parents were resilient. It was a good thing. It meant they could protect him from the things young Ralph wasn't yet capable of dealing with.

As he released his hands from his face, he breathed out slowly to savour the moment. It finally hit him the level he was playing at now. With people like Stella Mitchell and Tom Novak. That's what had driven him into making the mistake in the first place: getting carried away and making a demand of an unknown and potentially dangerous contact that could have had grave consequences for his family. It hadn't been intentional, but the fact was that he'd put his family, his children, in danger. It was a mistake he would never make again.

He exhaled heavily one more time, then rinsed his face with water so any traces of tears would be indistinguishable from the rest of his damp face. He had cried. It had felt good. Now it was time to get back to work.

* * *

Downstairs, Novak rejoined Stella in the kitchen, which had turned into a temporary newsroom, with laptops and phones and notebooks and empty coffee- and tea cups cluttering up the small, round table.

'What did she say?' asked Stella.

'It's confirmed,' Novak replied. 'They make the announcement at Frankfurt Book Fair tomorrow evening at seven. She wants me there, front and centre. The marketing team's pulling an all-nighter for the presentation. If Hathaway announces sooner rather than later, Anne says that losing

Hugo during the writing process will look more like bad fortune, rather than anything that could lead to accusations of rushing out something exploitative.'

'I can't find any updates on Hugo. Have you seen anything?'

'Nothing yet. If it was suicide, I expect the snow would have preserved him well overnight.'

'But you think foul play.'

'It must be.'

Stella wanted to be a friend, but she also knew she had to be an editor. 'Novak, if you go out there on that stage–'

'I know.'

'Gary Shepherd could have ordered Ian Ferguson's death. Maybe even Sebastian Dunhill, too. You cannot put your name to that book. Even if Gary is innocent of any crime, you can't do publicity for a book that you know to be fatally flawed, then put your byline on a story with us exposing it.'

'I know,' he repeated, fully accepting his position. 'We've got until the announcement to prove who's behind all this, or I'll have to walk away from it all.'

They both knew what that would mean for him, but neither felt it necessary to dwell on his imminent financial collapse. Even if they did find the person pulling the strings, if it turned out that Anne Cochrane had been involved, Novak would still be ruined. The only option he had left was to keep Hathaway onside for as long as possible until they got to the truth.

Novak asked, 'Did you speak to her?'

'Anne?' asked Stella. 'Yeah. Just before you.'

'You called her that earlier. You're done with "mum" then?'

Stella leaned against the kitchen worktop, something else clearly on her mind. 'I need to tell you something...'

Hoping to make it easier on her, Novak tried to get ahead of what she had to say. 'As long as you've stopped now, Stel.'

'I have,' she said. Her eyes filled. It was the shame at having lied to her best friend. The person she was closer to than anyone else. 'I'm sorry I lied, Novak.' She told him everything. Every morning, arriving at her desk feeling nothing but dread. Each passing hour bringing only more of it as she felt herself slipping further behind in her work. Where every edited piece only kept her head barely above the water rather than definitively pushing back the tide. Now, standing with Novak, being truly honest with him about her drug use, she felt her head rising out of the water. It was like accepting a life ring from a passing ship, and he was pulling her to safety.

Novak put his arm around her.

Stella said, 'The pills were never helping. Not really. They just gave the illusion that I was getting the help I needed.'

'I shouldn't have left you,' Novak said, releasing himself to look her in the eyes. 'I thought the reviews, book sales, attention, money... that they would take me away from it all. Everything that happened after Angela Curtis. But I know now, standing here, that *this* is what I do. *This* is what I am. Being a reporter, chasing stories with *you*. That's what I am.'

Stella reached back to release her hair from the tight ponytail it had been in every day since Diane died. Brushing it free with her hands, she said, 'Me too.'

Ralph appeared just as the pair were getting themselves together. 'I'm going to say goodnight, guys. I've not seen Christine all day.'

Novak and Stella were glad to hear it. They both looked at each other, sharing the same thought.

Stella said, 'We're going to stay up for a while with the Suvorov records. See if we can make some progress for the morning.'

'I'll be up super early with the girls anyway,' said Ralph.

'It's time to bring this home, gents,' Stella told them. 'Seven o'clock tomorrow night, Novak has to go out on stage and announce that book.'

'Which I can't do,' he added.

'We have until then to get on top of this thing. We need a plan for tomorrow. And we need to land every piece of the puzzle or it's lights out.'

'It's got to be Julian Darby,' said Novak. 'If Ian Ferguson completed a version of the manuscript, there must be some evidence of it with Darby. He's in charge of all of Ian's book-keeping and digital life.'

'He doesn't have it,' Stella maintained.

'Or he doesn't *realise* he has it,' suggested Ralph.

Novak took a sip of coffee that had long since gone cold but he was beyond caring. 'Hugo wanted me to find that code,' he said. 'He wanted me to know about the backdoor on Griffin's system. If he helped *me*, I'm certain he would have helped Ian. A completed manuscript could have the answers we need. If we can positively ID the Russian poisoners, then we can get a concrete link to Polonius and Christopher Benedict. That keeps our heads above water, at least.'

Stella said, 'With Hugo dead, his laptop will have been destroyed. And with Sofia in custody, her laptop is with the police and MI5 now. Which leaves us high and dry.'

'All we have left is that Suvorov yearbook and finding Ian's completed manuscript.'

'It's a long shot,' said Stella.

'And it's all we've got.'

Ralph sighed in acquiescence. 'My stories with Verax are more like police investigations. We don't get into motives much. We find suspects and we point to the people responsible with logistical evidence and data that supports it. I don't know how much more I can help you guys. And the last thing I want to do is slow you down.'

Novak said, 'We need you more than you realise, Ralph.'

Stella concurred.

Ralph seemed to hesitate by the door, hearing Christine coming downstairs. She hugged him from behind.

'Sorry to interrupt,' she said, squinting at the harshness of the kitchen lighting after the darkness of the bedroom. 'Are you staying up?' she asked.

'No, I'm just coming,' Ralph replied, tenderly pushing her hair out of her eyes.

Novak and Stella felt truly like intruders for the first time. They both turned their backs, finding minor tasks to occupy themselves – tidying mugs away, refilling the kettle for yet more coffee for the long night ahead.

Christine whispered to him, 'I'll get the girls in the morning. You should work tonight.' She nodded towards Novak and Stella while they weren't looking.

'Are you sure?' he asked.

She rubbed his upper back. 'They need you, Ralphy. You're not just some blogger in his kitchen. You're a reporter now. So be one.' She kissed him on the lips. 'I'm so proud of you. Now go nail those bastards.'

When she was gone, Novak and Stella turned to Ralph expectedly.

He made for the table to sit at his laptop. He told Novak, who was holding the kettle, 'Mine's black, no sugar.'

Novak smiled and turned the kettle on. It was going to be a long night.

43

There were no shortcuts when it came to searching the yearbook of the Suvorov military school. No quick-scanning function or app. It was just page after page of photos of graduates to compare with the photos from Gorkov and Nikolevka's cover passports.

Ralph split up the files so that everyone had an equal share of students to look through, then created a shareable folder where possible matches could be dropped. Stella emphasised that if there was any doubt at all about a match, they were to be put in the folder with the other possibles. They couldn't afford to spend all night searching photographs, only to miss the two they needed.

The intention was to stay in the kitchen throughout the search, for practical reasons as well as psychological ones. It meant ready access to coffee – which was being chugged like plastic cups at a marathon water station – and the stiff wooden chairs meant that no one would get too comfortable and feel like nodding off.

That had been the theory, anyway. By half past three,

everyone was flagging. Staring at an endless stream of faces against the same light blue background, eyes darting back and forth between the passport photos, caffeine no longer held back tiredness. All it did now was accumulate an uneasy sense of jitteriness. An infectious spate of yawning and wide-arm stretching broke out.

When the thought of more coffee made everyone feel sick, they decamped to the living room where they could spread out across the carpeted floor and three-seater couch, rather than being in a tight huddle around the kitchen table.

Novak lay on his front on the carpet, while Stella and Ralph shared the couch. Stella had her legs crossed and her hair dangling in front of her face, enjoying the newfound freedom of it. For the first time since New York her nausea had dissipated, the only upside of quitting cold turkey: the drugs left her body quickly.

Ralph sat upright out of fear that anything else would send him immediately to sleep. All of them had been running on fumes even before then, but they had no choice other than to keep going. The folder of potential suspects was filling up. Some were encouraging without being definitive. Others were only lukewarm, with radically different hairstyles, and in the case of Gorkov, vast changes in physical build and facial hair compared to the passport photo where he wore a bushy goatee and distracting square-rim glasses.

By half past five, there were thirty-three suspects in the folder. Both Novak and Stella had fallen asleep, leaving Ralph the last one standing. Literally. To keep sleep at bay, he had got to his feet, and had been pacing the living room holding his laptop underhand.

The moment he laid eyes on the photo, Ralph knew. It was the eyes. Even looking past the glasses in Gorkov's passport photo, he could see it. They never lied. The colour. The shape. The heartlessness.

'Guys,' he said quietly, the first word out of his mouth in over an hour sounding like a foghorn to him.

No one stirred yet.

He said it again, louder this time.

Novak slowly opened his eyes. Stella jolted awake with the panic of having slept in for an exam.

'I've got him,' Ralph said, showing them the laptop screen.

'That's him,' Novak croaked.

Stella agreed. 'One down.'

Ralph shook his head, clicking into the folder of suspects. 'I found Nikolevka twenty minutes ago. She was in the same class as Gorkov.'

'Why didn't you wake us when you found her?' asked Stella.

'I didn't see the point until I also found Gorkov. One was useless without the other, so I thought I'd let you guys rest. Two sources, right? I read about Diane Schelsinger's rule in *True Republic*. It has to be two sources or it doesn't get published.'

One side of Stella's mouth arched in subtle delight. 'That's still the rule.'

Ralph made fists and pumped his arms. 'We're on the way. Anyone need more coffee?'

Novak recoiled at the mere suggestion. 'Lord, no.' He opened his eyes as wide as they would go and pulled his laptop onto his knees. 'Give me their names, Ralph.'

Ralph couldn't even contemplate sitting down. He was hopping weight from foot to foot, savouring the momentum that had finally flowed their way. 'So, he's Evgeny Firmov–'

Stella broke in, 'Could you spell both names, Ralph? I

don't want to go down a cul-de-sac because we got a Y confused with an I.'

After spelling the names of both male and female suspects, Novak filtered both into Verax's residential database of Russian residents from the past five years. 'Hang on,' he said. 'There's a link to an attached file here for her.' Having clicked through and enjoyed a few glorious seconds to himself with the result, he showed the laptop screen to Ralph and Stella.

'Wouldn't you know it,' she said.

Ralph said, 'They're married.'

Novak concluded, 'Evgeny and Yelena Firmov.'

Ralph had never lunged so quickly for his laptop, opening up the telephone databases he had. Along with their dates of birth, their personal registered phone numbers were only mouse clicks away. 'Sending you now, Tom,' he said, pinging the results to him by encrypted messenger.

'Do you have location data for the past, I don't know, ten days?' asked Stella.

Ralph was typing feverishly. 'Already on it.'

Novak and Stella waited in silent anticipation for the results. Ralph's typing went on for far longer than seemed necessary. Once he'd set the parameters for searching, he hit the enter button at the end like the triumphant final note of a pianist's concerto.

'Okay, the results are spooling,' Ralph said.

Novak and Stella perched on either side of him, watching a world map apply links and dotted lines connecting phone call data, pinpointing the location of each from call received to call made.

Novak and Stella both pointed at the UK, reacting with excitement to different phone calls that seemed promising.

'That one,' said Novak, zeroing in on a call made from Moscow to London. 'That was the night before Ian's murder.'

'What direction is that going?' asked Stella.

Ralph said, 'That's incoming. From London to Moscow.' He clicked through to uncover the London number. 'That's Upper Brook Street. Polonius.'

'For sure?' Novak checked. 'We need exact, not this within twenty metres-type stuff.'

'It's exact,' he confirmed. 'It's a landline in Polonius's building.'

Their focus had been so entirely on London and Moscow and the dozens of results back and forth with different dates and times, that only Novak noticed a single stray dotted line much farther north.

'What's that one?' he asked. 'That was the night before as well.'

'To Moscow,' Ralph said, clicking for further data. 'Incoming to Evgeny's mobile in Moscow.' He took a deep breath as the map zoomed in on the location of the call's origin. 'That's Badanloch House, guys.'

A part of Stella felt relief that it was nothing to do with Anne.

Novak covered his mouth in horror. 'But who made the call? Magnus, Hugo, or Sofia?' As the possibility that they could be left agonisingly short of evidence dawned on him, Novak said, 'There's got to be some other data you can use to check.'

Ralph didn't know how to soften the blow. 'We don't have exhaustive phone records of all of these people's calls. All we have is calls to and from the Firmovs' personal mobiles.'

'Wouldn't they use burners for business?' asked Stella.

'Yeah, you're looking at them,' said Ralph.

'Then how do we have them on record?'

'Because they assumed that no one could uncover their real identities. So they got sloppy. As soon as you use a burner for anything other than contacts you want to keep secret, you blow your cover. Evgeny and Yelena were making calls back and forth to each other on these two numbers, as well as receiving calls from abroad for what they likely refer to as business.'

'We have to assume that whoever called the Firmovs from Badanloch House was using a burner too. How do we identify them?'

It was only then that Ralph and Stella realised that Novak had his head in his hands, and it wasn't due to tiredness.

'I think I know who ordered the hit,' he said, dragging his hands down so they only covered his mouth.

'How?' asked Stella.

Novak pointed out the time of the phone call from Badanloch House to the Firmovs in Moscow. He said, 'Sofia said that Hugo had caught Ian on his laptop that night. The timing of that fits with the call. The motive was always there. Now we have this connection from Badanloch to the Firmovs around the same time. I saw with my own eyes how Hugo reacted to what he saw as a lack of loyalty. And there was his temper. What if Hugo has been working for Polonius all this time? Using Griffin as a sort of spider web of extortion?'

Ralph could see the angle. 'The backdoor that Hugo wrote into the code lets them see whoever contacts them and what sensitive documents they have. A perfect tool for blackmail or extortion.'

Novak said, 'Prince James donates to Griffin via Polonius and Benedict. Then Griffin publishes the hacked material on Princess Rose... And it all looks like an anonymous leak.'

Stella nodded. 'It's possible.'

Dawn was breaking behind the gap in the living room curtains, while the three of them sat in silent contemplation, filling in the gaps of the puzzle that they had been holding –

Ralph, Stella, and Novak, each with different ones. Now that they had come together and bring their share of information about the case, those gaps had become much smaller. Though more than a few still remained.

'So if we're saying it's Hugo, what's next?' asked Ralph.

Everyone was struggling. Yawns were stifled. Faces rubbed with increasing aggression.

'It's not Hugo Byron, though, is it,' said Novak. 'It's Gary Shepherd.'

The central heating was on, but exhaustion had made Ralph's internal temperature plummet. He pulled on a jumper. 'I've been down that road, Tom,' he said. 'I mean, if you want a crack at it, be my guest.'

'What about a reverse image search?' Novak pointed out, 'We don't just have the data from the CPS file. We have the Gary Shepherd photo.'

With each subsequent second that passed, the more it sounded like a good idea to Ralph. 'If what we need is a concrete link between Gary Shepherd and Christopher Benedict, then we could do a dual search on both of their images.' Ralph started typing, bringing up a Google image of Christopher Benedict, taken from one of the newspaper articles on Polonius. 'Face-on. Well lit. This should do it.'

Traditional journalists like Tom and Stella had come up through the ranks using searchable resources like LexisNexis that aggregated news stories, online publications, and research papers. Where Ralph Ogden and Verax had made their name was the championing of a type of search that was fast becoming essential in the war on fake news. A reverse image search took a digital picture and found all likenesses of it online. It could be the exterior of a building, or a person's face. In a world where almost everything left a digital trail and with few places to hide already, reverse image searches were making it almost impossible to disappear forever.

'Aren't you using Google?' asked Novak.

Ralph smiled as if someone had just recommended he use a lighter to cook a steak. 'If you're trying to find someone who ripped off your Facebook profile picture, maybe. But for our needs, we need something substantially more refined. See, where Google really falls down is facial recognition. If you upload an image to reverse search for a middle-aged male wearing, say, a yellow shirt, you'll got a ton of results of middle-aged males wearing yellow shirts. It latches onto the wrong detail. We don't need to find duplicates. We need similar faces.' He opened up a website neither Stella nor Novak had heard of before. 'This is Yandex. It's like a Russian Google, and it's the king of image searches. It pulls mostly from user-generated content rather than press-agency photos and website images that make up most of the material you find on Google images. Yandex, however, has got remarkably accurate facial recognition software. Some say it's pulled directly from GRU or FSB technology, but no one really knows. What it has in our favour is a really strong return in results from eastern Europe and Russia specifically.'

After uploading the passport photos of the Firmovs along with the CPS picture of Gary Shepherd, the results came back with lots of group shots – what appeared to be from social media sites. Mostly obscure Russian ones.

Ralph explained, 'Some say Yandex is a little too cosy with the Kremlin, so I'm hiding my IP address with a VPN so the image searches can't be traced back here.'

Stella said, 'What we really want is something, anything, with Gary Shepherd and Sir Christopher Benedict. How will Yandex handle the one picture we have of Hugo when he's so young in it? And pictures useful to us might have Benedict from over a decade ago?'

Ralph said, 'Yandex looks for common elements. Bone structure, shape, eye colour, facial construction, like how far apart your eyes are. In short: the elements that age generally doesn't affect.'

He uploaded the one picture they had of Gary, along with one of Benedict.

'How long will it take?' asked Novak.

'Looking for two separate matches? It might return zero results. But if such a result does exist, Yandex is so good, it won't waste your time with hundreds of wildly wrong guesses. If there's only one match, then that's all it could well...' Ralph broke off, stunned by what he was looking at. '...show you.'

The search had returned one result.

Novak and Stella came in closer.

'I can't believe I'm actually seeing that,' he said. 'I mean, you think about how good it would be if you could find it. But to actually...'

'I know,' said Stella.

The three of them were looking at a picture of Gary Shepherd, as he was still known then, standing at what looked like a busy ambassador's drinks reception, drinking a tumbler of water next to Sir Christopher Benedict. Gary was in a cheap suit and poorly tied tie, while Benedict was in a tuxedo like all the other men in shot. Neither was looking at the camera, but it was unquestionably them.

'What's that taken from?' asked Stella.

'It's a pool photograph from the British embassy in Paris. Full-time photographers will take pictures for certain events–' Ralph managed to stop embarrassing himself further. He nodded. 'You know what a pool photograph is. Sorry.'

Novak threw up his hands. 'That's it.' Imagining the headline, he said, 'Sir Christopher Benedict's ties to Hugo Byron. Let's see him deny this.'

Stella turned to Ralph. 'It's time.'

He looked nervous. 'You're sure?'

'We need to sit on this Benedict thing for now. But what we have on the Firmovs would get Diane's two ticks. It's time to publish the Firmovs' names and pictures. Everything we've found so far on them.'

'What about the police?'

Novak said, 'We publish first. Then we inform them.'

Stella scrolled quickly through her phone. 'I'm going to hook you up with Mark Chang in our New York office. The first co-publication between *Republic* and Verax. It's going to be a big day, Ralph.'

'What about you guys?' he asked.

Novak said, 'We need Ian Ferguson's manuscript to fill in the rest of the blanks. And there's only one place I can think of where it might be.'

44

When Julian Darby reached his office, he found Novak and Stella sitting on the front steps waiting for him.

Darby turned as if to flee the scene altogether. 'I thought you were bright enough to understand I was ignoring your calls,' he told Stella.

'That's what I thought,' she replied.

'What do you want?'

'Ten minutes of your time.'

'I can't. I have a meeting with an author at half past then I'm catching a flight to Frankfurt. The Book Fair starts tonight.'

'Yeah, we heard,' Novak said.

Stella stood up. 'What if I said it'll help catch the man who ordered Ian's murder?'

Darby checked his watch, although he already knew the time. It was stalling to consider the offer. 'Let's try to keep it closer to half an hour, if possible.'

Inside, Darby's staff had a cafetière ready for him in his office. He offered some to his two guests, who both took a cup.

Their exhaustion had come back full circle again to the artificial-help-required-to-stay-standing phase.

Darby removed his Trilby hat and shuffled out of his overcoat. 'I told you everything I know last time, Stella. I really don't see how much more use I can be.'

While Stella stood in front of his desk, Novak hovered in the background. Craning his neck, Darby told him, 'Will you sit down, please? You're making me nervous.'

They had agreed on the way there that, as Stella had the established rapport with Darby, she would take the lead. 'Mr Darby, I came back with my colleague because we believe you might have Ian's completed manuscript.' Anticipating the inevitable denial, Stella put out her hand to stop him interrupting. 'We think he hid it somewhere behind the scenes. You said that Ian left you in charge of all his online log-ins and passwords. We were wondering if we could check his emails to see if there were any attachments, or anything that might have been missed.'

'I'm not a total bloody imbecile, Stella,' Darby barked. 'My biggest client was murdered. Yes, I checked his emails. For the love of...' He gesticulated wildly behind his desk. 'Is *this* what you came here for?'

Novak spoke up, if for nothing else than to direct some heat away from Stella. 'Mr Darby, it's my understanding that Ian was planning to self-publish–'

He didn't get any further with his question as Darby's secretary could be heard in the background, telling someone, 'You can't just barge in here!'

The door was thrown open by a man in a suit, holding out a police badge. 'I'm Detective Inspector Scahill. Metropolitan Police.' He had eyes only for Novak. 'Mr Novak, I need you to come with us, please.'

He got reluctantly to his feet as Scahill's partner appeared behind him. 'Am I under arrest or something?' Novak asked.

'We've got some questions we think you might have the answers to.'

'I'm working. I'm in the middle of something right now, in fact.'

Stella stood up, 'Will it involve going to the station?'

Scahill took up a wide, defensive stance. 'I'm hoping that won't be necessary.'

Stella gave Novak the nod.

On the way out, he reminded her, 'Tell him about Gary Shepherd.'

Darby, who had removed his glasses and was currently rubbing an aching forehead, suddenly lowered his hand. 'How do you know that name?'

Stella turned in shock. 'You know Gary Shepherd?'

Darby scoffed. 'Well, of course I do.' He paused, thinking he didn't have to explain. When it became clear that he did, he said, 'That's the pen name Ian said he was writing his next book under.'

Just as Novak was about to press further, Scahill pulled Novak out of the room. 'Come on, two minutes. I promise it won't be painful.'

* * *

Scahill took him to the street outside. Novak considered the offer of a cigarette for longer than Stella would have cared for before ultimately declining. Scahill pocketed the pack without taking one himself. They were just part of his toolkit.

He motioned to his partner. 'This is DI Wood. We're holding Sofia Alvarez currently, and I was wondering if you could answer a few questions for me.'

Novak hugged himself against the bitter chill swirling through Bedford Square. 'On what charge?'

'I'm sorry?'

'On what charge are you holding her? You realise you can't touch her on hacking charges, or malicious communications, or whatever you call it here. I know your game.'

'Do you?' said Scahill, nodding sagely.

'CIA, FBI, it's exactly the same. It's spurious intimidation.'

Scahill glanced at DI Wood. 'I don't think that's a thing, Mr Novak.' He was done with explaining himself, and opened his notepad for his questions. 'Where were you at the time of Mr Shepherd's disappearance?'

Novak hadn't thought about it until now. He couldn't answer a question like that, not without a lawyer. The ramifications for Sebastian Dunhill, for the story that was still unfinished, and for everyone else in the margins, were too big. 'I was outside on a walk. I went to Forsinard Flows.'

'Uh-huh,' Scahill said, scribbling the answer that he had expected to be given. 'And who were you meeting there?'

Novak paused.

'You did meet someone there,' said Scahill. 'Didn't you? That's what you told Sofia Alvarez.'

'You know what,' said Novak. 'I think I want to talk to a lawyer before I answer anything further.'

'Then you can come to the station with us.'

Novak pulled back half a step. 'I can't do that. Not now. I can't afford to lose even a few hours to this.'

'Mr Novak, I don't think you realise the seriousness of what you're in the middle of right now.'

He couldn't help muttering to himself, 'I've heard that a lot the last few years.' He said, 'Two Russians murdered a novelist on the streets of London and are responsible for the homicide of a publishing intern. I'm just as committed as you to breaking this story.'

DI Wood stepped in. 'This is a murder investigation, Mr Novak. Not a story.'

Chastened, Novak struck a more conciliatory tone. 'I think I have something you need. Hugo caught Ian Ferguson going through his laptop the night before he left for London. They fought about it. Hours later, a call was made from Badanloch House to the suspects you know as Alexander Gorkov and Ludmilla Nikolevka.'

Scahill shot Wood a quick glance, acknowledging that they didn't have that. Rocking on his feet, Scahill asked Novak, 'How do you know that?'

'Because I do. Hugo had some kind of link to a private spy company called Polonius.' Novak pointed, then realised he had no clue in what direction they were. 'They're in Mayfair. They're near here. It's owned by a guy called Sir Christopher Benedict. He and Hugo go back years together. This is all...' He tried to continue, but he was out of energy. There was too much to explain to them. About Prince James. Princess Rose. And he knew how mad it would sound coming from him on the street, without any of the context he and Stella and Ralph had acquired in the last three days. 'I think Ian knew what Hugo was up to, and came here to London to confront his publisher about it.'

'Anne Cochrane,' Scahill said. 'Yeah, we spoke to her.'

'Hathaway had paid three million pounds for a book by a guy who was in the process of either working with Prince James to try and bring down the royal family, or to extort James for the conspiracy Hugo knew about involving hacking Princess Rose. In short: not what Hathaway and Anne Cochrane signed up for.'

'I have several witnesses that saw her and Ferguson arguing in her office.'

Trying not to get too off-topic, Novak put out his hand. 'Look, I know there are some inconsistencies with what Anne Cochrane has been saying, but she can't have anything to do with this. She was a target herself.'

'I don't disagree. Whoever targeted Ian Ferguson likely had designs on Anne Cochrane too. It certainly explains Ferguson's paranoia in Hathaway's office.'

'What do you mean?' asked Novak.

'Ferguson wouldn't even take his phone into Cochrane's office. He left it outside.'

Novak's gaze fell to the ground, scanning it, out of focus. His mind elsewhere. 'If he went there to confront her, why wouldn't he take his phone in to record the conversation?'

Scahill and Wood both leaned in a little at the same time.

'What do you mean?' asked Scahill.

'Ian knew what was going on. He told his agent that he had completed the manuscript, but he never told Anne that. He would have wanted to get her on the record. Yeah...' he nodded to himself. 'He must have.'

Scahill snapped, 'Tom, you're not making any sense.'

He looked towards Darby's office. 'Can we go in? Quickly? I think it will be worth it.'

* * *

When they re-entered, Darby was fending off Stella who had taken control of his keyboard.

'I've told you ten times, I've already looked there...' Acknowledging DIs Scahill and Wood, and Novak's return, Darby announced, 'Ah, excellent. I was getting worried this place wasn't full of total time wasters already.'

'Mr Darby,' said Novak. 'Do you have access to any of Ian's cloud software? Anywhere he could upload something remotely?'

He shrugged dismissively. 'He didn't use it much. It was supposed to be a back-up place for when he sent me a new manuscript. But he hadn't used it for months. He changed the password shortly before he died. He didn't leave me it.'

'He changed it? When?'

'I don't know. I can' t tell! All I know is that it wouldn't let me sign in.'

He came round to join Darby on his side. 'May I?'

Darby opened up the cloud software, then wheeled himself back from the desk. 'Go on then,' he grumbled.

When the password screen appeared, there was only one word that Novak had in mind to try. If it failed, he had nothing else. He typed carefully:

c-i-n-c-i-n-n-a-t-u-s

The man Ian Ferguson hoped his successor would find inspiration from, and thought was one of the bravest men who has ever lived. The man who had the power of an emperor but did the honourable thing and handed back power to the people.

When the password was accepted, there was no extensive catalogue of manuscript files, Word documents, or Notepad entries. Just a solitary audio file.

'Look at the date. The time,' said Novak.

Stella leaned over to see. 'The morning he died.'

'Judging by the time it must have been done on the bus.'

'What have you got?' asked Scahill.

'Do you have speakers on?' Novak asked Darby.

Considerably more modest now, Darby reached forward to turn them up. He was as keen as anyone else to hear what was on the file.

45

The recording was murky at first. The atmosphere of an office. A quiet one.

Office chairs moving around on thin carpets. Phones ringing. Distant conversation. Then louder renditions of good morning. Eventually one of 'Good morning, Mr Ferguson.'

After they had put their phones outside the office, there was a thump as Ian put down his bag – where the audio recorder had been left. A slap sound followed as Ian dropped a copy of *The Bookseller* on Anne's desk, and got into the argument over his being outed as ghostwriter on the Hugo Byron book.

Discussion soon turned to what Ian had come to confront Anne with.

'You have no idea what's going on up there,' he told her. 'What's been going on this whole time.'

There was a long pause while Anne consulted the evidence Ian had given her. 'Who else knows you have this?'

'No one.'

'Apart from the source who gave it to you.'

Things quickly deteriorated as Ian refused to name the source, ending with Anne instructing him to lose the document and forget about ever having seen it.

He couldn't understand why she wanted no part in what he'd found. So he moved on to his next piece of evidence. Very much the calmer of the two, he explained, "I saw it all on Hugo's computer last night. I got him shit-faced drunk on Magnus's stash of Talisker and Lagavulin. He was passed out by sunset, and I got more than enough time with his unlocked laptop to see what he and Griffin have been doing.'

'What are you talking about?'

'I found a donation for two hundred and seventy-four thousand pounds from a shell company that leads back to Prince James, and I've got the documents from inside the Sovereign Grant to prove it. I've also got this...' He laid out another document. 'A sealed CPS file–'

Anne asked gravely, 'How did you get this?'

Ian charged on. '–that shows a clear link with Hugo and MI5 that goes back years. His real name is Gary Shepherd.' He paused to let it all sink in. 'I think he's working for MI5, Anne. I think Griffin is a disinformation tool, and MI5 are using him–'

'Stop talking, Ian!' she snapped. Once she'd calmed down, she told him, 'You should forget about this. All of this.'

It then dawned on Ian what was really going on. 'Of course,' he said. He chuckled. 'It was you that brought Hugo into the fold. You brought him to Julian...'

'Ian, I'm warning...' She rethought the phrase. 'I'm asking you to stop this.'

'You're with them, aren't you? What are you, his handler or something?'

'This is ridiculous... Absurd!'

Ian's voice dropped an octave. 'I'll publish,' he said, prompting a dreadful silence.

Anne finally said, 'Not with Hathaway, you won't.'

'I don't need you or Hathaway. I'll publish it myself.'

'You don't have copyright on the material. That would be totally reckless. We have no idea where these documents are from...'

'I might not have copyright on Hugo's autobiography. But that's not what I'm going to publish. I'll publish the manuscript I've been writing. The manuscript I finished on the train down here. Exposing everything I've seen.'

'Is that a threat?'

'You can't stop me, Anne.'

For a moment, she didn't reply. It was hard to tell in the audio recording, but she was building up her reserves. 'I dare you, you mass-market piece of shit,' she seethed. 'I *dare* you to threaten me.' She shut her eyes. The outburst seemed to take even her by surprise. She took time to reset. Recompose herself. 'Ian, I know what you must think of me right now. But I'm urging you to step back.' She sounded genuinely afraid for him. 'If you do that, I don't know that I can protect you.'

'Sounds a lot like you're threatening me now, Anne,' he said.

'Ian,' she warned him, 'if you walk out that door, I can't be held responsible for what happens next.'

Ian picked up his bag and stormed out, passing Gayle Ademi – holding one coffee cup – on the way.

The audio recorder picked up Gayle's last living words: 'Mr Ferguson, I'm a big fan...'

But Ian kept walking, too angry to even hear her.

46

Everyone held their breath for what felt like in inordinate amount of time once the audio file had clearly come to an end.

Stella was first to speak. 'I don't know what you call that, but it's not a smoking gun. There's no proof that–'

'It's not Anne,' Novak explained. 'She didn't do it.'

Scahill stepped forward. 'What are you getting at?'

'When I was at Badanloch House, Sofia told me that Hugo caught Ian looking on his laptop and they had a blazing row about it. That contradicts Ian's story. Why would she lie?'

Stella put a hand to her forehead as she saw the truth unravelling. 'Unless she was covering her own tracks.'

Novak told Scahill, 'You were right to take her into custody. You just took her in on the wrong charge. She ordered the murder of Ian Ferguson, and is responsible for the homicide of Gayle Ademi.'

DI Wood went outside to make some urgent phone calls to the station regarding Sofia Alvarez.

Inside, Novak remained at the helm of Darby's computer. 'You said that Ian told you his next book was going to be written under the name Gary Shepherd.'

Darby was in something of a daze. 'Yes, that's right.'

'Did Ian have a homepage for Amazon?' Trying to think of the right term, Novak said, 'A dashboard.'

'Yes, I'll open it for you.' Darby made his way over.

Scahill and Stella joined them at the computer.

'What's the dashboard?' Scahill asked.

Novak said, 'Whenever you publish a book, you get access to a publisher page that shows you all of your sales, your covers and blurbs, and press reviews – somewhere that pulls together all of your data. And if you upload manuscripts directly to Amazon yourself – like Ian talked about doing – there's a separate place for that too.' He recognised the heading on the page. 'There. Bookshelf, it's called. It shows you all of your upcoming titles.'

Darby put his glasses on, his attention caught by something. 'There's an alert here for a new title that's pending.'

Novak said, 'It's not listed under his author name.'

'Look,' Darby pointed, more familiar with the page layout. 'We're under the pen name "Ian Ferguson".' He started typing "Gary". He didn't have to go further than that, as the rest automatically filled with "Shepherd".

Darby clicked on the one title showing under the name.

Captive State.

Darby opened the manuscript, which started with an official introduction from Ian Ferguson.

"I write this from a carriage on the Caledonian Sleeper from Edinburgh to London, and after what I've found on a young man's laptop tonight, I'm not entirely sure that I will live to see this passage – or the rest of the manuscript – in print."

For the past three months I've been ghostwriting an autobiography of a man that the world knows as Hugo Byron. Founder of Griffin. Home of the most explosive and damaging classified leaks in the world. But Griffin has been hiding a terrible secret all this time. One that I reluctantly must expose as one of the great corruption scandals of our time."

It's about the untouchables in society. The people above the law. Who can buy anything. People who walk between the raindrops. This book is about a flawed young man with nothing left to lose. And my attempt to tell his story."

After ten straight pages, no one had spoken. The material building in intensity, incendiary in both tone and content.

Novak was first to comment. 'Is anyone else...'

'Yeah,' said Stella. 'Pretty much.'

Scahill pointed at the screen. 'I'm going to need a copy of this.' He texted Woods. 'I better get back to the station. Sofia Alvarez has got some questions to answer.'

Darby said, 'Let me be the only literary agent in the room for a moment and ask what the hell we're going to do with this damn thing now? We can't just hit publish. We've got no idea what else is in this manuscript.'

'Then we read,' Stella said.

'Then what?'

Novak said, 'I've been thinking about that, actually. You're on your way to Frankfurt Book Fair tonight, right?'

Before Scahill left, Stella took him aside. 'Detective Inspector, I want to let you know that we've come into some information regarding the Russians that poisoned Ian Ferguson. We've got names.'

'Real names?'

'Yes. We're going to publish in a few hours.'

He nodded. 'I appreciate the heads up. You didn't have to do that.'

'I was wondering... You don't really think my mum has anything to do with this, do you? Gary's death? There's no evidence of foul play there yet, right?'

'We're investigating all available lines of enquiry, Ms Mitchell. That's all I can say.'

47

FRANKFURT, GERMANY

Book fairs were a fundamental part of the publishing industry. A place where publishers from all over the world could do business and sell book rights to each other.

There were many things that made the Frankfurt Book Fair different to any other trade show in the publishing industry. The most obvious one was its size. Nowhere else even came close. The London Book Fair held in the Olympia Grand Hall was not much bigger than an aeroplane hangar. The sprawling collection of halls that made up Frankfurt took a full fifteen minutes to traverse from end to end.

What really made Frankfurt stand out from the crowd was its focus on rights sales. It had always been the go-to marketplace for publishers to sell the translation rights of their existing titles. Then there were the new book deals themselves. All the agents and publishers held back their biggest hitters to sell at Frankfurt. It wasn't uncommon for agents and publishers to hold back titles for as long as ten months just to pitch them at Frankfurt. The time of year the fair was held was a factor. Due to the time required for editing, marketing, cover design, and building pre-release buzz, it normally took nine months to a year for most published books to see the light of day. With autumn bringing the most potential bestsellers, warming up for the run into Christmas, selling rights in Frankfurt was crucial to time a book's release just right.

For a trade that revolved so heavily around social media, Frankfurt was also where the publishing industry let its hair down in a party atmosphere, and different publishers could actually mingle outside of their own organisations. The early-evening drinks at *Grandhotel Hessischer Hof* – where almost all delegates stayed – followed by later drinks at nearby *Hotel Steigenberger Frankfurter Hof* were legendary in the industry.

There had been no such party atmosphere on the plane there for Novak and Stella. Because of the late additional bookings, they had ended up separated multiple rows away from each other, leaving them alone with their own thoughts. And fears. Occasionally, both would glance over at Anne Cochrane, who was busy running through the hectic schedule that was planned out with military precision. There wasn't a single block of fifteen minutes at the fair that her time wasn't accounted for, or booked in with a domestic agent or foreign-rights agent or foreign publisher. As she sat blissfully unaware of what her two travelling companions now knew, she also had no idea that of all the meetings she had planned, she wouldn't take one of them.

Novak's presentation of the Hugo Byron biography – rumours of which were already spreading, thanks to Hathaway's PR team – would see to that.

* * *

There was barely time to dump bags in hotel rooms before making for the venue at *Messe Frankfurt*. Anne had stopped by

Stella's room to check on her, finding her in hushed conversation with Novak as they ran through their plan one last time. Anne couldn't understand their secretive behaviour, or Stella's emotionally distant responses. But she had bigger things on her mind. Namely, the imminent announcement of one of the biggest non-fiction books of the year.

Before Novak left with Anne in a taxi, Stella asked him, 'You sure you want to do this?'

'I have to,' he replied. 'For Ian. And Gary.'

* * *

Across multiple halls, the interior of the fair covered nearly 200,000 square metres. Fortunately, Stella had the ideal guide for such a vast and strange place. Julian Darby.

He walked briskly through the crowd, making it clear that it was Stella's responsibility to keep up with him. 'I've got ten minutes, then I need to get to my stall before the evening presentation.'

On each of the fair's five nights, a major publisher booked the stage to present the fair with a single book for its consideration. Only true behemoths like Hathaway could even consider spending the money required to book such a slot, and the one for opening night was always the biggest title of the fair, and the year to come.

'Forgive me for asking,' said Stella, 'but what exactly is it an agent does here?'

Darby spoke over his shoulder, as it was almost impossible to walk two abreast in the packed hall. 'We're a kind of quality control filter between authors and publishers. That's why publishers won't touch you if you don't have an agent. Your manuscript won't even get read. In fact, publishers hire interns for round-the-clock destruction of unsolicited manuscripts and the mass-deletion of email submissions. Authors actually think they have more chance of being noticed by sending a manuscript recorded delivery, when nothing will condemn them faster to the nearest bin.'

Stella felt her attention being pulled in several directions at once. 'How do you know which book is going to work? I mean, all these posters and promo materials make every book look like it's going to be the biggest thing ever.'

Darby said, 'To quote the great William Goldman on Hollywood, nobody knows anything. You can pay two million for the next big thriller, but no one really knows if it's going to work or not. That's where people like me come in. Publishers trust that if I represent an author that I believe in so much that I think my twenty per cent cut of their royalties is worth my time and effort to flog their blood, sweat and tears, then it's probably worth their time and effort too. Publishers like Hathaway need me, because frankly there are too many authors and too many books published. They have to sell a lot of something to make up for the fact that ninety-five per cent of what they buy isn't going to sell. They won't even recoup their costs. And why?'

Stella said, 'Because nobody knows anything.'

'Exactly. Name for me any other industry that would tolerate a ninety-five per cent failure rate?' He lifted his arms as they reached the main presentation stage. 'Welcome to publishing Valhalla.' He shook Stella's hand. 'Ian would be proud of what you and the others are doing. I don't want to get too Godfather Part Two on you, but I know how to return a favour. I won't forget what you're doing for Ian. And for me. I'll be watching on the big screen.'

Behind the stage was a screen large enough to grace any cinema. And the logo for Hathaway Parker House was currently filling most of it.

48

Backstage, Anne Cochrane was in her element, lost in conversation with Wendy Halbach who had flown in early to make sure she made the presentation. Novak paced in circles, going over his notes, stopped only by a technician to hook a microphone around his ear.

The murmur of the assembled crowd grew with each passing minute, a sense of anticipation in the air.

Wendy delivered a final handshake to Anne, then winked to Novak. 'Light 'em up, Tom.'

Oh, I will, he thought. He pursed his lips, knowing that when he was done, he would be dead to Wendy Halbach and she would likely spend years plotting her revenge. He could kiss goodbye to being offered a major publishing deal again for quite a while. If ever. This was publishing's Super Bowl, World Cup final, and Olympics all rolled into one. And Novak was about to use it to humiliate Hathaway and wipe millions off its share price. Putting them at the centre of a scandal they might never recover from.

'Just another book event,' Novak told himself breezily,

then grabbed hold of his thighs – his legs were actually shaking. He quickly let go when Anne patted him on the back.

She looked deep into his eyes as the lights went down on stage and the introductory music – modern atmospheric electronica – filled the vast hall. Wherever you were, regardless of whether you could see the stage, you could hear what was happening.

'Are you ready?' Anne asked him.

'Yeah,' he replied, taking one last deep breath that did absolutely nothing to dissipate the nerves he was feeling.

'The tech guys have the PowerPoint ready. Go out there and kill it, Tom.'

A technician got a nod from the stage director, then signalled Novak to the stage.

As soon as the crowd recognised him, their cheers grew even louder. It meant that the rumours circulating for the past two hours were true. Hathaway really had brought Tom Novak on as some kind of superstar substitute writer on their lead title for the next year. If the book trade loved its biggest authors, there was nothing it loved more than when a celebrity outsider graced the industry. It came as validation. And Novak brought not only notoriety and cool points, he also brought credibility to a book project. If expectations had been high already, they were now Empire State Building high.

In typical New Yorker style, he held a hand up like a golfer accepting applause for a sunk putt. 'Thanks. Appreciate it,' he said, flinching internally at how loud his mic was. The slight shakiness in his voice was impossible to ignore.

Back a few rows stage right, Stella looked on, phone in hand, arms folded. There was nothing more she could do: everything was in Novak's hands.

'I'm sure a lot of you have heard what I'm here to present

tonight,' he said, holding court at the front of the stage. 'Whatever you think that is, I can tell you you're wrong.'

The crowd wasn't sure whether or not to cheer this, creating an awkward murmur while Novak tried to elaborate.

'The book that I am here to talk about was started by a writer called Ian Ferguson.' He waited for the inevitable applause, which was sustained and deeply felt. Encouraging them to keep it going, he applauded too. 'Yep,' he said. 'Ian dedicated himself to this book like no other. And this was a guy who always put the time in. This book was a little different. For a lot of reasons.' Novak hit the remote in his hand to move to the next slide.

Novak's intro had been a little off-script already, but the second slide was when Anne had an inkling that something was definitely wrong. It wasn't the slide that she and the marketing team had prepared. It was, however, one of the slides that Stella had reworked on the plane, out of Anne's sightline, then swapped out from the real one by Novak while Anne was unintentionally distracted by Wendy Halbach.

A picture of Gary Shepherd filled the screen. The one taken from his CPS file.

Novak explained, 'This is someone you've almost certainly never seen before. But you've heard of him. This is the man you know as the founder of Griffin. Hugo Byron.'

The crowd broke into enormous applause at the revelation: the first publicly available picture of his face.

Novak went on, 'Hugo's real name was Gary Shepherd. This photo was taken when he was nineteen years old when he was arrested on computer hacking charges...'

Backstage, Anne felt in the opening grips of a panic attack. 'What's he doing?' she asked no one.

'...Shortly after this arrest, Gary Shepherd would no longer be Gary Shepherd. He would adopt his online persona of Hugo Byron full-time. As part of his cover as an informer for MI5.'

The hall filled with a scandalised buzz of conversation, shock and dismay spreading through the crowd, then dying down as people urgently shushed to hear the rest of Novak's monologue.

'Facing thirty years in jail, a deal was constructed through this man,' the slide changed to a shot of Murray Morton, 'to hand Gary Shepherd over to work for MI5 in return for house arrest. For a scared, lonely kid, Gary thought he had no option but to agree. Despite the complete lack of *habeas corpus* or access to a lawyer actively working in his best interests. You see, MI5 had a plan. To take a website where people could upload files anonymously to blow the whistle on criminal behaviour, and turn it into a giant machine called Griffin, to entrap whistleblowers. Because those whistleblowers don't know that Griffin isn't anonymous. They have full visibility of leakers' IP addresses and locations, making it easy to identify them. And Gary had no choice but to cooperate with this scheme or be sent to jail. Except it all went wrong when Gary Shepherd decided to fight back. Like Solzhenitsyn, he refused to accept his fate, his imprisonment. Then one day, Griffin received a batch of files from someone senior – very senior – in the British royal family...'

The crowd was now almost silent. Their collective breath held.

'Prince James, the Duke of Salisbury. He hired a private spy company to hack the phone of his sister and next Queen of the United Kingdom, Princess Rose. Gary Shepherd saw his way out. He decided to blackmail the prince. The only man with enough power to extract Gary from his deal and help him escape. A large donation landed in Griffin's accounts. Two hundred and seventy-four thousand pounds, routed through a series of shell companies owned by Polonius. The private spy company who hacked Princess Rose. Everything was in place. Griffin was going to leak the hacked files as planned, keeping Prince James's name out of it as agreed. And Gary Shepherd and his close assistant would be extracted by Polonius. Until one night, Ian Ferguson makes a critical mistake. A fatal one: while Gary is passed out drunk, he takes the opportunity to look on Gary's laptop. Ian's technologically savvy and can see from the logs that Gary has removed the leaked documents from Griffin's system and quarantined them somewhere MI5 won't find. He also finds evidence of the extortion deal: the payoff masquerading as a donation from Prince James, which was backed up by evidence from a whistleblower within the royal family's bank. Now Ian has everything he needs to expose Gary's deal with Prince James, which is his last hope for escape from MI5. It also risks exposing Polonius's part in the deal, and Polonius doesn't do exposure. Ian's fate is sealed when he takes it to the one person he thinks he can trust with the information...'

Backstage, Anne already knew where things were heading. That Stella, Novak, and Ralph had put the pieces together. She whirled around to escape, only to find Detective Inspector Scahill accompanied by a couple of *Bundespolizei* officers.

Scahill said what Anne was already thinking. 'There's nowhere to go. Don't make this any harder on yourself.'

She didn't run. She had been running most of her life...

Scahill cuffed her. 'Anne Cochrane, I'm arresting you for the murder of Gary Shepherd...'

It was over and she knew it. She didn't put up a fight as Scahill read her her rights.

Feeding off the tense energy of the crowd, Novak said, 'Ian thought he'd found the truth about what they had done to Gary. Little did Ian know that his fate was already sealed.'

Novak pressed his remote to change the video screen to a shot of *Captive State* in its new form, with a cover delivered just an hour earlier from Ian's designer. A circular badge next to it declared it "OUT NOW exclusively online".

Far back in the crowd, Julian Darby consulted his phone with a satisfied nod. 'Good job, Ian,' he said quietly to himself. 'It's one of your best.' The screen showed that Ian's manuscript had uploaded successfully to Amazon and was now live for sale. As Novak had suggested, they listed the author as Ian Ferguson, meaning that all of his tens of thousands of followers were receiving a new release alert at the same time for *Captive State*. Along with the frenzied social media reaction from bloggers and industry insiders live-streaming the announcement – it was everything the book needed to fly up the charts by the end of the day.

In the crowd, Stella edged out as she called Mark Chang in New York, who had been editing Ralph's piece on the Firmovs up until a few minutes earlier. 'Are we ready?' Stella asked, shielding the mouthpiece.

'We're good,' Mark confirmed.

'Okay,' she said. 'Go.'

The story went live online under the banner of "*A co-publication with The Republic and Verax, by Ralph Ogden with additional reporting from Stella Mitchell and Tom Novak.*"

The headline: "*Ian Ferguson murder suspects named as former GRU agents.*"

Stella saw the link go live on her phone. 'Good job, Ralph,' she said to herself, then made her way back into the crowd.

Meanwhile, Wendy Halbach stormed across the backstage area and ordered security onto the stage. She wasn't going to have Novak up there under Hathaway Parker House's banner, promoting a book that wasn't theirs. She had always cut a fearsome figure at the book fair, and security had been well briefed on her importance. They and the technical team weren't about to refuse her demands. If she wanted to destroy her own publishing house's presentation, that was up to her.

The music intended for the closing segment – when Novak was meant to be accepting the applause of the crowd – now played, causing him to raise his voice to be heard as the tech team, on Halbach's orders, tried to drown him out. The crowd could tell what was happening. Loud boos rang out. It was hard to ignore, also, that the attendees now knew that whatever Novak was announcing wasn't with Hathaway's consent, and they didn't want it to stop. Many cheered him on.

Novak held his mic closer to his mouth, raising his volume against the audio onslaught from the monitors facing him, and the speakers facing the crowd. 'When MI5 found out about Gary's secret deal with Prince James and the secret leaks he was about to expose, they knew the threat it posed to political and cultural stability. Not least yet another crisis for the British monarchy. It was bad for business. Bad for security. And it meant that Gary Shepherd had to be silenced before the leaks came out. We don't know exactly who ordered the hit. But a hit it certainly was. *Captive State* is the result of Ian Ferguson's work to expose that deceit, corruption, and conspiracy from MI5 to hold a young man without charge and use him as a tool of the state...'

Wendy was now in the technical booth, demanding, 'Cut his mic. Do it! *Schnell!*'

The helpless operator did what he was told.

'...A young man who chose to rebel against his captors...' Novak's voice disappeared from the speakers, but that didn't stop him. He ripped off his mic as he strode to the very front of the stage and yelled to anyone that could still hear him.

'This is the truth that Ian and Gary died for! Don't let them silence the truth...'

As security charged onstage and dragged Novak off, the screen behind him went blank and the stage lights dimmed, leaving Novak kicking at the ground. From out of nowhere, Stella leapt onto the stage to help fend off the stocky guards, but she was no match for them.

Surrendering to the inevitable, she backed off as the guards carried Novak off the stage. He had got further in the presentation than he had thought. Catching her breath and straightening her suit jacket, Stella looked beyond Novak, seeing Anne's slouched figure as the police led her away.

Emerging from the technical booth, Wendy Halbach saw the same and set off in pursuit, clip clopping across the back-stage area in her high heels, taking half a tumble on the way. 'Anne, what's going on?' she called out.

Anne looked over her shoulder, calling out Stella's name.

Stella watched from the wings. Unsure of what she should be feeling.

The announcement had sent shockwaves through the fair. The entire arena was buzzing like a rock concert in the immediate aftermath of the band leaving the stage.

On Scahill's urging, the German police stepped in to insist the guards let go of Novak. He dusted himself down, heart still thumping from what he'd experienced on stage.

'Are you okay?' Stella asked.

Checking his nose for blood, Novak puffed to release some caged-up energy that the guards had restrained. 'I'm alright.' He wasn't buoyant or triumphant. Too many lives had already been lost for that. Now his closest friend was having to watch the last piece of her family be ripped away.

Catching Stella's eye, Anne called out, 'Stella, I'm sorry...'

Novak put his hand on Stella's back. 'It's over.'

'No, it's not,' she replied, showing him her phone screen – Ralph's story. 'It's a start. But if the Firmovs are back in Russia, I don't know how they'll see justice.'

'They made one big mistake,' said Novak. 'When they left the GRU, they lost the Kremlin's protection. As far as Moscow's concerned, they're mercenaries. Someone will cough up the Firmovs to Interpol eventually.' They both had bigger things on their minds at that moment. 'Are you okay?' he asked.

'I'm fine,' she said.

'I'm sure your mum is–'

'Don't, Novak. Don't say it. I know you're trying to help. But right now, I don't know what to believe about her.'

49

BALMORAL CASTLE, SCOTLAND

Prince James was waiting on the front steps of Balmoral when a navy estate car trundled along the thick gravel driveway, headlights piercing the gloom. The police guards at the main entrance of the grounds had been good enough to call a warning through to the house, that the Security Services were on their way and there was nothing the guards could do to stop them.

Even then, with the three intelligence operatives in smart business attire approaching, James didn't feel any fear. He was royalty, after all. What were they going to do? They had no powers of arrest. Even if they did, it's not like they could ever convict him of anything. A royal in jail?

The one female of the three went first, pulling her jacket closed in the breeze with sharp tugs. 'Your Royal Highness,' she said. 'My name's Duffy. I'm with the Security Service.' Having dispensed the formal address, she was now free to call him simply 'Sir'.

The two men held back at the car.

James leaned casually against the door frame, inspecting

his fingernails. 'If MI5 wants to talk to me, you're going to have to go through my lawyer.'

Duffy was now so close that she could speak quietly and have only James hear her. 'We know about Sir Christopher Benedict and Polonius.'

'Bollocks.'

Duffy showed him a photo of Benedict being arrested at a private airfield in the middle of the Suffolk countryside. 'The thing is, Sir Christopher is an ex-spook. We look after each other, you see. And Sir Christopher really doesn't want to go to jail. Which means he's desperate to tell us all about your little deal. So do yourself a favour.' She dropped her voice to a whisper. 'Invite me in. Sir.'

James showed her to the master study, where he had been spending the majority of his recent days. He sat on the leather Chesterfield, while Duffy stood in front of the towering open fireplace that was almost as tall as she was.

'You can't bloody touch me!' James spat. 'Sending me to jail is more noise than anyone wants. Least of all MI5. I mean, how are you going to explain to the country that the British intelligence services failed to stop the future Queen of the nation being hacked?'

'That's exactly right, sir,' said Duffy. 'Our failure should be your victory. Except, what you have on us is merely embarrassing. I don't even think it tops MI6's part in the dodgy Iraq dossier. People will forget about it in no time. But treason? Hacking? Conspiracy? That isn't just embarrassing headlines. That's hard time. But again, you're right. No one can afford that. Which is why we're going to keep it quiet. The details are being worked out with the Attorney General. As of now, you're under house arrest. Publicly, you're taking a step back from your royal duties.'

'I already have,' he snarled.

'Then you're going to have to take another step back. All the way back to the woodshed, where no one can see you or hear you. You will remain there until absolutely no one can remember how badly you've stained the royal family. Because a happy royal family is good for business. Everyone's business.'

James had never looked at anyone with so much contempt. He hated everything about her. Had done since he'd laid eyes on her cheap suit, frumpy haircut, and heavy legs. That she was pasting him intellectually on top of all that only added fuel to the fire. He was far beyond anger. He was at the boiling with rage phase, where anything beyond twenty decibels was unthinkable. 'And just why the hell would I agree to this?' he asked softly.

Duffy shot a glance towards the closed door. 'Because mama has already agreed to it. You can check with her if you like. But I believe she's rather busy right now, gouging your name out of the history books. And the public diary.'

'What do you want in return? Silence?'

Duffy laughed. 'Oh god no. We want you to talk our ears off. We want you to sing.' She pulled her trousers up an inch to give breathing room as she sat on the low-profile coffee table in front of James. 'You see, you're going to be our new Hugo Byron. Our man with connections. We're going to monitor your phone. You're going to wear an electronic tag. The only place you're going to go out will be abroad, under secure guard. You're going to repay what the country has given you. You're going to help keep us safe. And no one is going to know.'

'Impossible,' he said.

'We kept a permanent file on Harold Wilson, even while he was Prime Minister. The Queen herself allowed Anthony Blunt, a known KGB spy, to continue to work in Buckingham Palace. History is rich with these kinds of arrangements, sir.

You should be thrilled to be in such esteemed company.' Her smile faded. 'It's the only way you'll ever be mentioned in the same breath as them. In short: you're going to be the best spy this country's ever had.'

'Who was it that killed young Hugo?' James asked. 'It was you, wasn't it? I asked around. I can see it in those black eyes of yours. Hear it in your voice. That dispassionate, distant tone. Barely disguised anger. Did he make you feel it? Was he a wriggler? I'll bet he was. More guts than the entire Service put together.'

Duffy slapped him on the leg. 'Get comfortable. You're going to be here for quite a while.'

James rose as Duffy made for the door. 'What for?' he asked.

'Training,' she said.

'I haven't dismissed you,' said James. 'In my position, I dismiss whoever's in the room before they leave.'

'Yeah,' said Duffy, leaving, 'get used to this.'

50

CHARING CROSS POLICE STATION

Detective Inspector Scahill was quick-marching Novak, Stella, and Ralph down a corridor towards a window at the end, bright light streaming out of it. A two-way mirror. Behind the glass, sitting alone, was Anne Cochrane, wearing the same clothes she'd been wearing six hours earlier at Frankfurt Book Fair, minus jacket and shoes – jacket replaced by a heavily pilled fleece that had been worn by hundreds before her, along with laceless canvas shoes.

Scahill kept his voice low. 'I want to be well heard on this: there will be no addressing the suspect. She will not know that any of you are here, because if she does, then it could be my job. But there are details about this case you know that I don't, because while I was out arranging overseas warrants and making arrests, you lot read that book. As there aren't any York Notes available and I can't have you in the room, I want you to use this if you hear something that doesn't sound right, or that you want me to press on.' He put in a small earbud, then held out a radio, waiting for someone to take it.

Ralph didn't even consider taking it.

Novak kept his hands behind his back.

Stella took it.

Scahill opened the door to the interview room and sat down with his back to the mirrored window.

Anne faced the three in the corridor, with no clue her daughter was only a matter of feet away.

Stella whispered, 'She looks so small. I never thought I'd see her so fragile.' It felt like a long time had passed before Stella next spoke. Looking through the glass, she asked Novak, 'Do you think she did it?'

Returning the honesty that she had given him at Ralph's, Novak replied, 'I think she might have.'

* * *

Scahill began the audio recording, going through the legal preamble of confirming she had declined legal representation, and she was being held on a charge of murder.

Once Scahill had presented the conversation that Ian Ferguson had recorded in Anne's office the morning of his death, Anne imperceptibly slumped. 'It's not a crime.'

'What isn't?' asked Scahill.

'Being a spy.'

'It doesn't give you immunity from prosecution.'

'I did everything I could to protect Hugo.'

'You mean Gary Shepherd.'

Anne paused. 'He was only ever Hugo to me.'

'How did it work, then? This arrangement between you and MI5?' He could see Anne's fear working her over. 'You don't have anything to worry about other than your own future, Anne. It's not like any of this will ever make it into open court.'

'In over thirty years, Detective Inspector, I've never gone on the record about my past.'

Novak glanced down at Stella's hand on the radio. Her knuckles white with tension. She couldn't believe that after all these years she was finally getting answers.

Scahill said, 'I've got three dead bodies in Westminster mortuary that I'm accountable to. The Security Services are leaving you holding the bag on at least one of them. I'd say now is as good a time as any to start talking.'

She knew Scahill was right. Nothing she had to say would ever be reported or heard in open court. MI5 would see to that. While she still had time, she wanted to tell someone what she had been doing all this time. To clear her name. 'It started in the secretary pool when I was twenty-three. We were editing a spy novelist who introduced me to Sir Christopher Benedict. Back then, he was still just Chris to me. A young intelligence officer looking to change the world and end the Cold War. We all had such big dreams back then. Chris was convinced that our novelist had ties to a KGB informer – that his inside information was a little *too* inside. It was all so low rent but at the time it felt glamorous. Dangerous. The Service back then was run on paranoia. Chris was no different. He saw enemies everywhere. Traitors. Spies. At the head of government. In the arts. In culture. I became his contact. An asset.' She stopped for a sip of water from a paper cup in front of her. 'Inevitably, we started an affair. It was on-off for many years. I got married. He got married. And one night the call came through: Chris needed me for a job. He had secured me a senior editor job with Hathaway in London and I had to leave everything right away.'

'You left your daughter?' asked Scahill. 'Stella.'

On the verge of saying she didn't have a choice, she changed her mind – she knew that that wasn't completely true, though it had felt it at the time. 'Chris had this idea of planting me inside Hathaway, a job that gave me access not only to London's literati, but the political establishment. He gave me the option of bringing John, my husband, and Stella with me, but it would mean living a secret life, and I didn't want to have to hide that from them. I thought it would be best if I just left altogether. I knew it was wrong but I did it anyway. In my head, I thought I would come back eventually. I'm not sure how she did it, but Stella turned out to be twice the woman I'll ever be.'

On the other side of the glass, Stella resisted showing any emotion.

Anne went on, 'When Chris retired from the Service it seemed that my secret life was over. It was too late to go back then, of course. I had caused too much damage. Then his replacement took over his files and I was brought back into the fold again as an asset on a classified operation.'

'To do what?' asked Scahill.

'The Service had blackmailed a young computer hacker, Gary Shepherd, into taking a deal to cooperate with them. He was young, terrified. He was willing to do anything to avoid jail. So the Service put one of its lawyers, Murray Morton, onto the case to cut a deal. The idea was that Gary would run and operate a website called Griffin that would be used as a honeytrap for whistleblowers. To find them, flush out any threat to national security, and destroy their intel. One thing the evolution of the war on terror has taught the intelligence agencies is that there's only so much they can do. The most devastating recent attacks have been from fringe fanatics. Young men who were assessed as reformed or no longer a threat to society. De-radicalised. Meanwhile, you've got foreign governments trying to influence elections, and wars being derailed by classified intelligence leaks. Griffin was a way to gain back some control of all that.'

'What about all the successful leaks?'

Anne snorted. 'Look at who suffered. The Germans, Italians, the Vatican, the United Nations. The UK doesn't give a stuff about any of them. It was all intelligence that the Service already had or was loaned from the across the river.'

'MI6?' asked Scahill.

'Yes. Though normally at each other's throats, they do occasionally come together on a project. Griffin was one worth doing. Of course, the Service did a great job leaning on newspaper editors to talk the leaks up. They stoked the fires online, and before they knew it, they had a movement that claimed to be about truth, and it was all run by the Security Service.'

Stella couldn't hold her tongue any longer, taking control of the radio to speak to Scahill. 'If it was going so well, why risk it all with the book?'

Scahill asked it – he had been going to ask it anyway.

Anne answered, 'That wasn't their idea. It was mine.'

'Yours?' asked Scahill.

'I told the Service it would help them in the long run. Bolstering Hugo's image would draw in bigger targets. Not just individuals, but foreign governments. The Service realised that in building this almost mythical figure of Hugo Byron, they had a powerful asset that could pull in bigger targets. The Russians. The Americans. Not just individual whistleblowers. It started as a place to entrap, but what it was going to grow into was a tool for massive disinformation. The best way to make that tool seem credible to the public and the international community was by building up Hugo Byron. That meant crafting a story, a compelling narrative about him. The Service liked the potential but not the risk. I decided to tout Gary to Julian Darby anyway, to get a ghostwriter onboard. Ian Ferguson was a perfect choice. A little too perfect, as it turned out. He saw through the Service's legend for Gary.' She pleaded, 'When I saw what Ian was risking I tried to stop him, just like I was trying to help get Gary out...'

Her voice trembling with anger now, Stella radioed, 'What did she try? When? She's lying.'

Scahill didn't respond.

Anne went on, 'I assumed that's why the Service tried to take me out along with Ian. Once he pulled on that first thread, he just kept pulling and pulling. Until the thread stopped with Prince James.'

'Anne,' said Scahill. 'Was Prince James involved in the murder of Gary Shepherd?'

The question stopped Anne in her tracks. She shook her head. 'It was the one thing none of us saw coming. What James promised him I can only imagine: a new passport. Extraction. When Gary went missing, that's what I assumed it was. I never thought he'd actually turn up dead. Whether it was James or not, I couldn't say. It's possible. But it wasn't me!'

Scahill said, 'Oh, we know that you're not connected to Ian's death. We've heard Ian's recording of your last meeting, where he clearly states that Gary was passed out drunk all night. Which contradicts Sofia Alvarez's claim that Gary caught Ian at the laptop.'

'It was Sofia,' Anne said in shock.

'Someone called it in from Badanloch House. Magnus was out walking. He'd already fulfilled his part of the bargain: giving up his mansion to MI5 as a safe house on the promise of reconnecting him to the business world. Sofia was the only other person it could have been. When Sofia caught Ian going through Gary's laptop and found out he planned on meeting you the next day, she knew it would expose her and Gary's deal with Prince James: their last chance of escape. So she called it in to two Russian assassins-for-hire. Evgeny and Yelena Firmov.'

Anne said, 'She targeted me as well.'

'To bump off the woman that had kept the man she loved imprisoned by MI5. Sofia and Gary's deal with Prince James brought a connection to assets belonging to Polonius. A company run by former MI5 spy Sir Christopher Benedict. He was pictured with Gary a year before Benedict left the service. A connection I'm sure Benedict didn't tell Prince James about.'

'Christopher didn't know I was going to be a target or he would have stopped it.'

Unconvinced, Scahill said, 'Really? Benedict was only too happy to provide some ex-GRU assets to protect Prince James's deal with Gary and Griffin. Exposing their deal risked exposing Polonius just as much as it did Prince James.' He leaned across the table. 'Can't you see, Anne. They've all left you holding the bag here. MI5, Benedict. Give us a statement. We'll charge him.'

Anne shook her head.

Scahill didn't let up. 'Did you plan or have knowledge of a plot to kill Gary Shepherd?'

'No,' she said categorically.

Stella spoke into the radio. 'She's lying.'

Scahill reworded. 'Ian Ferguson came to your office and told you that he knew the truth about MI5 and Griffin. He'd seen the code on Hugo's computer. Julian Darby used his connections to find the CPS file on Gary Shepherd's original arrest. Ian showed you what Gary was going to leak next through Griffin, and it was going to destroy the royal family's reputation for years, and expose MI5's operation. Gary Shepherd was going to bring the whole house of cards down. He had to be silenced–'

'No...' said Anne.

'–before the next Griffin leaks. Someone had to give the order. Was it you?'

This time she yelled, 'No! You've got to believe me. I had nothing to do with Gary's death or Ian's!'

In the corridor, Stella sensed it was time. 'Detective, she's dying. She has six months to live. Tell her she might as well do the right thing now.'

Scahill seemed to hesitate, breaking off for a few seconds.

Stella insisted, 'Tell her that there's still time to redeem herself. To do right by Gayle and Ian and Gary by telling the truth. She's going to die just like them.'

Scahill's eyes narrowed as he asked Anne, 'Did you tell your daughter you're dying?'

The question seemed to hit her like a sledgehammer. Not realising that Stella was watching, Anne put her head in her hands.

She said, 'I didn't mean... I just needed...' She lifted her head, tears accumulating on her eyelids before spilling down her cheeks. 'I thought if I could get her to stay, just a little longer, that we might...'

In the corridor, Stella could only stare through the window in shock. She dropped the radio.

Ralph didn't know what to do with himself.

Novak whispered after her, 'Stella...'

'I'm fine,' she replied blankly, disconsolate that she'd fallen for the story.

Scahill tried to redirect things in the interview room. 'I want to get back to Gary Shepherd.'

Anne hung her head. 'I protected him as long as I could. I swear...'

From the far end of the corridor where Novak, Stella, and Ralph were standing, a bright light appeared as a door was thrown open. Striding towards them was an anxious Murray Morton followed closely behind by Chief Superintendent Lancaster.

He told the three, 'Show's over.' Then he crashed into the interview room as Anne was in mid-sentence.

'...I begged them not to,' she explained to Scahill.

Murray pulled Anne out of her chair. 'Get up,' he said sharply.

Scahill looked towards Lancaster, who regretfully nodded.

'Whatever you've got,' she told him, 'will need to be destroyed.' She handed Scahill an official order.

'The Attorney General,' Scahill muttered in wonder. 'You're pulling her under Anti-Terror Legislation,' he said to Murray.

Murray tried not to grin, helping Anne to her feet. 'My client is protected under Section Four A of the two thousand and nine amendment, as a potential corroborating witness to an act of–'

Scahill had to be restrained by Lancaster. 'You're going to put her on a plane and bury this whole thing!'

'It's over,' Lancaster told him. 'Thames House have called it in.'

MI5's headquarters on the stuffy Westminster side of the river.

'What about Sofia Alvarez?' asked Scahill.

'MI5 have pulled her as well. Part of the same deal.'

Scahill sighed. 'The fix is in. They're covering their tracks.'

'She'll be on a flight back to Colombia by this time tomorrow. And there's not a bloody thing we can do about it.'

Murray led Anne out to the corridor. She froze in shock at the sight of Stella, realising that she must have heard her startling admission. While also knowing that it would likely be the last time she would ever see her daughter.

'I'm sorry,' Anne said.

Voice cracking, Stella said pointedly, 'You'll live.'

Murray marched her off before she could say anything further.

Lancaster and Scahill joined the three in the corridor, watching a prime suspect in a murder being walked out of their station under the orders of the Attorney General.

'I gave you as much time as I could,' said Lancaster. 'I'm sorry.'

Scahill removed his earpiece and took back the radio from Stella. 'Thanks, boss.'

'What about Dunhill?' asked Novak. 'Was that Sofia too?'

'It was the same poison,' said Scahill. 'Proving it could be another matter entirely.'

'So that's it?' said Stella. 'They're just going to get away with it?'

Novak knew that Stella needed to let out her anger, her hurt, but he still wanted to comfort her. He reached out for her. 'Stella...'

She pulled her arm away. 'No, Novak! She can't do all this and just walk away...'

Novak pulled her into an embrace anyway.

Ralph felt like he was intruding. After laying a consoling hand on Stella's hand, he said softly, 'I'll be outside.' He left the pair of them alone in the corridor.

'It's okay,' Novak said.

That was when she let it all out. What had been necessary since her mother took off that fateful night. And since Diane had died. Stella began to cry the tears she'd so badly needed to cry for such a long time. The tears she had denied herself for so long.

51

With a heavy heart, Villiers knocked on the door to Princess Rose's private study in Clarence House.

'Come,' came the muffled response on the other side.

Villiers' stomach was churning. He hadn't been summoned to the princess's study for weeks. Had he been found out? Was this how she wanted it to play out? To confront him herself, followed by a swift arrest back at his office?

She was standing. Not a good sign, thought Villiers. She didn't even stand for her mother.

'Villiers,' she began, then broke into a smile. 'I wanted to thank you for your diligence in that whole sordid Sebastian Dunhill affair.'

He wanted to drop to the floor in relief, but he wasn't out of the woods yet. Was it merely a preamble to something far worse? With little else that he could safely venture, he decided to say, 'Thank you, Your Royal Highness.'

'I've spoken to the Director of the Security Services

personally,' she explained. 'You don't have to worry, George. It's already figured out.'

'Behind us?'

'Dunhill would have understood. He did what he did to defend a noble institution. As you have.' She walked out from behind her desk and held his arm reassuringly. 'If Dunhill had successfully leaked the documents that he had, there's no telling where we would be now. That's thanks to you. In defence of the realm.'

The phrase made Villiers take a hard gulp.

Rose went on, 'By any means necessary. Right?'

Villiers nodded, still unsure if he was in the clear. 'By any means necessary, ma'am.'

'I look forward to having that sort of courage by my side when we move in to the Palace.'

'We, ma'am?'

She laughed. 'Yes, George. If you want the crown, you must be prepared to risk the guillotine. Isn't that right?'

'Yes, ma'am.' He bowed, then made towards the door.

That word – guillotine – put a knot back in his stomach. Reminding him of how close he had come, how much he had risked in taking down Dunhill. Now he had everything he wanted. Private Secretary to the next monarch secured. Fiona Bingham cast out to exile with James.

Then Rose said, 'Unfortunately, George, you've shown courage for the wrong person. The man who was all too happy to betray me and risk this family's future.'

Villiers spluttered, 'But... but ma'am, I was protecting the family.'

'You wrote that memo asking for MI5 to reopen the investigation into my phone hacking. Then framed Fiona Bingham to make it look like she had deleted it. You thought I was going down, so you tried to protect James instead. Clinging to that old life raft. No matter who was in the Palace, you knew you would never be the one to be Private Secretary there.'

'Ma'am, I–'

She didn't want to hear it. 'It was a smart move to have Dunhill killed with the same poison. It nearly fooled them.'

The study door opened, and in walked Duffy of MI5.

'The guillotine has to fall on someone, George,' Rose explained. 'I'd like to thank you for your service to the family. It's greatly appreciated.'

As Villiers protested and Duffy moved in, accompanied by her two male colleagues, he felt a black cloud swarming above him. His steps began to falter. All he could see was Dunhill's face. Twisted, writhing in agony. The death that he had caused. The death he had ordered.

Once Duffy and the others removed him, Fiona Bingham passed him on the way in.

'You broke rule number one, George,' she said. 'No blood on the front pages of the newspapers.'

Villiers' feet barely touched the ground the whole way to the car outside. He was leaving Clarence House for the last time.

EPILOGUE

NEW YORK CITY

Novak and Stella were walking through the crowds of downtown Manhattan. It was a freezing winter day, the sky azure, in contrast to the Christmas decorations and lights hanging in every shop window around Fifth Avenue. Tiffany & Co. was twinkling from ground floor to rooftop, and the entire frontage of the Cartier building had been wrapped in an enormous red bow.

'I'm sure you miss home, Stel,' said Novak, waving to a stranger who had announced that she recognised him, 'but you've got to admit, absolutely no one does Christmas like New York City.'

Stella smiled. 'I will concede that, Novak.'

He smiled back, enjoying her relaxed demeanour. He held up a length of her hair, which was down. 'You suit your hair like this.'

'I like it too,' she said. 'I think I'm going to keep it this way.'

'So tell me. How the hell did I get you out of the office at lunchtime?'

'It's time for a break. Time for a change.'

'Oh yeah?'

'I'm handing the reins over to Mark.'

'Mark Chang, chief editor. I like it.'

'I'm a reporter, Novak. That's what I am. I mean, yeah, in time, I can see myself in Diane's chair. I just feel like there are too many other stories out there.'

'So you're not quitting.'

'Does that sound like me?'

Novak needed a short break in conversation before he could ask his next question. 'Have you heard anything from Anne?'

'No,' said Stella, genuinely unaffected at the mention of her. 'If I had, I wouldn't reply.'

'MI5 have likely buried her in some witness protection scheme.'

'I wanted to talk to you about that.'

'What about it?'

'Ralph's got a source in the Service who says Anne's going to testify at the Gary Shepherd inquest.' Novak checked on either side of him, saying quietly, 'Apparently she's got some compelling forensic evidence that was covered up. It seems to implicate someone in MI5 named Duffy being behind Gary's murder.'

'I'll believe it when I see it.'

'Ralph says she's waiving immunity.'

Stella stopped walking. 'They could charge her with aiding and abetting. Perverting the course of justice, for failing to come forward.'

'It will likely be jail time, Stel. I thought you should know.'

She sighed, taking in the beautiful surroundings during such melancholy thoughts. 'I think... it's time for a clean break.'

'With her?'

'With everything. I feel like myself again.'

'Great,' joked Novak.

'What's that supposed to mean?'

'Oh, nothing. It's just that, historically, that's generally involved breaking my balls, correcting my grammar, my spelling...'

A picture of innocence, Stella said, 'I don't do that *all* the time, do I?'

Novak put his arm around her and pulled her closer to him as they reached a large bookstore. 'Look at that,' he said, pointing at the window display. 'Three books about Gary Shepherd and Griffin. And not one of them is *Captive State*.'

'It's funny,' said Stella, turning in profile to get through the crowds at the front door where the bestseller chart was. 'The biggest book of them all and it can't be sold in bookstores.'

'I checked last night. It's doing just fine. There are four of Ian's books in the top twenty on Amazon here and the UK. *Captive State*'s still the number one.'

'What is that, like, eight weeks now?'

'Close to it. Speaking of which, Julian Darby emailed me. He wants me to write the definitive book about Ian's murder.'

Stella stopped her browsing. 'What did you tell him?'

'I told him it will never get past whatever injunction MI5 slap on it.' He squinted, noticing a book piled high among many others on a table. He picked it up and showed Stella. 'That look familiar to you?'

Stella read the title to herself. '*A Right Honourable Death*. By Gayle Ademi.' She turned the book on its back and saw the Hathaway Parker House logo. 'They never miss a trick.'

'It's all just units, isn't it,' Novak suggested. 'Pile them high, sell them cheap.'

'Way to get in the Christmas spirit, Novak,' Stella said

sarcastically, reading the blurb of Gayle's book. 'I don't know. Some of these books might not change the world, but maybe that's alright. Someone somewhere gets a little bit of distraction from this messed-up world for a day or two. The bad don't always prevail. Justice wins out. That's worth something.'

A bookseller with purple hair, carrying a stack of *True Republic* hardbacks, gestured at the book in Stella's hand, telling her, 'It's really good, by the way.'

'Oh yeah?' she said.

'It's about this politician who's a murderer. I couldn't put it down.'

Stella and Novak shared a knowing glance.

Novak said, 'I don't know. Sounds a little far-fetched to me.'

Stella nodded, clutching *A Right Honourable Death* at her chest. 'I'll take it.'

The bookseller's cheeks were flushed. 'Excuse me for asking, but aren't you guys Tom Novak and Stella Mitchell?'

Unsure whether she was going to be a nice one or a crazy one, Novak said cautiously, 'Yeah.'

'I really love your work in *The Republic*,' she said. 'I've been waiting for some follow-ups on the Ian Ferguson and Gary Shepherd story.'

'Didn't you see the news this morning?' asked Stella. 'The Firmovs have been arrested in Italy. The British government's working with Interpol and the Italians to have them extradited.'

'I'm glad,' said the bookseller. 'That must be so... strange. To know that you did that?'

'It doesn't always work out,' said Stella. 'We did okay on this one.'

Novak said, 'Plus, we had some help this time.' He peered

down at the copies of *True Republic*. 'Hey, do you want me to sign those?'

'Would you? My manager would love you for that. And, well, me.'

Novak took out a pen from his inside jacket pocket, and set to work signing the books. 'It's still selling well, huh?'

'Oh yeah, it's doing great. Reality's crazier than fiction these days.'

'Tell me about it,' said Novak.

Stella muttered to him, 'Not so concerned now about pile them high, sell them cheap, are you...'

Novak said to the bookseller, 'I never said that. She's a crazy person, really... In fact, could you direct her to self-help?'

Stella punched him on the arm.

When he was done signing, he considered writing his phone number on the bookseller's hand, thinking it might be cute, but worried what Stella might say. He pocketed the pen. 'Merry Christmas,' he said, shaking the bookseller's hand.

'Merry Christmas,' she replied, then gave Stella a brief wave.

'Let me guess,' said Stella. 'If I wasn't here, you would have given her your phone number, right?'

Novak thought about denying it. 'How did you know?'

She sighed. 'She's all of twenty-five, Novak. You're a bankrupt, old reporter. Do you really think she wouldn't head straight for the restroom and wash your number off her hand?'

Novak checked his watch. 'Where did we say we were meeting Ralph again?'

'FAO Schwartz at Rockefeller Center. He and Christine wanted to do some Christmas toy shopping for the girls.'

'Great,' said Novak, rubbing his hands. 'I love that place.'

Stella laughed at his infectious enthusiasm and put her arm around him. She was savouring the crowds, everyone wrapped up in winter coats, the chirpy Dean Martin version of "Let It Snow" playing overhead. It was the only situation in life in which Stella would take Dean Martin over Frank Sinatra.

Novak asked, 'What time do you want to get back to the office later?'

'I don't want to think about that yet,' she said, linking arms with him as they emerged back onto Fifth Avenue. Having reconsidered, she added, 'Soon.'

* * *

THE END

* * *

Novak and Mitchell will return

ACKNOWLEDGMENTS

This book is dedicated with love to my sister, Cathie.

Without the incredible editing, support, and love of my wife Emma, this book wouldn't be half of what it is. I couldn't do this without you.

Some of the material on Hugo Byron was inspired by Andrew O'Hagan's searing essay about Julian Assange called *Ghosting*. I can't recommend it highly enough.

I would also like to acknowledge the incredible reporting done by Eliot Higgins and Bellingcat – the inspiration behind Ralph Ogden and Verax. Ralph will definitely feature in future books, by the way. He's been one of my favourite characters to write.

***

Finally, to all of you, dear readers, thank you for all of your lovely emails, Facebook comments and messages, and anything else. They are truly appreciated. As I always say, a writer is nothing without readers, and you lot are the best out there.

Your good humour and encouragement really keep me going.

- Andrew

Glasgow, Scotland

Printed in Great Britain
by Amazon

16250293R00212